The Funeral Dress

Center Point
Large Print

Also by Susan Gregg Gilmore and available from Center Point Large Print:

The Improper Life of Bezellia Grove

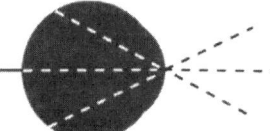

This Large Print Book carries the Seal of Approval of N.A.V.H.

The Funeral Dress

SUSAN GREGG GILMORE

CENTER POINT LARGE PRINT
THORNDIKE, MAINE

This Center Point Large Print edition is published in the year 2014 by arrangement with Broadway Books, an imprint of the Crown Publishing Group, a division of Random House LLC, a Penguin Random House Company, New York.

The text of this Large Print edition is unabridged. In other aspects, this book may vary from the original edition. Printed in the United States of America on permanent paper. Set in 16-point Times New Roman type.

ISBN: 978-1-62899-130-7

Library of Congress Cataloging-in-Publication Data

Gilmore, Susan Gregg.
 The funeral dress / Susan Gregg Gilmore. — Center Point Large Print edition. pages ; cm
 Summary: "Leona befriended Emmalee, taught her to sew, and offered a home to the unwed mother. When Leona dies tragically, Emmalee decides to honor her by making her a beautiful funeral dress. While half the town rallies behind her, others try to take her child from her. Emmalee will learn she has more strength that she thought possible" —Provided by publisher.
 ISBN 978-1-62899-130-7 (library binding : alk. paper)
 1. Women—Southern States—Fiction. 2. Single mothers—Fiction. 3. Self-actualization (Psychology) in women—Fiction. 4. Large type books. I. Title.
 PS3607.I4527F86 2014
 813'.6—dc23
                                                    2014007841

for my mother, MARY,

and

for VALLERIE who welcomed me home and
led me over a mountain

My Father's house has many rooms; if that were not so, would I have told you that I am going there to prepare a place for you?

—JOHN 14:2
New International Version

EMMALEE

The Tennewa Shirt Factory

1974

Emmalee Bullard became a Tennewa girl on the
last Thursday in May. She woke early that
morning, like always, in the back of a two-room
house squeezed in tight at the foot of Pine
Mountain. But today she'd slipped away beneath
the oaks and cedars without waking her father.

A steady line of cars pulled into the Tennewa
parking lot, and women, mixed in conversations,
spilled out of each automobile and herded past
her. They giggled and pushed against one another
as they funneled inside the one-story building,
not noticing the willowy teenager lingering
behind them. Standing on the rough asphalt drive
outside the shirt factory, Emmalee listened to the
hum rolling from the building's open doors as it
swelled and deepened. The sound coursed through
her body and lured Emmalee closer.

The shift bell rang. Emmalee climbed the concrete steps leading to the sewing room and slid
onto the factory's floor, hugging the wall like a
shadow skimming along smooth and silent. A

dozen fans spinning from the whitewashed ceiling provided the only relief from the thick morning air. Fluorescent bulbs cast an artificial glow about the room, and the hardwood flooring, its patina burnished with age, sparkled beneath the light. High-set windows spanned both sides of the building, but most of the panes had been painted gray.

Heavyset women with thick, flabby arms and weathered skin sat in perfect rows next to younger girls with slender frames and long hair clipped behind their heads. Concentrating on the fabric streaming through their hands, they looked almost dwarfed in the large space. Their bodies nearly touched as they hunched in front of their machines, trying to make ends meet with every single stitch. Even those who had rushed past her in the parking lot had already taken their places and begun the day's work.

"You hunting your mama? Go on in, girl," said a man in oil-stained coveralls with a tool belt hanging low on his hips.

"No, sir."

"What you need?"

"A job."

The man took another look at Emmalee.

"How old are you?"

"Old enough."

He grinned and pointed to a closed door. "Office is over there."

"Thank you," she said, her eyes turned to the floor.

The office walls were painted the color of butter beans not quite ready to pick. A few metal folding chairs and a rack for hanging coats were the only furnishings in the small space other than a tall wooden counter anchoring the right side of the room. A woman perched on a stool behind the counter peered over the rim of her cat-eyed glasses and smiled.

"Can I help you?" she asked and adjusted the glasses on the bridge of her nose. A wad of blond hair teased and piled on top of her head held a ballpoint pen and a yellow pencil. Emmalee thought this woman beautiful and caught herself admiring her pearly skin and perfect red lips.

"Sweetie, you need something?" the woman repeated.

"I was wanting to know . . . I mean I was wondering if . . ."

"What is it, hon?"

"I'm wanting to work. Here. At Tennewa."

The woman studied Emmalee.

"How old are you?"

"Old enough."

"Well, you need to be eighteen. Anything younger than that and you'll have to get a permit. It's not a big deal, but we'll need it on file here. So how old are you?"

"Seventeen," Emmalee said. She tucked her

hair behind her ears. "Come September. I'll be seventeen in September. I'm sixteen."

"Okay." The woman shuffled a stack of papers but kept her eyes on Emmalee. "That's fine. You graduate from high school early?"

"Don't go no more." Emmalee did not confess she had quit only yesterday. She had run late for the bus again, and Nolan refused to drive her the four miles in the pickup. He said it was time for her to get a job, not waste her days listening to a bunch of bullshit. He wasn't carrying her nowhere near that school, he told her.

"That's okay, hon. We always ask. I don't recognize you though. You from Cullen or you drive over from Pikeville or Jasper?"

"Cullen."

"Who your people?"

"Bullard."

"Hmm." The woman tapped her pencil on the counter's smoothed top. "You by chance Nolan Bullard's girl, the one that makes them crosses when somebody dies?"

Emmalee looked away. She knew people in Cullen had heard of her cross-making. She had seen plenty walk back into Red Chert to inspect her handiwork. Some thought it interesting, pretty even, while others poked fun. Emmalee didn't want to talk about it no matter how this woman judged her habit of commemorating the dead.

"Yes, ma'am," she said.

"How about that. I'm Gwen Whitlow." She extended her hand over the counter. Emmalee hesitated but shook the woman's hand. "I heard you made a cross for my daddy when he passed two years ago. Landis. Landis Williams. You remember him?"

"Yes, ma'am. I remember them all. Their names, that is."

Emmalee knew the full names of all those who had died in Cullen in recent years: George Chester Lamb, Floyd Wade Kenner, Berta Grant Price, Landis Bell Williams. She had made a cross for each one of them, even those she didn't know or didn't much like. But she had lost count of the number of crosses made since starting eleven years ago come June fifteenth, only five days after her mama died.

"Heard they're all nailed to an old tree. Nearly covered up by now."

"Yes, ma'am. A white oak. It's dead too."

"Huh. How about that." Mrs. Whitlow pursed her lips and rolled her stool a few inches back. "Kind of a peculiar thing for a young girl to be doing," she said. "But you look normal to me, and we are hiring. Can you sew?"

"Yes, ma'am. Some." Emmalee could place a button on a shirt and stitch a simple seam on a machine, all things she had learned at school. She made a two-pocket apron last spring, even placed the hem by hand.

"You don't really need to know how. We'll train you. This is real specific work. It just helps a bit, especially in the beginning. Any chance you had Easter Nichols for Home Economics?"

"Yes, ma'am." Emmalee stifled a small laugh. She had never heard anyone call her teacher by her first name.

"Easter's been working here since she retired from the high school end of last May. She's a wonderful seamstress. Does beautiful work. Always meets her quota unless she gets to talking." Mrs. Whitlow tugged on the ballpoint pen buried within the beehive heaped on top of her head. Emmalee expected the woman's hair to fall, but it held in place. "Go ahead and fill out this application. Get comfortable, as best you can in one of those old chairs, and take your time. Only got a couple of positions open, but you might be the very girl we're looking for."

Emmalee chewed on her left thumbnail while she wrote her name, address, and birth date with her other hand. She didn't know her Social Security number or what that was. She didn't even know if she had one, although Mrs. Whitlow reassured her they were easy to get and handed Emmalee another form. Emmalee bit some loose skin between her teeth.

She didn't have any past work experience, which worried her some. But she didn't have a criminal record, which made her feel better.

Emmalee left those parts blank and handed the clipboard and pen back to Mrs. Whitlow, who was coaxing her hair higher on top of her head.

"Let me talk to Mr. Clayton," Mrs. Whitlow said. "He's the general manager here at Tennewa. I'll be back in a minute. Here's a magazine you can read if you like." She handed Emmalee last month's issue of *Ladies' Home Journal*, featuring a four-layer yellow cake with chocolate frosting on the cover.

A young man with a bolt of denim fabric balanced on his shoulder and a stubby pencil wedged behind his ear passed through the lobby on his way to the sewing room. The noise roared loud as the door opened, and Emmalee bent forward to steal a peek. But the door slammed closed behind the man, shutting out the din of the machines.

"Emmalee." Mrs. Whitlow walked in front of the counter, stopping to check her lips in a small mirror mounted on the wall. "Mr. Clayton is on the phone with a vendor down in Georgia, but he said if I felt good about you, we could go ahead and offer you a job."

Mrs. Whitlow pointed to a man in a crisp blue shirt and red tie leaning against a window frame in the office behind her. He held a telephone receiver to his ear. His hair was white along the temple and deep lines marked his face. Emmalee thought he was handsome for an older man.

When he laughed at something said on the other end of the line, Emmalee saw a gap between his two front teeth. He winked at her and continued his conversation.

"How's that sound?" Mrs. Whitlow asked.

Emmalee nodded. "Sounds good. Real good. And I'll work hard. Real hard. I promise."

"I have no doubt about that. But aren't you the least bit curious to know what you'll be doing?"

"Yes, ma'am," Emmalee said. She tucked her feet underneath the chair and rubbed her hands together.

"Well, you'll be making collars."

"Making collars," Emmalee said, repeating the words carefully.

"That's right. You'll be a Tennewa collar maker. You know what that is, dear?" Mrs. Whitlow asked.

"No, ma'am."

"Simple really. You'll be making collars for men's shirts and women's housedresses mostly." Mrs. Whitlow reached for a notebook on top of the counter and opened it to a sketch of a plain yellow dress. "See, here, this is a housedress." She handed the notebook to Emmalee. "Thought about starting you on pockets or lapels, but I think you can manage collars fine, what with your experience and all."

"Yes, ma'am," Emmalee said, studying the dress's wide rounded collar.

"You'll work from seven in the morning until four in the afternoon with thirty minutes for lunch. Take a break whenever you need it. Just get your work done. We pay piece rate. I think collars run about a hundred and fifty a dozen for an eight-hour shift," Mrs. Whitlow said.

"A hundred and fifty dozen." Emmalee's eyes popped.

"Of course, you'll never make less than minimum wage, and that's running right at two dollars an hour."

"A hundred and fifty dozen," Emmalee said again.

"Sounds like a lot, don't it. It's really not bad," Mrs. Whitlow said. "Some women nearly double their quota, and that means more money for them. Two make more than seven dollars an hour. That'll take some time, though."

"Seven dollars an hour."

"That's right. But all we care about right now is that you do quality work. Mistakes cost money. Mr. Clayton there," Mrs. Whitlow said again, motioning toward the man wearing the stiffly starched shirt, "don't like mistakes. He's a nice man, a family man, got four boys of his own and a lovely wife from a real good family outside of Montgomery. But he don't like careless mistakes." Mrs. Whitlow stepped back behind the counter. "Don't worry, we'll help you along for the first month or so till you get the hang of things."

"Yes, ma'am."

"I'm going to put you next to Leona Lane. She's worked here forever, probably wasn't any older than you when she started out. She don't talk much. But she's real good, and you'll learn a lot just from watching her. Probably the best seamstress we got. But don't go telling Cora Hixson I said that or we'll have another fight to referee." Mrs. Whitlow threw her hands up in the air; her gold charm bracelet jangled as she stressed her point. "Those two are always suspecting one another of hoarding bundles or slipping work beyond the four o'clock bell. But enough of that." She folded her arms in front of her waist. "Don't want to scare you off before you get started."

"No, ma'am."

Mrs. Whitlow reached for a manila folder and fingered a piece of paper inside it. "Here's the application for the work permit. Fill this top part out. Have your daddy sign here and bring it back to me as soon as you can. We like to have everything processed and on file within thirty days of your start date. So we have a bit of time."

"Yes, ma'am," Emmalee said, knowing she would forge Nolan's signature. He could write his name well enough if his hand was steady, but he had been drinking hard for the past two days. Besides, Emmalee had grown accustomed to signing his name and believed she did a better job of it than he did, even on his good days.

Mrs. Whitlow pointed at the clock. "It's only eight. You want to come back tomorrow, or you want to go ahead and get started today?"

"Today. I want to work today."

"I figured as much." Mrs. Whitlow undid the top button of her mint-green sweater. "Just promise to get that permit form signed."

Emmalee nodded. "I promise."

"Well, come on then." Mrs. Whitlow slipped the sweater off her arms and draped it across the counter. "This time of year it starts out cool in the sewing room, but it gets hot quick. There's nearly three hundred machines running nonstop in there, so I can promise you'll never freeze here at Tennewa. I keep telling Mr. Clayton that should be our company motto," she said and pulled on the sewing room door. "So wear something comfortable. And best bring a lunch. A few of us walk down to the drugstore but that gets expensive real fast. Most the seamstresses eat here, outside on the picnic tables on the west side of the building."

She motioned for Emmalee to follow her. "After today, you'll enter and leave through those double doors there at the end of the building. That's where you'll punch your time card. I'll show you where all that's at." Emmalee stepped close behind Mrs. Whitlow, clipping the heel of her pretty black shoe. "Right here are the sleeve setters. Myrtie there has been at Tennewa for nineteen years come Monday week," Mrs. Whitlow said as she nodded to a woman snapping a long thread between her fingers.

Emmalee caught the stares of the other seamstresses. Some slowed their work; a few stopped and rested against the backs of their chairs as they examined the new employee. Emmalee pressed her hands down the thin cotton skirt she bought at the thrift store in the basement of the Methodist church and brushed her hands across her head. Still her skirt hung wrinkled on her body, and her hair fell messy about her face.

Young men dressed in blue jeans and short-sleeved shirts darted between the rows of seamstresses checking canvas baskets for finished work. In the back of the room, two long tables stood end to end, both covered in layers of pale yellow fabric stacked six inches thick. Three or four men stood around each table positioning patterns for what looked like a dress or maybe a man's extra-large shirt. They lifted the pattern pieces and positioned them again and again, working for the tightest fit.

"Only men set the patterns," Mrs. Whitlow said as she leaned close to Emmalee. "Don't ask me why. Just the way it's always been."

They walked deeper into the room. Mrs. Whitlow pointed to the right. "They're bottom hemmers over there." She pointed to the left and turned her face to Emmalee so she could be heard over the roar of the fast-spinning machines. "They're pocket makers. And them there, behind the pocket makers, are the lapel makers." Emmalee nodded.

She spotted Easter Nichols sitting among the other pocket makers in the far left corner of the room. Easter had a large goiter underneath her right cheek, and it looked as though it had grown some, further thickening Easter's already fatty neck. Some of the kids at school said the sight of that awesome goiter killed her husband, shocked him right to death. It was an ugly thing to look at, but Emmalee had seen worse. She waved to her teacher, but Easter was focused on her work.

Pearl Tribble sat behind Easter. Pearl lived in Red Chert, too, and Emmalee had seen her walking to work many times. She hoped they might walk together soon and talk like the other women who arrived at the factory in cars. Next to Pearl sat Laura Cooley. Laura was a couple years older than Emmalee but had left school after the ninth grade. She lived on the back side of Pine Mountain near the small lumber mill Emmalee's uncle Runt operated on his own. Laura had pale skin and pale blue eyes and kept her bright red hair cut short like a boy's. She looked up and stared at Emmalee before returning to her work.

"There. There's the collar makers. That's where you'll be," Mrs. Whitlow said. She pushed on through a tight aisle formed by a row of sewing tables to one side and the backs of women curled over their machines to the other. Baskets, already filling with finished collars, sat beneath each table. Mrs. Whitlow pointed to the floor, cautioning Emmalee to watch her step. She stopped in front of an empty chair and patted a woman on the back. With her hands, she asked again for the woman's attention.

The older seamstress did not look up or slow her machine.

"Leona," Mrs. Whitlow said, "I want to introduce you to Emmalee. She's new here. She's going to be working collars next to you. She knows how to sew a bit, but I need you to show her the ropes. You know. Get her started."

Leona remained fixed on her work. Mrs. Whitlow tapped her high-heeled shoe on the shiny wood floor by Leona's chair. She placed her hands on her hips. "Leona, I'm not asking for more than twenty minutes of your time. She'll learn fast. She took sewing from Easter at the high school."

Mrs. Whitlow leaned in close. "Go on and take a seat," she said. "Leona ain't going to stop until she gets through with that batch. She don't like anybody messing up her rhythm. But she'll get to you. I promise. Good luck today." Mrs.

Whitlow spun sharp on her heels and walked back toward the office.

From behind Emmalee, a woman half stood over the top of her machine and introduced herself as Wilma Minton. She had full cheeks shaded a bright pink and eyebrows drawn on her face. The tail of her left eyebrow was smudged, and Emmalee held her hand to her mouth, careful not to snicker.

"Wish I could help you, hon, but I'm a lapel maker," Wilma said, holding up a raw lapel. "Have been for eighteen years. Gwen's right, though. Leona'll get to you in due time. She's the best." Wilma grinned. "Don't go telling Cora I said that, ain't that right, Leona?" She laughed out loud and talked on as if Leona was not there. "Don't pay Leona Lane and her moody ways no mind. She's a good woman even if she acts sour most the time. Ignores you most the other."

Leona slipped another collar under the machine's presser foot.

"You from Cullen?" Wilma asked. "I'd even go so far as to bet you're a Bullard girl."

"Yes, ma'am." Emmalee looked back at Wilma.

"I knew it. I could tell by those big brown eyes of yours. You're a pretty thing. Your daddy done one thing good and that was marrying your sweet mama." Emmalee smiled. No one spoke of her mama anymore. "I heard Gwen say you had Easter for Home Economics. Me and Easter are roommates, and I'll tell you right now she'll want you calling her by her first name. None of that Mrs. Nichols talk like you had to do at school."

"Yes, ma'am," Emmalee said, but Wilma had returned to her sewing.

Emmalee faced her own machine. She ran her fingers across its top. It was larger than any she had ever seen, and its casing was slick and cool to the touch. She wanted to press her flushed cheek against its metal. Silver lettering along the front read *Union Special*. She traced the letters with her index finger and then raised and lowered the presser foot as she had watched Leona do. She turned the wheel attached to the right of the machine and watched the needle rise and fall. She picked up a spool of thread and pretended to examine its color and quality as if she knew what she was to do next.

She slumped in her chair and fingered the lettering again, trying to look busy while Leona and the other women around her tended to their work. The noise of the machines ebbed and flowed, at times roaring so high Emmalee wanted to plug her ears. But as fast as it grew to a fevered pitch, it fell to a more gentle level as if the seamstresses were following notes on a sheet of music.

Emmalee pushed her foot against the floor pedal and the machine lurched forward. She yanked her foot back and her hands fell to her sides. She stared up at the painted windows and focused on the bits of sunlight peeking through glass where the gray had chipped away. Even for a girl raised in the dimness of the holler, it bothered her not to see the sky. She looked at the large clock on the wall behind her, rubbing against Leona's arm as she turned toward the wall.

Leona snatched another bundle of collars tied with a piece of cotton twine and dropped them onto her lap. "Look here," she said to Emmalee.

Emmalee rubbed her eyes and sat up straight.

"These are for housedresses," Leona said and held the bundle out in front of her. "We usually make for housedresses and men's work shirts, more than anything else, sometimes women's blouses. But mostly housedresses lately." She tugged on the collar of her own dress. "Some'll go to J.C. Penney. Some'll go to Sears. Same dress, just different label. Now there's only a couple hundred in these bundles here," Leona said, holding up a bundle in front of her. "More in shirt bundles. See this ticket. Attached to the bundle. This is like cash to you and me. Proof of your work."

"Like cash," Emmalee repeated.

"Don't try stringing them all together like I do." Leona reached behind her machine and pulled on the collars threaded together like a piece of ribbon. "That'll come later. I've probably sewed a million collars since starting at Tennewa.

Blue, green, yellow, denim, flannel, cotton—don't make no difference to me. Don't even ask if it's going on a housecoat or a shirt no more. That don't matter. All that's important is that I go past production."

"Production?" Emmalee asked.

"Your quota. You don't know nothing about this, do you?"

"No, ma'am."

"Put the collar under the presser foot starting here." Leona pointed to a corner. "Then stitch all the way around like you're drawing a line. Stop here at the other corner and leave this end open. See?" Leona pulled apart the collar pieces. "It's not up to us to turn them. When you're done, let it fall into the basket on the other side of the table. The bundle boys come by every couple of hours and pick them up. It's as simple as that."

"What if I make a mistake?" Emmalee asked.

"Inspectors'll check your work. You make your own repairs. And don't go arguing about them, just do them. Saves time in the end. The finishers'll press them before they go to the collar setters."

Emmalee nodded.

"And girl, be sure your threads always match the color of your fabric. Seems plain, don't it? You'd be surprised how often that don't come out right. Some days I think half the girls in here gone color blind." Leona pushed her glasses down on her nose. "You got yellow on there so you're good to go. Your thread's in that cabinet there on your left. These here are mine, you understand? When you need you some more, go to the supply closet. Don't take from nobody else. Most important, you don't draw but one bundle of them raw collars at a time."

"One bundle," Emmalee said.

"Some here struggle more than others to meet their quotas. Some work real fast and don't take no break like Cora there." She pointed to a heavyset woman with long gray hair pulled into a loose bun. "They're the ones putting food on tables that would've gone bare without them. And some here mostly to get off their husbands' farms like Sarah over there." Leona nodded to the right. "Tired of picking beans and cooking for hired hands. But don't matter to me why you're here. Just do your work."

"Yes, ma'am."

"And girl, these machines run fast, real fast. Watch your fingers. They'll slide right under that needle in the blink of an eye. Seen too many women stitch their fingers together. Just last week Ida Lawson done stitched her tit."

Emmalee held her arms across her front. "That must have hurt," she said, hugging her chest tighter. She'd never heard of such a thing, and she'd never heard a woman say the word *tit* before.

"Lord, no, it was her fake one. Lost the real one to cancer years ago. But Gwen didn't know that. Passed out right there on the sewing room floor." Leona tilted her head back and laughed. "That poor woman. Can't stand the sight of blood." Leona handed the bundle of collars to Emmalee. "Go on. Enough talking."

Emmalee picked up a raw collar and placed it on the machine, positioning the needle at the far-left corner. She lowered the presser foot and stepped on the floor pedal. The machine's needle sped up and down, and Emmalee fought to keep a straight seam. She jerked her foot off the pedal, adjusted the collar, and started again. She finished one, and then another, but her sewing was slow and messy compared to Leona's. Her bottom grew numb and tiny beads of sweat formed on the tip of her nose as she worked to finish her first bundle.

Emmalee guided two layers of thin cotton fabric underneath the needle. She eased her foot off the floor pedal, struggling to keep the pressure steady like Leona. Instead the machine hesitated and lurched before climbing to a steadier purr. The needle rose and fell at awkward spurts while Emmalee stitched the collar closed, and the motor burned hot on her legs.

While Leona neared the end of a bundle, other women stood up and pushed their chairs underneath their worktables. Their talk was fevered as they bunched together and hurried out of the building.

"Lunch, hon," Wilma said as she touched Emmalee on the shoulder. "You bring something to eat?"

Emmalee looked up at Wilma, but she was already pushing back her chair, intent on joining Pearl and Easter walking on ahead of her.

Emmalee pressed her hand against her stomach.

With her canvas loafer, Leona tapped a brown paper bag on the sewing room floor.

"There's a sandwich in this bag down here. Take it if you want." She pushed another collar underneath the presser foot. "Go on. From looking at those bony arms of yours, I'd say you need it worse than I do."

Emmalee inched closer to Leona's chair like she was reaching toward an angry dog. She pulled the bag to her lap and peeked inside.

"Curtis made it, so guess it's fried bologna." Leona stood and pushed her chair underneath her sewing table. "You ain't supposed to eat in here, not anywhere near the machines or the fabric. But go ahead this time. No one's watching but me, and I sure ain't going to tell." Leona walked away, leaving Emmalee alone in the sewing room, the paper bag in her hands.

EMMALEE

Red Chert

- - - - - - - - - - -

Three Years Later

Light leaked into the holler, slow and quiet. Emmalee lingered by the front window, waiting for the first speck of sun to crown the trees crowding her view. Dressed in a pair of blue jeans and a faded green T-shirt stretched too tight around her belly still swollen from giving birth, Emmalee pulled a wool coat across her shoulders.

The baby had fussed during the night, never sleeping for more than an hour. Even when Kelly Faye did drift into a peaceful slumber, Emmalee lay there wide-eyed, thoughts spinning. Hidden in the dark underneath the quilts her mama had stitched long ago, she plotted every detail of her last day in Red Chert. Now with morning about to break, Emmalee was eager to set about her chores while the baby finally slept in the back room.

She would pack the few things she cared about, careful to leave the house appearing as though nothing had changed. She would bake a fresh skillet of cornbread for Nolan if there was enough meal in the cupboard and cook up the pinto beans she had soaked overnight. When her chores were done, she'd hike to the small cemetery at the top of the mountain. Come spring the azalea would bloom fierce there but for today Emmalee would carry a bundle of cedar and holly ripe with red berries to place on her mama's grave. A shiver ran through her body, but Emmalee tossed it off as she looked behind her.

Nolan's cot sat empty, pushed into the far corner of the room. It wasn't suspect for her father to go missing for a day or two, but it was never something Emmalee could plan or schedule. Even as a child, she had treasured those days she woke to find herself alone in the holler. Besides, she had never felt truly lonely there—at least not until Kelly Faye was born. But for the first time Emmalee interpreted her father's absence as more than good fortune. It was an omen, a sign from Jesus or God or perhaps her mama, that her leaving was right.

An early gray light washed the top of Pine Mountain. Emmalee buttoned her coat snug around her neck and rushed outside. Her body shook against the cold, but she treaded deeper into the wet mist already clinging to her face and hands. A towhee with snips of fuzzy oak gall in his mouth darted past her, nearly brushing her left cheek as he flew to a low-hanging branch. Emmalee did not flinch.

She primed the pump set off in the yard and filled two large buckets with water. She carried them back to the house, stopping only once to rest her arms. A couple of pots sat ready on the wood-stove. Emmalee struck a match and tossed it into the open hole. Once the fire took hold, she replaced the iron plate and poured the water into the kettles, leaving it to heat while the baby slept on.

She walked back outside, this time heading toward the narrow dirt road twisting through the holler's tallest pines and cedars stretching to find the sun. She dug the tips of her boots into the compound of leaves and twigs carpeting her path and kicked them up into the air. The red rocky chert covering this land was still soft and thick from the recent rains, and Emmalee stumbled as her toe sunk too deep into the mud.

She stopped sharp at the edge of her father's property and listened for any hint of his beat-up truck rumbling toward home. She leaned forward and turned her ear closer toward the main road. Someone in the far distance hammered a steady note. Emmalee shuffled through the leaves toward the trunk of the large oak left misshapen from a bolt of lightning long before she was born. The trunk stood thick at the bottom and tapered thin like a sharpened pencil at the top. Its woody flesh was nearly camouflaged in her crosses, each no more than half a foot long and crafted from twigs collected from the hillside behind the house. Those from the oak and poplar were Emmalee's favorites, although not as fragrant as those from the cedars speckled about the holler.

On occasion Nolan carried a twig home from his long walks among the mountains if the shape called to him right. He'd leave it on the table without ever saying a word, but Emmalee knew its purpose. She preferred to hunt for her own. There was a time when she had felt close to her mama whenever she was in the woods gathering twigs for her cross-making. She had sworn she once heard her mama's voice skittering through the tops of the pines, calling her name. But eventually Emmalee felt her mother ease away, and her voice grew silent.

She continued making her crosses, somehow convinced that with each one she kept a tiny bit of the person passing with her in Red Chert. Even the dead she didn't know, she was desperate to keep close for a time, preferring to believe that this ever-changing family of angels watched out for her. Emmalee stood a moment longer and studied the trunk.

She fingered Ida Lawson's cross. The wood looked fresh and new compared to the others. The cancer that had teased Ida once long ago took her life fast this time. Emmalee thought that was particularly unkind, and for that reason alone, she made Ida's cross a little larger than the others. Leona told Emmalee they had buried Ida without a bra or her fake breasts. "Ida was tired of pretending she had something that wasn't there and didn't want nothing binding her in heaven," Leona said. Ida had even insisted she be buried barefoot, wanting only a pair of knitted socks "to keep her feet warm."

Emmalee smiled at the memory of the older seamstress who had always been kind to her. Then she looked toward the top of the trunk and to the only cross she couldn't leave behind when she left this place for good. Balanced on her toes, she tugged on the one belonging to her mama. But she stumbled backward empty handed. She approached the trunk a second time, stepping onto a knotted root. Emmalee reached for the cross with her other hand and lifted it free from a nail driven deep into the oak. She stood steady among the leaves and raised the cross to her lips.

A creaking, rattling sound echoed in the distance and disappeared. Again Emmalee turned her ear toward the main road. She tucked the cross inside her coat and ran back to the house. Tomorrow she would carry Kelly Faye out of Red Chert to where Leona and Curtis would be waiting for her.

LEONA

Old Lick

- - - - - - - - -

Late Afternoon

Worn out from another long day at the factory,
Leona eased from the pickup, her navy purse
and a grocery sack dangling in her right hand.
Curtis lingered behind the steering wheel,
jiggling the key in the truck's ignition. He
pounded the dashboard with the palm of his fist,
but the engine sputtered and coughed as if it
had taken ill. Leona turned her back to him and
walked across the gravel drive, staring with
glazed eyes at their home of twenty-one years.

The trailer was bled dry from a lifetime of rough
living, its aluminum skin turned chalky and
pocked with rusted sores. Her gaze was steady as
Leona remembered seeing the trailer for the first
time. It was shiny and new and she was so young,
her hair black and her skin smooth. But what
once gleamed brightly in the late afternoon sun
stood dying, a metal carcass left to rot on a frame
of cinderblocks. Through the years, Leona had
grown accustomed to the trailer's slow and subtle
deterioration much as she had the ever-deepening

lines around her eyes and mouth. She frowned and furrowed her brow, worried how it might appear to Emmalee.

Leona tugged on her sweater, stretching it further across her body. The temperature in the valley had dropped fast since lunch, and it was already a good five degrees colder up here. Curtis said they might even see the season's first snowflakes by morning. A redbird rapped at the trailer's far window, but it flitted off before Leona could blow a kiss and wish for something better. "Maybe," she whispered, "something better is already on its way."

A strong wind gusted against her back, and leaves swirled and danced about her body, reminding Leona there was other work to be done. She shifted the paper sack holding a box of cornflakes to her left hand and walked on to the trailer door, scraping her canvas loafer across the metal threshold and letting the door slam shut behind her.

Low-hanging clouds had kept the trailer dark most of the week. But the sun, hovering just above the mountain's crest, at last carved a slim path through the drifting cover. An orange glow spilled through the wide window set by the trailer's only door, and Leona welcomed the traces of warm light cutting across the floor. The trailer rocked to and fro like an anxious mother trying to soothe a fussing baby as a cold front swept fast from the west. Leona planted her feet square beneath her shoulders and surrendered to the subtle pitch and sway of her home. Some said the wind blew backward on Old Lick, but Leona knew that wasn't so. There was nothing peculiar or magical about the living there.

She closed her eyes and reached for a crib once shoved tight below the window, where a wooden table stood laden with fabrics of different textures and colors, including the pieces of three damask slipcovers needing to be finished by morning. She smiled as her hand fell through the air grasping nothing but memories. She pictured her body, full and round, squeezing past the baby's bed standing ready to cradle her newborn. She scooted on toward a young Curtis with his tanned face and broad shoulders. He pulled her into his arms and rubbed his calloused hand across her belly.

The narrow trailer had never allowed for any missteps. Yet it felt so much bigger then—back when Curtis worked in the coal mines and brought home a steady paycheck and she lounged on the sofa for hours in the evenings, resting up for the birth of their first child. She hand stitched nearly a dozen day gowns, cut from Curtis's old shirts, and embroidered little bunnies along the hems. But even Leona's most treasured memories had grown fragile, and so she stood a moment longer, straining to hear the sound of a baby cooing and crying in the trailer. In her mind, there was no prettier melody than that.

Leona reached for the lamp on her sewing table. The room, which she usually kept tidy, was strewn with unfolded laundry in need of mending, glasses half-filled with day-old soda, and two stacks of outdated copies of the *TV Guide* Leona had intended to burn days ago. Thin green carpeting worn bare in places, fake wood paneling bowed from the walls, and deep cracks spidering across the ceiling looked even worse in the warm lamplight. But Leona had accepted the trailer's tired condition long ago. She ran her fingers through her wiry gray curls, desperate to cast off the remnants of another exhausting day.

The windows rattled as the wind seeped past their metal frames, and Leona tugged harder on her sweater. She had fought a chill most of the afternoon, but there was no time to take sick. Too much needlework had left her hands stiff, and a fresh blister was brewing on the tip of her index finger. She grimaced as she twisted and pushed the sweater's buttons into place. She held the sore to her lips. She knew better than to keep touching it, that it would never heal if she did.

"Damn," Leona said as she tripped on the table's thick square leg. She dropped her navy purse and the paper bag on the floor, then slipped her foot from her canvas loafer and bent to massage her toe. She stared at the pieces of damask stacked high on her sewing table. Her finger throbbed harder.

Leona reached for a large piece of fabric and held it out in front of her. She examined the seam along the zipper's edge and picked at a loose thread with her fingernail. Out of the corner of her eye, she spied Curtis still struggling to quiet the truck. She shook her head and picked at another thread. Curtis had always called Leona a miracle worker. He said the way she handled fabric was like watching the Lord turn water into wine. He believed her sewing was a gift, a gift from God. But Leona never came to think of it that way.

She had planned to finish these slipcovers for a large sofa and two club chairs by early evening. Mrs. Brooks had come from Chattanooga and was adamant that all three pieces be ironed and folded and sitting in a cardboard box outside the trailer door early the next morning. Leona should have finished them yesterday, but the fabric was thick and difficult to manage.

Her old machine struggled to keep pace as she pushed her foot harder and harder against the floor pedal. She had been forced to do much of the work by hand, and she had been preoccupied all week cleaning and tidying the extra room for Emmalee and her newborn daughter. They would come tomorrow, but Leona wished Emmalee was already there. She could have used her young eyes with the tedious hand stitching. Even Leona had to admit that the girl's pickstitch was now almost as good as her own.

Leona had tried to explain to Mrs. Brooks that another fabric would be easier to handle and might drape her furniture more smoothly. But the young woman, outfitted in her neatly ironed dress and fine pearl necklace, refused to listen. She held her palm up toward Leona's face, indicating Leona was to hush.

"The only reason I've come this distance at all is because I hear you do fine work at a fair price," Mrs. Brooks said as she handed the bolt of fabric to Leona. "Considering this cost more than sixty dollars a yard, and I've driven all this way to find you, I hope I'm not disappointed." Mrs. Brooks cocked her head to the right and tried to steal a peek into the trailer, although she refused to come inside, even when Leona offered her a cold glass of lemonade and a piece of fresh cake. She preferred to handle her transaction standing on the wooden stoop, slipping Leona no more than twenty dollars folded and tucked neat inside the palm of her gloved hand.

"I'll leave the rest in an envelope when I pick everything up Thursday morning." Mrs. Brooks's speech slowed and an exaggerated smile had stretched across her face. "You know my mother-in-law prefers I use *her woman* down in Saint Elmo. I'd hate to prove her right."

Leona rubbed her tongue across her blistered spot and glanced at the clock on the wall. She spent too much time this week sewing baby gowns, flannel blankets, and bibs for Kelly Faye. She had fallen behind in all her chores, but today she blamed Curtis for her running late. He forgot the cornflakes, and he knew damn well she could not make her hash brown casserole for Wednesday-night church supper without them. He had offered to run to the store five miles down the road, leaving her to finish her sewing. But she was too mad to be reasoned with and insisted on riding along for no other purpose than to remind him every mile of the way that his error had cost her valuable time. Her heart raced and her sore finger throbbed in perfect rhythm with every beat.

Outside the trailer, the pickup spit a final hacking cough. Leona glanced out the window to find Curtis standing with his head buried underneath the truck's hood. She picked up another piece of the red damask with pinned seams. She had no choice but to finish the slipcovers after church supper. She always had done most of her sewing late at night, after the dishes were cleaned and put away. But she was tired, more tired than she had been in years, and the thought of staying up late into the night left her both weepy and cross.

With the arch of her foot, Leona pushed a bucket

of potatoes and two large sacks of birdseed against the refrigerator's side and stepped into the kitchen. November's cold percolated through the holes in the dingy linoleum, and she shivered thinking of the winter months to come.

"Damn," she repeated, loose birdseed sticking to the bottom of her thin wool socks. A wave of cold air rushed into the trailer, and Leona turned to see Curtis at the door.

"Shut the damn door," she said and turned to the morning dishes sitting dirty in the sink.

Curtis's eye cut in Leona's direction. He did not like to hear any woman talking with a foul mouth. In all their years of marriage, the only times he raised his voice to Leona was when her tongue got ugly, but she was too mad to be concerned with his opinion or reprimand. She thrust her hands on her hips and tossed him a mean look. Curtis's expression turned soft, and he scooted farther inside the trailer. He placed his hat on a peg fastened to the trailer's wall and shook his body as if he was casting off the cold. His frame was lean and his arms muscular, but his pace had slowed in the past few months, leaving him to look much older than his fifty-two years. Curtis held his hand in front of the living room window.

"I better head down to the hardware store first thing in the morning after dropping you at the factory and get some more plastic sheeting to tape outside here. What do you think, Ona?" he asked, pushing the curtain to the side. Leona had made the curtains years ago with cheap cotton fabric bought at the five and dime in Pikeville. She hadn't bothered to line them then because she had believed they were only temporary. Now the curtains hung limp, long faded like her dreams of a different life. "I really think it helps keep the cold out, don't you?"

Leona ignored him. She hated the thick plastic obscuring what little view she had. She stacked the dirty dishes on the counter, slapping the plates one against the other. With the edge of her hand, Leona swept the crumbs into the sink and tossed a dishtowel over her shoulder.

"Sweetie, you got time," Curtis said in a soothing voice. "Nobody's going to put a bit of food on their plate till you get there anyways."

"I can't work magic," she said. "Hell, Curtis, you passed the store twice today coming and going. You couldn't think to stop and get one box of cereal?" Leona did not like to rush, especially when it came to making her hash brown casserole, the same dish she had prepared for Wednesday-night church suppers since she had officially joined the Cullen Church of Christ two days after she married. Although her attendance had never wavered, Leona's opinion about God and church had grown angry through the years.

"Don't worry, Ona girl. Like I said, church supper ain't going to start without you." Curtis plucked a white handkerchief from deep within his hip pocket. "Everybody knows you're bringing the very best dish. Even the preacher's convinced your hash brown casserole draws more people to the Lord than his Sunday preaching." Curtis rubbed his nose with the cloth and folded it into a perfect square. "You could make that casserole in ten minutes flat if need be," he said, tucking the handkerchief back into his pocket.

"I know good and well what time it is, old man, and I know good and well how much time we got. And it ain't enough." She pointed to the clock and turned the oven on high.

Leona bent low from the waist and reached for the bucket of potatoes on the kitchen floor, holding her forehead in her left hand as she dipped forward. Her neck had been hurting off and on since leaving the factory that afternoon and now the pain radiated behind her eyes. She dumped the potatoes under the running water and pulled herself up on her toes. She reached for the yellow mixing bowl stored high on top of the refrigerator.

Curtis flipped on the television set and lowered his hips into the reclining chair. The sound of the evening news mingled with his exaggerated groans as he fell the last few inches into the worn cushioned seat that held his body's impression even when he wasn't in it. He stared at Leona, busy yanking ingredients from deep within the refrigerator, while the weatherman talked about relative humidity and atmospheric pressure.

Leona didn't need an official explanation for what she felt in her bones. Although her joints already tightened and ached, she was ready for a respite from the sweltering heat inside the Tennewa sewing room. She knew to be extra careful this time of year not to let her fingers, drawn with arthritis, slip underneath the needle as she released a finished collar and began working on the next, never slowing the fast-spinning motor or breaking a thread as she moved from one piece to the other.

"Lord, Curtis, I can't barely hear myself think," Leona said as she stepped in front of the tele-vision and turned a small knob set underneath the picture. "My head's about to split wide open as it is." She leaned forward and patted Curtis on the knee. "Don't go falling asleep on me. We'll be leaving sooner than you think."

Leona's tone spun softer. She felt guilty she had talked so harsh to Curtis since he picked her up at the factory. Truth be told, she'd noticed Curtis acting more forgetful lately, and she was ashamed to admit she found his declining memory more frustrating than worrisome. Her days were tiring enough as they were, and she could not bear to think what her life would be like if Curtis lost his mind to hardening of the arteries like Burnett Daws, who wandered out from his house in the middle of the night. His wife found him the next morning facedown in a pond about a quarter mile from the road wearing nothing but his underclothes. Surely Curtis was too young for that, she reassured herself and turned the oven down to three hundred and seventy-five degrees.

"You hear me? I mean it. Don't go falling asleep. We're going to need to be on the road here soon."

"I'm just resting. I cut near a half cord of wood today."

"I saw that. You got a buyer?"

"Most of it promised to the preacher," Curtis said.

Leona rolled her eyes, knowing Curtis's day's work would not earn him one dollar, only another jewel in that damn heavenly crown he talked about all the time.

"Bring me a glass of water, girl. Not sure I can get out of this chair right yet." Curtis pushed the recliner back farther and released a deep sigh.

"Don't have no ice. Or any chilled for that matter." Leona held up the empty jug. "You know you can fill this and put it in the refrigerator as good as I can. It sure ain't going to fill itself. You'd think I was the only one on earth that knows how to work this faucet."

"Don't matter. Tap water'll be fine. Too cold for ice today anyway."

Leona handed Curtis a glass of water filled from the kitchen sink.

"Is that all? Water? No sugar?" Curtis feigned an exaggerated frown.

Leona couldn't help but laugh. Curtis had always been able to do that, to make her laugh when she felt more like crying. She did love that about him. She really did. She took a step back toward her husband and kissed his bald head. He'd do anything to make her happy, even if it meant agreeing to let a young unmarried collar maker and her baby come and live with them for a while. It had all happened so fast, and maybe Leona had made the decision in haste. But for the first time in years, she found herself looking forward to something, not back. Leona leaned down and kissed his head again.

"That's more like it," he said and grinned, his blue eyes bright after all these years. Leona laughed and held her blistered finger to her mouth. She turned back to the kitchen, her foot gliding across the thin metal strip separating the green carpeting from the kitchen's linoleum floor. She chose a sharp paring knife from a drawer, and with the confidence of a master sculptor approaching a block of stone, she whisked away the potatoes' dirty skins.

Mayonnaise, creamed chicken soup, onion, salt, and grated cheddar cheese—she measured the ingredients by sight and tossed them into the large yellow bowl. She spooned the mixture into a Pyrex dish greased with a thick layer of Crisco and admired her work before sprinkling the top with the entire box of cornflakes, well bathed in a stick of melted margarine. Leona set the casserole in the hot oven.

"See, Ona, I knew you could do it," Curtis announced. "You could make them potatoes with your eyes shut."

She smiled, knowing that indeed she could.

Leona turned to the sink filled with the brown peelings. She reached for the counter and stared into the thick stand of white oaks, maples, and pines insulating their property from the main road. A mockingbird darted across the field, pecking at the remnants of her summer garden, a few stalks of withered corn fluttering in the evening's breeze. She spied another redbird and puckered her lips. She was certain this time her kiss caught its tail as it flew across the clearing.

Leona suddenly felt as though the room was spinning around her. She clutched the edge of the kitchen counter and dropped her head. She got like this when she raced too fast from one task to the other. The dizzy spell would pass as quickly as it came on. But right now she felt weak and alone, even though Curtis sat no more than three feet away. She reached for the refrigerator handle and stood a little straighter, then walked to the reclining chair, tapping Curtis on the shoulder as she passed him by. He did not bother to open his eyes.

She maneuvered past her sewing table and into the tight hallway leading to the trailer's two bedrooms and only bath. The wall to the right displayed a collection of miniature spoons from faraway places like Niagara Falls and Yellowstone Park. Leona bought them at flea markets and yard sales for no more than a quarter each. Curtis had laughed whenever she added another piece of silverware to her collection and asked what she was going to do with such little spoons.

"You'll starve to death if you intend to feed yourself with them things," he warned her.

She thought they were pretty. That was reason enough. Curtis crafted a curio box for her collection and gave it to her on her forty-third birthday. Now all of her spoons were encased in glass and nailed to the wall.

A large photograph hung on the opposite wall. A tiny baby wrapped in a white blanket and wearing a white bonnet trimmed with blue satin ribbon lay asleep on a satin sheet. Leona sat next to him. Her hand cradled the baby's head. Curtis stood tall behind them both, with his eyes fixed on the newborn.

Leona looked at this photograph every time she walked down the hall, even when she was rushing from one end of the trailer to the other. Sometimes she saw herself in the young mother

47

with dark curls falling against her neck, and sometimes she was certain she was staring at a stranger. Either way, the photo was her most treasured possession. Today she stopped and straightened it. She kissed her son's cheek, leaving a damp smudge on the glass.

"I ain't replacing you, baby. I can't ever do that," she whispered. She wiped the glass clean with the dishtowel hanging across her shoulder. "This girl needs a little help is all. She ain't got no one else."

Leona had tried hard to ignore Emmalee when she first came to Tennewa, knowing if she started a conversation, it would surely lead to something more and possibly slow her work. But from looking at Emmalee's sad eyes and scrawny legs, Leona knew from the start that Emmalee needed mothering as much as she needed a job, and the young girl was bound to her for good now.

Leona slid into her room and slumped onto the foot of the bed.

"Ona," Curtis called from the other end of the trailer, "I'm going to drag myself out of this chair and head out to the truck. Let it warm up a bit. Don't want you catching a chill tonight."

Leona dusted her face with a fresh coat of powder and smeared some lipstick across her mouth. It was a small improvement. She lifted her chin and ran her fingers down her neck. She tugged on the skin around her eyes. She had the energy, she told herself, to care for a newborn. Besides, it was what she had always wanted. Leona rubbed some lotion on her hands and pulled a brush through her hair.

The oven timer buzzed. Leona tossed the brush on the bed and went into the kitchen, skating along beside the wall as she fought to regain her balance. She pulled the oven door open far enough to see that the cornflakes sprinkled on top had turned a crisp golden brown and the cheddar cheese was bubbling around the edges. Leona clapped her hands, relieved that in her rush she had not burned the topping, some would argue the very best part of the hash brown casserole. She turned off the oven and left the door open so the heat would spill into the trailer.

Leona forced her tired feet into a pair of low-heeled navy pumps. Her feet wobbled in the only dressy shoes she owned as she hurried out the trailer door, the basket holding the casserole secure in her arms, her navy purse swinging on her wrist.

Curtis sat ready in the truck. A fresh, mint-flavored toothpick appeared glued to his lower lip. He reached across the seat and opened the door wide enough for Leona to wedge her shoulder and round hips inside the pickup. She handed Curtis the basket and pulled herself onto the seat patched with odd-shaped pieces of a vinyl table-cloth she had stitched secure with thick nylon thread. As they headed out toward the main road, Curtis smiled at Leona and shifted the toothpick to the other side of his mouth.

"Them potatoes sure do smell good, Ona," he said.

Leona sank against the seat, the first time she had stopped to relax all day. She rolled the window down an inch or two and turned her face toward the stinging cold. She felt better, knowing she was on her way. Leona looked at her watch, tapping the crystal with her blistered finger. The preacher was probably standing in front of Sally Greer's china platter loaded with fresh buttermilk biscuits and her own pineapple-glazed ham. He was surely asking everyone to bow their heads and thank the Lord for the meal they were about to receive. Leona hated walking into the fellowship hall once the preacher had begun to pray. No matter how deep or shallow her faith, she thought it rude to interrupt.

Curtis moved both hands higher on the wheel and maneuvered the truck down the dirt drive pitted with ruts and holes left by last week's heavy rains. He groaned as he turned the wheel to the right.

"Too old to be chopping wood," he said and grinned wide.

Leona smiled back at him. "How about I rub them shoulders with some Ben-Gay when we get home?"

Curtis raised his right brow and steered sharp into the first hairpin turn. The pickup eased down the mountain road, coughing and spitting as it had earlier in the day. "Come on, old girl," he said and rubbed his hand across the truck's dash. Curtis glanced into the valley, studded with a sprinkling of lights.

"I never tire of looking at that. How about you, Ona?" he asked, patting his wife's knee.

But Leona had already observed the truck loaded with fresh-cut logs coming up the other side. She watched as it eased into their lane. She didn't think much of it at first. The road was particularly narrow there at the top. The driver would surely realize he was drifting and pull his rig back to the right.

The truck's lights only grew closer, brighter. Leona lifted her left hand out in front of her face and shielded her eyes from the blinding white light. She pulled the basket tight against her stomach. Curtis clapped both hands firm around the steering wheel. The truck strayed farther into their lane. Leona thrust both feet against the floorboard.

"Lord, Curtis, you think he sees us?" she gasped, pushing her feet harder against the floor of the truck.

Curtis did not answer. He threw his hand on the horn.

The truck eased back into the other lane. Leona

exhaled. They were safe, she thought, and dropped her chin to her chest as if she was lost deep in prayer. But Curtis had worked the pickup too far to the edge of the road. Their old truck, with four balding tires, skidded through some gravel and spun to the right. Leona stared at Curtis with bulging eyes as he fought with the wheel, navigating into the turn as best he could. The toothpick, which had been held firmly between his teeth, fell to his lap.

"Oh God!" Curtis cried as the tires left the rough asphalt road. Every loose thing in the truck slid in one direction. And then everything fell quiet. The sky was clear, and the evening's early moon hung low and full and perfect above the horizon, like it might burst open, explode like a firecracker, spilling stars all over Sequatchie Valley. But in seconds the world had grown too quiet, too perfect. Leona arched her back and screamed. The hash brown casserole fell away. Leona reached for Curtis.

A tree snapped.

Somewhere down in the holler, a baby was crying for her mother.

EMMALEE

Red Chert

- - - - - - - - - - - -

Deep in the holler, the baby wailed. Emmalee held her hands to her ears, unsure if she was trapped in another bad dream or just in the tiny bedroom she shared with Kelly Faye. She spied the dark beyond the window and pulled the bedcovers snug against her chin, careful not to smother the newborn tucked close to her side. Her father snored loud in the other room, his labored breathing leaving her anxious and jumpy. She had gone to bed early hoping morning would break sooner that way, but it was still hours before Leona was to come for her.

Emmalee twisted the end of her shirt between her fingers. She needed to pee but refused to confront the cold that had settled inside the house wrapped in plywood and pieces of tar paper. In the winter, it grew so bitter sometimes, a glass of water left by the bedside froze solid by morning, even when the stove burned hot in the other room. In the summer, the house was stifling, until a rain swept through the valley and offered

53

a rest from the heat and humidity. Emmalee tried to think of summer.

She rolled onto her side and lifted her knees to her chest. In the dim light offered by a clock radio set next to her bed, Emmalee studied her baby girl. Kelly had fidgeted off and on for the last hour, and her tiny arms grew rigid and flailed in the air. Her fists clenched tight and her cheeks reddened as she whimpered for her mama's attention. Emmalee could see she was gathering strength for a more vicious yell.

"Hush girl. Hush up," Emmalee begged. She thrust her nipple into her baby's mouth, trying to squelch Kelly's shrill cries. Emmalee flinched as the baby latched on to her tender breast, cracked and sore from the constant feedings. There was no money for bottles and formula, and she shuddered every time her baby grew hungry.

The nurses at the hospital had promised mothering would come natural. The way they talked, Emmalee had expected it to blow into the holler on the tail of a thunderstorm. Instead, she gritted her teeth as the baby's tongue pressed again and again against her raw skin. Only when her milk began to flow did her body relax some. Emmalee had tried to be a good mama with what little she knew about mothering, but she hadn't wanted this child. And now she felt tethered to her like a dog staked to the ground, not knowing which way to run to free herself of it. But things were about to change.

Emmalee had spent most of the day readying herself and the baby, first washing soiled diapers in a tin pail beside the house. She left a half dozen of the dirtiest ones to soak in water with a bit of bleach and hung the others to dry on a line held between two oaks. Then she hauled a couple more buckets of water from the outdoor spigot to warm on the stove so she could wash her own body and wipe the baby clean.

Nolan had stayed away from early morning till night, but Emmalee hurried, not knowing when her father might return. She threw what little belonged to Kelly Faye in a brown paper sack: a couple of gowns; a pair of socks; a thick sweater and matching hat Uncle Runt and his wife, Mettie, had brought to the hospital; and a pink crocheted blanket, a gift from Leona.

Leona had told Emmalee not to worry with bringing much of her own. When she got to the trailer, the two of them would make new clothes. They would shop for the fabrics together, maybe even drive to Chattanooga, where the selection was best. Leona admitted she did that if she was making something extra special. Emmalee rubbed her hand up and down her arm, imagining what a new dress would feel like. She smiled as she placed an old blue sweater that had belonged to her mama on top of her baby's things. She tucked the wooden cross she had pulled from the tree trunk inside the sweater's sleeve.

Leona had warned Emmalee her home wasn't much, but she promised her that she and Kelly Faye would have a room of their own without anybody having to sleep on the couch. They would be safe and comfortable, and Emmalee would have two people there to help care for the baby. Leona said she even had a real crib, not one made of cardboard.

Emmalee didn't fully understand why Leona had taken to her and made such a generous offer. She was a private woman and kept most of the details of her life quiet, but Emmalee had felt drawn to Leona from the first and had come to count on her perfect attendance at Tennewa as the backdrop for her days. It was a constant in her life she had never known growing up with her father. Leona's presence was as predictable as the sun rising in the east over the top of Pine Mountain or an easy spring rain that left the land smelling clean and new. It was as regular as the season's change or the nuthatch, outfitted in his slate-gray feathered coat, hammering his beak at a walnut wedged into the bark of a nearby tree.

From seven in the morning until four in the afternoon, Monday through Friday, Emmalee had listened to the hum of Leona's machine as she threaded one collar and then another underneath the presser foot. It was as if a practiced melody permeated the air, surrounding and soothing her, before being swallowed by less fluid tunes spewed from the hundreds of other machines crowding the room.

Emmalee had ached for that sound in the few weeks since the baby came, and last night she could barely sleep for imagining her new life on top of Old Lick. Leona said it was beautiful up there even when the fog lay thick on the ground. But on a clear morning, she could see for miles. "Curtis'll tell you that you can see all the way to Kentucky, but don't you go believing him," she warned Emmalee. "When we first married, it took me two whole years to figure out he was pulling my leg." Leona laughed out loud when she told Emmalee this. "I was a silly thing then."

Emmalee clapped her hands. "Kentucky," she said, repeating the word in a long, slow breath. She had once felt comforted there on her father's piece of land where Pine Mountain stood big and gentle behind her. She had loved to roam the woods near the house as a child, nesting under a tangle of mountain laurel, knowing Nolan could not find her there. But things were different now, and Emmalee longed to escape and stretch her arms open wide.

Kelly suckled hard for her mama's milk. Her tiny body stiffened as she worked for another sip. "You ain't filled your tummy yet? Lord knows I'm about to run dry," Emmalee said as she guided the baby to her other breast. She gasped as Kelly took hold. "Damn, you're a mean thing when you're hungry," she said and raised her head, listening for the familiar sounds drifting from the front room where Nolan slept.

When Nolan moved in his sleep, the cot squeaked and whined as if it, too, was wincing in pain. When he was awake, the thick soles of his work boots rubbed against the raw wood floor worn smooth with age. Floorboards were so warped in places, Emmalee spied the dirt ground a few inches below her feet. She never went to sleep without looking underneath her covers first, making sure a chicken snake or a field mouse hadn't nested in her bed. She fingered the baby's fine hair, knowing this would be the last morning she would wake in the back of her father's house.

A harsh, jarring knock came at the door. The baby pulled from Emmalee's breast and started to whimper.

"Nolan, it's me, Basil," a voice called from the yard, followed by a deep, wet cough. The town's only funeral home director worked a wad of phlegm into his mouth and spit it onto the ground. The noise rang so clear, Emmalee thought Mr. Fulton might as well have been standing by her bedside, hawking his crud right onto the floor.

Mr. Fulton knocked harder, and Emmalee understood someone in Cullen was dead.

She knew the sound of death, its tone and

rhythm, as well as she did that of a popular song played over and over on the radio. At her father's house, death never acted hesitant or shy. It came barreling out of nowhere, walking straight up to the front door and announcing itself with a bold and repetitive rap.

More experienced in the protocol of dying than her nineteen years would suggest, Emmalee was convinced the precise moment of a life's passing was determined long ago, probably before the life itself ever took root in fertile soil. And she had come to believe nothing was sadder than someone dying without warning, with no family or friends standing vigil or singing their loved one over to the other side.

Her mama had promised there was nothing sad about going on to heaven. She had talked about a place above the clouds where the streets were lined with gold and gates were crusted with pearls. She said Jesus died hanging on a cross so we all could go there someday. "Dying ain't nothing to fear," she told Emmalee. "We all got a beautiful room in a beautiful house waiting for us up there."

Emmalee never fully understood her mama's stories. They sounded more like fairy tales told to soothe a child at bedtime or the desperate ramblings of a dying woman, muttered to ease her own fears about the unknown. But after her mama passed, Emmalee spotted these crosses everywhere. She found them strung on chains around people's necks and perched on top of the church roofs in Cullen. She saw one tattooed on a man's forearm and another painted on the rocky face of Pine Mountain. She fixated on these crosses. She wrote them on paper and drew them in the mud long before she made her first one out of twigs. Back then, she hoped they might be some sort of key to that house where her mama had gone to live.

Still Emmalee believed a death was more intimidating in the dark, when the world stood quiet and defenseless and the funeral home director came looking for her father. Mr. Fulton called on Nolan when that sort of thing happened, when someone slid out of this world unnoticed in the deep of night and his passing needed to be officially confirmed and properly noted. A man who had been weakened by an early stroke, Mr. Fulton had come to count on Nolan to do the heavy lifting for him whenever a body needed to be hauled up out of its predicament and carried back to town.

"Nolan," Mr. Fulton said, calling from outside, "wake up, sir. There's work to be done. You hear me? You leave me out here in the cold much longer, and you might have another body to contend with."

Emmalee placed the baby against her thighs and pulled her knees a little closer to her chest, wrapping Kelly in a leggy cocoon. The baby's wet diaper chilled Emmalee's skin.

"Nolan!" Emmalee hollered her father's first name, both of them agreeing years ago anything more would not suit him well. "Open the damn door! Let the poor man in."

Nolan was once a good-looking man with a shock of dark hair slicked back against his head. His smile was as honeyed as his talk, and Emmalee imagined he had conned many men into hiring him and women into loving him, including her own mama. But his charm had run thin like his hair.

Another knock echoed at the door.

"You hear me, Nolan Bullard, I'm not paying you twenty-five dollars a call to stand out here in the freezing cold. I can do that on my own dime."

"Hold on," Nolan said, shouting back as he fumbled across the floor. "I was dead asleep. What the hell time is it anyways?"

Emmalee glanced at the clock radio by her bed. It read seventeen minutes past two. Then again, it always did. Pulled from one the garbage cans behind the Ridgeview Trail Apartments, the radio was a rare gift from her father, handed to her on her sixteenth birthday.

"Here," he said and jumped into his truck and sped down the dirt drive winding its way out of the holler.

Nolan searched through other people's garbage like a miner panning for gold, but Emmalee always considered the clock radio one of his better acquisitions. It picked up a couple of stations from Jasper and one from Chattanooga if the weather was good, and it always glowed bright enough so she could see her hands out in front of her even when the moon hid behind a dark sky. Besides, keeping time didn't really mean much to her anymore. In that way, she believed she was no different from the dead her father drove about town.

Another knock. Nolan fumbled with the latch, and the two men exchanged a quick hello. Emmalee rolled onto her other side and pushed her bangs from her eyes. She inched to the edge of the bed and lifted her head, struggling to make sense of the conversation in the next room.

"Listen here, there's been an accident on the other side of the valley," Mr. Fulton said. "Sheriff called about twenty minutes ago. A trucker from up near Manchester was hauling logs over the plateau and saw a pickup fly off the side of Old Lick. Trucker admitted he drifted out of his lane but thought he righted his rig in time."

Emmalee cupped her left hand over her mouth. She forced a fierce cry back down into her belly and pushed her face into the pillow. The baby squirmed against her back. Emmalee twisted toward Kelly Faye and slipped her pinkie finger in the baby's mouth, hoping to soothe her before her crying took hold. Kelly Faye suckled her mama's finger.

"Who from Old Lick?" Emmalee only mouthed the words. She was frantic to know who had passed, always finding it easier knowing than wondering. But it was foolish to think it was Leona and Curtis. They weren't the only two people who lived on that mountain, and Curtis was surely a careful driver. Besides, when a passing came sudden in the night like this, it was more often than not a teenaged driver racing too fast up and down these narrow mountain roads, chasing some fleeting thrill eluding him there in Cullen.

Mr. Fulton cleared his throat. "That poor trucker said he won't ever get that picture out of his head. Upset him so much he ran his own rig into a shallow ravine on the other side. Sheriff said it took three shots of whiskey to calm him down enough to talk." Mr. Fulton's voice grew louder with each bit of news he shared. "Rescue team's been there most of the evening. Sissie Boyd's headed out with the wrecker. Preacher Herd's probably already there. Runt's clearing trees."

"Shit, what's the sheriff calling Runt for? I can handle that chain saw better than anybody in Cullen. Runt knows it too."

"You may not care for your brother, Nolan, but there's nobody quicker at taking down a tree."

"That ain't so."

"Look, Nolan, this isn't about you. They're not reporting any survivors. But you know the sheriff—always remains hopeful to the very end. He's got to move fast. Get the best team together he can. And now we got to do our part."

Nolan shuffled toward the door.

"I'm just glad we don't have those heavy rains we had last week," Mr. Fulton said.

"Muddy as hell, ain't it?"

"True." Mr. Fulton quieted another phlegmy cough. "Only other problem I see is the rescue squad's taken the ambulance over to Chattanooga with Arbutus Spangler's boy. His fever spiked, and he started convulsing. So if there is a survivor at this point, we might be running the hearse over to the hospital ourselves."

Mr. Fulton stepped a few feet further into the room, his right foot dragging across the floor. "You know something about all this reminds me of that night back in sixty-nine when those three Signal Mountain boys out riding in that brand new convertible ran right under that semi. Remember? Two of them got their heads shaved right off." Mr. Fulton's voice rang as light and friendly as it always did. He could talk of mangled and broken bodies all the while smiling and nodding sweet. Emmalee figured he had spent so much of his life comforting the bereft that his face and voice just got stuck in that reassuring way.

"Give me a minute to get the fire going here," Nolan said. "Got to keep the baby warm." Nolan stepped outside, and Emmalee knew he had gone to steal another piece of wood from an unsuspecting table or chair he had carried home and tossed along the side of the house.

"How is Emmalee? Sure was surprised to hear she had a baby," Mr. Fulton asked, raising his voice.

"Yep," Nolan said as he returned to the stove.

"I guess you knew Hester delivered her." It sounded as though Mr. Fulton followed Nolan to the woodstove on the other end of the room. "She took Billy with her in case she needed help. Not sure the boy's recovered from the sight of it yet." Mr. Fulton laughed. "You know we haven't run Cullen's ambulance in more than ten years, since the county took over service, but the old-timers at the factory still call on Hester whenever there's a womanly problem of any kind. Guess they feel more comfortable with her than one of the men from the rescue squad." Mr. Fulton paused. "Hester said Emmalee was convinced she had the flu was all."

"Yeah. Thought she'd gotten fat." Nolan tossed the fresh wood into the stove, and Emmalee could hear the fire crackle and pop. "But it wasn't looking like there was a baby in there."

"Well, Hester said it was a tiny thing. Not more than five pounds. Is she growing good?"

"Guess so. Got some lungs, that's for damn sure." The stove's metal door clanked shut.

"Saw Runt the other day," Mr. Fulton said. "Said he brought some formula and bottles by, but you run him off. Why'd you do that, Nolan?"

"Don't need one damn thing from him."

Nolan stumbled back to his cot.

"Sure this isn't about Runt getting your daddy's mill? Nolan, that was a long, long time ago. You got to do what's right for Emmalee and the baby."

"She's doing fine. Baby too."

Emmalee clenched her fists and sucked in another fierce cry.

"Well, what about the daddy? Has he been around to help?"

"Don't know. Girl won't say. And I ain't seen a boy back here."

"Hmm. You better keep an eye on her or you'll have a houseful before long." Mr. Fulton walked back to the door. "I was always telling our Rachel you can't trust a boy till he puts a ring on your finger. Of course, I tell Billy to keep away from a girl looking for you to put a ring on her finger," Mr. Fulton said and laughed.

Billy's name was only a quick mention, but Emmalee repeated it in her baby's ear. Billy had promised to marry her long before Kelly Faye was brewing deep inside her. He asked her outright, even talked about a life together. They would live in Cullen and run his daddy's business.

Said he never knew a girl so comfortable around the dead. When they could, they'd buy a house of their own, one with two stories and a big backyard. He called Emmalee beautiful and pure then.

Emmalee had worked hard not to imagine her life married to Billy. It was foolish dreaming. But she had worked harder not to love him, even after that day he had crawled on top of her and pushed his way inside. Looking back, she understood the girl from Red Chert was only a novelty for a boy like him, not much different from the bearded lady on display at the state fair. Besides, Nolan always told her that it would take a mindless fool to fall in love with her, and Billy Fulton was a real smart boy.

Emmalee traced the outline of her baby's lips with her fingertip as she had once traced Billy's before pressing her mouth against his. Even though Billy had not claimed his baby girl, he was always there now, staring back at her. Sometimes she swore this baby taunted her on purpose. The flecks of green in Kelly Faye's eyes and her slender nose, both features stolen from the Fultons' blood, worried Emmalee. She was afraid Mr. Fulton might see his own son in Kelly's face soon. Or worse yet, Nolan would see it, too. And nothing good could come from these two men learning they shared a grandchild. If Nolan grew demanding and were to lose the only job he had ever performed with any consistency, he would surely blame Emmalee for that like he did most other things that left him cross.

"Worst cases always in the dead of night. Wonder why that is, Nolan?" Mr. Fulton asked.

"No shit."

"Stop that cussing, old man."

"Yes, sir."

"Don't seem right—cussing and tending to the dead at once. We promise dignity at all times. From pickup to burial, always respectful. That's what our ad in the paper says every single week, and I mean to honor those words. And you work for me."

"Yes, sir."

"I'd just think after all these years, you'd know where I stand on that kind of talk." Even when Mr. Fulton reprimanded Nolan, his voice sounded kind. "Come on. Sheriff's probably waiting on us, and I want to get those bodies to the funeral home before daybreak if possible. This is not a spectator sport, and this one's already drawing plenty of attention. Three calls came in before midnight. Hester says these people can't get enough of a good funeral."

The cot squeaked and moaned, and Emmalee knew Nolan was lacing his boots, preparing for the night's grim work. "Go on and get the hearse running," he said. "I'll fetch my coat and meet you out there."

"All right, but hurry it along. Like I said, I want

to get on with it." Mr. Fulton opened the door. "Why don't you follow me over there in your truck. We might need it given the circumstance." The door shut.

"Who is it, Nolan?" Emmalee said, sitting straight up in bed. "You hear me? Who was it?"

Nolan slid across the floor. "Sounds like a couple from Old Lick."

"But who? What couple?" Emmalee crawled on her knees to the end of the bed. "Nolan!"

The door slammed closed, and the house shook. This time Emmalee's body heaved forward as though she were going to retch. Her head grew dizzy, and she dropped back onto the bed. She reached for her baby, looking for someone, even a newborn, to comfort her.

The hearse rolled past her window and down the drive, kicking up mud and rock in its wake. Nolan followed in the pickup. Its suspension rattled as it hit the holes washed deep by the week's rains.

Emmalee tried to move her arms and legs, but her body felt weighted to the bed. Tattered pieces of tar paper flapped against the sides of the plywood covering the house, and bare branches from the forsythia bush rooted outside the bedroom window scraped the panes as if begging for her attention. The baby whimpered some more, kicking her legs and straining to lift her head. Emmalee lay frozen on her back, peering through the pinpoint holes that peppered the tin roof.

The clock read seventeen minutes past two. Emmalee pulled herself out of bed and began the long wait for her father's return.

LEONA

Old Lick

- - - - - - - - - -

1956

Leona fiddled with the thin gold band on her finger. Curtis had placed it there that morning promising to love and cherish her forever. The young bride followed close behind her boyish husband, holding his hand tight, as he led her to a patch of open land flecked with purple crowned thistle and wild lettuce. She listened without interruption as he gushed about the house he promised to build her some day—a frame house, he told her, painted yellow, her favorite color.

Curtis planned to add a wraparound porch in a year or two so Leona would have the perfect place to watch the sun set while rocking their babies that were sure to come. With his warm blue eyes, he nodded toward the laurel hell rooted among the pines and hardwoods and promised by the time they bloomed bright again she would have the home of her dreams.

Leona stood in the spring grass and admired the new home. She watched intently as Curtis pointed with his free hand and etched into the air the tin roof he imagined. It would cost a little more, he warned her, but he wanted his bride to hear the rain falling on a summer's night even when she was standing in the kitchen, cooking him a pot roast dinner. He winked, and she kissed him on the cheek. The blue trailer sparkling in the sun like a piece of fine crystal there on the bluff of Old Lick Mountain was only temporary, he said.

"My wife is going to live in the prettiest house in all of Sequatchie County. Can't you see it?" Curtis asked. The hem of Leona's skirt lifted in the breeze, and she laughed as she pressed the fabric against her thighs. She leaned into Curtis and snuggled against his broad chest. He wrapped his arms around her waist and slipped his hands beneath her panties.

"Yes, I do see it," she said and fell further into Curtis's embrace.

Curtis pulled Leona to the ground. He yanked on her skirt and kissed her long on the mouth. Leona raised her arms above her head and closed her eyes, easing into her husband's touch. Curtis stroked her neck with more kisses and tickled her ear with the tip of his tongue. His talk grew quiet as his arms tightened around Leona's body. He unbuttoned her blouse and cupped her breasts against his cheek.

"I love you," Leona said softly, answering her husband's caress.

Curtis wrapped her slender body between his thighs and pushed the palms of his hands against the ground. And when he was done loving his wife, he fell back into the tall grasses by her side and kissed the tip of her nose, his rough lips tender on her smooth skin.

Leona tugged on Curtis's belt and cooed in his ear, "Carry me inside, Mr. Lane."

Curtis took her by the hand and lifted her onto her feet. A meadowlark hidden in the field's tall grasses flew high above their heads, but its sudden flight did not startle Leona, still dazed by their lovemaking. She moaned, longing to linger there in the nest they'd shaped with their bodies. But Curtis pulled her along.

"Keep those eyes closed," Curtis said as he held on to Leona's hand. With eyes closed, Leona followed in her husband's path across the field and up three short steps. "Now keep 'em shut. I ain't told you to open them yet." Curtis lifted Leona into his arms. She giggled and gripped his neck. She kissed his lips, and he carried her into the trailer.

Leona took a deep breath and held it in her lungs, savoring the scent of a home untouched.

"I love it," she said.

"You ain't even seen it yet."

"I don't need to."

Curtis laughed. "Go ahead. Take a look. I didn't spend all that money for you to stand there and sniff." Curtis set Leona on her feet and kissed her cheek.

"Oh Curtis," she said as she opened her eyes.

Leona slipped her canvas shoes from her feet and ran her bare toes across the carpeting. She reached for the wall looking like real knotty pine and smiled. She walked deeper into the trailer and stood between low bookcases mounted to the left and right sides of the room, separating the kitchen from the rest of the living space. She already imagined the books and curios she would place there over time.

She glided across the kitchen's glossy white linoleum. The window above the sink allowed plenty of light. She knelt low and stroked the floor with the palm of her hand. She had never seen a kitchen gleaming like this one.

"I love it, Curtis. I really do." She jumped to her feet and hugged his neck. But Leona turned back to her kitchen and admired her new green refrigerator. She opened the door to find a half gallon of milk and a pound of butter already cold on the top shelf. She paused in front of the stove and looked for her reflection in its shiny top. She opened the oven door and pictured the casseroles and peach pies she would cook for her husband. She took another breath and savored the newness.

"There's more," Curtis said. He took his wife's slender hand in his and led her down the narrow hallway to the other end of the trailer.

Leona grinned as she tiptoed behind him, stopping at the first bedroom door. Curtis admitted it was a tiny room, but Leona did not see it that way. He promised by the time their first child came along, their house would be finished and the nursery would be at least twice this size. Leona already imagined a baby sleeping sound in his crib tucked in the corner near the window. "It's perfect," she said and walked on behind her husband.

"This is our room." Curtis said. He tugged on Leona's skirt again. She giggled as she gently pushed his hand away.

A bed was placed against the far wall. It was made up and draped with a creamy white cover. "You done all this?" she asked while she stroked the cover with her hand.

"All for you."

"Nobody's ever been so good to me," she said.

Leona suddenly spotted the blue sky outside the room's window. She crawled across the bed to get a better look. "It's so pretty here. The valley. The sky. It's all so beautiful," she said and pointed out the window. She pictured herself floating on a passing cloud.

Curtis told her that on a clear day, like this one, she could see all the way to Kentucky. She leaned closer to the window, hoping to catch a glimpse of the Kentucky bluegrass from her spot there on Old Lick.

"Take me there someday, Curtis," Leona said and collapsed on the bed, pulling her husband along with her. "You know my mama told me not to marry some poor boy from Old Lick. She can't imagine anyone with any sense wanting to live way up here. Said it's twenty minutes farther to everywhere but heaven." Leona petted Curtis's cheek. "Mama said only people up here are no-good fools. Are you a no-good fool, Curtis Lane?" Leona whispered in his ear. "Tell me now."

EMMALEE

Red Chert

- - - - - - - - - - - -

A band of fast-moving clouds slid in front of the moon, shrouding the Bullards' land in darkness. But the dark did not scare Emmalee. She had grown up there at the head of the holler, when even on the brightest days, long shadows crossed the mountain's folds.

Wrapped in a quilt thinned with age, she raised a flashlight and cast its beam across the clearing. The neon-lit eyes of a wandering possum, spotted low beneath a patch of rhododendron, lanced the otherwise pitch-black night and reminded Emmalee she was not alone. She lowered the light and huddled on a stool under the plywood porch cover extending across the front of the house. She relaxed her shoulder against a broken-down refrigerator Nolan had hauled home before she was born. It was only good for leaning against.

Emmalee was drawn outdoors whenever Nolan was driving for Mr. Fulton. Whether she knew the dead or not, she believed it was a somber time.

And she felt comforted behind the copse of tall white oaks and pines even on a cold night like this when the trees' branches danced above her head and the valley prepared for its winter's sleep.

She raised her arms above her head and stretched her back. Her spine creaked and popped as if her bones belonged to an ancient hag, not to a teenaged girl left to mother a child of her own. Her breasts hung heavy and ached from the weight of too much milk, yet she did not dare disturb the peace of her baby sleeping in the back room. She pulled the quilt up around her waist and stroked the fabric, a kaleidoscope of faded hues. She wondered if there was anything left of Cynthia Faye Bullard among these worn threads.

Emmalee didn't carry many memories of her mother anymore, other than those final ones of her lying sick in bed—her skin a pale yellow stretched loose across her bony frame, her lips split and dry, her eyes vacant. Sometimes, when she was real quiet and alone in the back room, she felt her mother's lifeless body next to hers or smelled the sour scent of urine and death tainting the air. But even after all these years what haunted Emmalee most was the silence that came at the very end.

Nolan said Emmalee "liked to drove him crazy," balled up next to her mama for hours after she died. She clung to her mama's neck, screaming when anybody tried to pull her free.

He said she whined and moped about the house for days until he finally had enough of it one night and took his hand to her bare behind, spanked the sadness right out of her. He took off for the woods, said he couldn't stand looking at the child that had drained the life right out of his wife. Emmalee remembered sitting alone in the holler that night, too. Back then, she swore she heard the house weeping along with her.

Nolan certainly had not planned on raising his daughter by himself, and he had reminded Emmalee of that almost every day since her mama's death. Now she worried she might not do much better by her own baby girl, but Leona had promised things would be different on Old Lick. She had promised life would be good up there.

"Leona, are you out there?" Emmalee's teeth chattered and her toes stung in the cold, but she did not dare leave her post. Another hour or more passed as she sat and waited for any measure of her father's return—the rough sound of the tires rolling across Red Chert Road or a quick flash of the truck's headlights bobbing in the distance.

"Oh, Lord, please don't take Leona Lane from me!" Emmalee hollered her plea, but only an owl in a far tree answered her cry. "I ain't making another cross. Not for you, Leona. I won't do it. You can't leave me."

Emmalee rocked back and forth, and the quilt dropped to her lap. She hummed a low note. She did not want to know the details of this night's accident. Yet she predicted with absolute certainty Nolan would return home all too ready to divulge what he had witnessed firsthand. He would walk into her room and sit down at the foot of the bed and proceed with his telling of the broken bones and torn flesh he had seen on the side of Old Lick Mountain.

"Stop!" she'd yell, already picturing the fear in Leona's face as she fell from the mountain's edge. But Nolan would not stop. He'd prattle on while Emmalee sat limp, trying to crowd her thoughts with prettier things. Sometimes she sang "The Star Spangled Banner" loud in her head to drown her father's voice. Other times she pretended to be in a deep sleep, hoping to avoid his talk altogether. But Nolan was a patient man when it came to his storytelling. He'd seat himself at the foot of her bed slurping a cup of yesterday's coffee and wait for her to wake.

She came to understand that when her father returned from working with Mr. Fulton, he was desperate to purge his thoughts of another lifeless body, too often bloodied and bruised, like the one of Grady Denton who drank too much beer one Friday night and steered his motorcycle square into a tree. Emmalee was barely nine years old when Grady was killed. He was nothing but a name to her, but she had closed her eyes and held her hands tight to her ears. She had sung louder and louder of rockets' red glare, but her father sat at the foot of her bed, not once looking at his daughter who was desperate to drift away.

"No shit, Emmalee, we done near had to peel the boy's face right off the trunk of that split oak out on Highway One Twenty-Seven," Nolan said. He took a swig from his bottle and wiped his mouth with the back of his hand. "Little bit of his brains here. Little bit there. Like a damn bomb blowed up. Shit. We done found his girlfriend fifty yards on down, hanging limp cross some barbed wire fencing like a damn rag doll. Not a scratch on her. Shit. Pretty girl too."

Emmalee shifted her weight against the refrigerator as images of Grady's and his girl-friend's bodies, even her mother's, flashed in her head. She saw them clear in front of her as if she could reach out and touch them. Preparing for another death always conjured up the ones already done.

The baby hollered in the back room.

Emmalee took hold of the refrigerator's door handle and pulled herself to her feet. She hugged her breasts with both arms as she straightened. She imagined her father was well into his work, and she feared the preacher had already offered up a prayer, willing the souls of the newly departed to a better place, perhaps a place where the streets really were lined with gold and speckled with pearls.

"Oh Mama, not Leona. Don't take Leona. Do this one thing for me. Just this one thing. This one time. Please, Mama, please."

The baby wailed again.

Nolan cut the engine, and the headlights dimmed. He stumbled out of the pickup and into the familiar morning gray. A knit cap, pulled down over his forehead, highlighted his bloodshot eyes. His cheeks were streaked with dirt and a cigarette hung limp between his lips. His boots were covered in mud and the hem of his pants was stained dark. Even in the dull morning light, Emmalee knew these markings on his clothes had not come from the orange clay varnishing the mountains of East Tennessee. The truck's rusted door screamed as Nolan slammed it shut, and a mourning dove's first attempts to greet the day fell silent.

Emmalee's long legs had grown stiff and numb. She gripped the post at the edge of the house to steady herself as she stood, holding the baby tight in her other arm. She met her father's stare head on. "Who was it?" she asked.

Nolan took a drag on the cigarette as he pinched it between his fingers. He plucked an empty beer can from his coat pocket and tossed it on the ground behind him, turned his mouth up to the sky, and blew a long stream of white smoke in the air. He pulled the cigarette back to his lips and took another drag.

"Nolan, tell me who."

He stumbled past his daughter, smoke spilling from his mouth and nostrils. "The Lanes."

The woods grew dark, and Emmalee's body slid down onto the packed dirt, her long legs tucked underneath her. The baby rocked her head back and forth, rooting for her mother's nipple. Kelly Faye squirmed and fussed while Nolan rambled on about shattered bodies, not noticing or caring his daughter was slumped on the ground.

"It was bad, girl. The woman done flew right out of the truck. Found her maybe a hundred feet on down the mountain," Nolan said. He flicked the stub of the cigarette to the ground. "Shit, must've been some more ride. I done thought we'd be looking for pieces here and there, but the body held together pretty damn good. She turned out better than her husband, that's for damn sure. He was done near crushed flat as a pancake."

Emmalee lifted her head. She tried to speak, but her chin dropped to her chest. The baby screamed fiercer. Nolan paid them no mind. His footsteps were clumsy and his speech slurred as he stumbled inside the house.

"Where'd you put my bottle? Where's my damn bottle, girl?" he asked, not waiting for an answer before his tone grew rough and anxious. "I ain't in the mood for a damn egg hunt. I told you quit hiding my stuff."

Any other day, Emmalee would have understood her father's desperation to drown these gruesome pictures in a bottle of alcohol. Any other day, she might have offered it to him, even if she knew his talk and temper would swell with every sip.

"Damn it, girl, I mean it. Quit messing with me." He staggered out the door and knelt low behind his daughter, his sour breath washing over the back of her neck and his fist growing tight around her arm. "Get my stuff," he said.

"I don't keep up with your bottle no more. Got enough to care for if you ain't noticed," Emmalee said, her cheek resting on her baby's head.

"Shit. I see what you care for. Whoring around. Dropping those pants for any boy come your way. Now I got a baby to feed as if your butt ain't enough."

"Shut up, Nolan. I ain't no whore. And you don't feed me nothing." Emmalee leaned away from her father, trying to scramble to her feet and escape his words and foul stench.

"Don't know the daddy's name, do you? Don't see him coming around here helping none, do you? Uh-huh. He figured you out right quick. They all do."

Nolan's eyes were red and fiery, and Emmalee grew limp as he tightened his grip around her arm. She drew the baby close. "I don't need nothing from you!"

Nolan grabbed her shoulder. "Cindy Faye, I've told you, woman, not to hide my bottle from me." He hissed his wife's name in Emmalee's ear and slid his finger down her bare breast toward the baby's mouth. "It ain't right the baby got hers, and I got nothing." Emmalee slapped at his hand and struggled to her knees.

"I ain't Mama. I ain't Cynthia Faye. Wake up, you drunk fool!" Emmalee yelled, her voice choked with anger and fear. She worked to pull free from his grasp, but with the baby bound to her chest, she floundered.

Nolan tangled his fingers around Emmalee's long brown hair and yanked her head backward. Cursing and spitting, he dragged her toward the house. Emmalee cradled the baby in one arm. She pushed her heels into the dirt.

"Under the cot, you damn fool. It's under the damn cot." Emmalee cried out and grabbed on to the doorframe with her free hand. Nolan wrenched her deeper into the house and fell onto his back, his head snapping against the wood floor. He let go of Emmalee and covered his face with the palms of his hands, the cuffs of his blue work shirt stained dark with blood.

"Shit," he spewed and coiled over and onto his stomach. He lay quiet for a moment and then slithered across the floor, ferreting for his bottle amid crumbs of cornbread and bits of dried orange clay.

Emmalee crawled back outside, the baby squalling in her arms, and huddled in the dirt on the far side of the refrigerator. The mourning dove plucked another note of its melancholy song while Emmalee waited there in the cold for Nolan to calm himself with his drink.

Later from her room, Emmalee listened to her father slurping from his bottle and rambling on about all he had seen on the side of Old Lick. She pulled the quilt over her head and hummed another bar of "The Star Spangled Banner," but his talk sputtered on.

"Shut up, you old fool." She did not want him talking about Leona that way. "Just shut your mouth," she said and rubbed her arm where he had grabbed her, certain to find a bruise there.

The baby slept in the middle of the bed while Emmalee sat stiffly in a chair placed against the door. The chair legs were uneven, like the broken-down sofa in the front room. She rocked back and forth while she pictured Leona's death in vivid detail as if she was watching a movie, each frame rolling too slowly across the screen.

Leona's eyes grew big, and her arms flailed about the truck. She reached for her husband, desperate for his hand, but she could not find it. She screamed his name as the pickup dropped to the ground. Emmalee wondered if Leona had told Curtis she loved him. She wondered if there was time or the presence of mind to say such a thing as the truck hurtled through the air and Leona's body was flung against the truck's roof. Emmalee wiped a tear from her eye and played the scene again, and again. When the house at last grew quiet, the baby woke, angry and loud. Her diaper was sopping wet and her belly empty.

"Damn it, Kelly," Emmalee said, her tone harsh. "I ain't up for you right now." Kelly's cries boomed louder, and she kicked her little legs, tossing the covers from her body. "Hush up." Emmalee stood by the bed and pulled the baby in front of her. Kelly's face was red and her fussing, sharp. "Stop it. Everybody in Red Chert's going to hear you if you don't hush up." Emmalee's breath blew white in the room. "I'm doing the best I can, can't you see that?"

She slipped the wet gown over her baby's head and stripped the wet cloth from her bottom. She held her hand on Kelly's tummy while she reached for a dry diaper on the table next to the bed. "Damn it," Emmalee said. A half dozen diapers had been left soaking in the tin pail outside the house and were likely frozen hard. A dozen others had been left hanging on the line. "Damn it. Damn it." Emmalee glanced about the room for a suitable cloth for diapering. "What with you pulling on me all day, I gone and forgot all those damn diapers."

Emmalee scrounged about the room for something more to wear. She pulled on a pair of jeans tucked under the bed and a ratty sweater left across the back of the chair. She bundled herself in what else she could find: a hooded sweatshirt and some thick wool socks. "Hush Kelly. Hush now," Emmalee said as if reciting a mantra. "Hush baby. Hush your crying." But the baby carried on for her mother's care.

Emmalee tugged on the jeans' denim waistband and drew in her stomach. She wondered if she would ever look or feel like she had a year ago. As her tummy had grown with the baby, Emmalee had never once believed she was pregnant. She never got big like the other women she had seen at the factory. The doctor at the hospital said sometimes that happens. Besides, he figured the baby came a bit early, barely weighing five pounds. Nolan had called Emmalee fat a time or two there at the end, and she guessed she had rather believed that than the truth. Once she suspected her condition, she had hidden her body inside large shirts and baggy housecoats.

Emmalee crept into the front room. With the baby wrapped in a blanket and held in her arms, she tiptoed to the table and grabbed a dishtowel used the day before to wipe the baby's face and hands. It was dry and clean enough for diapering. Nolan slept facedown on his cot, dressed in his muddy work boots and blood-

88

stained overalls. He did not stir, and Emmalee rushed past him and back into her room.

"This'll do you fine," she said to Kelly Faye, who turned her head toward the sound of her mother's voice. Emmalee placed the baby on the bed and opened the blanket, again exposing the baby's skin to the bitter cold. Kelly cried harder and her lips quivered as her mama tended to her bottom, already growing blotchy and red. Her pink lips shaded icy blue as she worked herself into another breathless tantrum. Emmalee rushed to dress her, struggling to slip Kelly's rigid arms into the flannel gown the collar makers at Tennewa had given her.

"Dressing you is like trying to tame a hornet," she said, jerking matching pink socks onto Kelly's bare feet. "Shut up. I mean it," she said. "My head's full of your wailing."

Emmalee wiped her baby's tears with the tail of her shirt and put her to her breast. The baby tugged hard for her morning meal, only stopping to catch her breath. "Hurry on up," she said, having grown impatient with her daughter and her demanding nature. She had never understood babies were such a constant thing.

She listened for any sound of her father's stirrings, certain Kelly's fussing would rouse him from his sleep. But the steady rise and fall of Nolan's breathing was the only noise drifting from the front room. "That's enough," Emmalee said and lifted Kelly onto her shoulder. She thumped Kelly's back, steady and even, as the nurses in the hospital had taught her to do. She held Kelly against her shoulder and carried a long, sturdy stick with her free hand. Emmalee had pulled the stick from a poplar back of the house after one of Nolan's tantrums and hid it under the bed. Now she kept it close as she went to wake her father.

"The bodies at Fulton's?" she asked, poking Nolan's thigh with the stick's rounded end. Emmalee repeated her question. "Nolan, you hear me? The bodies at Fulton's?"

"Huh, what . . . you what?" Nolan mumbled and eased onto his back.

"I'm taking the truck to Fulton's. Hand me the keys."

"I ain't going nowhere," he said, slurring his words and not bothering to open his eyes.

"That's right. You ain't going nowhere. Hand me the keys. I'm the one going to see Miss Leona. Not you."

"Miss Leona's dead. Thrown out the windshield. Shit, girl."

"Shut up, Nolan. Give me the damn keys."

Nolan held his hands to his head. "Girl, don't do that," he said with a softened but exasperated tone. He focused on Emmalee even though his eyes had yet to open. "That woman don't look right. I know you cared about her, but hell, girl, let Mr. Fulton do his work. I'll take you later. They ain't putting her in the ground today no way."

"Don't need you to take me. Don't want you to take me," Emmalee said, rapping the end of the stick against the wood floor. "I mean what I say. Give me the damn keys."

Nolan rubbed his right hand across his stubbled chin. He hadn't taken a razor to his face in weeks and yet his beard was short, mostly black, with just a sprinkling of white. After drinking heavily, Nolan always looked feeble, not the mean and threatening man he had been only hours ago. Again, she rapped the end of the stick on the floor and waited for an answer.

"All right," he said and swiped at the stick, but his reach fell short.

"The keys, Nolan."

"Coat pocket," he muttered and rolled onto his left side, turning his back to his daughter.

EMMALEE

Fulton-Pittman Funeral Home

Cars and trucks loaded with men passed Emmalee as she drove into town. She figured most of them were headed over to the DuPont plant in Chattanooga where they made nylon for tires. There was a time when Nolan had talked big about working there. Said he could make a lot of money. But that's all it was. Just talk.

Emmalee peeked down at the baby, nestled in a cardboard box set next to her on the seat. Kelly Faye stared back at her mama and cooed dulcet notes. Emmalee gently rocked the box and drove on toward town. The nurses had given her a proper seat for the baby to ride in, but Nolan dropped it on the sidewalk in front of the hospital the very next day. He pulled a box from the Dumpster behind the Ridgeview Trail Apartments. "It's fine for hauling a baby," he told Emmalee.

Emmalee glanced at the dials set in the panel above the steering wheel. "Damn," she said. The tank's gauge registered empty, and she carried only enough change in her pocket for maybe a half gallon. She didn't have far to go; Fulton's was only a mile ahead. But with the baby in tow she didn't want to be walking home in the cold. She leaned on the steering wheel as if encouraging the truck along. The PURE station sat on the very next corner. As the truck rolled toward the pumps, a bell rang out.

A young woman walked out of the garage wearing blue jeans pushed into a pair of heavy black work boots. She waved to Emmalee and flashed a toothy smile. Sissie Boyd had worked at her mother's filling station since she was thirteen, less than six weeks after her father died of a heart attack while checking the oil filter under a customer's hood. Sissie was a year older than Emmalee, but she graduated valedictorian of her high school class. She left three months later for college somewhere in Nashville but came home three months after that. She told her mama she wasn't going back, and she'd been at the filling station ever since.

Emmalee had always envied Sissie, and not because she pumped gas and discussed spark plugs and distributor caps with the men in town as if she was their equal. It was Sissie's loss that Emmalee envied. Her father had died, not her mother, and Emmalee wished she had been that fortunate. She knew it wasn't right to think so. Mr. Boyd had been a good man. But nothing about life and death was ever right or fair.

Sissie motioned for Emmalee to roll down the window. She flung her arms inside the truck and peered across the seat. Sissie's fingernails were cut short and the tips were stained black with grease. Her hair was long and smooth but she kept it tucked on top of her head underneath a baseball cap most days. Emmalee imagined Sissie could look real pretty if she wanted.

"Hey there, Emmalee. Haven't seen you around since you had the baby. You got her with you?" Sissie pushed her head farther inside the truck.

"Yeah, she's right here." Emmalee lifted the end of the cardboard box.

"Oh, she's precious. Look at those little bitty hands. What's her name?"

"Kelly. Kelly Faye."

"Mighty tiny thing. You feeding her enough?"

"Feed her all the damn time. My tits so sore I can't stand it."

Sissie grimaced and shoved her hands inside her jeans' pockets. "That doesn't sound fun."

"Fun? It ain't fun."

"Well, what can I do for you? Fill her up? The car, I mean," Sissie said and laughed.

"Ain't got but a little change. Hate to bother you, but can I get a couple of gallons on credit?" Emmalee reached into her coat pocket for the coins. "Not sure when I can get the rest to you. But I will. You know I'm good for it."

Nolan had always taken most of Emmalee's

pay when she worked at Tennewa. He said she owed him every penny of it after sixteen years of mooching off him. Emmalee handed over all but a few dollars of it, knowing anything less would only end in a fight. But in all her life, Nolan had never bought her much of anything, and she remembered too many nights going to bed with her stomach screaming to be fed.

"How about I fill the tank, Emmalee, sort of a baby gift from me and Mama. Only hitch, you'll have to bring Kelly Faye back around for her to see. Mama'll die to get her hands on her." Sissie unscrewed the gasoline cap. "Already begging me for grandchildren. But I can guarantee that's going to be one long wait. Told her I need a husband first, and I'm certainly not interested in getting me one of those anytime soon." Sissie's smile faded fast. "I'm sorry, Emmalee. I didn't mean nothing by that. Just blabbering nonsense. I'm sure you and the daddy got it all worked out."

Emmalee looked at the baby. "Yeah, we got it all worked out."

Sissie shoved the nozzle in the tank and returned to the truck's open window. "What are you doing out so early anyway? Baby not sleeping?"

"She don't sleep much. But I'm headed over to Fulton's. Heard you ran the wrecker last night. On Old Lick?"

"Sure did," Sissie said, her voice turning somber. "Sheriff called a little before ten o'clock to let me know there'd been an accident. I didn't get there till nearly two. Didn't want to get in the way of the rescue." Sissie pulled a faded blue rag from her back pocket. "We never could get the pickup down the mountain, what with the equipment we got. I think they're going to call in some help from Chattanooga or Nashville." Sissie rubbed her nose with the rag. It left a spot of black grease on her skin. "I can't believe Mr. and Mrs. Lane are both gone. And what an awful way to go, flying off the mountain like that. Such nice people."

Sissie wiped the windshield with a wet sponge and then dried the glass with the same blue rag. "Mr. Curtis was no doubt about the nicest man I've ever known. Pretty voice, too. He was a song leader at the church. And a deacon. He always had something kind to say about everybody. I don't think he hated a single living soul." Sissie pulled the nozzle from the tank and screwed the tank's cap back on tight. "You friends with them or out running some kind of errand for your daddy? I saw him over there last night. That was some tough work those men did. They weren't giving up till they got Mr. and Mrs. Lane down that mountain."

Emmalee drummed her fingers against the steering wheel. She liked thinking her father had done something good for Leona there at the end, although she had not expected that of him. In fact, she always found it difficult picturing him kind and respectful around the living or the dead, never knowing him to give either much attention.

Emmalee looked straight at Sissie. "Tennewa. Leona and me worked together at Tennewa going on three years. Side by side. Curtis came by the factory with a cold orange soda whenever he was in town. He knew Leona wouldn't buy one out of the machine. You're right. He was a real nice man. Sometimes he brought me a sandwich and a bag of potato chips."

"I didn't know that about you and Miss Leona. I'm so sorry, Emmalee. Really I am. Think sometimes friends hurt more than family, but nobody pays them much attention."

Emmalee nodded. She thanked Sissie and promised to bring the baby back later in the week for her mama to admire. The truck lurched forward, and Emmalee steered onto the main road with a full tank of gas and fifty-two cents in her pocket. The sun shone in her eyes, and she lifted her hand above her brow to better see the road that led into town and to the Fulton-Pittman Funeral Home.

The downstairs curtains were pulled shut at Fulton's. The large wood-framed house with a broad wraparound porch looked grander than the other homes on the street, and Emmalee considered it to be the prettiest one in town. Mr. Fulton's granddaddy, George Pittman, had been a furniture man who saw the money to be had in making caskets, not tables and chests of drawers. He opened his home to Cullen's grieving families nearly sixty years ago, all the time making caskets in a shed in the far back of the property.

When Mr. Fulton married, he took over the family business and moved into the home's second story. Mr. Fulton told Emmalee once it had been the perfect place to raise a family, although he admitted his wife had grown tired of the town's grief-stricken taking over her home as if it were their own. Some kept their vigil going all night and wandered into her kitchen in the early morning to scramble up eggs and cook a pan of biscuits. She even found a relative of the deceased sleeping off a bottle of whiskey in an upstairs bedroom, on her finest cotton sheets. Mr. Fulton said his wife pitched a fit that could have waked the dead down in Georgia. But this morning, the house looked peaceful, as if it might be sleeping, too.

A paved drive led around to the back where deliveries were made and caskets, which Nolan had told her were now ordered direct from a company in North Carolina, were hauled in and out of the house. Large clay pots brimming with purple and white pansies accented either side of a wide concrete stoop. Emmalee bent to finger one of the purple petals, believing something so perfect must be fake.

She wondered if the Fultons were lonely in this big house. Their daughter had moved to Birmingham with her new husband at the end of April, and Billy had started school up in Knoxville the first of September. Standing there on the porch steps, Emmalee missed Billy more than she had in months. She missed the way he twirled her hair between his fingers and kissed the tip of her nose. She missed the way he held her firmly in his thick, strong arms but never squeezed her too tight. She missed the way he spoke with a soft tone never seeming to fit his large, muscular frame. She wondered if he thought about her or if he had found someone new to love, someone he could bring home to his mother. It made her crazy to think so.

Emmalee shook her head, trying to rattle the image of another girl out of her thoughts. She stared up at the windows on the second floor, wondering which room belonged to Billy. She had been inside the house only one other time. Her mama's body had been kept at the house back in Red Chert. Nolan said he didn't trust anyone, not even the Fultons, to stand vigil over his Cynthia Faye. Mr. Fulton came to the holler with a black bag in his hand and prepared the body right there in the front room. Emmalee had no memory of that day, only of her uncle Runt holding her in his arms.

When her mama's mama died, Emmalee had walked to the funeral home alone. She was only ten and carried no memories of the woman Nolan called a red-eyed snake. But she figured they should meet at least once before her grandmama was dropped in the ground for good. Emmalee leaned over the casket and studied the woman with the thick layer of beige makeup on her skin and a blue scarf tied around her head. She couldn't see the color of her eyes, and she struggled to find traces of her own mama in the woman's deeply lined face.

"Never seen a girl get so close to the dead before," Billy said and blew in her ear. He had eased up behind Emmalee without warning, but she did not frighten. "Wouldn't get too close, you know. She might reach out and grab you. I've seen it happen."

"No, you ain't, Billy."

"Yes, I have. They'll hang on to anybody passing by. Some just not ready to go on, I guess." He moaned like a ghost might and blew another blast of warm air on Emmalee's neck. Emmalee swatted him away.

"They can hear you, you know. Keep an eye on her. She'll blink fast if she's listening. You'll miss it if you don't keep a close watch. Sometimes they even talk back."

"Shut up, Billy. She don't scare me, and you don't either."

"She don't?"

"Hell no. Only the living can do that."

Billy snickered. "Guess so." He steadied his elbow on the edge of the casket and stared at Emmalee.

"She's my grandmama," Emmalee answered, not daring to take her eyes off the woman boxed up neat in front of her in case there was some truth to what Billy had said. "Why she wearing that rag on her head?"

"She didn't have any hair except for what the family brought to my daddy in a paper bag. Heard them asking if Daddy could put it back on her." Billy pointed to the wisps of white hair protruding beneath the edge of the scarf. "He did the best he could. Got some of it on. Mother helped him. Family seems pleased. Daddy says that's all that matters."

"She looks good. Don't know what she looked like before. She's got some hair though sure enough. Your daddy done good, I guess."

Emmalee examined the woman a while longer. "Yep, he done real good," she said and pushed her way past Billy and the other mourners. She walked back home, holding one lasting memory of her grandmama in her head.

Standing outside the funeral home all these years later, Emmalee pulled the crocheted blanket over the baby's face and stepped onto the wide wooden porch. She knocked on the door and waited. She glanced up and down the street and knocked again.

Mr. Fulton opened the door a few inches, appearing in a bathrobe and black slippers. He scratched the top of his head. Then he held his weak hand to his mouth, cleared his throat, and offered up his familiar smile.

"Young lady, what in the world are you doing here? Nolan forget something? Is something wrong? Something wrong with the baby?" he asked, his tone growing anxious as he rubbed his fingers across his short-cropped hair.

"No sir."

Mr. Fulton stared at Emmalee.

"I come to see Miss Leona."

He tied his bathrobe shut. "What time is it anyway? I was about to head upstairs." He turned and hobbled down a long hallway toward the kitchen, motioning for Emmalee to follow. He looked around as if searching for a wall clock or a pot of coffee warming on the stove. "I don't know what all your daddy told you about last night, but the bodies aren't in good shape. I can't let you see them this way." Even his smile broke tired. "Come back tomorrow. Better yet, the day after. I'll have time to do most of the repairs by then. Mrs. Fulton'll hang the white wreath on the door like she always does when the bodies are ready for viewing."

Emmalee planted her feet firm. "No. No, sir. I come here to see Leona."

Mr. Fulton shook his head.

"Look, I know she ain't in good shape," Emmalee said. "And I know you ain't even been to bed. But if you don't let me see her—" She paused and pulled out a kitchen chair. "Well, I'm going to sit right here at this table till you do." Tears welled in her eyes. Emmalee shifted the baby from one arm to the other and sat down at the table.

"Don't start crying. Lord, I hate to see a woman cry. I know. It sounds crazy for a man in my line of work to say that. You'd think I'd be used to it by now. But I'm not." Mr. Fulton handed Emmalee a dry dishtowel. "Hester says I'm too tender hearted for the funeral business."

Emmalee dabbed her eyes with the terry cloth.

"You look as worn out as I do." Mr. Fulton poured a cup of hot coffee and placed it on the table in front of Emmalee. He poured another for himself. "Babies'll wear you out, but you got to be real careful with a newborn, especially a tiny one like that. I've seen too many get sick this time of year and die. I don't mean to be scaring you, but I don't want to be burying yours next, you hear me?"

"Yes, sir." Emmalee blew on the coffee and took a sip.

"And you got to take good care of yourself so you can take good care of her."

"Yes, sir."

"You know I buried one no bigger than yours right before Christmas the year I married Mrs. Fulton. Tore my heart out. We kept the casket there by the Christmas tree in the living room."

"Under the tree?"

"Right next to it." Mr. Fulton smiled. "Funny thing though, Hester wanted no part of tending to the dead back then. I asked her to diaper that baby for me, said I didn't know the first thing about working a diaper. After she did it, I looked at her and said, 'There, now you've touched a dead person.' She was fine after that. Been doing most of the makeup for me ever since."

Mr. Fulton leaned against the kitchen counter as if he had forgotten the purpose of Emmalee's visit. "Sorry, I'm talking to no end. Ask your father, I do that when I haven't had enough sleep."

Emmalee cradled the baby in her arms, careful to keep her child's face from Mr. Fulton's view.

"You look pretty certain about this, Emmalee."

"I am."

Mr. Fulton squinted at the clock above the oven and set his mug on the counter. "You need to understand that once you've seen her, there's no taking it back. No erasing it from your thoughts.

It's there for good. Are you sure you're ready for that?"

"Yes, sir," she said and sat a little taller.

Mr. Fulton set his mug on the counter. "Okay then, come on." He motioned for Emmalee to follow him this time down a short, dimly lit hall running off the back of the kitchen. "You know the wife and me were supposed to be leaving in another hour to drive down to Destin for a week of deep-sea fishing." Mr. Fulton tapped the blue-colored fin of a large fish mounted on the wall. Emmalee had never seen a fish that size in the creeks around Cullen. "Mrs. Fulton hates that tuna. Makes me keep it back here hidden from plain view."

"You caught that?"

"Sure did, back when my arm was good." He pretended to cast a fishing line into the water. "This one was just too pretty to eat, don't you think?" Mr. Fulton turned to a closed door. "Seems every time we plan another fishing vacation, someone in Cullen ups and dies. Usually Claiborne's over in Jasper'll cover for us, but they're short-staffed this week. My brother and his wife are already down in Destin. Called me a few minutes ago to remind me to bring the ice chest."

"Destin?" Emmalee asked.

"Florida, hon. Ever been to Florida?" he asked and pulled a set of keys from his robe's pocket.

"No, sir."

"Water's so blue and clear. You can see the dolphins swimming right by your boat. Maybe one day you'll get down there." Mr. Fulton winked and scanned all the keys before easing a smallish silver one into the lock set above the knob.

Emmalee noticed a photograph hanging on the wall next to the door. Mr. Fulton stood in the water on a sandy shore. His chest was broad and his skin, tan. A small boy was perched on his shoulders, dangling a tiny fish next to Mr. Fulton's ear. Emmalee saw Kelly in the boy smiling back at the camera.

"You recognize that man?" Mr. Fulton puffed his chest out big. "Believe it or not, that was me. Long time ago, but it was me."

"I believe it," she said and winked like Mr. Fulton had.

"You're sugar talking me now," he said and gripped the doorknob tight. His knuckles washed a pale white. "Look here. I don't want to be scooping you up off the floor. So if you feel lightheaded, you let me know. Nothing to be embarrassed about. You won't be the first to faint," Mr. Fulton said. He stooped a bit and looked straight at Emmalee. "You know, I wouldn't be doing this if it weren't for your daddy." Emmalee's eyes widened. Being Nolan's daughter had never served any obvious advantage, and she tried to reconcile this thought with the fresh bruises already coloring her arms and legs.

Mr. Fulton opened the door into a small room, the only light coming from a long fluorescent tube mounted on the ceiling. Emmalee quickly covered her nose with her left hand while keeping the baby snug in her other arm. The smell was odd and discomforting, more disturbing than that of a dead animal left to rot underneath the house.

"That's formaldehyde you're smelling," Mr. Fulton said. "Always in the air. It's a preservative."

Emmalee mashed the palm of her hand against her nose.

Two stainless-steel tables stood in the middle of the room. Leona was on one. Curtis, the other. But each was covered with a crisp white sheet, and Emmalee could not tell them apart. Both tables were positioned at a slight angle, a small pitch forward, just enough to leave the feet of the deceased several inches closer to the ground. Whatever washed over or flowed from the bodies spilled into large stainless toilets mounted on the wall, one at the foot of each table.

A stainless cart footed with wheels and loaded with an array of oddly shaped knives, scissors, spatulas, and a spool of thick cotton thread stood ready between the two tables. Emmalee studied the draped bodies and then the cart, not wanting to speculate on these instruments' purpose or past use.

Mr. Fulton stood beside the table closest to the door. He looked at Emmalee as if asking for permission to proceed. She nodded, and he lifted the white sheet only far enough to expose another covering. This one was made of a thick plastic, but Emmalee could already see bits of Leona's gray curly hair, matted with a mixture of dirt and blood.

Mr. Fulton peeled the plastic sheeting from the body, revealing Leona's head and bare shoulders. Her skin was pale, almost white, drained of all life and color. Her lips were too full and colored a grayish blue. Her forehead was split from her right eye clear to her left temple, leaving an open wound, wet and raw. Her eyes were swollen shut, her right cheek twice its normal size. Emmalee had seen death before, but it had never looked so wounded. She did not shrink away. Instead she nuzzled her nose against her baby's head and drew a deep breath, trying to fill her head with the infant's sweet scent.

"Can you fix her?" Emmalee asked as she further studied Leona's face.

"I'm going to do the best I can." Mr. Fulton held Leona's chin between his forefinger and thumb and turned her head slightly toward him. "Life never was fair to you," he said in a melancholy tone.

"What?"

"Oh nothing. She may not look perfect is all," Mr. Fulton said and straightened the sheet covering Leona's body. "Most families want an open casket, although I'm not sure what they'll do in this case. Mr. Lane's worse off, and I don't know how it would look to have one open and one closed. We'll see how he turns out before making any final decisions."

"They got family here?"

"Not really. Not anymore," Mr. Fulton said. "Mrs. Lane doesn't have any relatives in town. She had a brother out in Oklahoma, but he died a couple of years ago. I believe she's got a younger sister somewhere in Virginia."

"Does she know?" Emmalee asked, not taking her eyes off Leona.

"Not sure the preacher's gotten word to her yet."

Mr. Fulton rested against the other table. "Mr. Lane's mama is here, over in Jasper, but she's nearly ninety-eight. I'm not sure she's been told either, and if she'll even really understand what's happened. I hear her mind's been slipping." Mr. Fulton patted Curtis's arm. "Preacher will stop by the convalescent home and talk to her later today."

Emmalee spotted a navy dress, folded neat and placed on the counter behind her. She stroked the fabric and lifted its collar. The collar looked no different from those she and Leona had made at the factory, except the cloth was a little heavier than the lightweight cottons they used most often at Tennewa; and this collar was soaked with blood, shaded brown under the room's harsh light. Emmalee imagined this was Leona's best dress, and she wondered if the frugal woman who ate bologna-and-tomato sandwiches most every day had anything else hanging in her closet appropriate for eternity.

"What are you burying her in?" Emmalee asked, rubbing the collar between her fingers.

"Don't know. Hadn't given it any thought. Family usually brings something," Mr. Fulton said. "Of course, given the circumstances, I'll probably go up to their trailer later today and look around."

Emmalee held on to the collar.

"But we got some dresses here that'll do fine if we can't find something of her own that's suitable. As I was saying earlier, Mrs. Fulton helps with the hair and makeup. So I usually leave these kind of decisions to her."

Emmalee fingered the small band of lace stitched beneath the collar's edge. She had never seen Leona wear anything so frilly or fine. She came to work most days in one of the cheap cotton housedresses they made there at the factory, the same ones that were shipped to Montgomery Ward and J.C. Penneys and sold to the public for no more than twelve dollars apiece. In the colder months, sometimes she'd wear a hand-knitted sweater with a thick cotton skirt, although the same pair of canvas loafers covered her feet summer or winter unless the ground was wet or buried deep in snow.

"Let me do it," Emmalee said fast, breaking the silence blanketing the small room. "Let me make her something. I want to do it. I want to make Leona something special for burying."

"That's not necessary, Emmalee. Like I said, we've got dresses here if need be. Come on, I'll show you." Mr. Fulton led Emmalee out of the room and to a closet door at the other end of the hallway. "Let me see here," he said and pulled a pale pink chiffon dress into the light. "See, this'll work fine. It's even open in the back, no buttons or zippers. It's actually made for this kind of thing."

Emmalee held the sleeve of the dress in her hand. "This ain't Leona. She'd never wear something like this, and I can sure enough tell you she'd never wear pink."

"It doesn't have to be pink. We got them in yellow, blue, peach, and a real pretty shade of green. I think Hester calls it *celadon*." Mr. Fulton pulled another dress into the light. "Hester picks them out. I think they're shipped from New York City or Saint Louis. These are very nice dresses, Emmalee."

"I ain't arguing that. But Leona's earned better than this. She should have a dress with meaning. It should be special. Real special. It shouldn't come from New York or somewhere else or made by somebody she ain't ever seen."

Tears streamed down Emmalee's cheeks, dripping onto the baby's pink blanket. "Leona sat next to me every day, Mr. Fulton. She looked after me like nobody else ever done." Emmalee caught her breath and wiped her face dry. "Let me make her burying dress. I really want to do this for her. I want her to have something special, and if it don't work out, you can use one of these here. Please."

Mr. Fulton thumped the palm of his hand against his forehead. "These are real nice dresses, hon. Maybe nicer than anything Mrs. Lane ever bought or made for herself. And she gets to wear this one for the ages." He waved the hanger and the celadon-colored dress fluttered in the air. "Besides all that, you've got a new baby to care for. You don't have the time to be making a dress. Or the money. Where are you going to get the fabric?"

Emmalee shifted the baby onto her shoulder and patted her bottom. "I got plenty of time for Miss Leona. Just tell me when you need it. And the fabric . . . I don't know. I'll figure something out. Maybe she's got some scraps of something up at the trailer. She had extra sewing most every night. I can use anything I find up there, can't I?"

"I guess so." Mr. Fulton rested his forehead in his hand. He stood silent like that till Emmalee wondered if he had dozed off. "Okay, listen to me," he finally said as he focused on Emmalee. "I'm going to need this dress at the very latest by Sunday morning. We'd like to get the visitation under way later that afternoon with burial on Tuesday." He hung the dress back in the closet. "That'll only give you a little more than two full days. Can you manage that? Two days?"

"Yes, sir." Emmalee's smile grew wide.

Mr. Fulton stood quiet for a moment longer. He looked at both bodies and then back at Emmalee. "We don't need anything fancy here."

"Oh thank you, Mr. Fulton. Thank you." Emmalee hugged his neck.

"Don't get too excited. I got to see it first. But you go ahead and get started," he said and straightened his robe. "Like I said, we don't even need a zipper down the back. It's actually easier if there's not one. Nobody's going to see it no how. Remember, people are only looking from the waist up. Something simple is usually best, and Leona Lane was definitely a woman of simple means." Mr. Fulton walked back to the kitchen. Emmalee followed him. "Lord, I hope Mrs. Fulton don't skin me for this. So keep it real tasteful, hon, or you and me both are going to be in trouble. Big trouble."

"Yes, sir, tasteful."

Mr. Fulton reached for the coffeepot but stopped and lowered his head, and Emmalee wondered if he might be falling asleep standing there in front of the counter.

"Mr. Fulton, you okay?"

"I'm fine." He waved his hand but kept his back to Emmalee. "Can't believe what all has happened. Some sure to say this is God's plan, but I don't know about that." He poured a fresh cup of coffee and turned toward Emmalee, a bright smile returning to his face. "Here, you might need this," he said and reached for a key with a rubber band looped through its head, hanging on a nail by the kitchen door. "This here is to the Lanes's trailer. Don't think they ever locked it, but take it with you just in case. See what you find. There may be a perfect dress already up there in her closet. If not, maybe I can sneak you a little money for fabric if you need it. But let's keep that to ourselves."

Mr. Fulton handed Emmalee the key. "Have you been there before? To Leona's?"

She looked out the kitchen window toward Old Lick, knowing if Leona had not died during the night, she would be on her way to the trailer now. She would be sitting between Curtis and Leona. Leona would be holding the baby on her lap, cooing at Kelly Faye and gushing on about her bright eyes and fine hair. She'd only stop long enough to remind Curtis to slow his speed around those mountain curves so as not to make the baby sick. Then she'd talk more gibberish to Kelly Faye and tickle her cheek with the tip of her finger.

"You are absolutely sure you can handle this, hon?" Mr. Fulton asked.

Emmalee nodded.

"Okay then. When you get to the top of the mountain, go three miles to the fork. Then veer to the left." Mr. Fulton set his coffee on the counter and picked up a pencil and worn envelope. He flipped it over and started drawing a map on the back as he spoke. "Go about another hundred yards. It's the first drive on the left after that." He drew a big star at the end of a thin line and handed Emmalee the paper. "Hey, while you're up there, why don't you see if there's a suit for Mr. Lane. If not, we got some of those here too. Got them in black and dark navy. You mind checking for me? Unless you got plans to sew him a suit while you're at it."

"No, sir." Emmalee hugged Mr. Fulton, squeezing the baby between them. "I'll get on out of here and let you be." Kelly squirmed and began to whimper.

"Let me get a good look at this little girl. She's been so quiet, almost forgot she was there."

Mr. Fulton lowered the blanket from Kelly's head.

"You're a sweet thing. Yes, you are. Such a pretty girl." Emmalee had never heard Nolan gush over the baby like this. "Look at that head of hair. Our babies were born bald as cucumbers. This one here'll be asking for pigtails before long." Mr. Fulton's tone grew soft. "I really mean it, hon, you two doing all right?"

"Yes, sir."

"Runt said he and Mettie offered to help with the baby. Said they came to the hospital to tell you that but Nolan ran them off."

Emmalee covered Kelly Faye's head with the blanket. "Nolan said they wanted to take her home. Keep her as their own."

"I don't know anything about that," Mr. Fulton said. "Runt didn't get real specific, but I know how your daddy feels about charity of any kind. That's why I'm telling you this in private. If you need anything, let me know. Nolan doesn't need to know about it either."

The baby's fussing grew louder. Emmalee jostled Kelly Faye in her arms and rushed out the back door. The baby grew quiet in the cold morning air, and Emmalee pulled the blanket farther over Kelly Faye's head.

"You keep that little thing covered up, Emmalee," Mr. Fulton called after them. "You hear me? I don't want her catching sick."

Emmalee hurried down the paved drive. She settled the baby in the box in front of the pickup and pulled away from the funeral home. She headed straight for Old Lick, the strange smell of the mortuary lingering in her nose.'

LEONA

Old Lick
- - - - - - - - - -
1957

Leona never knew Curtis to worry about much of anything. His good nature had attracted her in the beginning. She called him solid and sweet back then. So when he stepped into the trailer with coal dust smeared on his face and a vacant look in his eyes, Leona understood it was bad news.

"The mine's shut down," Curtis told her straight out. Leona watched as her husband stood slumped against the kitchen counter, cradling a small savings book between his large, calloused hands. She closed her eyes but could feel Curtis staring at the dwindling numbers scribbled inside the tiny green book.

"Don't go worrying, Ona," he said and rubbed her pregnant belly. "I'll find another job soon," he added, pulling his wife into his arms.

Leona dropped her head against his chest. She heard his heart beating, strong and steady. She had always hoped Curtis would find a better job someday, a safer job, one not thousands of feet below the earth's surface. When they first married, she even dreamed of him joining the Teamsters Union and driving a big truck across the country. She watched him talking to the drivers who stopped to fill their tanks at the gas station near Kimball. She spied him admiring their shiny rigs, lolling around the pumps as the truckers chatted about destinations she could only imagine. Maybe, she thought then, she'd ride with him across the country, even dip her toes in the cool waters of the Pacific Ocean. But a baby was coming, and there was no time or money for dreams like that.

Curtis found work the following week in a poultry processing plant thirty miles south in Chattanooga. It was only temporary, he promised her, till he could find something better and closer to home even though businesses in town were shutting their doors, not looking to hire more men. But Curtis told Leona something was sure to come his way. The Lord would take care of them. At least for now, he came home every Friday evening with a paycheck in his pocket and a roasting hen wrapped in brown paper tucked underneath his arm.

Leona knew very little about her husband's day. She really didn't want to know more than his hourly rate. She saw him leave for work wearing clean pants and a clean shirt, and return home some twelve hours later wearing clothes stinking with the urine and feces dropped from nervous birds. He eased out of the pickup most days to find Leona waiting for him with a rag and a bottle of bleach.

"Wipe that seat down, Curtis, before you step another foot near this house," she said, waving the rag in her hand. Curtis did as he was told, dousing the rag with the liquid that sometimes burned his hands. He'd walk toward Leona with his arms open wide, begging for a kiss. "Uh-huh, Curtis Lane, I mean it. Don't you take one more step till you get out of those nasty clothes," Leona warned him.

Curtis stripped down to his underwear right there in the yard. He teased Leona about her wanting to see his body bare and strummed his hand in front of his chest as if he was playing a guitar. Some nights he danced in the moonlight in nothing but his white underpants, singing a love song to his pregnant bride. He'd take her by the hand and spin her across their grassy ballroom floor. "There's no need to worry," he whispered in her ear, "this is only temporary."

Then one cool June morning, Curtis left for work as he always did, a few minutes before six. He carried a cup of sugared coffee in one hand and an egg biscuit Leona had wrapped in a paper napkin in the other. He stopped to kiss Leona's cheek before rushing down the porch steps. The early-summer sun already lightened the sky as he steered the pickup toward the main road cut across the top of the mountain, waving another good-bye out the truck's open window.

It was nearly nine o'clock before Leona scrambled a couple eggs for herself and poured a full glass of milk. She wasn't going to the factory these days. The doctor told her it was time to stop for a while. Rest up for the birth of the baby. This morning she sat on the sofa with a breakfast plate balanced on the top of her tummy while she listened to the newscaster on Channel Nine yabber on about construction and roadblocks in downtown Chattanooga. She wasn't feeling hungry but forced herself to eat another bite of egg. Curtis promised to bring her a bottle of ginger ale tonight, but she wished she had it now.

Leona slipped the breakfast dishes into the sink filled with soapy water and left them to soak. She noticed the kitchen floor needing mopping but walked back to the sofa instead. She woke tired today, and her back had been aching since yesterday evening. It was hurting worse this morning, but she hadn't mentioned that to Curtis. There was nothing to be done about it anyway, and there was no money for another doctor's visit. Besides, a cotton gown for the baby needed hemming, rows of strawberries needed picking, and jars of jam needed to be made. Once the baby arrived, there'd be no time for such chores.

Leona studied the empty crib shoved tight under the living room window and pictured herself patting the baby's back as she sang a lullaby to soothe him. She leaned over the railing to smooth a flannel blanket already in place when a fierce, stabbing pain seized her back and radiated fast around her tummy. She gasped, struggling for her next breath.

"Oh God," she cried out and gripped the crib's railing. A stronger, fiercer pain moved swift around her tummy, and Leona fell to the floor. She took short breaths and pulled herself onto her hands and knees. She crawled to the trailer door and banged her head against it. "Help me. Curtis, come back." She raised her body far enough to open the door and then fell back on the floor. "Curtis," she cried. "The baby."

Leona crawled down the hall toward her bedroom, believing if she could lie down for a moment, this pain would surely pass. She wanted to scream, to release the hurt mounting in her belly, but Leona did not want to admit what was happening. Instead she called out for Curtis, but he never came.

She hugged a blue-ticked pillow, dug her fingers into its feathered mass. And when she could no longer bear the pain, she finally screamed for God to save her. As her body heaved with another contraction, Leona felt something wet seep between her legs. She looked down at her panties and the white sheets beneath her, both stained brown. The smell was foul, and her fear was ripe. She had no more strength for crying or calling out for help.

Her body grew hot and beads of sweat dripped from her nose. Then she grew cold, and her body shivered as if she had been left too long in the snow. She tugged on a blanket and slipped into a shallow sleep, only to be startled awake by another sharp pain brewing deep inside her belly. "Curtis," she moaned. She repeated her husband's name over and over, hoping he would sense her need. But sometime later that morning, Leona birthed her baby alone.

The boy came fast, too fast. His body was small and weak, and his cries sounded more like those of a new kitten than those of a newborn child. Leona pulled him on top of her belly and kept him warm against her body. She stroked his cheek and encouraged him to take her breast. "Please baby, please. Look at your mama." She hummed her plea in his ear. But the baby grew still.

She rubbed her finger, wet with her breast's first milk, across her son's lips, but he held his tiny mouth closed. She patted his bottom with a firm hand. She pulled on his chin and tickled his tongue, but he would not suckle. His breaths grew fainter and farther apart until she heard only quiet, sporadic gasps.

"Wake up, baby. Please wake up," Leona cried till her voice sounded raspy and weak, but her little boy never opened his eyes. And by the time the sun fell behind Old Lick Mountain, the baby boy born on the first day of summer was dead.

Leona named her son Curtis Brown Lane, Jr., and held him in her arms, even as his skin grew cold and a deep shade of blue. She kissed his cheeks, washing his tiny face with her salty tears, and lightly stroking the tip of her finger along his back. Curtis came home that evening and found his wife unconscious in their bed, a bloody towel stuffed between her legs, and the baby lying limp across her chest.

"Where's my boy," Leona mumbled as Curtis carried her to the truck. "Where's my baby boy?"

"Right here, Ona, right here," Curtis said. He had wrapped their son in a flannel blanket and placed him on the seat of the truck. "He's right here, Ona. He's right here."

Leona came home from the hospital two days later to find the crib sitting empty. She blamed herself for the baby's death at first. Next she blamed God. Then she blamed Curtis. If her husband had been on the mountain, he might have heard her cries. He might have felt her pain. He might have found her and the baby before it was too late.

• • •

Leona and Curtis stood side by side at the cemetery next to the Cullen Church of Christ and watched as their baby's casket was lowered deep into the ground. Leona had refused to let Mr. or Mrs. Fulton dress her baby. Instead she slipped the pale blue cotton gown she had stitched by hand, the one with little white feathers along the hem, over his tiny head. She eased his arms into the sleeves and held him against her chest as she buttoned the three pearl-like buttons down the back of the gown.

Leona had insisted on embroidering Curtis's name on the collar, afraid God might not recognize the little baby boy from Cullen, Tennessee. She tied a matching cap on his head and wrapped him in a knitted white blanket with a lacy edge. Easter had hurried to make the blanket so Leona would have something pretty for swaddling her baby for his eternal sleep.

Leona had insisted a family portrait be made before her infant son was placed in the casket for good. Mr. Fulton offered to take a picture with his camera, but Leona refused. So Curtis called the Olan Mills studio in Chattanooga and asked them to send a photographer to Cullen by the end of the day. He paid ten dollars extra for the photographer's trip to Sequatchie County.

Leona knelt by her baby's tombstone. She had insisted on this, too, that the marker be in place right away, with her son's name already engraved on it. She couldn't stomach the thought of her little boy lost among the other dead buried there. Mr. Fulton had said it usually took several weeks for the final tombstone to arrive, and they would use a temporary marker instead. Curtis only pulled his wallet from his back pocket, insisting Mr. Fulton do whatever he could to rush the order along. "He's just so little," Leona said as she sunk closer to the ground. "He's just so little."

She stayed on her knees while the preacher promised the Lord never delivered more than one could bear. He spoke of Curtis, Jr., sitting happy on Jesus's lap and loved by the family gone on. A short black veil covered Leona's face, and the preacher could not see her sad, angry eyes.

"There'll be more babies, Ona," Curtis promised his wife, kneeling by her side, holding her hand tight in his.

Leona hated Curtis for saying that. She hated him for not crying. She hated him for not talking about this baby like he was their son, instead only speaking of the others to come.

There'll be more became a hollow refrain Leona heard too many times in the months after their baby's death. *There'll be more.* Somewhere in its singing, Leona no longer trusted the young man who had promised her a life better than the one she had known.

The preacher lifted his Bible toward the heavens. He held it above Leona as she rested on bended knee in the short grass carpeting the hillside. A thick ribbon of clouds streamed across the sky.

"Be with Leona and Curtis, dear Lord, as they carry on. Reassure them that their baby boy is safe, happy, spared the difficulties and pain of this world," the preacher said. "He is with our Lord and Savior."

"No, God, no," Leona said, her cheek pressed against the concrete lamb set atop the small granite headstone. A blue carnation hung limp in her hand.

Curtis lifted his wife and led her to the truck. Tears stained his cheeks, too, and his shoulders fell forward. He pulled Leona close, but she pushed him away.

"Leona, please, let me help you."

"No," she said and collapsed against the side of the truck. "Don't touch me, Curtis Lane. I heard the preacher talking to Easter and Wilma. I heard him carrying on about what a man of God you are. How devoted you are to the Lord." Leona's voice had strengthened and grown sharp. "He said you stopped by the church on your way home from work the day Curtis, Jr., was born."

Leona tossed the back of her head against the door of the pickup. Curtis reached out for her, but again she pushed him away. "He said you come by the church to take a look at the plumbing in the bathroom. He said you worked on it for near an hour. You hear me, Curtis?" With the palms of her hands, she slapped Curtis's chest. "You hear what I'm saying?"

Curtis stepped back but did not take his eyes off Leona.

"If you had come on home instead of stopping to do one more good deed," Leona said, her voice rising with every syllable before coming to a full stop—she turned her back to Curtis and fumbled with the truck's handle—"our son would be alive."

Leona threw the door open wide and crawled inside, quickly righting herself on the seat. "You did this, Curtis. You and that God of yours did this to us, to our child. Can you live with that?" she asked and slammed the door.

Curtis walked around the front of the truck, stopping to shake hands with men outfitted in dark suits. He nodded at their kind words but kept his face to the ground. Muttering a short, plaintive prayer, he climbed into the truck. He did not look at Leona. He did not speak to her either. Instead he steered the truck out of the parking lot and onto the road heading to Old Lick. Curtis stared ahead as he drove past Tennewa on the other side of town.

Leona spied the women gathered around the

picnic tables outside the factory building. They talked and laughed in between bites of the lunches carried in brown paper bags. Not long before, Leona had sat there among them and chatted about names and dreams for her new baby. Some had brought her presents, knitted booties and caps. Now she hated these women, almost as much as she hated Curtis, for going about their day as if nothing had changed.

EMMALEE

Old Lick

- - - - - - - - - -

A spray of white flowers hung from the factory door. Emmalee spotted the familiar bouquet as she passed in front of Tennewa on her way to Old Lick. This was not the first time she had seen these flowers. Mrs. Whitlow placed them there whenever someone from the factory died. It was a nice gesture, she guessed, even if it was a fake one.

Nolan hated plastic flowers, said there was no need to use artificial when so many wildflowers and greens graced these mountains. "There ain't no plastic roses growing out there. You ever seen one?" he asked Emmalee once after returning from Fulton's. "I hauled more than twenty plastic bouquets over to the cemetery. The shit people spend money on."

Nolan could call out every flower, tree, and bird in these parts, something that impressed Emmalee, especially knowing her father couldn't write much more than his own name. He loved the mountains. He walked them almost every day. He even told Emmalee not to bother calling

Mr. Fulton when he finally passed; just drag his body to the top of Pine Mountain so he could seep back into the earth like the autumn leaves.

Emmalee shifted the pickup into neutral and drifted near the factory parking lot. Kelly was calm by her side, the truck's vibration already lulling her into a deep sleep. Women, gathered on the dark pavement, held one another in their arms. Their heads were bent forward, and their backs heaved up and down as their cries broke the late-morning quiet. Their grief appeared honest, as though they truly loved Leona. Surely they had gasped when they heard the news of her tragic death. Emmalee spied Wilma and Easter locked in an embrace. They stood apart from the others as they rocked to and fro.

Emmalee had heard too much gossip to believe the women's tears were true. She had listened as many of them had called Leona *cutthroat, coldhearted,* even *unfaithful. She hoards the bundles,* they said. *She lies about her time,* they said. *She'd do about anything to make a dollar,* they said and rolled their eyes toward the front office.

Emmalee never believed this talk, and today she watched as these women lamented their loss. Surely this morning their words were kind. Maybe they were complimenting Leona's work—her attention to detail, her quick hand, and her life-long commitment to Tennewa. *But poor Curtis.*

Poor, sweet Curtis. What an awful death for such a good man. Emmalee was sure that's what they were saying.

There had been times when Emmalee had loved sitting on the picnic tables among these women, especially when the air was warm and she had enough change in her pocket to buy a cold drink. She remembered the day Easter had called out to her.

"Come over here, girl." Easter was sitting on the end of a bench, her short, sturdy legs crossed at the ankle, her head cocked to the right toward her goiter as if she was resting on a pillow. She and Wilma were listening to Cora, who was chattering about her three grown children while the others around them puffed on their cigarettes. "Hang on there, Cora," Easter interrupted. "I want to introduce you to Emmalee. She sits about ten rows in front of you."

"I seen her," Cora said. "You work collars by Leona."

"She sure does but don't go holding that against her." Easter chuckled and took a sip of her Coca-Cola. "And Emmalee, this here is Cora. She's one of the oldest and best at Tennewa. Loyal too, no one's going to argue that. Walked to work once in a snowstorm. Two miles here. Two miles home. Nobody else but Mr. Clayton showed up that day. And he only drove a couple blocks in that big truck of his. Ain't that right, Cora?"

"Had to feed my babies. Nobody else was going to do it."

Emmalee extended her hand as she had watched Mrs. Whitlow do. "Nice to meet you," she said. Cora nodded but kept her hand to her side.

"Emmalee was a student of mine at the high school," Easter said and tugged on Emmalee's shirtsleeve. "A real good student."

Cora looked Emmalee up and down. "How you liking it here?" she asked. "Leona treating you right?"

"Now, Cora, don't go putting none of your foolish thoughts in this girl's head. Ain't that right, Wilma?"

Wilma nodded.

"Leona don't talk much, but she shows me what needs to be done," Emmalee said.

Easter and Wilma laughed a little louder. Cora leaned her head back and soaked up the afternoon sun.

"She don't talk much to nobody. Don't take it personal," Wilma said. "We've all known Leona Lane since she was a tiny thing. She's a good woman."

"She sure is," Easter said, "but she don't want you to know it."

Cora harrumphed and folded her arms across her full, rounded waist.

Laura Cooley, dressed in blue jeans cuffed at

the ankle, walked straight up to Emmalee and tapped her on the shoulder, not bothering to apologize to the other women for interrupting their conversation. She handed Emmalee a cigarette and turned her back to Easter and Wilma.

"Me and Georgia over there," she said, pointing to another young girl also wearing jeans cuffed at the ankle, "we're riding over to Pikeville later tonight to meet up with a couple of boys. They got a friend. You want to come?" She offered Emmalee a lighter and promised she would have a real good time.

Emmalee rolled the cigarette between her fingers.

"Emmalee!" Leona hollered from just inside the sewing room. She waved her arm, motioning Emmalee back to the factory door. "Emmalee Bullard!"

Laura laughed and the smoke spilled from her nose and mouth. "Ooh. You better go on. Looks like you're in big trouble."

Emmalee ran to the concrete steps. She looked up at Leona, the cigarette slack between her fingers.

"Listen to me, if you ever want to amount to anything, girl, you'll stick to your work, not waste your time out there swapping silly stories and day-old gossip," she said and snatched the cigarette from Emmalee's hand. "And you sure enough won't be hanging out with that Laura

Cooley. She could make something good of herself, but she don't care to. You hear me?" But Leona spun around, not waiting for an answer. Emmalee had followed Leona back to her machine, and Laura never again offered to take her to Pikeville.

Today Laura was talking fast to Georgia Mitchell, grins stretched broad across both their faces. From her pickup, Emmalee watched as Georgia giggled at something Laura said. They wrapped their coats around their bodies in unison as if they had choreographed their movements and walked on toward the others already gathered out front. With cigarettes drawn to their lips, they pulled their breath deep in their lungs and released perfect rings of smoke into the clear morning air. They chatted some more, not acting the least bit sad that only hours ago Leona had fallen off a mountain and tumbled out of this world. An older woman threw them a stern look, and their smiles vanished for a moment. Then they leaned their heads together and giggled some more.

"Shut up," Emmalee whispered.

A redbird nipped at one of the plastic roses hanging on the door and danced along into the day amid the women's tears. Emmalee blew a kiss into the air. Leona had told her blowing a kiss to a redbird would bring good luck. Nolan had told her this, too, but Emmalee had never believed him. She had blown thousands of kisses waiting for her luck to change, but not until she met Leona did she believe this could be true. As Emmalee imagined her kiss floating toward the clouds, she wondered if Leona was happy this morning, or if she was darting about, frantically searching for Curtis.

Emmalee pushed the clutch and quickly shifted the engine into first gear. She patted the baby's tummy and sped straight into second, guiding the truck past the factory and the women, left huddled in her rearview mirror. She spotted Wilma and Easter, pointing in her direction. The engine sputtered and coughed as the truck barreled faster through town and toward a sky turning gray and bitter.

A couple of men milling in front of the hardware store looked up from their coffee and tipped their hats as the track passed in front of them. The taller of the two men pushed a long-handled broom across the sidewalk, and a ball of dust rolled into the street. Emmalee headed on west toward Old Lick.

As the road narrowed, she gripped both hands on the wheel, careful to manage the tight turns while keeping the cardboard cradle secure on the seat by her side. The truck climbed a little higher. Emmalee glanced back at the smoke pouring from the stone chimneys speckling the valley's floor like spring daisies growing wild along the riverbank. The wood-framed houses built long ago to shelter the families of the Tennessee Mining Company grew smaller and smaller till they looked no bigger than the dollhouses Emmalee had once admired in the dime store window. These homes with their thick stone foundations weren't wrapped in tar paper like hers. It seemed like a fairyland to Emmalee as she looked back at the houses growing smaller and smaller.

She pumped the accelerator, and the truck lurched forward. The mountain road, once traveled mostly by loggers like her uncle Runt, who hauled loads of timber in and out of the valley and across the Cumberland Plateau, was rough in places, where the asphalt was cracked and drawn. Runt had come by the house a few days after Kelly Faye was born, offering to pay Nolan two hundred dollars to cut trees on the far side of Old Lick. He had two acres to haul and needed help. Instead Nolan cursed and yelled like a gambling man who thought he'd been cheated at his own game, claiming he didn't need a handout from his own kin.

The truck's engine fought the steep climb, spitting fumes and coughing hard. Emmalee looked quick at the baby who was kicking her feet and lifting her arms in the air. She shifted the truck into a lower gear and pushed the accelerator to the floorboard. She thumped the gearshift. The truck climbed higher, obeying Emmalee as she guided it through one hairpin turn and then another. The road grew rougher as she neared its top, and she tightened her grip on the wheel, trying to avoid the deep ruts and the slim shoulder.

Two wooden crosses stood in the ground to the left of the road, already placed there earlier in the morning to mark the very spot where Leona and Curtis flew off the mountain and fell head-long into a dark November night. These were painted white and much larger than the ones Emmalee made of twigs. Red and yellow carnations were scattered among the crosses and the rock and mud. Emmalee wondered who had done this, who had cared enough to memorialize Curtis and Leona this way. Her eyes grew wet again as she pictured Leona's face, stricken with fear as the pickup left the road.

Emmalee idled the truck and bowed her head toward her chest as if praying for a winged angel to come and guide her the rest of the way there. Her straight brown hair masked her eyes. She had seen Leona's bloodied face at Fulton's, and she had stared at her without growing sick or lightheaded. But at the sight of these crosses, Emmalee felt hopeless, abandoned, maybe even orphaned.

If Leona were alive, she would be tending to the baby. She would have told Emmalee to rest while she fed Kelly Faye her bottle and rocked her to sleep. And when Emmalee woke from her own nap, she would have found Leona cooking dinner with Curtis sitting nearby, maybe reading the evening paper or holding the baby on his lap. Now this was all gone, and Emmalee wiped her eyes on her shirtsleeve. The truck rattled as it climbed a little higher.

The fog lay heavier in patches on the top of Old Lick. Emmalee had watched these white clouds blanket the mountains around her many times in the winter months, keeping the sun from shining on the people who lived there. She eased to a full stop before heading deeper into the marshmallow-white sky. She sucked another tearful sob back down her throat and shifted the truck into a higher gear. She counted each mile and searched for the fork in the road Mr. Fulton had drawn on the back of the envelope. The fog thinned in places, and Emmalee found her way. She turned sharply into the drive marked by a black mailbox painted with large white letters that read LANE.

As she straightened the wheel, the tires spun in place, kicking up pine needles and wet leaves before grabbing onto a patch of drier ground. The engine roared and the truck lurched forward. Emmalee bounced on the seat. She eased her foot off the accelerator and then pressed a bit harder. The truck barreled on into the fog.

She spied enough road in front of her to steady the truck in the middle of the gravel path. Emmalee knew it made no sense but she felt as though she was headed home even though she had never been there. She slammed her foot against the brake when the fog suddenly thickened. Her head jerked forward, and the cardboard cradle fell against the dash. The baby screamed a shrill bitter cry, and the truck pinged and moaned.

"Oh shit," she said. "Shh, baby. Hush up." Emmalee was desperate to soothe the newborn with a few frantic words, but the baby hollered louder, her tiny fists clenched tight and her legs pulled to her stomach.

"Shh, baby," she said and pulled the baby onto her lap. Kelly's tiny heart beat fast, and her skin was hot to the touch. Emmalee was sick of the baby's crying and tired of her own. She tapped the accelerator and the truck eased a few feet farther. The sky's white cover had thinned even more, and she quickly spotted the trailer's aluminum frame. She shifted the truck into park and hugged the baby on her lap. Kelly's cries had softened, and Emmalee lingered there behind the steering wheel waiting for her own nerves to calm.

Suddenly, the trailer door slammed shut, the jarring sound ringing loud across the clearing. Emmalee jerked straight up to find a tall man dressed in a dark suit rushing down the porch steps. He hurried toward a long black sedan left at the far end of the trailer. Emmalee placed the baby back in the cardboard cradle, not once taking her eyes off the car she had seen at Tennewa nearly every day.

Mr. Clayton must have come to Old Lick to pay his respects. Maybe he figured family might have gathered in the trailer, and he owed them a personal visit. After all, Leona had worked at Tennewa too many years for him not to come. Surely he did this sort of thing for all of his employees, an official farewell for a career of dedicated service. Emmalee had never heard the other women talk about him doing that, but it must be so. That's right. That's all it was.

Mr. Clayton ducked his head and slid into his car. He raised his coat's collar about his neck and pulled away from Leona's home, navigating his sedan far from the pickup idling in place.

"No," Emmalee reassured herself. "It ain't so. It just ain't so." She sat behind the wheel of the truck till the sound of the car had faded down the drive. Then she sat a while longer, glancing in the rearview mirror for any sign of Mr. Clayton's return. When the fog lifted in earnest, her heart beat more steadily.

For the first time, she could see Leona's trailer perched there on the bluff like a giant blue bird ready to take flight and soar above the valley's floor. The pale grass was trimmed around its aluminum skirting, and a neat pile of fresh-cut wood was stacked off to the side. The land around it was not cluttered with other people's garbage. It was open and broad.

With the cardboard cradle in her arms, Emmalee eased from the seat and walked past a concrete pig standing stiff in the cold like a swinish sentry. One ear was missing and his snout was badly chipped, but it looked as though he had once held flowers in his back. Emmalee admired this bit of whimsy set outside Leona's home. She steadied the box on her knee while she pulled on the hair blowing across her eyes, trying to rid her thoughts of Mr. Clayton.

Emmalee climbed the wooden stoop leading to the trailer's door, the baby held quiet in her arms. "Leona," she called across the clearing. "Miss Leona?" She waited for an answer, but nothing came. She thought she might be better at talking to the dead after all these years with her mama gone.

"Leona," she called once more and turned the knob, not needing the key stuffed in her pocket.

The lamp on the table set just inside the door was already lit and cast a warm glow about the room. Emmalee moved slowly into Leona's home and set the box holding her baby on the carpeted floor next to the brown reclining chair. "There you go," she said and stepped to the table where a vase of white carnations and roses sat wedged between a sewing machine and yards of a thick crimson fabric.

Emmalee fingered one of the flowers with her left hand as she unbuttoned her coat with the other, believing it was Mr. Clayton who had placed such a beautiful arrangement there. Then she stroked the fabric piled high on the table. She studied the different shapes and the pinned seams but could not make sense of it and could not imagine sewing anything so large. Whatever Leona had been making, it was surely a hundred times bigger than the collars they had stitched at the factory.

Emmalee glanced at the baby and noticed a pair of reading glasses balanced on the recliner's arm. She figured these belonged to Curtis, and she pictured him sitting in his chair, browsing the morning paper. Curtis's face was always kind—fuller than her father's and with warm blue eyes not dulled with age and drink. When he stopped by the factory to bring Leona her lunch, he would hesitate by her chair, like a teenaged boy hoping to steal a kiss. Maybe it was there, inside the trailer, that Leona talked sugary to him. Maybe there she kissed him on the cheek and told him she loved him. Emmalee rubbed her hand across the back of Curtis's chair.

Leona's home was both cluttered and ordered at once. And every piece in it, even the scraps of fabric scattered under the wooden table, told something of her friend's story. Cast-iron skillets, paperback books, a boxed set of checkers, a leather-bound Bible, and a pair of sewing scissors with handles shaped like a bird's head—all looked like treasures to Emmalee. She took it all in and ambled on into the kitchen.

Dishes were piled in the sink, and potato peelings were stuffed about the drain. Leona had left in a rush. Emmalee was certain of that. She had known Leona to wash her coffee mug every afternoon before quitting the factory, wiping it dry with such a thoroughness that Emmalee knew leaving the day's dirty dishes in the sink was not something she had done by choice. Emmalee spotted an empty glass on the counter and turned the faucet. She rinsed the glass and filled it. She drank it fast and filled it again.

The trailer groaned, and the walls shimmied as the wind gusted over the bluff. The sudden movement did not scare Emmalee. She felt as safe there as if she were held in a tightly woven nest. There, she felt Leona was close by.

Emmalee knelt by the cardboard cradle. She gently rocked the box, encouraging Kelly into a deeper sleep. "You got nothing to fuss about. Get to sleep and let me be," Emmalee said soft but firm. She stood and tugged on her jeans. She walked into the narrow hall leading to the back of the trailer. She studied the large photograph hanging on the wall. She stared at Leona and

Curtis but could not take her eyes off the baby boy, lying peaceful on a satin sheet.

At Tennewa, Leona never bragged about children or showed off pictures of grandbabies like the other women did. She retreated from conversations when the others commenced such talk, claiming she was behind on her bundles. Easter said Leona had a baby a long time ago, but he had died only hours after coming into this world. She said his death was rough on Leona and she had never been the same, never able to pick herself up and move on.

Emmalee had never dared ask Leona about her son when she was living, somehow never thinking he was real. Now this photograph both startled and mesmerized her, and she searched for the smallest gestures on this boy's face—a faint smile, a slight dimple. She looked for a misplaced hair or a curled fist, pursed lips or furrowed brow.

"Have you found *your* baby yet?" Emmalee asked a much younger Leona sitting proud behind the glass, her husband standing tall behind her. Leona's complexion looked pale, but her mouth was painted a deep shade of pink, a hint of vanity Emmalee had never seen. Her eyes were dazed and her expression was blank. Emmalee knew the baby in the picture was dead, that Mr. Fulton had only made him look real. "I hope you found him."

Emmalee turned to a closed door behind her, placing an open palm on the wood panel as if she was checking for a heartbeat. She hesitated and then opened it far enough to see a bed, covered with a white spread, sitting in the corner of the room. A rocking chair was placed at a slight angle next to it and held a baby's pink blanket and a doll made of cloth. A white dresser, its top wiped clean, was pushed against the opposite wall, and hanging above the dresser was a picture of a rabbit dressed in a blue coat. He held a watering can in his hand.

A crib stood on the other side of the dresser, almost behind the door. It was stained a dark brown and was prepared with sheets and blankets of varying shades of pink. At one end, a stuffed bear sat smiling back at Emmalee. And hanging from the crib's rail was a cloth bag filled with diapers, disposable ones that would not need washing out in the yard. Emmalee tiptoed into the room and pulled a diaper out of the bag. She held it to her nose. It smelled like soap.

Leona had readied this room for her and Kelly Faye. Everything had been done for them, and Leona's hands had touched everything in it. Emmalee inched backward and closed the door. She wanted to keep the room this way, just as Leona had left it. She brushed her cheeks dry. She did not have time for all this crying, Emmalee told herself.

She scooted farther down the hallway and into the bedroom at the end of the trailer. A bigger bed sat underneath a narrow, high-set window. A chenille cover lay rumpled across the mattress, and a hairbrush looked out of place on the foot of the bed. A larger window set in the wall to the right framed a view of the bluff's edge, and Emmalee wondered what it must be like to wake to such a big sky.

An oak dresser underneath the window left little space. Bobby pins were spread across the dresser's top. A bottle of lotion, a jar of loose face powder, and a swatch of yellow fabric were shoved to the back below an oak-framed mirror hanging low on the wall. A small photograph, set in a gold frame, sat among the other clutter. The picture was of a baby, the very same one Emma-lee had seen in the hallway, only here he was by himself, his head resting on a satin pillow.

Emmalee thought the room was cozy and warm, and she pictured Curtis and Leona sidling through the tight spaces, bumping into each other and stopping to hug or maybe shoo each other away. If there was a dress suitable for burying, Emmalee figured it would be here. She squeezed past the bed to a narrow closet. A couple of skirts, three pairs of blue jeans, a half dozen house-dresses from the factory, four or five plaid flannel shirts surely belonging to Curtis, as well as three heavy cotton work shirts and a man's winter coat were all packed inside. She did not see a suit of any kind, but a couple pairs of work boots and one pair of terry-cloth slippers were strewn across the closet floor.

Emmalee sifted through Leona's clothes, but found nothing fancier than a pleated skirt and a matching blouse. She wondered if she had missed something and lifted a blue housecoat off its hanger. The sound of a car's engine pulling close in the drive quickly drew Emmalee's attention back to the front of the trailer. She tripped over the foot of the bed as she raced to the curtained window next to the front door. She looked out at the gravel drive as she reminded herself she had every right to be there. Mr. Fulton said so. Yet she felt like a child caught doing something wrong. She patted the key in her jeans pocket.

A woman dressed in an olive-colored suit stood beside a deep blue sedan. Her figure was slender. Her neck, her nose, every feature looked thin and perfect. Her hair was a brilliant blond, swept into a ponytail dropping gracefully down her back. A green satin ribbon was tied neatly in her hair.

The woman stared at the trailer, walked a little closer and stared some more, as if she was looking for something that was not there. Emmalee opened the door, startling the woman climbing the front steps.

"Oh, Lord, you scared me!" the woman said, holding her manicured hand across her chest. "I was not expecting, well, you." The woman took a deep breath and grabbed the handrail. "I'm looking for Leona. Is she here?"

Emmalee shook her head.

"Are you her daughter?"

Emmalee stared straight ahead, the house-dress hanging over her arm.

"Who are you?"

"Nobody you know," Emmalee said.

"All right." The woman's expression turned cross and her voice harsh. "Leona was supposed to have my slipcovers ready and sitting in a box by the door first thing this morning. I don't see them anywhere." The woman pointed at the ground. "I got a little delayed, but I did try calling. More than once. No answer. I assumed she was at her factory job. Bottom line, I don't see my slipcovers."

The woman stared at Emmalee, and a silence lingered between them.

"Leona ain't here."

The woman shook her head. "Yes, I see that. But I almost killed myself getting up this mountain in this weather. Leona promised to have my slipcovers ready."

"I don't know anything about slipcovers."

"Look, young lady. I made it very clear my slipcovers must be ready this morning. Not tonight. Not tomorrow. You understand me? This morning. I can't be chasing Leona around when I've got a dinner party to prepare for."

Emmalee stood firm in the doorway and glanced at the red fabric on the table to her left. "Like I said, she ain't here."

Emmalee did not care for this woman who looked only a few years older yet insisted on talking to her as if she was a child. She did not bother to tell her Leona was dead and that she had left this world in a horrifying manner only a few hours ago. She knew this woman in her pretty green suit did not care about the seamstress she had hired to do her work. Her only concern was these slipcovers she prattled on about, still lying in pieces needing Leona's hand to give them structure and shape.

"Well, that's great. Just great." The woman shoved her gloved hands onto her hips. "When you see Leona next, you tell her I am not coming back up this mountain. She promised these slipcovers would be ready, and she is going to have to get them to me. Today."

Emmalee picked at her thumb.

"Listen here, I will not be recommending her to any of my friends. My dinner party is tomorrow night, and she has left me in a terrible bind. I cannot entertain my husband's associates without those slipcovers. Do you know when she'll be back?"

"Nope."

"Do you know where she's gone?"

"Don't know for sure."

"Who are you anyway?"

Emmalee only stared at the woman.

"Fine," the woman said. "Be sure and tell Leona to call Mrs. Brooks the minute she returns. Can you do that much? Are you going to write this down so you don't forget?" The woman tapped the point of her shoe on the top of the wooden stoop. "I'd feel better if I saw you write this down."

"Ain't got a pencil."

Emmalee shut the door and fastened the lock. She watched the woman stalk to her car, her high heels sticking in the damp ground.

As she backed into the trailer, Emmalee tripped across a pair of canvas loafers. She had not noticed them there before, and something struck her sad about these shoes waiting for Leona's return. Emmalee felt emotion bubbling up again. She hurriedly placed the shoes side by side where she had found them, in case Leona came looking for them in the middle of the night. Then she sat on the metal folding chair in front of Leona's sewing machine. She scooted close to the table as she had at Tennewa as though she were preparing for a day's work.

Silver lettering across the machine's black casing spelled *ATLAS deluxe*, the name shining brightly under the warm lamplight. This was a much smaller machine than those at the factory, but Emmalee wondered how many hours Leona had sat in this very place, her foot pushing the floor pedal, her fingers spinning and slowing the hand wheel. How many hours had she sat there at the end of another long shift at Tennewa? What all had she made guiding the needle through countless yards of fabric—shirts for Curtis, the drapes hanging there on the window, slipcovers for other women who stood there at her door, demanding and angry, gowns and blankets for Kelly Faye? This old machine knew Leona's story better than anyone.

Emmalee picked up a piece of the thick red fabric and held it in her hands. She set it aside and picked up another, and one more. Every stitch already pulled taut through the fabric was uniform and perfect. Although Emmalee did not know what a slipcover was, she imagined these unfinished pieces were what the woman in the olive-colored suit had wanted. No matter what Leona had or had not done, she had not deserved those woman's harsh words. Had she not flown off the side of Old Lick, Leona would have finished the sewing as she had promised. It would have been ready, sitting in a cardboard box, first thing this morning. Emmalee knew that for certain.

The baby slept sound in her cradle box, and

even though Emmalee was tired and wanted to sleep, too, she stepped back into the kitchen and pulled the old potato peelings from the drain. She filled the sink with hot, soapy water and placed the dishes there to soak. Emmalee would make a dress for burying, but she would start in the morning. First there was cleaning to do. Leona would not want anyone to see this mess. Only when everything was neat and tidy would she head back down to Red Chert.

EMMALEE

Red Chert

- - - - - - - - - - -

"Hey girl. Get up," Nolan hollered from the front room. "Preacher's here to see you." Emmalee yanked the pillow over her head, but Nolan's yelling only grew louder and sharp. "Get out here! Preacher ain't got time to waste on you."

Emmalee held the pillow tighter to her ear.

"You hear me, girl?" A loud knock followed at her door. "Preacher's got business with you, and he's got more to do today than to sit out here staring at me. Get your butt up out of that bed!"

Emmalee dragged herself from underneath the covers and oriented herself in her tiny room. She had returned from Old Lick late and fell asleep listening to her baby whine. She did not want Nolan waking her.

"Come on, girl."

"Damn it, Nolan." Emmalee scrambled to her feet and tucked the quilt around the tiny lump in the middle of the bed. She tossed her coat over her shoulders and stumbled through the bedroom door, swaying from side to side like a drunk, although she had never once touched a drop of her father's alcohol. "I heard you the first time," she said, talking gruff to her father.

The preacher stood in the middle of the room. His chin, blistered with white-tipped pimples, left him looking more like a high-school boy than a full-grown man responsible for others' salvations. He toted a black-bound book in his hand and rocked back and forth from his heels to his toes.

Nolan took the chair by the wood-burning stove. He held a plug of chew in his mouth, locked between his cheek and gum. He fixed his eyes on the preacher as if he were a cat playing with a trapped mouse.

Nolan rarely opened the door for anyone, other than Mr. Fulton or the sheriff, and Emmalee was particularly surprised to find the preacher standing there in front of her. Nolan did not care for any of the church men in Cullen, especially those who had come to pray over his Cynthia Faye when she lay dying in the back room. He called them liars. All of them. He said they marched into his house and dropped to their knees and begged God for his wife's healing. They promised God could work a miracle, even in Cynthia Faye's withered body. The very next day they claimed her death was part of God's great plan and Nolan needed to accept her passing.

"They ain't to be trusted," he had told Emmalee. He pushed his chair back on its rear legs and stared cold at the young man standing in front of him. Emmalee pulled her coat farther across her body.

"Good morning, Emmalee. I'm Brother Herd." The preacher cast his eyes toward the ground as though he had already seen too much of her. Emmalee slipped her arms inside her coat sleeves and pulled her arms together, struggling to hide her body from view. "I need to talk to you, child. I understand you're wanting to make a dress for Mrs. Lane."

"I ain't a child, and I ain't *wanting* to make a dress. I *am* making a dress." Emmalee spoke her mind as fierce as Nolan when need be.

"Yes, I heard that," the preacher said, keeping his voice calm and steady. "Why don't you sit down. That little baby of yours must be wearing you out." The preacher directed Emmalee toward the sofa. "I'm curious why you want to do such a thing, a young girl like yourself? Especially with a new baby and all."

"Leona needs a dress, don't she?"

"Yes. And I'm sure you do beautiful work. No one's questioning that." The preacher paused and glanced about the room as if he was searching for the right words. "It's just that, uh, why don't you make Miss Leona one of those crosses. You know, like all the others down there on that oak by the road?" He slipped his right hand in his pants pocket and jiggled some coins together. "That would be such a lovely gesture."

Emmalee shook her head. "I don't want to."

The preacher shifted his weight from his toes to his heels. "Let Mrs. Fulton pick out this dress since she's a grown woman and all, more Leona's age. And you make a cross—"

"I don't want to."

"We could place it on the casket during the service at the church. You could hang it on your tree later. You can make one for Mr. Curtis too?" The preacher talked faster, not pausing long enough for Emmalee to interrupt. "So what do you think, Emmalee? You'll make two crosses for me?"

"This ain't about me or my cross-making. And it ain't about you either." Emmalee tugged on the coat, hoping to cover her bare legs. "My friend needs a dress. A special dress. Not one that half the other women buried in Cullen are wearing."

The preacher pressed his palms together and lifted his index fingers to his mouth. Emmalee wondered if he was praying, and she wondered if she should bow her head or if that was only something you did inside the church building.

"I guess you know Leona and Curtis were headed to Wednesday-night supper when the accident happened," the preacher said. "You can imagine their church family has taken this loss real hard." The preacher squatted on his heels in front of the sofa. "Curtis did so much for us. He

157

just cut a huge load of wood for the fellowship hall earlier in the day. He was a great man of God, and his heavenly crown is surely heavy with jewels. I really do think the stars shined brighter in the sky last night since he left this world for his eternal home."

"How come you think them same stars ain't shining for Miss Leona?"

"Oh, I'm sure they were. All I'm saying is that Curtis was a man of deep commitment to the Lord. He was what my mama called bitterstrong in his faith."

"So," Emmalee said, tucking her legs underneath her and stretching her T-shirt over her knees.

"You see some of the women at Cullen Church of Christ would feel a lot better about all this if you left the dress selection to Mrs. Fulton." The preacher stood and looked to Nolan. "This church is really all the family they got."

Emmalee had not been raised in the church like most of the others in Cullen. Sometimes she believed it was her absence from the church rolls that left her feeling more like an outcast in this town than the fact she was Nolan Bullard's child. If her mama had lived, Emmalee figured she would have been a *churchgoing* girl, too. She was sure of it. All she really knew about God had come from those beautiful stories her mama told her before she died. In Emmalee's mind,

God had a long white beard and sat on a golden throne. His son sat beside him. His hair was brown and fell past his shoulders. He was kind and spoke sweetly to the little children.

Emmalee did not know scripture like Brother Herd, but she was certain she believed in God as much as he did. Sometimes she even felt Him blowing past her neck when she was out walking in the woods. Her mama had told her God was everywhere. She said He'd whisper to you like that if you stopped and listened, opened your heart to his calling. But Emmalee didn't understand what her Sunday attendance had to do with her sewing a straight seam.

"I liked Mr. Curtis. But Leona was my friend," Emmalee said. "And I want her wearing something real nice. When a woman goes to being buried, she ought to be wearing a dress that's got some meaning." Emmalee thought back to her mama and wondered what Nolan had dressed her in, if he even considered putting her in something special. Emmalee quickly pushed away the thought of her mama in rags and stared back at the preacher. "Leona deserves a dress made by hands that knew her and loved her."

The preacher exhaled, loud and frustrated. He bowed his head and clutched his hands tighter around his Bible as if he was choking the Holy Spirit straight out of it. Emmalee thought he might be praying again, talking to God in the middle of her own father's house. She glanced at Nolan, whose cheek was fat with chew.

The preacher raised his head. "You know, child, I can tell you care for Mrs. Lane, and her dying surely is upsetting you. But sometimes the Lord works in ways we can't comprehend, that's for sure."

"I ain't looking for an answer," Emmalee said. "People die every damn day. And I'm no more a child than you."

Nolan raised his eyebrow and spit a full load of tobacco juice near the tip of the preacher's polished shoe. Brother Herd clenched his jaw and sidestepped the watery mess on the floor. He turned his back to Nolan.

"You see, girl, the Lanes didn't play at church like some people do. Curtis read the Bible every day. I think he had it memorized. He tithed regular. He even adopted a little black girl in Haiti, sent money to her every month. That girl's going to grow up a Christian, rescued from her heathen ways."

Nolan laughed. "Haiti," he repeated it as though the name sounded funny.

"True. I don't know Mrs. Lane as well. But I know she did good things people here don't know about." Emmalee pulled on her hair, gathering it into a ponytail and letting it fall against her neck. The preacher talked on. "Every year she bought the graduation gowns for at least four or five seniors over at Cullen High who couldn't otherwise afford one. Not sure Curtis even knew about that. She swore me to secrecy. And I do know of two or three times she sewed a girl's prom dress, stayed up past midnight to get it all done. And she made a Christmas box every year for one of Cullen's less fortunate families."

Emmalee had never known Leona to gush about anything she did for others. She kept to herself even though she stopped at the end of most every day to show Emmalee a new hand stitch or to help correct the ones she was learning. Emmalee had watched Leona come to work in tattered sweaters and worn housedresses. She ate tomato sandwiches on white bread and never splurged on a cold Coca-Cola from the machine at Tennewa. Leona said that machine robbed you blind and you'd only pay half that amount for a bottle of Coca-Cola down at the corner store. Water was free. Even Emmalee dropped her change in the drink machine now and then. Truth be told, Emmalee was shocked when Leona had asked her to come to Old Lick.

But Emmalee had seen the trailer. She knew Leona had worked hard to ready her home for her and Kelly Faye. Emmalee had seen it first-hand—the crib, the diapers, the rocking chair. It was all perfect. Leona had done it all for her and Kelly Faye, never once talking about God or heavenly crowns.

"I ain't meaning to be ugly, Preacher, but I don't see what all this has to do with my sewing a dress."

The preacher closed his eyes. "Nolan, what do you think of your daughter making this dress?"

Nolan pushed the chew against the side of his mouth.

"Look, I know you're not a churchgoing man, Mr. Bullard," the preacher said, his voice sounding tired. "But surely you can appreciate that Mrs. Lane's burial garment should be made by someone who at least seems to have some understanding or some respect for the Lord's commandments. Not by a girl who's just had a baby out of wedlock." The preacher nodded toward the back room where Kelly was starting to squeal.

Nolan shot another wad of tobacco juice on the floor, this one landing even closer to the preacher's shiny black shoe. A thin line of juice stained his stubbled chin, and he leaned forward in his chair as if he was contemplating spitting again. The preacher took another step from Nolan.

"So what bothers you most is Emmalee got herself a baby before she got herself a husband," Nolan said. "Seems to me the girl can do what she damn well pleases whether it's making a baby or making a dress." Nolan wiped his mouth with the back of his shirtsleeve. "Mr. Fulton said it was okay for Emmalee to make Miss Leona's dress, and his word's the only one that matters to me. He's the one dressing the bodies."

The preacher pulled his Bible to his chest. "Yes, but this is one time Mr. Fulton and I do not agree. He doesn't go to the Church of Christ. He's a Baptist man."

"Yeah," Nolan said.

The baby's cries grew stronger. This time Nolan held a tin can to his lips and let some spit fall into it.

The preacher turned toward the door but glanced back at Emmalee. "You really think this is what your mama would want? You raising a baby without a daddy and without God. From what I've heard, I can't imagine she'd be happy with the ways things are."

Nolan jumped to his feet and landed in front of the preacher. With his finger, he poked the preacher in the chest, pressing harder and harder as he spoke. "I don't want you talking about Emmalee's mama. You hear me? The girl's done answered your questions. Best you get on your way."

The preacher's lips quivered as he reminded Emmalee she was the one responsible for her child's salvation. He raised his Bible over his head and reached his free hand out toward Emmalee. From the way the preacher stretched his body, Emmalee grew scared he might be placing a hex on her. Even Nolan tilted back from the preacher's reach.

"For the wages of sin is death, but the gift of God is eternal life in Christ Jesus our Lord!" The preacher looked up to the ceiling as he spoke. When he was done talking, he stepped backward out the door and returned to his church and a more compliant flock.

"What the hell did that man say?" Nolan asked and spit another load of tobacco juice in the can. Kelly was screaming fierce, and Emmalee could feel her milk starting to wet her shirt.

"I don't know. Baby needs feeding."

"Hold on there, girl." Nolan's voice was firm. "Look a here, Emmalee. I don't like no one talking about my blood, especially a preacher. I wouldn't of let him in here, but he said he'd been talking to Mr. Fulton."

Emmalee pulled her bangs down in front of her eyes.

"You know I don't care to see you hauling that little one off to some church just 'cause he brings your mama's name into this. But it's time you tell me who this baby's daddy is. You got knocked up. You ain't the first girl, but I want the daddy's name. He needs to do right by you. You hear me?"

Emmalee pushed her hair to the side and eased off the sofa. "I got to feed the baby."

"Girl, believe it or not, I'm trying to help you here. Now tell me his damn name."

"Are you? Are you trying to help me? 'Cause I ain't looking for you to do nothing."

"Girl, you are making it so damn hard." Nolan bounded toward Emmalee, but she did not back away. Sometimes Emmalee wished he would go ahead and wrap his hands around her neck and choke the breath right out of her, instead of dragging her through this life slow and painful. "Preacher's right about one thing," Nolan said. "Your mama wouldn't care for what's going on here."

He spit on the floor before walking straight out the door. He took to his truck and sped out of the holler, leaving Emmalee to tend to the baby alone.

LEONA

Christmas

- - - - - - - - - -

1962

Leona spooned the remainder of the batter into a second loaf pan, careful to allow room for the gingerbread to rise as she had with the first. She set both pans inside the hot oven and checked her watch. She scraped what was left of the thick brown mixture from the sides of the yellow bowl and licked the spatula clean. She dropped the bowl and spatula into a sink of soapy water and rinsed her fingers, drying her hands on the apron tied around her waist.

Her calves ached from standing in the kitchen most of the day. She longed to sit for a minute but instead kneeled in front of a large cardboard box straddling the linoleum floor and thin green carpeting. Scattered around the box were piles of canned vegetables and meats and tins of baked cookies and biscuits, even a fresh pineapple upside-down cake wrapped in aluminum foil.

Leona was eager to finish her Christmas box. She had promised the women's mission at church she would have it delivered by early evening.

Most any other time of year, she was tight with her pennies, saving every one of them for something she could no longer name. She kept her money hidden in a shoebox in the back of her closet and added a few dollars to it every week. She once thought she was preparing to send a child or two to college. Later she thought about taking a trip around the world, but Curtis never wanted to travel farther than Nashville or Birmingham. Now Leona figured she saved the money out of habit more than anything else; just knowing it was there seemed reason enough. Curtis said his woman could stretch a dollar all the way to West Tennessee, and Leona knew this to be true. She spent some when the cause called to her, but she never did tell Curtis about the money stashed behind her slippers and his old work boots for fear he'd give it all to the church. She'd find a purpose for it someday.

Leona spent most of the week baking sugar cookies and sweet potato biscuits, loaves of pumpkin, banana, and gingerbread. She shopped for canned goods and a five-pound box of Russell Stover's assorted chocolates from the drugstore. She even gathered enough pecans from underneath a tree on the outskirts of town to a fill a cloth bag and sent Curtis to the backside of Brown Chapel Mountain to fetch one of Mrs. Haygood's fresh cured hams.

When Curtis wasn't looking, Leona wrapped a

lace-trimmed nightgown and matching robe in brown paper and hid it in the very bottom of the box between the cans of Spam and Blue Lake green beans. Curtis would never think it appropriate giving such an intimate gift to a stranger, especially inside a church box. But Leona figured every woman needed to feel pretty every so often, even if it was in the dark of night.

Christmas had been a sad time in Leona's house growing up. She was only eight years old when her daddy died in the mines along with nine other men from Cullen and Whitwell on December twenty-first. She and her mama were making Christmas cards out of red and green construction paper when a knock came at the door. She remembered her mama collapsing at the feet of the dark-suited official from the Tennessee Mining Company when he delivered the news. The company man apologized for her loss, said he spoke on behalf of everyone at Tennessee Mining. He gave her a meager check and a week to gather her things. Another miner and his family were set to move in the first of the year.

Leona was convinced her daddy left his family shackled to this valley, bound by poverty or weariness or fear. She wasn't really sure which it was, but she watched her mother raise three children, taking in wash and sewing from women she didn't know. They never had much for Christmas, other than a skirt or dress her mama had stitched together from scraps. But what saddened Leona most was that her mama never had a present of her own, other than what her three children had assembled from the school's supply of craft sticks and glue. Leona grew up determined to find more out of living than filling her babies' stomachs on hoe cakes and white beans, but nothing had worked out like she planned.

"You got the ham in there?" Curtis pulled a plastic comb from his rear pocket and stretched back in the reclining chair.

"It's right here."

"Who's it going to?" Curtis asked as he combed his thinning hair, careful to work the part on the right side of his head.

"Nolan Bullard and his wife."

"Nolan Bullard found someone to marry?" Curtis asked.

"Yep." Leona shook her head. "About a year ago. A pretty young thing from over in Whitwell somewhere."

"Bet he told her some more tall tale to get her to say 'I do.'"

"Curtis Lane, you're calling Nolan Bullard a liar," Leona said and laughed.

"Well, even the Lord knows there ain't any other way he could get a woman to marry him."

Leona placed her hands on her hips and laughed some more. "Hey, go on and get out of here and quit wasting your time jawboning with me. You said you were going to cut down a tree for the trailer an hour ago. We're never going to get this box delivered by dark if you don't get on with it."

"I thought you might want to go with me?" Curtis pushed himself up from the chair.

Leona shook her head. "You ask me that every year, and every year I tell you the same thing. No, I don't want to go hunting for a tree. I got enough to do. Go on."

Curtis slipped his hands in his pants pockets. "I doubt we'll have time to decorate it tonight."

"Those skinny things you bring in here ain't hardly worth decorating. Can't fit a decent-sized tree in this room."

Curtis pulled on his wool jacket. "I don't need to get one, Ona, if you don't want me to."

Leona had once loved to walk with Curtis into the woods. He scouted for the perfect tree while she hunted for pinecones. The big ones were her favorites. She'd dip the tips of their woody scales into glue and roll them in different colors of glitter. She hung them on the tree, giving thought to where she placed each one. The glitter sparkled against the strand of white lights Curtis wrapped around the tree's branches.

But Leona didn't care much about decorating the trailer anymore. She said it was a waste of her time. Surely Curtis could see she had enough to do without trimming a tree or making other silly decorations, especially with no one there to admire it all but the two of them.

"Maybe next Christmas, Ona. Maybe we'll be in our house by then, and you can pick the tallest cedar on Old Lick." He pointed above his head and stared at his hand as if he was admiring his imaginary tree.

"Hush up, Curtis. I'm tired of that talk," Leona snapped, her mood changing fast.

Curtis's smile faded. He opened the door and stared out at the woods.

"First Baptist is using real live animals in the nativity this year. They hadn't done that since I was six years old." Curtis placed his hand at his hip, indicating the little boy he once was. "One of the sheep got spooked and ran off with baby Jesus in his mouth, ran all the way to Pine Mountain."

"Curtis Lane, I wouldn't be lying about the baby Jesus," Leona said.

"I ain't. But it was a good thing the live baby Jesus come down with a fever earlier in the day. They ended up putting a baby doll in the manger instead."

"You're pulling my leg," Leona said and opened the oven to check on her gingerbread.

"I ain't." Curtis smiled big. "Some say that goat's still living up there, tending to that little baby doll like it was his own. You listen real close on a quiet night and you can hear him baying on the other side of the valley."

Leona waved her hand. "Go on. Get out of here."

Curtis buttoned his coat and looked back at his wife. "You want to go by and take a look at the nativity? I mean after we deliver the box?"

Leona pounded her fist on the windowpane. "I hate them old crows. Shoo. Go on now," she said to the birds pecking at the remnants of a dead possum or squirrel a few feet from the trailer's end. "Where's my pretty redbird?" she asked, her voice falling and rising as if she was calling an old friend to come pay her a visit.

Curtis stepped outside, and the door swung shut behind him.

Leona finished up the box, even tucking a new bottle of Jergens lotion she had bought for herself between the cans of green beans and the pineapple upside-down cake. She left the box ready on the kitchen floor for Curtis to carry and hurried into the bedroom to change her clothes smeared with butter and flour from her long day of cooking.

Later inside the truck, Curtis pointed to the band of thickening clouds settling across the valley. "Looks like we might have a white Christmas, Ona," he said. Leona said nothing as she spied the small cedar resting against the trailer as the truck lurched into reverse.

A long silence drifted between them as Curtis steered the truck down Old Lick Mountain. As the road straightened near the bottom, he licked his lips and pushed his nose into the air. "I can't take it much longer. Hmm. Hmm. That bread smells mighty good. When do we get ours, Ona?"

"Not till we get home. Need to do our good deed first."

Curtis pressed harder on the pedal and crouched behind the wheel like he was taking off for the moon. Leona screamed, and Curtis slowed the truck. He grinned big and patted his wife's knee.

"That ain't funny, Curtis," Leona gasped, holding her hand to her chest.

"Sorry, sweetie. Just having a little fun."

"I told you I ain't in the right mind for that kind of fun."

"I'm sorry. Where we headed anyway? Last I heard Nolan was living in a rented room on Cloverdale Loop. Surely he didn't take his new bride over there."

"No, he's moved into some old shack in Red Chert," Leona answered and pointed ahead with her finger as if Curtis did not know the way. "Easter said it was at the very back of the holler. And then to the right some."

"Nolan's a stubborn old mule. What makes you think he's going to take this box?" Curtis asked.

"His young bride. At least I hope he's thinking

about his wife this time of year. This one time of year."

Curtis grunted.

"Okay. I'm hoping he won't be there."

Curtis accelerated and steered the pickup on through town. He paused before turning left onto Red Chert Road. "You're a good woman, Leona," he said as he pulled onto the gravel and dirt road. He placed his hand on Leona's knee and kept it there as they wound their way deeper into the holler.

"You think that's it?" Curtis asked and nodded toward the house sitting back from the road. A long tail of smoke rose from a metal pipe pitched a few feet above a rusted tin roof. Any other time of year, the dwelling might not have been visible, but the winter's cold had left the wooded lot naked and the house in plain sight. Pieces of tar paper tacked to its plywood sides flapped in the wind and left the house looking as though it was shaking from the cold.

"I guess so," Leona answered. "You forget sometimes that somebody's always worse off."

Curtis nodded and guided the truck through a patch of thick mud. A bank of low cedars scratched the sides of the pickup as he maneuvered farther down the narrow drive. A dog ran toward them, barking and lunging at the truck's rolling tires.

"Don't hit him," Leona said, pointing to the

animal looking more like a skeleton wrapped in a loose hairy coat than a family pet.

"He'll get out the way," Curtis reassured her. "Poor thing, wonder when he was fed last. Sit tight while I take the box to the door." Curtis dipped his hand into the box. "You got a bone in there by any chance, Ona?"

Leona tugged on Curtis's sleeve. "You ain't funny. Listen, you be careful around that mangy thing. Something that hungry might take a bite out of even your scrawny leg." She rolled down her window and leaned forward, keeping a close watch on Curtis as he walked toward the house.

Curtis carried the box in one hand and with the other swatted at the dog trotting behind him, nipping at his every step. The dog circled Curtis as he knocked on the door and waited for an answer. Curtis looked back at Leona, who motioned for him to try again. With a tight fist, he knocked harder.

"Hello. Anyone home?" he called. "Curtis Lane here, from Cullen Church of Christ." Curtis waited a minute and knocked again. "Got a Christmas box for you. If you want, I can leave it right here outside the door."

Leona waved at Curtis and pointed at the dog.

"Sure hate for some animal to get into it is the only thing," Curtis said, raising his voice. "Maybe I can put it here on top of this refrigerator." He looked to Leona for further direction. She held up her hands, unsure of what to do next.

As he turned to walk away, the door opened, only a sliver at first, and then wide enough to reveal a young woman full with child. Her bare, skinny legs were visible beneath a thin cotton dress, and she yanked on a sweater too small for her swollen body. Her hair hung wild and loose from a bun pinned to the back of her head. Her eyes were deep-set and her cheeks, hollow. She looked more ghostlike than human, more child than adult, but Leona fixed her stare on the woman's pregnant belly instead.

It had been nearly five years since Curtis, Jr., died in Leona's arms, and Curtis's promises of another child had never come true. Every month she watched for her bleeding to stop, but every month, her bleeding came, regular and steady. She said nothing to Curtis of her hopes and disappointments, but she was growing afraid the Lord might never trust her with another baby. Dr. Greer told her it had nothing to do with trust. Her uterus was fierce or angry. She couldn't remember exactly what he called it, but she knew what it meant.

Leona had grown so tired of the disappoint-ment and wondered if that was why she found herself avoiding her husband's arms these days. She spoke shortly too often and her temper flared whenever Curtis wanted to take her to bed and love her like he had when they were newlyweds. The only reason Leona went along with him most times was the lingering hope that another baby would take root inside her. All she knew was she'd never have a family of her own.

Curtis said something to the pregnant girl standing there in front of him, and she opened the door a little wider. He took the box from the top of the refrigerator and disappeared inside. He was only gone a moment, and then he stepped back to the porch. He tipped his hat, and the young woman scooted backward into the darkened house. The dog sat by the front door and watched Curtis as he walked to the truck.

Snow fell on his shoulders, and he held his hands open wide and smiled at Leona. A single tear ran down Leona's cheek, but she wiped it dry before Curtis could see.

EMMALEE

Red Chert

- - - - - - - - - - -

The rain came shortly after Nolan left the house, striking hard against the metal roof. Comforting at first, the noise grew deafening as the storm strengthened and settled between the walls of the holler. What remained of the tar paper nailed to the house's exterior offered little protection from the wet weather, and the plywood cladding turned a full shade darker as the heavy rains persisted.

Emmalee was tired and worn out, but the preacher's visit had left her shaky and too anxious to sleep. Besides, she was eager to get back to Old Lick and start on Leona's dress. She didn't have much time if she was going to have it ready for Mr. Fulton by Sunday. She wanted it perfect.

Emmalee paced the length of her room, staring at what was once a pea-sized hole in her right boot that had spread wide across the toe. She figured she walked near a mile in these boots just this morning waiting for Nolan to return with the pickup. She walked to the window, but there was no sign of him.

She peeked into the front room and called his name even though she knew he was not there. His cot was empty, and the fire in the stove had burned out during the night. The room smelled of ash and stale greens and onions. There was no coffee warming, and her father's bottle was sitting empty on the table. There hadn't been much in it last Emmalee saw it, but what was there was now gone. Emmalee lifted the blanket covering the front window and crept about the house as she had when she was a little girl, worried Nolan might be watching from nearby, hidden on the wooded slope.

He used to hide out there often, especially when Mrs. Cain came from the county welfare office to check on Emmalee's condition. She would stand firm outside the door waiting for Nolan to answer. She threatened to wait all day if need be. "I see your truck, Nolan Bullard. You'd come out and show your face if you were a real man." Emmalee sat crouched behind the door while Mrs. Cain hurled more threats and pounded on the door.

"Nolan Bullard, quit playing these games with me. I know you're in there. Don't make me go back to town and get the sheriff. I'll do it. You know I will."

Emmalee had grown scared then and opened the door. Mrs. Cain's talk had thundered so big that Emmalee expected to find a giant standing in front of her, not a wrinkled woman who stood no bigger than a child and looked as though she might blow away in a strong gust of wind. She held a sack full of groceries in her hands and wore a sweet expression.

"Hello, Emmalee. How are you?" Mrs. Cain asked, her voice much softer. Emmalee was surprised this woman knew her name. "Your daddy here?" she asked and pushed her way into the house, her pretty pink dress swaying back and forth when she talked.

Emmalee looked toward the mountain.

"All right then." Mrs. Cain set the groceries on the Formica-topped table along with a stack of coupons. "Your daddy can use these like money at the grocery store in town as long as he's not spending them on cigarettes or beer. So there's no reason not to have some decent food in this house."

Mrs. Cain rapped the lid of a large jar filled with collards and chicken necks. "Is this all you got to eat, honey, this jar of greens? Lord, no telling how long that slop's been sitting there." Mrs. Cain muttered something to herself and tipped the grocery sack in front of Emmalee. "There's a package of clean panties in the bottom of the bag. Matching undershirts, too. Those are just for you. Mrs. Tate, your teacher, said you might be needing them." Mrs. Cain held Emmalee's chin in her hand. "I'll be back to check on you," she had said with a sad face and walked out the door, tossing orders for Nolan in the air, her voice growing shrill and high-pitched. "You got to take care of this child, you hear me, Nolan Bullard? And for crying out loud, wash her clothes."

Nolan had responded by throwing the coupons in the stove and taking his belt to Emmalee's bottom. Emmalee could feel the sting of the leather all these years later as she pulled a couple of dry biscuits from a tin box and tied them in a yellow cloth. She groused around the kitchen until she found a piece of cured ham Nolan must have missed. She untied the cloth's knot and added the salty meat to her pack. Emmalee hadn't eaten much since Leona died, and the baby drained her of what little she had. This morning she was feeling hungry and weak, leaving her hands shaking even when she slipped them inside her jeans pockets.

Emmalee buttoned her coat and went to fetch the baby, who was starting to fidget. She feared Kelly would want to suckle, and her breasts were more red and tender than before. Lately, she found herself growing angry every time the baby wanted to feed. She had hoped Doris Cain would come to the house all these years later and check on Kelly Faye, maybe bring some store-bought formula and a couple of bottles. Emmalee heard the county did that sort of thing.

Perhaps she had come, and Nolan had sent her away, too, like he had Runt and Mettie. Emmalee swaddled the baby tight in the pink crocheted blanket and hurried out the front door with her food sack looped around her wrist.

The rain was falling lightly, and another thick, white mist had settled among the treetops. The last of the fall's orange and red leaves, brilliant in their death, had dropped to the ground and were awaiting their slow, fertile burial. A lone rosette of shepherd's purse poked its flowery head through the fall's debris. Any other day, Emmalee would have stopped to admire its lobed leaves and delicate white blossoms, an unexpected spot of color during these colder months. But she walked on, cautious not to kick the leaves with the tips of her boots, something she had loved to do as a little girl. She did not want Nolan spotting her tracks. If he came home sober, he would follow her path down the muddy drive and onto the road winding its way toward the foot of the holler. She shifted the baby to her other arm and walked on down Red Chert Road. A wood thrush grew persistent in his morning song, and Emmalee focused on his warbled notes and the full rests falling between them as she walked on toward her uncle's house.

Runt and Mettie couldn't have a baby of their own no matter how hard they went at it, and Emmalee figured maybe there was some truth to what Nolan said. Maybe they were fishing for hers. Nolan told her they'd steal Kelly Faye straight out if they could, but Emmalee never believed all of that. Runt had been good to her when she was little, although she never saw much of him anymore.

The house Runt built after marrying Mettie was three times the size of Nolan's. It sat on a low rise about a hundred yards from the main road, and his land reached all the way to the top of Pine Mountain. There was no tar paper nailed to this house, and it was painted a clean white with a sturdy porch stretching across its front. A stone path was set in the ground all the way to the broad porch steps. A large twig wreath decorated with fake birds was fastened to the door. Emmalee stood and stared up at the house and the odd little birds nesting there. She hesitated and scooted backward, suddenly unsure of what she was doing at Runt's. She thought about turning around, running back to her father's or maybe all the way to Old Lick.

"Emmalee, hey girl," Runt called from an open door.

Emmalee jumped hearing her name but relaxed when she saw her uncle hurrying toward her, a wide grin on his face, his arms outstretched. Emmalee had not expected to find Runt home this time of day, but she imagined the rain had kept him off the mountain and away from the mill. She was relieved he was there and leaned into her uncle's embrace. Runt wrapped his arms around her and the baby and held them close.

"Look at you, Emmalee, a mama. My. My. You're looking more like Cynthia Faye every time I see you," he said.

"I wish Mama was here," Emmalee whispered back.

Mettie called to Runt from inside the house, wanting to know who had come to the door. Emmalee stood quiet and looked up at her uncle.

"Come on. Let's get you and the baby out of this wet cold." Runt kept his arm around his niece's shoulder and led her inside. The house was tidy and clean and smelled like wild jasmine. Emmalee savored the sweet scent. She took another full breath and held it in her lungs. No jasmine had bloomed in this valley for months.

"Come on in. Sit down," Runt said and pulled her deeper into the room. A blue sofa and two cushy-looking chairs covered in a bright floral fabric consumed most of the space. The furniture looked new, like it had come straight from the store, and Emmalee hesitated to sit for fear she might dirty one of Mettie's cushions.

Nolan had never allowed her to visit her uncle's house. He had warned her about coming with such venom in his eyes, Emmalee believed she was talking to a devilish haint, not her own father. Through the years, she had ignored much of what Nolan had told her about Runt and Mettie, but never this. She always feared what he would do if he found her there. Even today, her hands trembled some.

"You look beat," Runt said. "You okay?"

Emmalee bounced the baby in her arms. She tried to smile, although she wasn't sure if Runt had noticed the effort. Mettie walked into the living room and gasped. She cupped both hands over her mouth, and her eyes grew wide. "Emmalee," she said, drawn out and kind.

"Go on, sit," Runt repeated. Mettie kept her hands to her mouth. She stared at Kelly Faye, and a small smile pushed its way free. With her hand, Emmalee brushed the seat of her pants and sat on the sofa as her uncle had instructed. She looked at Mettie, hoping she had done right.

"Mettie, hon, why don't you get Emmalee some juice?" Runt said.

Mettie nodded. She stood a moment longer before turning for the kitchen. Emmalee and Runt didn't speak while Mettie opened and shut cabinets and clanked glasses together in the next room. She returned a moment later with a fresh glass of apple juice and set it on the table at the end of the sofa. Emmalee adjusted the baby on her lap and held the juice to her lips. It was cool and sweet on her throat. She gulped it down. It left her stomach feeling full and a little sick, but she wanted more. Mettie offered to fetch her another glass while keeping her stare fixed on the baby in Emmalee's arms.

"Why you here, Em?" Runt asked. "I know this ain't a social call. You need something? Something for the baby? Are you two all right?"

"You know we've been thinking of you," Mettie said from the kitchen. "We wanted to come down to see you. I even bought the baby a few gowns and a little pink sweater with a matching cap." Mettie grew giddy as she described the baby's new clothes. "You want to see them?" she asked.

"Hang on, Mettie. I think Em has come down here for a reason. What is it, hon? What do you need?" Runt asked, his face turning serious. "You know we'll help any way we can." Mettie nodded as her husband spoke.

Emmalee wished she knew what she needed most. Maybe it was someone to care for the baby, or maybe it was someone to care for her. She wasn't sure anymore. She said nothing while Mettie inched closer to her and Kelly cradled in her arms.

Runt had brought Mettie by her and Nolan's house when they first married. She wouldn't sit down on their broken-down sofa or drink or eat anything they had to offer. Mettie never let go of Runt's hand and insisted on calling him by his God-given name, William. Nolan called her a bitch after they drove off and said nobody in town would know who in the hell *William* was. Emmalee never blamed Mettie for acting skittish around Nolan. She didn't like much about her father's house, either, and imagined it was real off-putting to a stranger. Besides, *William* sounded nice to her, important even. Sure as hell beat *Runt.*

Emmalee was eight at the time, and she could not take her eyes off of Runt's pretty new bride. She thought Mettie was the most beautiful woman she had ever seen; even her skin smelled pretty. She liked Mettie then. She liked her a lot. More than that, she wanted Mettie to like her, too. But Mettie never came to the house after that, and Runt quit coming unless he had work to offer Nolan.

Emmalee drew Kelly closer to her chest and ignored Mettie's stares. She had grown to hate her aunt through the years, but not because of all the hateful things Nolan said about her. Emmalee never believed much of that. Instead she hated Mettie for never coming back.

"Can I hold her?" Mettie asked with a cautious tone.

Emmalee lifted the baby to her shoulder. "She'll be nine weeks tomorrow, fusses all the time. I guess that's what babies do. But it gets on my last nerve sometimes." Emmalee had never owned anything anybody else craved, and she enjoyed teasing Mettie by holding out on her.

Mettie's smile fell weak, but she did not take her eyes off the baby who was indeed starting to fuss as Emmalee had promised she would.

"Can I? Please?" Mettie asked again.

Again, Emmalee hesitated but then held Kelly Faye up in front of her.

Mettie slowly lifted the baby onto her shoulder and rubbed her tiny back. She nuzzled her nose against Kelly's neck. The baby's cries strengthened in pitch and volume, but the noise did not fluster Mettie. She swayed back and forth, back and forth, whispering in Kelly's ear. She patted her back with a tender hand and kissed her fuzzy head, and soon Kelly grew quiet. Mothering looked so natural for Mettie, Emmalee thought, and she had yet to birth a baby of her own.

"She's mighty tiny. You been feeding her good?" Mettie asked as she rocked the baby in her arms.

"Best I can. She's always hungry. Hard to keep up with her. Tit's so damn sore, can't barely stand it."

"I'm sure of that," Mettie said as if she understood from her own personal experience. "Are you eating enough? You know you can't feed her right if you're not eating good and drinking plenty of water."

Emmalee shrugged her shoulders.

Runt stared at her, and Emmalee lowered her

eyes to the ground. She picked at the electrical tape that held her boot together. Mettie wore shoes with a sharp point at the toe. Emmalee imagined Mettie's feet must hurt all the time scrunched up inside those shoes.

"Runt," Emmalee said, "you know Nolan would whip me good if he knew I was here. So you got to swear you won't say a word. I mean it. Promise. Hand on the Bible and everything. You, too, Mettie."

"I promise," Runt said. "You know you can trust us both." He reached out and patted Emmalee's arm. "We're sure happy to see you, hon, but I got to think you come looking for something more."

Emmalee wrung her hands and kept her eyes fixed on the floor, finding it easier to talk to Runt if she didn't have to look at him straight. "There's something I need to do, and Mr. Fulton was right. I can't do it and care for a baby at the same time. I ain't got no one to turn to, no one to hand her off to."

"Oh," Mettie said, fast to interrupt, "we'd love to take care of Kelly if that's what you're wanting." She hugged the baby tighter.

"You can't keep her, Mettie. I just need some help for a day or two. That's all."

"Yes, of course," Mettie said.

"It shouldn't take me any longer than that to get Leona's dress done without the baby hanging on me."

"The dress?" Mettie asked.

"For Leona. For burying." Emmalee nodded. "I'm making it. Mr. Fulton said I could."

"Oh. Well, that's wonderful." Mettie paused and whispered in the baby's ear. "And yes. We'd love to keep Kelly Faye for you. And Nolan won't know a thing about her being here."

Emmalee tucked her hair behind her ear. "Never thought you'd be wanting to do me a favor."

Mettie's body swayed more slowly. The baby had fallen asleep in her arms. "Why honey, I love you. I always have. You're family." Mettie gazed at the baby as she talked. Her smile grew bigger and her tone bright. "You are such a pretty girl. Yes, you are. We're going to need to put you on a bottle without your mama here to feed you. Yes, we are. Yes, we are," she cooed in the baby's ear.

Emmalee fidgeted watching Mettie care for Kelly Faye with such ease, but she was careful with her tongue. She needed Mettie now. "Fine with me. Bottle might do her some good. Know it'll do me some." Emmalee leaned back against the sofa and pushed her feet out in front of her. "I need one more thing, Runt. I need a ride to Old Lick."

Before leaving for Old Lick, Mettie wrapped Emmalee's chest in strips of soft white cotton, promising the binding would leave her more

190

comfortable while she was away from her baby girl. "You don't want to get all clogged, so be sure to take this binding off tonight and milk those breasts good. Probably best if you could do it more often than that, but promise you'll do it good before going to bed." Mettie held the edge of the binding against Emmalee's back. "That's real important. They can get infected if you don't. Your left one's already feeling a tiny bit warm to the touch. Probably nothing, but keep an eye on it."

Mettie pulled and stretched the binding around Emmalee's chest over and over. Emmalee stood in front of the mirror and admired her body wrapped up neat like a Christmas present. She looked smaller and flatter, more like the Emmalee she used to know. She felt mothered in Mettie's care as her aunt's slender fingers worked a pin into the cloth binding.

"There, that should do it," Mettie said as she fastened the pin closed. "If you have a hard time getting the milk to come, put some warm cloths on your chest. It'll help. Trust me."

"How come you know all this?" Emmalee asked as she examined herself some more, turning to the side and drawing her hands across her breasts.

Mettie laughed. "My mama had ten children. Surely you knew that. Figured everyone in Cullen knew that. I was the third, after my sisters

Dottie and Kitty." Mettie held up her hand as if she was counting out her siblings on her fingers. "Being the oldest girls, we three did our share of child rearing. Mama had her last at forty-nine. Two months short of her fiftieth birthday."

"Forty-nine," Emmalee repeated as though she could not believe it.

"Lord, we thought she'd never stop having babies," Mettie said as she sat on the edge of her bed, wrapping a scrap of the binding around her wrist. "Me and my sisters were so mad at her when she told us the tenth was on its way. That was my brother Calvin. Dottie wouldn't even talk to Mama for days. Can't blame her really. Dottie wanted to get out of that house. Out of Cullen. She was tired of sharing everything—clothes, beds, bathroom. Even your own toothbrush was up for grabs. But more than anything, we didn't want to raise any more of Mama's children. We wanted lives of our own and families of our own." Mettie kissed the baby's head, her lips smoothing the baby's fine hair.

"She feels a little warm, Emmalee. She been feeling okay?"

"I reckon. Seems fine to me. Sleeps, cries, poops, and eats. That's about it."

"Probably all this blanket she's wrapped up in is heating her up some." Mettie loosened the knitted blanket around Kelly's tummy. The baby stretched and curled her body.

"I thought your daddy was rich and could pay people to do for your mama," Emmalee said, twirling the end of her hair around her index finger.

"Where'd you get that idea?"

"Nolan."

Mettie rolled her eyes. "We weren't rich. We were comfortable. But not rich." Mettie's gaze got stuck in one direction as though she was lost in a memory. "You know when Mama told us she was pregnant that last time, our mouths dropped wide open. Kitty couldn't even speak. Don't think she said more than a word the whole day." Mettie shook her head. "Dottie, on the other hand, started screaming at Mama and wouldn't stop. Mama finally walked out of the house. We found her in the garden, working the ground with a broken hoe. She stayed out there till dark."

Emmalee and Mettie sat quiet for a moment, each staring at the other's reflection in the mirror. When Kelly started fussing, Mettie kissed her tiny cheek. "Baby girl, we done bound your mama up. Your uncle Runt's going to get you something to eat just as good. You're going to have to hold on, though," she said in a reassuring tone and rocked the baby some more.

"Don't take too long, Runt," Mettie hollered into the next room, careful to hold her hand over Kelly's ear as she spoke. "This girl's working up some more appetite. She's already rooting for her mama." The baby squirmed in her arms, and Mettie stroked her back. "And get me some of those diaper pins with the little plastic ducks on the end. And two or three dozen cloth diapers. Make it three. And a couple pair of plastic pants. Go ahead and get some of those disposable diapers, too."

"Mettie, you want to write this down?" Runt asked.

"Just ask Margaret for help. I haven't bought any baby things in years and don't know what's out there. Hurry up." Mettie's voice grew with excitement. She turned to Emmalee. "You know I'd drive up there with you, Em, but I think it's too cold to have Kelly Faye out for no good reason. She's already pretty fussy." Mettie jiggled the baby a little faster. "I think a warm bath might settle her down till Runt gets back."

Truth be told, Emmalee preferred it that way. She was eager to get to Old Lick and feared if she spent too much time with Mettie, her aunt might see clear inside her heart and find there was a part of her relieved, downright happy, to leave the baby in her care. Emmalee was tired of mothering on her own. She was tired of the baby's fussing and of sleepless nights and of washing diapers in a bucket under the outdoor spigot in the season's growing cold. She was worn out but had seen no escape until now.

"Don't matter, Mettie. I ain't going far."

Emmalee

Old Lick

- - - - - - - - - -

Emmalee stood in front of the Lanes' trailer and waved good-bye to her uncle Runt. She lingered there, soaking up the sun's warmth, the trailer door open wide behind her. Only as the truck's taillights disappeared behind the wall of hardwoods and pines did Emmalee feel a pang of sadness, perhaps a regret for leaving her baby in another woman's care.

There was no time for thinking such thoughts, she chided herself. There was important work to be done, and she could not make a dress and tend to a baby all at once. "It's best this way," Emmalee said and took hold of the flimsy rail edging the stoop. A stinging pain radiated fast and sharp down the left side of her chest as she reached farther up the rail. Already swollen with milk, both breasts were hard to the touch. It had been too many hours since she had nursed the baby well, much longer than she had confessed to her aunt. The pain eased some, and Emmalee stepped into the trailer.

She followed the steps worn in the green

carpet, a threadbare trail leading from the door to the kitchen at the right end of the trailer. She imagined Leona had walked this very path countless times over the years to prepare her family's meals. Foil pans of biscuits and baskets of muffins already crowded the counter, and Emmalee wondered who in their grief had brought all these gifts to the vacant trailer. It didn't surprise her, though. People need to do for the dead in whatever way they can. Nolan told her once that nothing pulled a woman into the kitchen faster than a dead body waiting at Fulton's. She looked out the window to see if someone else might be heading across the drive, carrying more offerings of flowers and food.

Emmalee wiped the sink clean and swept the linoleum, tasks she had done only the day before but found satisfaction in their doing. She dried her hands on a dishtowel hanging across the refrigerator's handle and dallied there a moment longer. She loved Leona's kitchen with its indoor faucet and electric oven.

Runt had packed a jar of freshly made pimento cheese and a loaf of white bread, a carton of milk, a half dozen eggs, and two cans of Vienna sausages. He told her to call if she needed anything else. He knew the Lanes had a working telephone because he had called on Curtis to help him at the mill just last week. He wrote his number on a slip of paper and handed it to Emmalee.

"Keep this someplace you won't lose it. And don't worry about Kelly. Mettie'll take real good care of her. She's probably already got her bathed and dressed up like a baby doll if I know my wife."

"She ain't a doll, Runt." Emmalee held the paper in her hands and studied the number scribbled in pencil. She traced each number with her finger. "And I ain't used a phone but a time or two."

Runt had winked and reassured Emmalee she was a smart girl and would have no problem placing a call.

Emmalee stared into the length of the trailer, cataloging the sum of Leona and Curtis's life there including the black telephone sitting on the floor by a worn brown chair. She spied a ragged *TV Guide* left on the chair's seat cushion; the rickety table set below the front window carried the weight of the old Atlas sewing machine and piles of different fabrics. She found family photos, miniature spoons, the clock tacked to the wall that kept perfect time, paper books by a man named Louis L'Amour, two bronze-colored hands clenched in prayer (the body nowhere in sight), a blue ceramic vase stuffed with plastic flowers, a wooden bear with the word *Gatlinburg* burned on his round tummy, and a yellow crocheted blanket draped across the back of the sofa, another piece of Leona's handiwork Emmalee had not noticed yesterday.

She took it all in as she traced her path back into the living room. Emmalee stood in front of the sewing table and ran her fingers across a piece of the deep red fabric the woman in the pretty suit had called *damask*. She glanced out the window as if she expected to see her standing in the drive with her hands pinching her slender hips.

The fabric was more beautiful than anything Emmalee had ever seen at Tennewa. Trees with vines hanging low from willowy branches and awkward-looking birds with long legs and skinny necks perched along a river's bank were all woven into the cloth. She pulled the fabric to her cheek and wrapped a piece across her shoulders like a treasured shawl. The crimson color would highlight Leona's gray hair.

With the fabric wrapped around her body, Emmalee rushed to the bedroom at the back of the trailer. She crawled over the bed as she hurried to the mirror mounted above the oak dresser. Emmalee stared at herself, the fabric draped around her neck. She imagined her hair white like Leona's. "It's perfect."

She opened the closet door and scanned the tight bunch of clothes, hunting for one of Leona's Tennewa dresses. Emmalee lifted a pale blue one off its hanger. She examined its simple A-line shape. Surely this could be adapted into a more attractive garment, one much more appropriate for a proper burial.

Emmalee picked the straight pins from the large piece of damask she had carried with her. She stretched it across the foot of the bed while she pictured the Tennewa dress adorned with an added belt or long sleeves trimmed with lace. Emmalee giggled with excitement as she imagined the dress taking shape. She placed the cotton housedress on top of the damask. There was more than enough fabric here, and there were yards more on the sewing table should she need it.

Emmalee hurried back to the front room, stopping at Leona's sewing table to grab a seam ripper she had seen there earlier. She settled into the reclining chair and kicked off the work boots she had left untied around her ankles. Emmalee flipped the dress inside out and slipped the tool's sharp point underneath a stitch placed right above the hem. She broke the thread and slipped the U-shaped blade underneath the next stitch, each gentle tug unraveling the work of women Leona had known. Emmalee settled deeper into the chair, pushing the blade underneath another perfect stitch. The seam disappeared as she moved the length of the dress, cutting one stitch after another and pulling it free.

She slowed her pace only as she neared the sleeve. This seam was set with double stitching, and Emmalee could see why the sleeve setters were held to a lower quota. She wondered who had done this work she now so carefully undid with the flick of her wrist. Maybe Patsy Brown or Ivory Daniels. Both of these women had been at Tennewa almost as long as Leona, and Emmalee wondered if they were grieving for their fellow employee or merely focused on their daily quota.

Again, Emmalee slipped the seam ripper underneath a stitch and tugged. The thread snapped clean. She moved quickly around the sleeve-to-shoulder seam until the sleeve fell into her lap with the breaking of the last stitch. Another sharp pain radiated from her left side. Emmalee gasped but ignored the breast now hard and growing hot. Instead she turned the dress and began working on the other side. She worked faster, following a familiar rhythm. But as she drew nearer the second shoulder, Emmalee stopped. She cut four or five more stitches. She studied the dress held together by a simple collar and wondered if perhaps she had stitched this one or if it had been Leona's work.

The threads pulled easily from their place. Emmalee's stomach churned, and her hand dropped to her lap. Her head fell against the back of the chair, and Emmalee closed her eyes. Her breasts throbbed from their heavy load, and a sharp pain moved fast from her chest down her left arm. She had been busy with her work and had not tended to them as Mettie had encouraged her to do, stopping to milk them if they grew too full. Her left breast was twice the size of the other and felt as though someone had struck a match to it.

Emmalee hated the baby at times for turning her body into something she did not recognize anymore. And she hated Emmalee for taking her from her work at Tennewa, from the collar makers and the other seamstresses there. The paycheck she received each week felt like a miracle, and she liked knowing she was part of making dresses worn by women she'd never know, in places she'd never see. She might not have shared a cigarette with Laura Cooley or have been asked to walk to the drugstore with some of the other women for a Coca-Cola after work, but Emmalee felt happy in their presence, like a baby starling snuggled cozily beneath its mother's feathered wings.

Emmalee knew they made fun of the girl from Red Chert who didn't have the good sense to know she was expecting a child. She knew some of the older women gossiped about her lazy work—her late arrivals and her quotas falling short, though she'd tried as hard as she could. Many of them took turns running to the office and confessing to Gwen about a cousin or a sister who could do a better job given the chance to sit in Emmalee's chair, but Emmalee had fought to stay and to belong, with Leona's help. Touching their work only reminded her how much she ached for them.

Emmalee rubbed her hand across the cotton. She fingered the buttons. "This is silly," she said aloud. "There are thousands more dresses like this one." But she hated to lift this collar from its place, to remove another part of Leona Lane from this world. The collar hung limp in her hands, held to the dress by a short piece of thread. "I'm sorry," she said and pulled the last stitch free.

Emmalee knelt on the floor and winced as she struggled to spread the damask across the carpeting in front of her. With one hand, she pressed the fabric flat between the sewing table and the reclining chair. It was too thick to cut double. She pinned the front of the housedress to the cloth, then two collar pieces, and four sleeves, adjusting their position for the best fit, working it like a jigsaw puzzle as she had seen the pattern makers at Tennewa do. Emmalee cut into the fabric, keeping the scissors' blades steady as she worked, tossing scraps of damask into a growing pile at the foot of Curtis's chair. On the floor in front of her, the form of a dress took shape.

When she closed her eyes, she saw Leona laid out at Fulton's. She looked beautiful, and every-one in town—the Tennewa women, Mrs. Whitlow,

Mr. Clayton, the preacher—filed by and admired her beautiful dress. They dried their eyes with a tissue and asked who had done such lovely work. They hugged Emmalee and complimented her design and obvious skill. In her imagination, she smiled in return and admitted Leona had taught her much of what she knew.

Emmalee spread another piece of damask on the floor and pinned the back of the housedress in place. Again, she guided the scissors along the pattern's edge, careful to make the rounded turns along the shoulder and neck. Only with the second piece cut free did she look at the clock on the wall and see it was long after midnight. She had been in the trailer since late morning and had not stopped to notice the passing of another day. Her eyes were weary, and the pain in her chest had spread across her back. Emmalee ignored the binding damp with milk and stretched out on the sofa. She covered her body with the yellow afghan. She would rest for an hour and then tend to her body. Emmalee slept while the trailer gently cradled her on the mountain's bluff.

She woke hours later to the sun shining on her face and a knock sounding at the thin metal door. Emmalee panted like a hurt dog, finding it difficult to catch her breath as she pulled herself up from the sofa. Both breasts were stone hard, and the binding was soaked with milk. She held her hands to her chest as she peered through a narrow opening in the curtains. Wilma stood on the stoop holding a bundle of mountain laurel. Easter stood behind her with a casserole in her hands. Emmalee opened the door and stumbled back to the sofa, not bothering to greet or welcome the women into Leona's home.

"Why Emmalee, we didn't expect to find you here," Wilma said, standing at the trailer's door. "What are you doing on Old Lick?"

Emmalee said nothing as she leaned into the pain.

"Not sure we really expected to find anybody here. Figured we should do something though," Easter explained, holding up the casserole in her hands.

"You know Easter looks for any excuse to make this chicken noodle dish. She knows there ain't no family to feed, everybody's dead or gone on, but we thought some of the church people might be stopping by." Wilma cleared a place on the sewing table to rest her vase of mountain laurel. She bent to smell the arrangement of carnations and roses already there. "Somebody done beat me up here," she said. "We were hoping Leona's sister might be in from Ohio. Or is it Oklahoma? I know it begins with an 'O.' Maybe it's her brother in Oklahoma. You know, Easter, which it is?"

Easter shook her head and headed into the kitchen. "Her brother died six years ago, remember? And I think her sister's in Virginia. I don't know for sure. I just know I need to cook at times like this. I figure somebody's going to turn up hungry sooner or later. You hungry, Emmalee?" Easter pushed a tin of muffins to the side and set down her dish in plain view. "Looks like I'm not the only one who needs to cook," she said and laughed.

Emmalee held her arms across her chest.

Wilma picked up a piece of the damask. "You know, I believe the preacher did say something about you making a dress for Leona."

"That's right, he did mention a dress," Easter echoed her friend. "Now where's that baby girl of yours? You never brought her around for us to admire. What'd you end up naming her?"

"Sure ain't *Viruslee,*" Emmalee said.

"Oh honey, we all knew she probably wasn't a virus," Easter said. "And you sure can't go paying attention to what those other girls say behind your back. Now what's her real name?"

Emmalee kept one arm across her chest. She didn't bother looking at Wilma or Easter.

"Kelly Faye. Her name's Kelly Faye. Faye's after my mama."

"That's pretty," Easter said as she eased back toward the sofa, her large body forcing her to maneuver carefully past the sewing table and reclining chair. The trailer floor rattled underneath the weight of her step. "You know, hon, I knew your mama when she come to town, right after marrying your daddy. Not sure I ever told you that. She come by the church looking for work. Such a sweet young thing. You look a lot like her," Easter said as she inched up behind Wilma. "She sure would be tickled to have a grandbaby to dote on. Ain't that right, Wilma?"

"She sure would." Wilma glanced about the trailer. "Oh Lord, I can't believe Leona and Curtis are both gone. I don't think I'm ever going to be able to walk into that sewing room without feeling blue." Wilma pulled a tissue from deep within her sweater's sleeve. "Leona worked right in front of me for more than fifteen years. You can't stare at a woman's back that long and not miss the sight of her."

Emmalee moaned.

"Emmalee, hon, are you all right?" Wilma asked while Easter talked on about casseroles and Curtis and the Cullen Church of Christ where she was also a lifelong member. Wilma tapped Easter's forearm, signaling her friend to hush. "Emmalee, you don't look right."

"I ain't right."

"Honey, what's wrong?"

Emmalee lifted her shirt only far enough to expose the cotton binding. Wilma eased next to her on the sofa. She touched the edge of the bandage. Emmalee flinched.

"Honey, where is the baby?" she asked, her voice calm.

"With Mettie and Runt."

"When you feed her last?"

"Don't know. A little bit yesterday morning. Night before some." Emmalee cried, and her chest throbbed even more with each heaving sob.

"Oh sweetie," Wilma said in a soothing tone, "you need to quit crying for one thing. Try to stay calm. Okay?" She gently pulled Emmalee's shirt over her head and wrapped the crocheted blanket across her bare shoulders and then directed Easter to gather plenty of hot cloths.

"This reminds me of the day Kelly was born. There ain't another baby coming, is there?" Easter asked as she walked back into the kitchen.

"Stop that kidding around and bring me them cloths," Wilma said as she stroked the hair from Emmalee's face. "I don't think this girl's finding that very funny." Wilma reassured Emmalee she would be better soon. With a gentle hand, Wilma removed the safety pin fastened near Emmalee's spine. "Easter, hand me those scissors."

Wilma placed the tip of a blade underneath the binding. Emmalee jerked as she felt the cold metal touch her skin. Wilma cautioned her to hold still as she cut away the cloth revealing Emmalee's breasts, swollen, veins bulging through the tautly stretched skin, nipples cracked and dry.

"Oh, baby," Wilma said. She reached for a warm

cloth. "Easter, better boil me some water with a handful of salt. This one here on the left feels real hot to the touch."

Emmalee moaned as her body absorbed the warmth of the wet cloths and the gentle touch of Wilma's hands. As each cloth cooled, Wilma replaced it with a warm one. Emmalee closed her eyes, trusting her body's care to the older women who talked in hushed tones as they hovered about her, stroking her hair and rubbing her arms and shoulders.

"They felt better all tied up. I didn't want to undo it like Mettie said. I didn't want to nurse no more, with or without the baby," Emmalee said, her voice choked with tears.

"It's okay. This is a lot for anyone, especially a young mama." Wilma leaned close and patted Emmalee's hand. "There you see, Emmalee, your milk's starting to come on its own. We just needed to get you all cozy and warm. But I'm going to touch you a little. Need to help it along a bit. You holler if I hurt you too bad."

Emmalee nodded. Her body stiffened as Wilma placed a dry towel on her stomach. "Honey, I haven't even touched you yet and getting all tight like that is only going to keep the milk from coming." Wilma rubbed Emmalee's shoulder first and moved her fingers in a small, circular motion down her chest. "Relax, baby," she said as she kneaded the hard, tight skin.

"Oh shit," Emmalee yelled as the pressure of Wilma's touch strengthened. "Don't touch me no more."

"Squeeze my hand," Easter said as Wilma mashed her fingers against Emmalee's breast. Emmalee screamed louder, but Wilma pushed her fingers into the hardened mass. Soon the milk flowed more steadily, wetting the towel spread across Emmalee's stomach. The women discussed collecting it for the baby but decided Emmalee was too uncomfortable to trouble with the effort. The milk flowed faster, and Emmalee relaxed on the sofa.

Easter replaced the wet towel across Emmalee's stomach while Wilma massaged the other breast. Emmalee grimaced, but this pain was not as sharp as the other. As the milk dripped onto the towel, Easter wrung out a small cloth soaking in a bowl of warm salty water and set it on Emmalee's chest.

"Easter, did you find any salve in Leona's bathroom? These nipples here are a mess, cracked and raw. No wonder the girl got so engorged. I doubt you was taking the baby to the breast like you should. Probably because it hurt too bad, am I right?" Wilma asked as she lifted the cloth to better examine Emmalee. "The problem is you can get real sick if you don't nurse the baby like you should. The milk gets backed up and you end up like this, or worse. You two need each other. The baby needs you to grow, and you need the baby to nurse real regular. When you going to see her next?"

"Soon as I finish with Leona's dress, probably tomorrow, maybe the day after."

"Well, first things first. Let's get you feeling better," Wilma said. She rubbed Emmalee's breasts with a cold white cream and wrapped her chest in fresh cotton strips cut from an old sheet Easter found in a bathroom cabinet. She handed Emmalee a glass of water and watched her drink it all up while Easter warmed the casserole in the oven. They fed Emmalee, spooning each bite of chicken into her mouth and wiping her lips clean with a paper napkin. They covered Emmalee's body with the crocheted blanket and kept vigil by her side as she slept on Leona's bed.

Leona

Old Lick

- - - - - - - - - -

1965

The sun kissed the horizon early as it climbed high into the July sky. The temperature would soar close to one hundred by afternoon even on top of the mountain. Curtis promised a thunderstorm would surely roll over the bluff later in the day, soaking the land with a quick but heavy rain.

Leona smelled the thick summer air as she stepped from the trailer. The katydids had already begun to sing, and she knew their oscillating trill would escalate along with the day's rising heat. This was her favorite time to work in the garden, before the day grew too hot and crowded with other chores. Curtis had bought her a new pair of work gloves, pink ones speckled with little white dots. The gloves were tucked in her back pocket as she reached to pick up a tomato that a squirrel had tasted and left behind.

Leona moved into the bright morning sun and shielded her eyes with her hand, but she swore her garden had grown twice in size since yesterday afternoon. The tomatoes were already heavy with fruit and their vines, bent from carrying such a burdensome load, rested against the metal cages supporting them. Leona pinched a weak rambler between her fingers. She examined the leaves, checking for any signs of blight or other disease, and tossed it onto the ground.

She grew beefsteaks for Curtis and Arkansas travelers and Cherokee purples for herself. She preferred the mild taste and tender flesh of the heirlooms. Leona spied another large cluster of green fruit with a hint of pink to their skins, and she daydreamed of the full jars she would put up for winter. Leona would start picking before long, and she would offer Curtis the first one, sliced and salted and served up on a paper plate. She would eat hers whole, sinking her teeth into its soft skin, its juice dripping down her chin.

This was the only day of the week when neither the factory nor the church forced Leona to keep an eye on her watch, and she paused to count the ears of corn with sprouted silks and the yellow squash with faded blossoms on their tips. Leona pulled stray weeds and sprinkled fertilizer on the ground. She cleared a spot for a late-summer planting, maybe another crop of beans.

Curtis had left a few minutes earlier to cut wood on the backside of Brown Chapel

Mountain. Runt Bullard had come looking for help, seeing how his brother never showed. Curtis never went back to the poultry business after they lost the baby. He never ventured far from home anymore and acted nervous when he did. He worked plenty of odd jobs around town while he claimed to look for steady work and was always eager to lend a hand at the church. But Curtis preferred spending most of his days on Old Lick, chopping wood for sale or tinkering with his truck.

"Things will get better soon," Curtis promised every morning when he dropped Leona off at Tennewa. "Yes, they will. They'll get better real soon." Then he'd lean across the seat and kiss Leona on the cheek. These days Leona was grateful whenever Runt called to offer Curtis a day's pay and she found herself alone on the mountain.

The rough sound of tires rolling across loose gravel suddenly drew her attention beyond the woods shielding their property from the main road. A large green wagon, with a cloud of grayish dust trailing behind it, headed toward the trailer. Leona had seen this car at Tennewa, parked outside the factory's office door. Most of the seamstresses carpooled to work, but this oversized wagon, with its wood-paneled sides, did not belong to any of them.

Leona ran into her garden and stood behind the wiry cages, planting her feet firmly in the fertile soil. She recognized Mr. Clayton sitting tall behind the steering wheel, his long sleeves rolled to his elbows and dark sunglasses hiding his eyes. The manager from Tennewa looked out of place up on the mountain in his crisp white shirt. Leona slipped her hands inside her apron pockets.

Her heart beat fast, and she feared Mr. Clayton had come to the mountain to reprimand her. Maybe he had noticed her staring every time he walked from the front office to the cutting room in the back of the factory building. She was ashamed of it, of the looking, that is, but Leona couldn't stop these feelings or her wandering eyes. She thought everything about Mr. Clayton was handsome, his crooked nose and his square jaw, his large hands and thick chest. Leona had looked at Curtis that way once. But she had done nothing wrong, she told herself. She had only looked.

"Leona," Mr. Clayton said, shouting out the open window. His broad smile revealed the gap between his teeth. "I guess by that look on your face my visit is not what you expected on this beautiful Saturday morning." The wagon rolled to a stop in front of the trailer.

Always dressed in suits and wing-tipped shoes during the week, Mr. Clayton looked more relaxed today in his blue jeans and faded sneakers. Although the sunglasses shaded his eyes, his face appeared more at ease.

Leona picked at another vine, snapping its brown tip between her fingers and tossing it onto the ground. "Good morning, sir," she said, reaching for another stem spilling beyond the metal cage.

"Good to see you, Leona. Don't worry. This is not an official visit of any kind. I've come about my wife." He pulled his dark glasses from his face.

Leona's heart beat faster, afraid Mrs. Clayton had heard of her wandering eyes.

"Your wife?"

"Yes. You see my wife wants to have a slip-cover made for a bedroom chair, and I heard you do that kind of work on the side. If I'm going to be completely honest with you, I've heard you're the best around."

Ever since Curtis lost his job in the mines, Leona took in sewing from women she barely knew—women who drove their fancy cars from Lookout and Signal Mountains and dumped their fine French fabrics in her tired hands so she could turn them into beautiful slipcovers for their ratty old club chairs and camelback sofas, pieces these women called antiques. They told Leona her sewing was beautiful, the best they'd ever seen. They praised her as if she were a child of their own, not a grown woman, although they pursed their lips and asked for discounts when they paid.

Leona was well aware of her excellent reputation as a seamstress, a reputation that had spread south to Chattanooga and north to Manchester. Yet when she met these women at her trailer's door, she avoided their eyes and instead focused on their fabrics and detailed instructions. Now with Mr. Clayton standing in front of her, Leona found she couldn't look at him, either.

"Anyway, I can't really show favorites, you know. Wouldn't be good for morale. I'm sure you can understand my predicament," he said and grinned.

Leona turned her eyes to the fresh dirt beneath her feet.

"That's why I came to your place. On a Saturday. Off the record. You know what I mean?" he asked, his pace slowing. "I hope that was all right?"

"Yes, sir." Leona tried to keep her gaze fixed on the ground.

"Good." Mr. Clayton grinned a little wider. "Would you mind taking a peek at this chair I've got here, and this bolt of fabric my wife's bought? I'd love to know what you think. And tell me what you charge for this kind of work."

Leona stepped from behind the metal cages. She glanced back at the trailer door, half expecting to see Curtis standing there, watching his wife with the factory manager. She pulled off her gloves, their tips stained with mud, and stuffed them in her apron's pocket.

"Looks like you're going to have a generous crop of tomatoes this year," Mr. Clayton said.

"Yes, sir," Leona answered as she followed him to the back of the wagon. "Kind of late getting some of them in the ground."

A small wingback chair and a bolt of pink-and-white gingham fabric sat next to a child's bicycle and a gray tackle box. Leona wondered about the little boy who must ride this bike with the blue seat and shiny blue frame. Maybe he was nine or ten years old and carried his daddy's same strong face and deep brown eyes. She wondered if they fished together down in Sequatchie River, if Mr. Clayton had taught him how to bait a hook with a fresh worm and how to scale a blue gill. Leona felt like she was spying, discovering a part of Mr. Clayton's private life not meant for a collar maker to know.

"So what do you think?" he asked, pulling the fabric into the sunshine.

"Yes, sir, a slipcover. When you need it by?"

"We're in no real hurry. My wife's expecting our third child, and she wants to use this in the nursery."

"Congratulations," Leona said. She cocked her head to the side and narrowed her eyes. "How she know it's a girl?"

"She doesn't." Mr. Clayton laughed. "She's hoping and praying and wishing on every star in the sky for a girl this time. I told her it was silly to spend the money covering this chair if the baby turns out to be another boy. But she doesn't care. She thinks if she plans on a girl, then she'll have one." Mr. Clayton sat on the wagon's open gate and held the bolt between his legs. "To tell the truth, I'm in no mood to argue with that woman right now."

Leona looked away.

"Oh, I'm so sorry, Leona, this is terribly insensitive of me. I wasn't thinking. I forgot you lost—. Please forgive me."

Leona fell quiet, and a crow called out in the distance. "It was a long time ago." She tried to speak but wasn't sure Mr. Clayton could see the effort. And with the toe of her canvas loafer, Leona pushed a chunk of gray gravel into the soft dirt.

"Let me ask someone else to do this. I should never have come up here with all this."

Leona fingered the fabric. "That's okay. I can do it for you," she said, her tone soft but resolute.

"Are you sure?"

"Yes, sir."

Mr. Clayton reached for Leona's hand. "I don't imagine a woman ever quits grieving the loss of a baby." He squeezed her hand in his.

Leona did not pull away. She knew she shouldn't linger like that. Nothing good would come of it, but she liked the warmth of his hand on hers. "I wouldn't feel right about taking your money," she finally said and withdrew from his grasp.

"Well, I wouldn't hear of not paying you. Not for this kind of work. I insist. How does forty dollars sound?"

Leona laughed. The sound surprised her, and she clapped her hand across her mouth. "That's too much."

"Not for quality work."

"Seems like an awful lot to me. Almost what I make in a week sewing collars."

"I tell you what, you feel like gambling a little?"

"I don't know about that." Leona lifted her hand to her brow, shading her eyes from the brightening sun. "Don't think it's a sin or nothing, just never done it. Doubt Curtis would care for it much."

"Hear me out. I'll give you fifty dollars right up front." Mr. Clayton reached for his wallet in his back pocket. "I'll hand it to you right now. But if it's a boy, you'll agree to make me another slipcover, a blue one, free of charge. If it's a girl, you owe me nothing. How's that sound? All legal, I promise. Don't even think the good Lord would have a problem with this one." He handed Leona a crisp fifty-dollar bill.

Leona giggled, excited about the prospect of placing a wager, even if it was a legal one. She would keep this to herself though, certain that Curtis would not approve of such an arrangement. Truth be told, she was relieved he was not there, catching her smiling back at Mr. Clayton.

"Remember, Leona, this is between you and me. Don't want to be making the other Tennewa women jealous, or we might not ever meet production." Mr. Clayton winked, revealing fine lines feathering from his eyes. "Can you keep a secret?"

"Yes, sir. I can keep a secret."

EMMALEE

Old Lick

- - - - - - - - - - - -

Emmalee woke to find Wilma and Easter standing in front of the refrigerator, cleaning out jars of food that were sure to spoil. They were talking real soft, but as soon as they spied Emmalee walking down the hall, they rushed to her side and guided her to the sofa. One examined her binding. The other kissed her forehead, checking for fever.

Wilma sat beside Emmalee and stroked her hair.

"Is this the dress you been working on, hon? The one for Leona?" Wilma asked and pointed to a piece of damask folded across the back of the metal folding chair.

"Yes'm," Emmalee answered. She pulled her feet up on the sofa, and Wilma adjusted the yellow afghan around Emmalee's legs.

Easter stood on the other side of the living room holding the front of the crimson dress in her hands. It looked small against her wide hips and broad shoulders, and Emmalee worried about its fit. Leona was a more trim woman, she reassured herself. Besides, Mr. Fulton said he could make most anything work.

"I thought the color would look real pretty with Leona's hair," Emmalee said.

"It sure will. I never seen a piece of cloth quite like this. It's beautiful. Where'd you get it? I know you didn't find it here in Cullen." Wilma motioned for Easter to bring the fabric pieces closer.

Emmalee confessed she had found the damask among Leona's sewing. Most of it had already been cut for another purpose. "A woman wearing fancy clothes come by the other day looking for *slipcovers*. I ain't sure what those are, but I got a strong feeling Leona's dress was part of it. I know it was wrong taking some of it, but it was so pretty." Emmalee explained the young woman in her high-heeled shoes had talked ugly about Leona. "She made me so mad, I guess I didn't care about cutting up her material. You think she'll come hunting for it?"

Easter and Wilma looked at each other and laughed. "I imagine so, but she's sure going to have to dig deep to find it," Easter said and laughed a little louder. The lump on her neck weighed heavy on her vocal cords and left her voice sounding raw and hoarse sometimes, particularly when she laughed real strong.

"I always envied Leona's hair," Wilma said as she pushed her own from her face. "It was such a pretty white, not like my mousy gray. It started turning that way when she was no more than forty. This crimson is absolutely perfect for her. It's a deep red, not too flashy or bright. Perfect for the occasion in my opinion. And it'll look a whole lot better on her than on a sofa, that's for sure."

"On a sofa?" Emmalee asked.

"That's what a slipcover is, hon, kind of like a dress for a sofa or chair. And nobody was better at making them than Leona."

"Cora makes them too," Easter said.

"You know, Emmalee, in all seriousness," Wilma added, "you ought to get Cora to teach you how to make them sometime. You can make good money with a skill like that."

Emmalee stared at the damask. "Well, I got to have the dress done by tomorrow. Visitation starts Sunday afternoon. I think Mr. Fulton really wanted to get things going today, but he didn't think he'd get the bodies ready in time."

"I bet the whole town turns out for Leona and Curtis. Last I talked to the preacher," Easter said, "he was even considering holding the service at the school gymnasium. I told him Curtis wouldn't like that. He was baptized at the church, and he'd want his funeral there too. I told him we'd need to make it work." Easter paused and cleared her throat. "I got to be honest with you, hon, the preacher told me you were making the dress. I can't lie to you. That's why we come up here. Thought you might need some help with it, what with the baby in tow and all."

Emmalee twisted her lips. "You didn't trust me either?"

"That's not what Easter meant, Emmalee." Wilma patted Emmalee's hand. "But I'm not going to lie to you either. The preacher was a little worried about the dress. You know, what with Leona being older and it being a funeral service."

"I bet he was." Emmalee's voice turned sharp and defensive. "What would a girl like me know about making anything *fine?*"

"He means well, hon," Easter said. She sat on the sofa next to Emmalee. As Easter's body sunk deep into the cushioned seat, Emmalee tipped toward her. "I don't think it was 'cause you come from Red Chert. Look at me. I come from Cloverdale Loop. It ain't no better."

Emmalee liked Easter being next to her.

"I think the preacher was really shaken up by the Lanes dying the way they did," Easter said. "I think if you get down to it, he feels responsible, seeing how they were coming to church supper. He's convinced if Curtis hadn't wore himself out chopping wood all day, wood for the church, he would have handled the road better. He only wants to do right by them. That's all. He's young, too, hon, not much older than you. He's never been through anything like this, and he really looked to Curtis as a father. You understand?"

"I understand he come by the house. Tried to talk me out of making it."

"I heard that, too," Easter admitted.

"Nolan told him I had every right to make this dress."

"And you do," Wilma said. "As long as Mr. Fulton agrees."

"But the preacher said something about the baby and sinning, and I don't know what all." Emmalee chewed on the tip of her nail. . . . "He got Nolan real worked up."

Easter wrapped her arm around Emmalee. "When you're young, sometimes you see everything black and white, tough to find the gray in life. Preacher hadn't found the gray yet. Give him time. He'll see it 'fore long." Emmalee dropped her head on Easter's thick, soft shoulder.

Emmalee did understand how much it hurt when you felt responsible for someone's passing. Nolan had reminded her too often that *mothering* was what wore out his Cynthia Faye. She grew frail, he said, from tending to Emmalee and had nothing left to fight the cancer.

"You know, I ain't going to lie to you while we're talking about this," Wilma said. "Some of the older women in the church were putting pressure on the preacher. They don't know you like we do. All they know is your daddy and that

225

you got this baby on your own. Don't pay them no mind though. I just don't want you to be surprised if you hear talk."

Emmalee nodded, the top of her head rubbing against Easter's goiter. "Heard it all before."

"I know," Easter whispered. "I know it, too. And I know it hurts."

Emmalee stretched her arm around Easter's full tummy. Easter pulled her closer.

"I got the front and back of the dress cut and pinned late yesterday." Emmalee spoke real soft. "I spent most of the evening working on the sleeves and collar. Took more time than I expected, but they're pretty much done. Need to set them in place is all."

"Need any help with that?" Wilma asked, stepping across the room to the sewing table. "Or placing the hem? What about a zipper?"

"Mr. Fulton said I don't need to worry with a zipper or nothing like that. I ain't ever worked one."

Easter laughed again, and Emmalee grew tickled as her head bounced up and down against Easter's stomach.

Wilma held one of the finished sleeves in her hand. "What's this here, hon?" she asked and pointed to a narrow blue band sewn to the end of the cuff, every stitch small and perfect. A cream-colored lace was set underneath the blue, its scalloped edge peeking behind the band of color.

Emmalee eased off the sofa and moved next to Wilma. "That cotton there's from one of Curtis's work shirts. I thought the touch of blue would remind Miss Leona of the sky up here on Old Lick. And I thought she should have some of Curtis close to her."

Wilma squinted and drew the collar closer. "I ain't got my glasses. Tell me what's this here?"

"Hang on there a minute," Easter said. She straightened her arms and pushed the palms of her hands into the sofa cushion. She rocked back and forth and lifted herself onto her feet. "Let me see that, Wilma. What are you talking about?"

"Look a here, at this detail work the girl's done?"

Easter pulled the damask from Wilma's hands. "Oh my heavens, those are needles and thread woven like a vine. I've never seen anything so delicate, so beautiful. Where'd you learn to sew like this, hon? I sure didn't teach you this in Home Economics."

"That's not so," Emmalee giggled. "I did learn some of the basic stitching from you and a little bit my mama showed me when I was real small. But mostly Leona. She was teaching me things here and there. Said I needed to know more than stitching collars together."

Emmalee explained how Leona would lean over her shoulder and correct her hand as she learned a new stitch. They had sat side by side in the sewing room at Tennewa while the other women settled on the picnic tables outside. Emmalee remembered holding a wooden hoop in her left hand, a square of thick cotton cloth stretched taut between its frames. With the needle in her right, she'd prick the fabric and pull it up from behind.

"Run the thread over here and push the needle through," Leona would say, "and then bring it back up one more time but without taking your hand to the back of the hoop. See here," Leona had said as she guided Emmalee's hand. "That's a stem stitch. Seems real simple, don't it. Go on and take this home with you and practice. Remember, every stitch needs to be of equal length and spaced even. You can use this stitch to outline. And it's perfect for making the stems of flowers. That's how it got its name."

Emmalee smiled big as she thought of Leona sitting next to her in the sewing room. "But I ain't done with the detail work. I got a few more things to add."

Wilma studied the sleeve some more. "What's this here underneath the blue?"

"Oh, I found that in the other bedroom there." Emmalee pointed down the hall. No one knew of her coming to live with Leona and Curtis. It had been a secret, but she knew that was about to change. She had been afraid of Nolan finding out about her leaving. She still worried when she thought of it, even with the Lanes lying stiff and cold over at Fulton's.

"That's a bit of lace from an old pillow sitting on the bed in there. Hope it was okay to take it apart." Emmalee explained her work, moving her hands in the air as if she was sewing with a needle and thread. "I took it from the bottom and stitched the pillow back together, can't really tell it's missing."

Wilma walked to the bedroom, and Easter followed right behind her. Standing in the open doorway, Wilma pulled on a tissue tucked underneath her sleeve and wiped a tear spilling from her eye. "This room. All of this was for you, Emmalee. For you and the baby?"

Emmalee nodded. "Yes, ma'am."

"Lord, Easter, do you see all this Leona has done?"

Easter sidled past Wilma and into the room. She stood in front of the crib as if she were admiring a sleeping baby. "Look at this crib all made up so pretty. And the curtains. And the rocking chair. Oh sweet Jesus. It's all so beautiful. Leona waited a lifetime for this nursery."

Wilma turned around and faced the framed photograph of Leona, Curtis, and Curtis, Jr., hanging on the other side of the hall.

"Oh, Easter, look at this." Wilma reached for Emmalee's hand. "Leona never did get over losing that boy. Don't think I would have done much better if I'd lost one of mine."

"How'd it happen?" Emmalee asked.

"Lord, I thought everybody in town knew about this," Easter said. "But I guess you was only a little thing when it happened." With the tip of her finger, Easter reached out and touched the baby behind the glass. "Curtis, Jr.'s dying was awful. Just awful. Leona birthed him all by herself, right back there." She nodded toward the bedroom at the end of the hall. "He was a tiny thing. Didn't live long. Died in her arms."

Easter sniffled, and Wilma handed her another clean tissue drawn from inside the sweater's sleeve. "After years of trying, Dr. Greer told her she couldn't have another. Leona only grew worse after that. Sadder. Meaner," Wilma said, twisting the tissue between her fingers. "I remember the baby's funeral like it was yesterday. Curtis carrying Leona in his arms. He was so brokenhearted, but I'm not sure Leona ever saw that. She was hurting too bad to see much of anything but her own pain."

"We'd all been pretty close up to then," Easter said, "but after Curtis, Jr., died like he did, everything changed."

"Can you imagine, Emmalee, how heartbroken you'd be if that sweet baby of yours was taken from you like that? In an instant?" Wilma asked.

Emmalee remembered the look in Leona's eyes

when she held Kelly Faye in the hospital only hours after she was born. Leona had seemed drawn to the baby in a way Emmalee did not share or understand. She had felt jealous, guilty even, for not knowing how to imitate Leona's expression. Now she stared at the baby in the picture, his face perfect, and thought of Kelly Faye's.

Wilma took Emmalee's hand in hers. "I do know if it hadn't been for her factory job, Leona might never have gotten out of that bed. She came back to work three days after Curtis's funeral."

"Three days," Emmalee said.

"Three days," Wilma repeated. "Mr. Clayton told her to take as much time as she needed. But there she was, sewing collars. She did it, I guess, because it was what she needed to do. I think a lot of women judged her for that though."

Easter nodded. "I'd be lying if I told you I didn't think it was odd at the time. I ain't got no kids of my own like Wilma, but after the accident Leona worked harder and longer than anybody else at Tennewa. When she wasn't working at the factory, she kept herself locked up here in this trailer sewing night and day, making them slipcovers."

She stepped to Leona's sewing table, piled with fabric. "I heard she took in so much work she never had a day to rest, not even Sundays. Some around here thought that was a sin, too. Probably some would still hold that up against her. Why she did it? For what? I really don't know. It was like she couldn't stop herself, like a drunk with his liquor."

"Too afraid of the quiet," Wilma said.

Easter picked up a piece of damask and draped it over her arms. She stroked it over and over again. "I understand that now. Only wish I had let Leona know."

Wilma turned to Emmalee. "Kelly Faye is a real pretty name, hon, real pretty."

Clutching the damask, Easter returned to Wilma and Emmalee. "Yes, it is. A real pretty name."

The three of them huddled together in the narrow hallway, their heads bobbing one against the other.

Emmalee's milk suddenly dropped through her breasts, and she wished Kelly Faye was there so she could fill her tummy. She wanted to kiss her cheeks and press her nose to Kelly's tender neck, drawing in the sweet smell of her newborn baby. Instead, the binding grew wet, and Emmalee pictured Mettie tickling Kelly Faye's lips with the tip of a bottle.

"You done good here," Wilma said, breaking the silence. "And I'm going to tell you exactly what Leona would tell you. Hold your head high. Way up high." Wilma took Emmalee's chin in her hand. " 'Cause you can't find your way clear, hon, if your eyes are glued to the ground."

• • •

Easter worked in the kitchen, humming an old hymn while she spooned her casserole into one of Leona's Pyrex dishes. She placed the dish on the top shelf of the refrigerator and set about washing the dirty plates and glasses left soaking in the soapy water. "Looks like the weather's changing," she said as she looked out the wide-set window above the kitchen sink. "Storm heading over the plateau."

"If that's so, I want you both off this mountain before the rain comes," Emmalee said. "I ain't going to lose anybody else."

Easter and Wilma hesitated to leave Emmalee alone. They offered to stay and help finish the dress. But Emmalee wanted to do it on her own. Besides, it felt good to offer a caring note to the women who had mothered her so well there at Leona's trailer.

They scribbled their phone number on a piece of paper and encouraged Emmalee to call if she needed help with her sewing or the baby in the weeks to come. "Anytime," Easter said. "We mean it." Emmalee promised she would, not bothering to tell them there was no phone at her father's house.

As they walked across the gravel drive to their car, Easter turned around and reminded Emmalee that three-fourths of a chicken casserole sat in the refrigerator. "Don't let it go to waste,"

Wilma added. "You got to keep your strength up what with nursing a little one. You're a mama now, remember."

"Mama," Emmalee said. She let the word simmer on her tongue as she waved good-bye. She liked being called that, at least the way Easter and Wilma said it. She blew a kiss to a redbird darting about the trailer and rushed inside, eager to return to her dressmaking.

The sewing machine sat quiet in front of her, and Emmalee wondered if it was missing Leona, too, waiting for her to come and guide another piece of fabric underneath its stainless foot. Emmalee believed the trailer and everything in it was aware of Leona's passing, and the redbird still darting about the window only punctuated her belief. She blew another kiss. "Go on. Bring me some good luck," she said and picked up a piece of damask.

Emmalee rolled the balance wheel and dropped the needle below the throat plate, then pulled it up, lassoing the bobbin's crimson thread. She held the thread and a similar length from the spool mounted on top between her fingers and pulled them both to the back, away from the machine. She placed the dress panels underneath the presser foot, allowing only a half-inch seam, and pumped the floor pedal. The motor moaned and Emmalee pressed harder until the machine surged forward. She remembered what Leona had taught her and steadied her foot against the pedal.

"This ain't a race, Emmalee, keep it steady," Leona once told her.

The motor fell into a steady purr, and stitches dropped in rapid succession, the needle bobbing up and down. With the tips of her fingers, Emmalee navigated a straight seam through the thick fabric, only slowing her pace as she neared the point where she would fit the sleeve. She turned the balance wheel with her hand and finished the last three stitches before breaking the threads free.

She raised the presser foot and quickly turned the dress but not before running a short seam along the left and right shoulders' edges. She worked the other side of the garment as she had the first, and the machine hummed along amid the early-evening calm.

She took to Curtis's chair and basted the collar and sleeves in place with long loose stitches. Pleased with her work, she decided to set them by hand instead of returning to the machine. Besides, Emmalee loved sitting snug in Curtis's chair with the yellow crocheted blanket spread across her waist. She made small, tight stitches, pulling and tugging the thread at the seam's edge. She grew giddy as she knotted the final threads, again not stopping to notice the late hour.

At last, Emmalee held the finished dress out in

front of her and admired her work. She pressed it against her body and ran into Leona's room to look at herself in the mirror. She turned to the left and then to the right, studying the crimson dress from every position. Emmalee rubbed her hand across the collar. She pressed it between her fingers as she stared at the photograph of the sleeping baby boy left on Leona's dresser. Emmalee ran back into the living room with the dress draped over her arm and the photograph in her hand. She plopped down on the carpeted floor in front of Curtis's reclining chair and opened the frame, careful not to tear the paper or cut her fingers on the glass. Emmalee removed the photo; and with Leona's sewing scissors in her hand, she cut away all but the baby looking back at her.

Emmalee placed what was left of the photograph inside the dress, over the darting on the left side. She pushed a needle into the damask, careful not to pierce the needle through to the other side. Working slowly, she whipstitched the picture onto the dress. For all eternity, Leona's baby boy would rest on top of her heart.

"There. Now it's done." She placed the dress on the carpeted floor and smoothed it flat with her hand. "Now it's perfect."

Emmalee had not noticed that the rain had stopped or that night had settled about the trailer. It was dark, too dark for Runt to come up the mountain for her tonight. She would call first thing in the morning and then finish the hem and press the dress under a hot iron.

Emmalee woke again on Leona's sofa with the sun warming her face. She snuggled under the afghan. Although her breasts were full, they did not ache as they had yesterday. But she was eager to see her baby.

She raised her arms above her head and arched her back. Her spine, stiff and sore from the hours spent hunched over her sewing, popped as she stretched her body backward. She had pinned the hem in place before going to bed, and it wouldn't take long to finish it. Mr. Fulton said this kind of detail was not necessary, but she knew Leona would never leave a dress undone, especially one as important as this one.

She was certain Leona had intended to finish that woman's fancy slipcovers. She would have folded them and left them ready in a box by the trailer door, just as she had promised to do. Emmalee knew that about her friend. Only then would Leona and Curtis have come down the mountain for her and Kelly Faye. She liked to think of Leona perched on the edge of the truck's seat, waiting for her first glimpse of Emmalee and the baby walking out of the holler. She smiled at the thought of it.

Emmalee went straight to the phone. She dialed

her uncle's number, and he answered after the first ring. She had finished the dress, Emmalee told him, and she needed a ride to town. "How's Kelly doing?" she asked.

Emmalee wrapped the yellow afghan around her shoulders and rubbed the sleep from her eyes. She stumbled into the bathroom, her bare feet sliding across the cold linoleum floor. Emmalee squatted on the toilet and dropped her forehead in her hands. Her toes scraped the side of the tub.

Two faded blue towels, trimmed with an eyelet lace, hung across a bar set above the back of the tub. The towel's cotton trim was another frilly detail Emmalee never expected of Leona. She wondered what all she did not know about the woman who had invited her to come and live on top of this mountain. Emmalee knelt by the tub's edge and held her hand under the water running hot from the faucet. She watched the water spill into the tub until it was nearly overflowing.

Back in the first grade, Emmalee had come home with notes pinned to her dress reminding Mr. Bullard his daughter needed to arrive at school clean, in clean clothes, with clean underpants. Even before she could read, Emmalee understood what the notes said. She imagined the other kids did, too, although Mrs. Tate said it was grown-up business. Her teacher folded the paper twice and pinned it to the thin cotton dress Emmalee wore most days. Emmalee kept her hand to her chest as she took her place in line by the classroom door, waiting her turn to board the bus for home.

Once a week, while the rest of her class walked on to the library, Mrs. Tate led Emmalee into the janitor's closet instead where she hurriedly washed Emmalee with a wet cloth and a bar of Ivory soap. Emmalee shivered in her teacher's care as the cool air touched her damp skin. "Sorry, honey, I can't get your hair washed. Maybe someday I can take you home with me and give you a good scrub in the bathtub," Mrs. Tate said, holding Emmalee's elbow firmly in her hand as she wiped underneath her arm. Emmalee looked away.

Emmalee thought of Mrs. Tate as she slipped out of her clothes, unwrapped the binding, and dipped her toes into the water, steam rising off its surface. Her skin tingled and burned as she touched the hot water, but she slowly lowered her body into the tub. A bit of milk leaked from her breasts but quickly dissipated into the bathwater. Emmalee relaxed and kneaded her breasts some more as Wilma had taught her to do. Milk spilled into the water.

The fullness in her breasts eased, but her back ached, a dull throbbing pain. She hurt for Kelly Faye from someplace deep inside, and the pain seemed to settle in the pit of her stomach. Emmalee pulled her knees to her chest. She wanted a better life for her little girl, but all she saw was Mrs. Tate leading her into the janitor's closet, her classmates staring as she followed her teacher down the hall. She could still smell the Ivory soap on her skin.

Emmalee held the terry cloth in her hand and scrubbed her body, washing away what she could and could not see. She soaped her hair and dipped below the water's surface. Holding her breath, Emmalee lingered there, rocking her head back and forth, rinsing her long hair clean.

Stepping from the tub, she wrapped her body in an eyelet-trimmed towel and then rolled the binding and tucked it under her arm. She would nurse her baby soon and no longer need this cloth. She felt exhausted from the bath, the hot water leaving her body limp. But Emmalee hurried to dress and brush her hair and take her place at Leona's sewing table.

She slipped a tip of crimson thread through the needle's eye and pulled the thread tight, knotting one end. Emmalee held the dress with its pinned hem in her left hand and pushed the needle into the fabric with her right, pricking a single thread from one layer of damask and then the other. Twice more she threaded the needle as she worked the circumference of the dress, each stitch setting the hem in place.

She stopped often to admire her work, not wanting to rush, even if no one would see it. Emmalee placed five tight little stitches, one on top of the other, careful not to push the needle through to the front. She cut the remaining thread close to the fabric. She would take the iron to it later and press the hem down.

Emmalee glanced out the window while she tidied Leona's sewing table—stacking remnants of fabric, collecting straight pins and loose threads. She positioned the scissors next to the machine exactly where she had found them, as if Leona would come looking for them. She walked to the kitchen and packed what was left of Easter's casserole and the other food that had been carried to the trailer. Easter had promised it was fine to carry all of it with her even though Emmalee didn't feel right about taking something that wasn't hers. In that way, she guessed she was like her father. But Easter had insisted the food would only go to waste.

Emmalee tiptoed into the bedroom readied for her and Kelly Faye. She reached for the crib and then patted the teddy bear's nubby head. "I'm sorry I didn't get to know you, but I bet you won't mind if I take a few of these," she said and pulled three plastic diapers from the cloth basket hanging on the side of the crib. These had been meant for Kelly Faye, Emmalee told herself, and scooted backward out of the room.

With her eye fixed on the clearing, Emmalee sat at Leona's sewing table and waited for her uncle Runt. The sound of a truck speeding down the gravel drive startled her even though she watched it barreling toward the trailer, kicking up bits of mud and rock in its wake. Emmalee grabbed the dress and the paper sack stuffed with her other provisions and headed outside. She was eager to meet Runt at the driveway. But standing on the stoop, Emmalee realized it was not her uncle who had come for her.

It was Nolan. He barreled farther down the drive and stopped his truck a couple of feet from the trailer. Emmalee's eyes grew big, and she leaned against the trailer as Nolan charged toward her.

"What are you doing here?" Emmalee called out to Nolan as he scrambled out of the truck.

He rushed toward her, stopping only inches from her face. She turned her head, but she could almost feel his whiskers prickling against her cheek. Nolan pressed closer.

"Ought to be no surprise to you I'm the one come to get you. Ain't you the one done give her baby over to Mettie and Runt," he said. The scent of tobacco stunk on his breath.

"I ain't gave her to nobody. They're just keeping her for a couple days." Emmalee pushed Nolan back. She held the dress out in front of her, crimson proof of what she had done and why she had needed her uncle's help.

"That ain't what Mettie's saying."

Emmalee's eyes widened. She had made it clear to Mettie she would be returning for her baby in a day or two. She was Kelly's mama, and with every stitch she had become more certain of her purpose. But Nolan's voice only grew louder, and Emmalee's fear grew sharp.

"You think I ain't going to know you gone and dumped your baby on somebody else. Can't keep no secrets in this town. I told you more than once Bullards don't give up their blood."

"I ain't dumped her on no one. And I ain't gave her to nobody. They're keeping her while I make this dress. And I'm done. I called Runt late yesterday evening and told him to come and get me. I was waiting on him. Runt. He told me he was coming for me."

"You see Runt here?" Nolan gripped Emmalee's arm and shook her hard. "Do you see Runt?"

"No. But he's coming any minute. He told me so."

"Runt ain't coming, fool. I done been to Runt's house. Went to see if you was there. I found Mettie rocking my grandbaby. My grandbaby. I told her the baby girl she got in her arms was Emmalee's. She said not no more she ain't."

"What?" Emmalee's knees weakened, and the dress slipped from her arms.

"That's right. She carried on about you not

taking care of Kelly like you ought. Said the baby not been fed right. Said her bottom was raw. Said she and Runt were doing the right thing, and we ought to be grateful they was so caring." Nolan looked toward the bluff. "Shit, us be grateful. For what?"

Emmalee slid down the aluminum and sat slumped on the wood stoop, the crimson dress wadded on her lap. She looked up at her father. "I want my baby, Nolan."

Nolan turned toward the truck. "Get your things," he said over his shoulder.

Emmalee held her tongue as Nolan steered the truck down Old Lick, cutting into the sharp turns with both hands firm on the wheel. The truck picked up speed till Emmalee felt as though they were the ones falling down the mountain's side. She pulled her coat collar tight around her neck with one hand while she held Leona's dress on her lap with the other. "Can't you go no faster, Nolan?" she pleaded.

Nolan tightened his grip around the wheel and pumped the accelerator. "A good mama don't go handing off her baby to a stranger."

"Damn it, Nolan. Mettie and Runt ain't no strangers."

"And that woman ain't your blood. She don't claim us. She don't ask us to her house. She don't call us family." Nolan pounded the wheel.

"You're a damn fool, Emmalee, for leaving that baby with that woman. Shit."

"Kelly Faye. *That* baby's name is Kelly Faye. Named her after Mama." Emmalee stared out the window. The ground passed fast alongside the truck; even the blue sky and the dull green fields in the distance melted into a blurry mass. "Come on, Nolan, can't you go faster?"

Nolan only slowed the truck as he made a sharp left turn into Red Chert followed by a quick right onto the drive winding its way up to Runt's house. Emmalee set the dress on the seat next to her father and readied her hand on the door.

"Hang on there, girl, you let me take care of this."

Emmalee paid no attention to her father's direction and jumped from the truck before he came to a full stop. She ran toward the house, but Runt met her at the top step. A shotgun rested against the doorframe behind him.

"Emmalee," Runt called and motioned for her to go around him. He stood square on the edge of the porch, not once taking his eyes off his brother.

Nolan spat and stepped closer. "Runt, I told you I was coming back for that baby. She's Emmalee's girl. You ain't got no right to her, and we've done come to get what's ours."

"Back off, Nolan," Runt said.

"The hell I will. Just 'cause that woman of yours can't give you a baby of your own don't mean you can go and take somebody else's."

Nolan jumped in front of Runt. His fists were clenched tight and his arms hung stiff by his side. He stood a head taller than his brother but next to Runt's sturdy frame, Nolan looked gaunt, worn thin from years of hard living.

Runt stood firm. "Listen, Emmalee," he said, "Kelly ain't been fed enough. Her bottom was beet red when you handed her to us. She was running a fever."

"That ain't so," Emmalee said, her voice cracking raw.

"If you really love her, Em, you'll leave her here with us. Even Dr. Greer thinks it's the best thing for her for right now.

"And Nolan," Runt added, "we done talked to the sheriff. All I got to do is call him, and he'll haul your sorry ass off for trespassing."

"Shut up, Runt," Emmalee yelled and pushed her way into the house. Runt kept his guard on the front porch.

Mettie sat in a rocking chair, humming a lullaby as she folded a stack of dry diapers.

"Where is she? Where's my baby, Mettie?"

Mettie hummed a little softer as she pushed the rocker back with the balls of her feet and let it fall forward. "Sit down, Emmalee."

"Where the hell is my baby, Mettie?" Emmalee

246

yelled out loud as she walked toward the hallway leading to the bedrooms in the back.

"She ain't here. A friend is keeping her for the morning."

"Damn it, Mettie. You got no right to keep my baby or hand her off to someone I don't know."

"Don't get upset, Emmalee. Come here and sit down and let's talk about this." Mettie extended her hand toward the sofa.

"Where is she?" Emmalee asked again, trying and failing to keep her voice from shaking.

"Honey, you didn't even bother to call us once to check on her. Just seems a mama truly concerned about her baby would've called after her a time or two."

"Hell, Mettie, I was making Leona's burying dress. You knew where I was the whole damn time. Not like I run off."

"Well, that doesn't really matter much." Mettie leaned toward Emmalee, and the chair tipped forward. "Look. Runt and I done a lot of thinking while you was up on Old Lick. We could see Kelly ain't been getting the kind of care she needs. She ain't thriving, Emmalee. *Failure to thrive,* that's the official term for it." Mettie reached for a piece of paper on the table at the end of the sofa. "That's what Dr. Greer called it. He wrote it down. See, I can show it to you in his own handwriting."

Emmalee swatted at the paper in Mettie's hand.

"Sweetie, Kelly's nearly nine weeks old and only gained a pound since you had her. That ain't enough. If she gets too weak, she could die, especially with winter coming on. You don't want that, do you, Emmalee?"

"Why'd you take her to the doctor?" Emmalee's eyes darted about the room, thinking Kelly Faye might be hidden somewhere nearby.

"She was running a fever. We was worried about her. She's fine, but it could have been bad." Mettie pulled another clean diaper from a basket on the floor and folded it into a square. She held it on her lap and pulled on another one. "The doctor thinks maybe this has all been too much for you. I told him you never had little sisters or brothers to practice on like I did. It ain't your fault, really it ain't. No one's blaming you. You don't know what to do with her is all. Goodness, Emmalee. You don't have running water. It's freezing cold in your house. You did the best you could. We all believe that."

Failure to thrive. Failure to thrive. These words made no sense to Emmalee. "Mama was no more than eighteen when I was born. She was a whole year younger than me, and she done good," Emmalee said, wiping away the tears spilling down her cheeks.

"Some women are more ready than others. I think some of us come into the world ready to mama. And Cynthia Faye, from what I've heard,

248

sure had some good mothering of her own to draw from. It don't mean nothing bad about you."

"I can do it," Emmalee said almost in a whisper.

"Maybe in time. But you can do the right thing now by letting Runt and me give her a good, loving home. I'm ready to be a mama, Emmalee. Been ready for a long time. I'll love on her right. So will Runt."

Mettie braked the rocker as it tipped forward and set the folded diapers aside. "She's beautiful, Emmalee, prettiest baby I ever seen."

Emmalee dropped her head in her hands, not even looking up when Runt and Nolan stepped into the room.

"Come on, girl," Nolan said, his voice slow but strong. "Come on now."

Emmalee walked to her father.

"You ain't stealing that baby from us, Runt," he said and took Emmalee by the arm and walked out of the house.

LEONA

Old Lick
- - - - - - - - -
1969

Leona held the palm of her hand to her cut and swollen cheek on the ride home from Tennewa.

"I ran into the bathroom door," she told Curtis twice before reaching the mountain road. "I was coming out. Cora was going in."

She dropped her head against the truck window, not able to look at Curtis when she was telling a lie. Leona did not confess about Cora following her into the bathroom at the end of the shift.

The other seamstresses sometimes bickered over the bundles, each one so determined to exceed her quota that she might sneak two or three instead of the allotted one. Leona had done it some, but this was the first time Cora had accused her of such doing. Mr. Clayton said nothing to either one of them, always choosing to ignore whatever happened inside the women's restroom. But Curtis stared at his wife, waiting for a more honest answer.

"Put your eyes back on the road," Leona said.

"It wasn't nothing but an accident. Just let it go."

The couple climbed the mountain in silence, neither daring to look at the other. Leona imagined Curtis had grown tired through the years of trying to coax her to a happier place and preferred riding on home in quiet. He pulled in front of the trailer and cut the engine.

"Leona, you don't need to work this hard no more," he said. "We're going to be fine whether you double your quota or not. If that's what all this is really about?"

"Of course it is," Leona snapped back. But she knew that wasn't so. She had been living with a secret for too long, and even though her cheek throbbed, a part of her felt better knowing Cora had beat the truth from her.

Leona had lost interest in Curtis years ago. She hadn't planned on it. She hadn't meant to do it. It happened slowly, without warning. She had come to blame Curtis for everything since the baby died. She blamed him for the hot summer temperatures beating down on her potted geraniums and the tomatoes she had staked out in the garden. She blamed him when she couldn't find her favorite program on the television, and she blamed him for smiling at her when she felt more like crying. In the end, Leona blamed him for moving on with his life when she felt shackled by the one that had left her barren.

But when Leona looked at Mr. Clayton she saw

none of that. Instead she saw a strong, powerful man. She saw a generous, kind man with a warm smile. Maybe his nose was a bit crooked. But it was only a small imperfection, one that left him looking even more rugged and handsome.

For too many months now Leona had stayed at the factory late, just to be near him, always telling Curtis she had mistakes in her sewing to correct or extra production to meet. Leona dallied at her machine and convinced herself there was no sin in only talking to the man.

"Mr. Clayton," she said, knocking on his open door late one Tuesday afternoon, "I hadn't seen you in the sewing room much today and wanted to make sure everything was okay."

"I was caught on the phone is all," he said and leaned back in his chair. "We're changing thread suppliers." He loosened his tie and undid his shirt's top button. "More important, how'd it go today for you, Leona? You beat another record?"

"No, sir, but I come close." Leona folded her arms across her waist. She lingered there till the silence grew awkward. "I guess I'll be getting on my way. Curtis'll be here in a little while."

"Don't run off, Leona," Mr. Clayton said and walked around his desk. He stepped right up to her, but she did not pull away. He reached for her waist and drew her into his arms, touching her lips first with his fingertip and then with his mouth. It was a short kiss, but Leona did not refuse it. Instead, she pressed her body against his and kissed him harder, this time wrapping her arms around his neck.

After that, Leona spied Mr. Clayton admiring her, too, sometimes even finding an excuse to come and ask her about production or daily quotas. He'd slip Leona a note, and she was careful to hide it in the palm of her hand. In his scribbled handwriting, Mr. Clayton asked Leona to come to his office after the four o'clock bell, careful to wait until Gwen Whitlow left for home. Leona folded the paper into a small square and pushed it deep inside her pocket. She would burn it later in the incinerator set back from the trailer.

"Ah woman, I need you," Mr. Clayton said in a hushed tone as he closed the metal blinds hanging in the windows. He undid the zipper in the back of her housedress and pulled it off her shoulders. Leona lay on the cold vinyl-tiled floor and tugged on Mr. Clayton's hand. He straddled her body and handled her rougher than Curtis ever had. He was a powerful man, a strong man, even in his lovemaking. But Leona realized in the darkened office, Mr. Clayton had never called her by her name.

Now sitting in the pickup next to Curtis, she could not look him in the eyes.

"Look, Ona, you don't need to be working late.

We don't need the extra money. We even got a little saved in the bank."

Leona said nothing. As they topped the mountain, Curtis tapped the truck's vinyl seat. "You know I've been thinking maybe it's time we take that trip to the Pacific Ocean you used to talk about." Curtis's tone was kind, more kind than Leona figured it ought to be. "I don't need to be driving a big rig to get us there. The pickup will do us fine. I'll have Jim Boyd take a look at her and get her all tuned up."

But Leona waved her hand at Curtis. "Stop that," she said and pulled her handbag onto her arm.

"Okay. We don't have to go there. Why don't you close your eyes and run your hand over all those spoons you got and point to one. Wherever your finger lands, that's where we'll go. Niagara Falls. Grand Canyon. Don't matter to me. We'll gas this baby up and hit the road."

"Quit it, Curtis. Quit talking such nonsense."

"I'm not talking nonsense, Ona. I'll go if you want." Curtis slowed the truck as he turned onto their property. He eased the truck down the long drive and parked in front of the trailer. Without bothering to cut the engine, he rolled down his window and whiffed the fresh air. "Not everything's my fault." His tone had turned serious.

"Curtis—"

"Hush, Ona. Let me say this. I should've done it a long time ago. Maybe I was afraid of what I knew or didn't know."

Leona slumped against the door.

"I didn't kill our son, for one thing, Ona. He died. That's all there is to it."

"I know that." Leona kept her head turned away from Curtis.

"Do you?" Curtis asked.

"Course I do."

"Well, here's the other thing. You will not be working late at the factory tomorrow or any other day from here on out."

With her back still to Curtis, Leona nodded and slid off the truck's seat. She walked toward the bluff, dropping her handbag on the trailer's stoop as she passed it by.

Curtis called after her.

Leona walked on, not bothering to turn back and face him.

The green grasses on top of the clearing had already assumed a more golden hue. And as the sun dropped behind the loblolly pines dotting the far edge of the bluff, the mountaintop looked as though it had been trimmed with a delicate band of lace. A towhee, dressed handsome in his black and chestnut colors, flew low across the field. His loud, ringing call reminded Leona winter would come soon and her mountaintop would be full of these birds nesting in the brush.

She sat down on the bluff and pushed her legs out in front of her, letting them drop over her rocky perch. Curtis never liked her sitting this close to the edge, but Leona felt freer there than anywhere else. Her cheek throbbed worse, and she imagined there'd be a bruise tomorrow. It had not been her nature to fight like that, but she didn't feel much like herself anymore. She hadn't felt like herself in years, and it had nothing to do with her body slowly morphing from mother to crone. Maybe Cora understood those feelings.

Cora had raised four children on her own, her deadbeat husband only showing up long enough to get her pregnant and steal what little money she had. Rumor had it she finally ran him off with a loaded shotgun. Leona never knew how much of this was fact or how much fiction, but she had seen bruises on Cora's face often enough for her to believe it, and she knew Cora was fierce when it came to protecting and providing for her young. Leona admired that about her.

Cora's children were full grown and scattered throughout Sequatchie Valley. They came home for holidays and sometimes Sunday meals, never as often as Cora liked, but they came. Cora talked about her children all the time, the one who'd gone to drinking like his daddy and the one teaching school over in Jasper, the one married to a preacher and the one who loved to paint pictures but was recovering from a bout of tuberculosis. Leona wanted all of that—the frustrations and the joys. Instead, all she knew was an empty, quiet trailer. But she also knew it hadn't been right to blame Curtis. And Cora knew that, too.

"Look a here," Cora had told Leona earlier in the day. "I don't care what you and Mr. Clayton are up to. Although Lord knows poor Curtis deserves better than that. But you ain't going to steal bundles from the rest of us and get away with it because you done caught Clayton's eye."

"Shut up, Cora. I ain't stealing nothing from you."

"I ain't shutting up when I'm speaking the truth," Cora said. "Hell, Leona, you got a good husband, and you can't see it. When that baby of yours died, it's like he took your sight right along with him. Women lose babies, Leona, all the damn time. They cry, and they grieve, but they keep on living. But not you. Only way you done found some thrill in life is lifting your skirt up for Mr. Clayton. You're acting like a no-good tramp, and you're better than that."

Leona had shoved Cora against the bathroom stall. Cora stumbled. She righted herself and threw a punch at Leona, her watch catching the skin above Leona's cheekbone. All these hours later, Leona held her hand to her cheek. She closed her eyes, and the wind washed over her face.

Someone suddenly called her name, but it was a voice more shrill and high-pitched than her husband's. She turned toward the trailer to find a sharp-dressed woman walking toward her, holding a bolt of fabric in her arms.

"You-hoo. Leona, it's me. Mrs. Campbell." The woman, dressed in flowing trousers and a matching blouse, called again to Leona and waved. "Sorry I'm so late but I took a wrong turn coming down Signal Mountain. I've got the fabric for the slipcover we talked about. You're going to love it. It's simply beautiful."

Leona stood up and brushed the dirt from her skirt.

EMMALEE

Red Chert

- - - - - - - - - - -

Emmalee sat in the truck long after Nolan walked into the house. With the windows rolled tight, she heard nothing but her own desperate cries as she numbered the ways she had failed her baby girl in the few weeks since she had been born. Mettie was right, she guessed. She had no reason calling herself a *mama*.

"Hey girl, come on, get out of that truck," Nolan said from underneath the plywood cover. He scratched his chin and hollered again, but Emmalee ignored him. He slogged into the yard. "Come on. Get in the house." With his fist balled tight, he pounded the truck's hood. "Ain't going to solve nothing sitting out here and looking off into space." Nolan opened the truck's door. "You're acting funny like you did when your mama died. I didn't like it back then, and I don't care for it much now. And I sure ain't got the energy tonight to find a switch and whip your butt."

Nolan grabbed Emmalee's arm and pulled her from the truck. She stumbled along behind him.

But as Nolan stepped to the door, she jerked away and dug the heels of her boots into the dirt. "No," she said, "I can't." She held her hands to her ears. "It's too damn quiet in there."

"Shit, Emmalee. You're wearing me out," Nolan said and yanked again on his daughter's arm.

"I ain't doing it. I ain't going in there without Kelly Faye." Emmalee sagged against the broken-down refrigerator.

"Hell, girl, you're acting like some kind of crazy fool done crept inside your body. Listen to me. This mess ain't all on account a you."

Emmalee looked at Nolan. "Runt and Mettie are right. I can't take care of a baby."

"They're stealing. That's what they're doing," Nolan said. "Putting doubts in your head 'cause you've got what they want." His voice sounded more frustrated and tired than hateful. He pushed his hands inside his pockets and leaned against the door. "You was getting better at it. Being a mama don't come overnight. Didn't for your own mama. Took some time."

"You said I was the one wore Mama out." Emmalee pulled her bangs down in front of her eyes. "You said it was me."

Nolan studied the narrow clearing there in front of the house. He said nothing for a while. A brief wind picked up some leaves and swirled them into the air. He turned to Emmalee. "Girl, I want the daddy's name. It's damn time you come clean. We need more than us to make this right."

"It don't make no difference no more."

Nolan grunted and spit a wad of brown juice from his mouth. "You must not want that baby like you say you do," he said and walked inside the house, leaving Emmalee out in the growing cold.

"No," Emmalee whispered, "that ain't so."

She walked away from the house and down the dirt drive. The oaks and pines danced above her head. Emmalee stepped faster. She thought about running straight to Runt's house and stealing her baby back. She thought about running clear to Old Lick and hiding inside the trailer. Instead, she stopped at the edge of their land and screamed into the holler.

She kicked the base of the large oak, its bark crowded with her twiggy crosses. A cross fell to the ground, and she broke it apart under the weight of her boot. She scratched at the tree, digging her nails into the wood, tearing one cross and then another free from the stump. She snapped them apart and flung the pieces into the air until all but one was lying in splinters about her feet.

These crosses hadn't been made for the dead. She had done them for herself, trying to soothe her own grief, trying to rid her own thoughts of gruesome memories. She was sick of Nolan's work. She was sick of the dead and dying. She hated every one of them for reminding her of her own loss, for miring her in a sadness she had wallowed in for too long. And of them all, Emmalee figured she hated her mama the most. Cynthia Faye was the one who had given up and left her daughter alone there in Red Chert.

If Cynthia Faye had lived, everything would have been better. Emmalee knew it to be so. They would have walked through the holler together and talked about boys and birthdays and the stars in the sky. Her mama would have stroked her hair and reminded her how beautiful she was. Emmalee would have gone to school every day washed and fed, her clothes mended and ironed. She would have felt warm kisses on her cheeks in the morning and heard lullabies sung sweetly before bed. She would have been raised a churchgoing girl even if she was poor and wore others' hand-me-downs. She would have been Cynthia Faye Bullard's girl.

There was a time when Emmalee had once felt her mama swirling through the trees like the wind, forcing the branches to bow toward the ground. She believed her mama had come to her that way, blowing right through her, but Emmalee hadn't felt her spirit in some time. She guessed all the hating she had done had run her off for good.

But at Leona's trailer, Emmalee had sensed a comfort or a presence she had not known in a long while. Maybe it was her mama. Maybe it was Leona. Maybe it was just Easter and Wilma being there and tending to her care. She did not know for sure, but back in Red Chert, nothing felt right. She screamed loud and kicked the tree again. She kicked it over and over. And she punched and scratched at the bark till her knuckles were bloody and raw. Emmalee begged her mama to come and save her and tossed her plea up to the heavens. Then she slid to the base of the old oak, not noticing Nolan standing there behind her.

"Girl," he said, kneeling behind her, "come on. Your baby needs her mama, her real one, not some woman pretending at it."

Emmalee rocked to and fro in the dirt, coughing and choking on her tears.

"Look," Nolan said, "I ain't been much of a father. I know that. Everybody in town knows it. Odds are that ain't going to change much. But you can be a good mama, Emmalee." He loosened a dirty rag tied around his neck and wrapped it around Emmalee's hand. "But you got to let go of the past. I ain't any good at that." Nolan shook his head and smirked. "You're better than me. But you ain't going to find your mama, or that God you pray to, in that stump or in all those little crosses you been making."

Emmalee stared at her father's outstretched hand.

"Come on," he said again.

Emmalee placed her hand in Nolan's, and he lifted her to her feet. She pulled her hair from her eyes and followed her father back to the house, the dead oak left bare. Again. she stopped at the refrigerator and grabbed its door handle for support.

"Oh, shit, Emmalee," Nolan said, letting go of his daughter. "What's it this time? I swear—"

"Billy Fulton." Emmalee tossed the boy's name into the air like a ball, waiting to see if her father would catch it or let it drop to the ground.

Nolan stopped and turned toward Emmalee.

"Say that slow, girl. Real slow," he said.

"Billy Fulton," Emmalee said again, letting the name simmer in the air. "That's it. That's the name you been looking for."

Nolan pressed his hand against the refrigerator, leaning closer to Emmalee. "You ain't told nobody else?" he asked.

"Ain't even told Billy. Figure he knows it. He saw Kelly being born."

A big smile spread across Nolan's face. He patted Emmalee on the shoulder. "You done good, Em. You done real good." Nolan scratched at his stubby whiskers. "Yep. The dead make for steady business."

"I ain't telling the Fultons," Emmalee said, her voice turning scared. "And neither are you. His mama and daddy are real proud of Billy. It'd break their hearts, Nolan. No point in it. He don't want me or Kelly Faye."

"Shit, girl. You know damn well I'm telling them. You wouldn't have spilled his name out like that unless you was ready for me to say something." Nolan pulled his keys from his pocket and dangled them in front of Emmalee. "Come on. You're going with me."

Emmalee said nothing as her father drove the couple miles to the Fulton-Pittman Funeral Home. She held Leona's dress in her lap, careful not to wrinkle it any more than it already was. Maybe Nolan was right. Maybe she did want the Fultons and everybody else in Cullen to know she had birthed Billy's baby. Maybe she wanted them to believe that for a little while Billy had truly loved her.

She knew she had dreamed too big in the past, imagining the Fultons welcoming her into the family as if she were a daughter of their own. Mrs. Fulton would help care for Kelly Faye and insist Emmalee and the baby live there on the second floor. Mr. Fulton would stand a little stronger, excited by the thought of his grand-daughter growing up in their house. He would want Billy and Emmalee to take over the family business someday so he could slow down and go fishing with his brother down in Florida. He and Mrs. Fulton would be downright tickled that their son had found a girl with such a kind heart. But more important, they would be thrilled he had found one not afraid of the dead.

No matter what people believed, she was more than Nolan Bullard's girl now. She was tied to the Fultons by something much stronger than death. They were bound by blood.

It had been only a little more than a year ago when Billy had first stopped Emmalee on her way to the factory. He worked for his daddy in the summertime and was returning from a run to the back side of Pine Mountain. A man had fallen from a ladder while replacing rotten shingles on the roof of his barn. He fell onto a pile of rock and split his head near in two. Never regained consciousness.

Billy had taken the hearse to wash it down and fill the tank with gas in case they got another call. His father insisted the wagon always be spotless, inside and out, and ready with a full tank. Billy had passed Emmalee about two blocks from the PURE station and pulled up to the curb.

"Need a ride?" he asked.

"Nope," Emmalee said, not even bothering to slow her step.

"You sure? It's mighty hot out there," Billy said as he wiped his brow with an exaggerated motion. "People have been known to die from heatstroke just walking about like you are now."

"I told you a long time ago, Billy Fulton, you can't spook me with that kind of talk."

"Oh yeah. I forgot I like that about you," he said and laughed.

Emmalee walked on down the sidewalk. Billy guided the hearse beside her, keeping it even with her pace. "Come on, let me be a gentleman and give you a ride."

Emmalee stopped and Billy braked sharp. The morning was burning hot, and she pulled on her blouse sticking to her chest. "Fine," she said and stepped into the front of the hearse. "It ain't but four more blocks." She tugged on her ponytail and straightened her skirt.

Billy took a long look at Emmalee. "You know my prom date backed out at the last minute when she heard I might be picking her up in this. Said it was too creepy going out with me even if I was the best-looking boy in school." Billy flashed an exaggerated smile.

"Best-looking boy, huh? She said that?"

"Okay, maybe I added that part."

"Maybe you did," Emmalee laughed, already feeling more at ease sitting next to Billy. "Why you being so nice to me today?"

"When have I not been nice to you?" he asked.

Emmalee crossed her legs and wiped the small beads of sweat from her forehead with the back of her hand. She glanced at her feet, a full shade darker than her legs and tinged a pale red from walking through the chert covering the paths around her house. She tucked her feet under the front seat as best she could.

"This is fine. Right here," Emmalee said as Billy steered the hearse down Second Street.

"But this is a full block from the factory. You promised to ride with me four blocks, not three."

"Stop the car, Billy," she said, her tone growing insistent.

"All right. All right." Billy pulled the hearse to the side of the road. Emmalee reached for the door handle, and Billy reached for her hand. "Thank you for letting me give the prettiest girl in town a ride."

The next time Billy offered Emmalee a ride, the leaves on the oaks and maples had begun falling and were blowing about the street like confetti. Billy had parked the hearse near Tennewa and was sitting on its hood, waiting for the factory's afternoon bell to ring.

"Hey there, I've been waiting for you," he called out to Emmalee and waved.

Emmalee stopped and looked around. She tried to slip away among the more than two hundred women walking from the factory, but Billy hustled toward her. "This ain't a good place, Billy. You need to go on."

"I'm not going without you. I've been sitting out here for the past hour just waiting for that bell to ring."

"Why you doing that?"

"Come on, let me drive you home," he said and reached for Emmalee's hand.

Emmalee jerked her hand away. "If your mama hears about you giving me a ride"—Emmalee looked around—"I can't be the one costing Nolan his job."

Billy nodded. "But the thing is, I like watching you walk to work, especially when you're wearing those clunky old work boots."

Emmalee blushed. "You been watching me?"

Billy grinned. "Hell, yeah. But to be honest with you, I like it even better when you're riding with me, and I can look at you right next to me."

Emmalee grinned, too, but was quick to shake the smile from her face. "Go on, Billy. Get out of here."

"Don't want to. Not without you."

"Damn it, Billy Fulton. Go on 'fore these women start talking."

"Fine," he said. "But there's an alley right over there behind the hospital." Billy pointed across the street. "Nobody'll think a thing about my being there, and nobody'll see you get in the car."

"What you got in mind?" Emmalee asked.

"I was thinking we could ride over to Pikeville. Get a burger and some fries. You know the French fries are better in Pikeville."

"No, they ain't."

"They sure are," Billy said. "Besides, I got to

deliver this casket to the funeral home over there. McGregor's buys them from Daddy when they're running short. They had a three-car pileup out on the highway. Killed four."

"That's awful."

"Yep, it is. But it's business."

Emmalee hesitated.

"Come on," Billy said as he turned to cross the street. "I'll even buy you a milkshake."

In the weeks to come, Billy drove Emmalee to Pikeville, Jasper, Whitwell, and anywhere else she wanted to go. He drove her to parts of Sequatchie County she had heard of but never seen. He bought her hamburgers and milkshakes and anything else she wanted when she was hungry, and even when she wasn't. He kissed her on the lips and told her he loved her, even if she was the kind of girl his mother would not approve of him seeing. He hadn't meant any harm by that, he promised. And Emmalee had told him she understood, even if she did turn away and wipe a tear from her eye. But she knew to duck her head low in the seat whenever another car passed them by.

Now Billy was gone, and Nolan sat next to her in the pickup.

Her father wore a smirk on his face, and Emmalee figured he was already counting the money he planned on collecting from Mr. Fulton. Nolan pushed the gas pedal and released it and pushed it hard again. Emmalee wondered if he was nervous, excited, or if he had the shakes. Whatever it was left his foot unsteady, and Emmalee grew sick as they lurched toward town.

Nolan pulled the truck alongside the curb, scraping the tires against the concrete edge. There was no wreath of fresh flowers hanging on the funeral home door yet, and Emmalee understood Mrs. Fulton was not ready for any company, particularly Nolan Bullard.

But Nolan ignored the bare door and jumped out of the truck. He rushed up the front walk, not waiting for Emmalee to fall in step behind him. He knocked on the door, and Emmalee joined him there on the porch with the red dress hanging over her arm. Nolan knocked again, but he did not wait for an answer. He opened the door and walked into the wide hallway leading to the living room where the Fultons watched the television most every night unless bodies were placed there for viewing, a detail about their life Billy had shared with Emmalee.

"Nolan Bullard, what are you doing in my house?" Mrs. Fulton asked as she stomped down the hall toward them with a towel wrapped around her head. She was wearing a yellow terry bathrobe and matching terry cloth slippers.

"It's the funeral home, ain't it?"

"Did you see a wreath on that door?" she asked with a sharp tone.

Nolan stared at Mrs. Fulton. "No, ma'am."

"No, you did not. Let me be very clear about this, Nolan Bullard. When there's a wreath on that door, you are welcome to come in this house. It's a public space. But when there's no wreath on that door, then this is my home. And you better wait for me or Mr. Fulton to open the door. You hear me?" But Mrs. Fulton did not wait for Nolan to answer. "What do you need?" she asked, her anger seeping between every word. She turned to Emmalee. "I see you got the dress made. Let's take a look at it."

Emmalee handed her the dress.

"Red," Mrs. Fulton said, her eyes narrowed. "Well, at least it's a deep shade of red. Where'd you get the fabric?" She held the dress closer and squinted a little tighter. "This looks expensive, and I know you can't afford nothing like this."

"I found it up at Leona's."

Mrs. Fulton cast her attention on the detailed work along the sleeve's edge. "What's this here?" she asked, pointing to the blue fabric and delicate trim.

Emmalee cleared her throat. "The blue come from one of Curtis's shirts. And the lace is from a pillow I found up at the trailer."

Mrs. Fulton nodded, obviously impressed with Emmalee's sentimental touches.

"I did this, too," Emmalee said and pulled a shiny piece of jewelry from her coat pocket.

"What's this?"

"A bracelet. I used a piece of ribbon and strung together these little spoons Miss Leona had all boxed up and hanging on the wall. Didn't take me long, but I thought it turned out kind of nice."

Mrs. Fulton took the bracelet in her hand and dangled it in front of her. The spoons made a soft clanging noise, and Emmalee wondered if Leona could hear it from where she was. "A spoon bracelet. Hmm. Well, all in all, you did a good job."

Emmalee inched backward toward the door. She wanted to leave. She wanted Mrs. Fulton to think good of her, and she knew if Nolan opened his mouth, then all of that would change.

"Lord, where's the baby?" Mrs. Fulton asked, her voice tinged with a note of panic. "You haven't left her out in the truck, have you? You shouldn't be leaving a child by herself." Holding in place the towel wadded on top of her head, Mrs. Fulton craned her neck toward the living room window.

"No ma'am," Nolan interrupted. "Emmalee done had her baby stole from her. That's why we come here."

Emmalee stared at the ground, knowing there was no way to hush her father now. She thought about running out the door. She even took another step toward it. But Mrs. Fulton slid in front of her. "Emmalee, what is your father talking about?"

Emmalee stood quiet, her eyes turned away.

"Emmalee, look at me," Mrs. Fulton demanded.

Nolan grabbed hold of Emmalee's coat and pulled her deeper into the hall. "Emmalee done gave the baby to Runt and Mettie while she went to the mountain to make that dress. Now they ain't giving her back. Said Emmalee's not fit to be her mama."

Mrs. Fulton again adjusted the towel on her head. "Well, it is hard work caring for a baby," she said in a softer, almost reassuring tone. "Maybe this is a good thing, for Emmalee and the baby."

"But I'm her mama," Emmalee said in a real soft voice.

"That's what I told Runt," Nolan said. "It's Emmalee's baby, not his. But he won't give her back."

Mrs. Fulton rubbed her forehead as if she had a headache. "I'm sorry about that, but what are you wanting me to do about it, Nolan? This sounds like a family matter for the Bullards to work out."

"You're right about that." Nolan shifted a plug of chew from one jaw to the other. "It is family business and that's why I figured you'd want to have some say in this, seeing how Kelly Faye is your blood too."

Emmalee shut her eyes. It was quiet for a moment, but then Mrs. Fulton took in a real deep breath. She held it in her lungs as if she might keep it there till she exploded in one thunderous clap. The front door opened and Emmalee looked up.

"Get the hell out of here, Nolan Bullard."

Nolan stood firm. "Can't do that. You're Billy Fulton's mama? Right?" Nolan did not wait for an answer. "Well, that baby of Emmalee's is your blood."

"My Billy is not the father of Emmalee's baby." Mrs. Fulton was shouting now. Her voice was shrill and sharp and bounced against the walls.

"He sure is," Nolan said, wearing a smirk on his face. "Your boy's the baby's daddy. Emmalee done told me so."

A loud hush suddenly fell among them. The only sound in the room was that of the grandfather clock keeping time, one second spilling into the next. Emmalee focused on the clock's steady ticking. Mrs. Fulton tried to say something but the words came out of her mouth garbled and nonsensical. She coughed and stammered, and Emmalee's heart beat faster. Emmalee braced herself for the storm brewing deep inside Mrs. Fulton.

"Is this true, Emmalee?" Mrs. Fulton's voice still sounded shrill.

Emmalee nodded.

"I don't believe you," Mrs. Fulton said. "I don't believe a word of this."

"Believe it or not, it's so," Nolan said.

"You, Nolan Bullard, are a drunk and a liar. You always have been. And you are either drunk or lying now. Or both." Mrs. Fulton pulled the door open wider. "I think it's best that the two of you get out of here. I mean it. Get out before I get Mr. Fulton and tell him all these foolish lies you're spewing around here. He'll fire you straight out, Nolan Bullard." The yellow towel fell from her head.

Emmalee snuck toward the door. She felt bad for Mrs. Fulton, who was trying to finger her wet, stringy hair from her face.

"Get back here, Emmalee," Nolan hollered, spit spraying from his mouth as his tone grew harsh. Even Mrs. Fulton staggered backward toward the hall stairs. "Like it or not, that baby is your blood." Nolan slammed the door shut. "Your boy done knocked up my girl, and you ain't washing your hands of it that easy." Nolan yanked Emmalee back to his side. His grip was strong, and Emmalee groaned as he squeezed tighter. "This here is the mother of your grandchild, Mrs. Fulton. You and your husband and that boy of yours need to do what's right by her and her baby girl."

"Nolan, let go of her." Mrs. Fulton was yelling now, too. "Get out of here. I mean it. I've always known you were nothing but trash. Go on. Both of you, get out of my house."

Nolan did not budge. "You ain't going to do right by your own grandchild?" he asked, his voice turned calm and low. "Fine. Then take this one. I ain't messing with her no more. And I ain't raising another one on my own." Nolan shoved Emmalee toward Mrs. Fulton. Emmalee stumbled and pitched forward, but Mrs. Fulton caught her in her arms. Nolan stormed out the door, not bothering to look back.

Emmalee ran after her father. She yelled for him and waved her arms in the air. But the pickup sped down the street, turned left, and disappeared behind a row of low brick buildings. The truck's engine sputtered and echoed in the early-morning calm.

"Don't leave me, Nolan!" Emmalee cried and stared down the empty street. "Please, come back," she said. "Please."

EMMALEE

Fulton~Pittman Funeral Home

- -

"Get in here, Emmalee," Mrs. Fulton called from the edge of the porch. Her voice rang out as she motioned for Emmalee to hurry along. "Come on," she said, her bathrobe swinging open and exposing her bare leg.

Emmalee stood limp on the sidewalk.

Mrs. Fulton glanced both left and right, checking to see who might be passing by or staring from a nearby window. "We don't need you out here cussing and carrying on and screaming for Nolan Bullard," she said, her tone stern.

But next door a pretty young woman with a full face and a chubby toddler perched on her hip had already taken notice. She leaned over her porch railing as she studied Emmalee standing on the dewy grass. "You got a visitation today, Mrs. Fulton?" she asked with a broad smile, revealing dimpled cheeks. She shifted her child to her other hip. "I've been at my mama's down in Mobile most of the week. Got home late last night. Robert doesn't get home till later today.

You know I don't like being here alone with the baby when he's on the road. Just a scaredy-cat, I guess."

"Glad you're home, Ruthie." Mrs. Fulton hurriedly tried to cover her wet hair with the towel hanging across her shoulder.

"So you got a visitation today?" The young mother repeated her question.

"We're hoping to be ready by early evening. No later than tomorrow afternoon," Mrs. Fulton said, not daring to take her eyes off Emmalee. "We'll hang the wreath when we're ready."

"Who you got this time?"

"Leona and Curtis Lane."

"Oh my, did they die?"

"I'm afraid so," Mrs. Fulton said.

"The both of them?"

"Yes, Ruthie, they did. The both of them. Thought most everybody in town had heard that by now." Mrs. Fulton glared at Emmalee while keeping her voice light and friendly. "Guess you being with your mama you didn't get the word. Tragic car accident Wednesday night on the way to church supper. Listen, hon, I really got to run. Haven't even dressed yet, and my hair's dripping wet." Mrs. Fulton hurried down the porch steps and linked her arm around Emmalee's, dragging her back to the house.

"Who you got with you there?" Ruthie hollered.

"Delivery girl dropping something off for the

visitation. Come by later if you want. Bring the baby too. We'd love to see her."

Mrs. Fulton tossed a wave over her shoulder and pulled Emmalee into the house. "We do not carry on like that," she said and locked the front door. She drew the drapes across the living room windows and pointed to a chair covered in a lush blue velvet. "Sit right there, and do not move one inch. You hear me?"

Emmalee sank into the chair and hugged her breasts. They were not as heavy as they once were, but her left side burned and the pain was sharp. She rocked back and forth, longing to be in Leona's trailer in the care of the older seamstresses, not trapped in a velvet chair inside the Fultons' living room.

Mrs. Fulton's footsteps fell heavy on the polished wood floor. Another door opened and slammed shut. Emmalee overheard Mrs. Fulton talking to her husband although she could not decipher the specifics of their conversation. The pain in her chest mounted as Mrs. Fulton's voice grew clear inside the living room.

"She is nothing but trash, Basil. I do not believe for one minute her child is any relation to us, and I most definitely will not claim it as my grandchild. You better get out there and make this whole thing disappear. You hear me, Basil?"

Mr. Fulton said something, but his voice was soft and mumbled.

"Our son is not going be the father to that Bullard baby. He's starting college. He's got his whole life ahead of him. He will not be tied to that trash and her no-good father!"

Emmalee thought about running back to the holler. She wasn't strapped to this chair. She had delivered the dress, and Nolan had spoken the truth about her baby girl. There was nothing more to do. Emmalee moaned as the pain stretched across her back. It was fierce and steady. There had been so many times when she had wanted Nolan to walk out of her life, but this was not one of them.

The door at the end of the hall slammed again, and Emmalee jerked straight up. Mr. Fulton appeared in the living room first, his wife close behind. He dried his hands on a faded blue cloth and tossed it across his shoulder. Mrs. Fulton stood with her arms folded in front of her. Her eyes were both wet and angry, and she tapped her right index finger against her left arm with a fierce beat. Her nails were painted a bright shiny red, an odd detail, Emmalee thought, for someone who handled the dead.

Mr. Fulton pulled a chair opposite Emmalee. His face was always kind, but today his expression had turned serious. Emmalee hunched forward.

"I'm going to come right to the point here," Mr. Fulton said and raised his right palm in the air, indicating his wife was not to interrupt. "I understand your daddy thinks our Billy is the father of your baby girl. I've known Nolan for a long time. He may not be perfect, far from it, but I've never known that man to lie, at least not to me."

Mrs. Fulton grunted and rolled her eyes.

"Hester." Mr. Fulton looked at his wife, and she stepped toward the front window. She pulled the drapes apart and peeked outside. "I don't know you as well as I do your daddy, so I need you to look me in the eyes and speak the truth, Emmalee. Is our son, Billy, the father of your baby?"

Emmalee placed her right arm across her chest as if she were reciting a pledge. She leaned further into the pain now consuming her whole body.

"I need you to look at me," Mr. Fulton repeated.

Emmalee raised her head. "Yes, sir," she said. "Yes, he is."

Mrs. Fulton stomped her foot and cried out loud. "It's your fault. You seduced him. He's a good boy. He's nothing like you. He's a good boy."

"Hester, that's enough," Mr. Fulton snapped.

"Billy's better than that, Basil. You know it as well as I do. You know she lured him into this. You're just too nice to say what you really think."

"I said that's enough, Hester." Mr. Fulton's

bony jaw twitched as he spoke. He rubbed his hand across his short-cropped hair and looked at Emmalee, the smile gone from his face. "Where's the baby now?" he asked. "And don't tell me you left her with Nolan. Please don't tell me that."

"No, sir. She's with Runt and Mettie." Emmalee leaned to the side. She wanted to curl her body into a tight ball but knew better than to put her feet on Mrs. Fulton's chair.

"You okay?" Mr. Fulton asked.

"Yes, sir. Just need my baby."

"Are you sure you're okay? Hester, check and see if she's got a fever. She doesn't look well to me. Her eyes are glassy and her lids are droopy."

Mrs. Fulton stood by the curtained window.

"Ain't nursed right in days is all," Emmalee said.

Mr. Fulton put the palm of his hand against Emmalee's forehead. "She's hot, Hester. Burning up. Go get dressed and pull the car around. We need to get her over to Dr. Greer."

"She'll be fine," Mrs. Fulton said, not bothering to look at Emmalee.

"Hester, what has gotten into you? We are taking this girl to the doctor. And we're doing it now."

"We can't go off and leave, Basil." Mrs. Fulton let the curtain drop and turned to Mr. Fulton with an icy gaze. "We got the visitation to tend to. Most of Cullen's going to be here in a matter of hours."

"We tend to the living first," Mr. Fulton said in a firm voice and a little louder than before. "Now get dressed and pull the car around front. Go on. Do as I say."

It wasn't the first time Emmalee had heard Mr. Fulton raise his voice. He spoke firm with Nolan whenever he cussed too much or smelled of liquor, but she was surprised anyone was brave enough to speak to Mrs. Fulton that way. Mrs. Fulton stomped out of the living room, leaving words like *trash* and *whore* bubbling in the air.

Mr. Fulton faced Emmalee. "Mrs. Fulton said something to me about Runt and Mettie wanting to take care of the baby. Is that so?"

Emmalee nodded.

"What do you think about that?"

"They've staked a claim to her."

"It could be a lot easier on you," Mr. Fulton said. "And they are your family."

Emmalee picked at a loose thread on her flannel shirt. She looked up at Mr. Fulton. "She's my girl."

Mr. Fulton tossed the blue hand towel over his shoulder. "Let's get you checked out first. We'll talk more later."

Emmalee hugged her chest a little harder. "You done with Leona?"

"Yes, except for dressing her. Mrs. Fulton

showed me the dress you made. It's lovely. Truly is."

Emmalee nodded. "Can I see her?"

"Now?"

"Yes, sir."

"Can't it wait till later? She's not going anywhere."

"No, sir." Emmalee's voice grew shaky.

"I don't really understand your needing to do this right now," Mr. Fulton said, helping Emmalee up from the chair.

"I don't expect you to understand anything about me, Mr. Fulton. What I want or what I don't want. What I need or what I don't need."

"All right. I hear you," he said and led her down the hall to the closed door. Their gait was slow, each one leaning against the other. "Remember, Mrs. Lane is there on the right, same place as last time. Not quite done with Curtis, so I'd appreciate it if you'd keep your conversation to her."

"Yes, sir."

"When you're done, turn off the light and shut the door. We'll be waiting for you out front." Mr. Fulton rubbed his hand across the top of his head. Emmalee recognized this gesture now as something Mr. Fulton did when he wasn't quite sure what to say next. And he lingered in the hall for a moment longer, looking as if he was hunting something he needed to find.

"Emmalee," he finally said, "you have to

understand this news has come as a huge shock to Hester. I can't say the thought of you and Billy hadn't crossed my mind. I had a feeling a while back he was real sweet on you." Mr. Fulton forced a smile as he opened the door into the embalming room. "But I want you to know my wife's not normally this hateful. And I also know Billy's not perfect, even if his mama thinks he is."

"Billy treated me good. Just so you know."

"I'm glad to hear that," Mr. Fulton said and placed his hand on Emmalee's shoulder. "We're going to need to talk to him later. Hear what he has to say. But we'll work things out."

"Yes, sir." Emmalee smiled back.

"Oh, and Emmalee, the dress, it really is perfect." Mr. Fulton pointed to the crimson dress hanging on a hook attached to the far wall. "You know I've buried men with their carbide lights, young women in their wedding gowns. Even buried a little boy no more than a year ago with a pocket full of change to take to Jesus for the Sunday offering plate. But I thought the way you sewed those little details into Mrs. Lane's dress was very, very special."

Emmalee smiled bigger. "Thank you."

Mr. Fulton nodded and disappeared down the hall.

The smell of formaldehyde lingered heavy in the room. Emmalee held her hand to her nose as she had the last time, still not comfortable with the strange-smelling odor. Leona's body was covered with a crisp white sheet. Her head was in plain view. She looked as though she was sleeping on the stainless table, the sheet folded neat around her shoulders.

The cuts and bruises on her face were gone, hidden behind layers of wax and beige-colored makeup. Her cheeks were highlighted with a soft splash of pink; her lips, painted with a slightly deeper shade. Curls lay soft against her head, crowning her forehead with bits of silver gray. She looked happy, and even if she could have, Emmalee knew better than to try to wake her and pull her back into this world.

"You really do look beautiful, Miss Leona. Nobody'd ever know you flew off a mountain," Emmalee said, stepping next to the body. "Mr. Fulton did real good work. And I hope you really like your dress. I made it all by myself." Emmalee pointed to the piece of crimson hanging on the wall. "Everybody in town wants to come and see you and Mr. Curtis. I guess some only want to see how you two turned out after taking a spill like that. But I know Wilma and Easter are coming 'cause they already miss you real bad. Two of them can't stop crying over you."

Emmalee brushed Leona's short bangs to the left. Leona was always pushing her bangs to the side. "Mrs. Fulton's done found out Billy is the baby's daddy. Guess it was bound to come out sooner or later. I'm sure Mr. Fulton wants me to think of handing Kelly over to Runt and Mettie. You know it's not about not wanting her." Emmalee placed her hand on top of Leona's. "It's hard to know what you do want when you got nothing to give."

Emmalee clasped her hands around Leona's as if she were praying right along with her. "Up in your trailer, I seen what a good mama you would have been. I seen it all around in everything you done for me and Kelly Faye. The crib. The rocking chair. It was all so pretty." Leona's hand felt cold, and Emmalee tried to rub it warm. "But I bet you're real happy to be up in heaven with your baby boy, you and Mr. Curtis both."

Emmalee looked over at the other table and shook off a gruesome image crowding her other thoughts. "But I got to be honest with you, Miss Leona. I wish you hadn't gone and left me like you did. I'm tired of being the one left behind."

Emmalee leaned over Leona's body and kissed her forehead. "Don't worry about Mr. Curtis. Mr. Fulton ain't done with him yet."

Emmalee stepped out of the room. She turned off the light and closed the door behind her.

LEONA

Old Lick

- - - - - - - - - -

1973

Leona stood in front of the kitchen sink, peeling carrots for supper. She had browned the chuck roast in the iron skillet when she got home from the factory and left it simmering on top of the stove, covered with a piece of tinfoil. She added some sliced onions to the pan and baby potatoes. She would start a cake soon. She had made the chocolate frosting before leaving for work early that morning. Chocolate frosting was Curtis's favorite.

Curtis would be home soon, and Leona wanted to have his birthday dinner ready when he walked through the door. He had spent most of the day down at the church, painting a fresh coat of white on the ceiling in the fellowship hall. Leona was glad he was gone. She needed the extra time to get everything ready and wrap his present. She had knitted him a new blue sweater, same color as his eyes. The temperature outside was warm and humid, but in another month or two she knew Curtis would be glad to have it.

Leona had never talked to Curtis again about those days when she stayed late at the factory. She had worked hard in the years since to make everything up to him, but she had come to wonder if that would ever be possible. Leona had caught a ride home right after her shift so she could start cooking, and she wanted to be sure she had time to take a bath and set her hair. She even bought a new pink lipstick, just deep enough to give her lips a bit of color. Curtis didn't like his wife all painted up like a clown, he said.

Leona put the roast in the oven and set about making the cake. The telephone rang, but she ignored it, imagining it was only someone wanting to check on slipcovers or another church member wanting to wish Curtis a happy birthday. She sifted the flour and added the salt and baking powder to the dry mixture. She pulled a couple of eggs from the refrigerator and the bottle of Wesson oil from the cabinet next to the stove. The cabinet door fell open at an awkward angle, its hinge pulling loose. Curtis had promised to fix that, but she would not mention it today.

Leona stirred the batter until it was smooth and greased and floured two round pans. She poured half the batter in one, and the rest in the other. She opened the oven, pushed the skillet to the side, and placed the pans one in front of the other. She set the timer for thirty-five minutes and swept the counter clean before glancing at the clock on the wall. Curtis would surely be here soon.

Bending low, Leona pulled out the good china from underneath the kitchen sink and placed a candle between two plates. She ironed cloth napkins and filled their glasses with sparkling cider, then rushed to the back of the trailer to wrap her gift and ready herself.

When it was time, Curtis pulled out her chair and seated Leona at the table.

"Everything sure is tasty, Ona," he said, already wearing the sweater she had made for him. His face looked much younger and handsome in the candlelight. Leona hoped hers looked younger, too.

"You got to be burning up in that thing," Leona said, laughing, "it's near seventy-five degrees out there with the sun down."

"Don't matter. I love it."

Leona blushed. "And I love you, Curtis, I really do."

Curtis smiled and rubbed his hand across his full belly.

"You want some cake?" she asked, rushing to change the subject. Leona pushed back her chair and stepped into the kitchen to fetch the choco-late cake.

"Maybe in a minute."

Curtis stood up from the table and walked to the trailer door. He opened it wide and the evening's moonlight poured into the room. "Katydids singing loud."

"They're singing happy birthday to you," Leona said. "I ordered them up special."

Curtis laughed. "Where are the bullfrogs? You know they're my favorites."

"I tried, but they're singing down in the valley tonight." Leona carried the dinner plates to the kitchen.

Curtis ducked his head underneath the door-frame and walked into the night. Leona cleared the rest of the dishes from the table and left them soaking in the sink. She blew out the candle's flame and stepped toward Curtis standing among the tall grass in the middle of the clearing. He looked both peaceful and lonely there, his gaze lost among the stars. Leona eased up behind him and whispered in his ear.

"You ever going to be able to say it again?" she asked. "You think you can ever tell me you love me? 'Cause I know you do. You show me every day."

Curtis was silent.

"I'm so sorry about what I done, but it's way in the past." Leona moved in front of Curtis. "I don't know what else to do to convince you that it meant nothing to me. I was hurt and angry and foolish. I wasn't thinking straight. Haven't you ever felt like that, Curtis? Everything so jumbled in your head."

Curtis said nothing.

Leona grabbed his hands and held them to her chest. "Please tell me you love me?"

Curtis pulled Leona into his arms. She rested her cheek against his chest still firm and strong.

"I don't know, Ona girl," he said and led her in a dance across the clearing like he had done once long ago.

Emmalee

Cullen

- - - - - - - -

Dr. Greer escorted Emmalee into the waiting room at the front of his office. A mismatch of chairs lined the walls, and an assortment of tattered magazines cluttered the top of a square table pushed into a corner. The Fultons stood in the middle of the room, adding a small spot of color to the otherwise drab space.

"It's mastitis," Dr. Greer said matter-of-factly as he reached to shake Basil's hand. "Hello there, Hester." Mrs. Fulton slipped her hands inside a pair of gloves and turned toward the outside window. The middle-aged doctor, dressed in a crisp white coat with a pair of black-rimmed glasses pushed onto the top of his head, looked at Mr. Fulton with a raised eyebrow.

"I've given Emmalee a bottle of antibiotics and explained she needs to take every one of them, even when she starts feeling better," Dr. Greer said. "As long as she does as I say, the infection should clear up quickly. But most important, Basil, she needs rest. She needs fluids. She needs to eat right. And if she's going to keep the baby, she needs to keep nursing. It's good for the both of them."

Emmalee sat on one of the chairs along the wall.

Dr. Greer shifted his attention to Emmalee. "So until a firm decision's been made, I do think it's best if mother and child are together. I told Mettie the same thing. Of course after talking to Emmalee here, I see there's a bit of a disagreement among the family about where the baby needs to be."

Mr. Fulton cocked his head to the side. "Well, there definitely seems to be two mamas staking claim to this one. From what I hear," Mr. Fulton said, "Runt and Mettie think the baby should be with them. And if Runt's got any of his brother in him, I can't promise I'll have much luck changing his mind. Stubborn seems to run in their blood."

Dr. Greer pulled the glasses down to his nose and examined a thin stack of papers tucked inside a manila folder. "Let's see. I saw the baby earlier this week," he said. "The day before yesterday in fact. There's no doubt she needs better care than she's been getting. Underweight. Severe diaper rash. Low-grade fever. But I do think with some guidance, Emmalee can be a good mother." The doctor looked up and pushed the glasses back on the top of his head.

"Emmalee?" Mr. Fulton turned to her.

"Yes, sir, I heard him." Emmalee looked away. The doctor tucked the folder under his arm, and Mr. Fulton shook his head.

"I've talked to Emmalee about feeding the baby on a regular schedule." The doctor continued with his instructions while making a few notes on a pad he pulled from his coat pocket. "And keeping her bottom clean, even letting Kelly soak in warm baths with a little baking soda. I understand none of that's easy for her to do at her daddy's place."

"No, it's not," Mr. Fulton said.

"I suggested maybe she stay with her aunt and uncle for a while. Thought it was a good compromise, and from what I saw Mettie does seem very comfortable with a little one. But Emmalee made it very clear she wouldn't do that." Dr. Greer tore the paper from the pad and handed it to Emmalee. "So I was wondering, Basil, if you and Hester might take her in for a few days?"

Mrs. Fulton spun around and walked out the office door.

"Sorry about that," Mr. Fulton said. "Hester's pretty upset. We just found out that the baby is Billy's. It's a lot to absorb in one morning."

"I'm sure it is," Dr. Greer said.

"I guess I've seen so much dying that it's hard to get upset about a beautiful little baby, no matter how it comes to be." Mr. Fulton looked as though he was tugging on a memory from somewhere back in time. "Hester'll get there."

"Does Billy know?" The doctor turned to Emmalee.

Emmalee stared at the dull green floor, and the two men talked on as if she wasn't there.

"I'm not sure," Mr. Fulton answered. "Thinking back on everything, I've got to think he's got some idea."

"Well, don't worry. I won't be saying a word about this to anyone. Let's get everybody feeling better first, and then we can take a fresh look at things." Dr. Greer slapped Mr. Fulton on the back. "But please consider letting Emmalee and the baby stay with you at least until the infection clears. I can't see her going back to her father's right now."

Mr. Fulton rubbed his hand across his head. "We'll work something out." He shook the doctor's hand and took Emmalee by the arm to guide her to the hearse. She slumped onto the jump seat. Mr. Fulton lowered his window as the wagon pulled onto the road. As the hearse picked up speed, the wind rushed harder across his seat, whipping Emmalee's hair about her face. Emmalee leaned against the back window and closed her eyes. The drive to the funeral home wasn't far, but Emmalee drifted into a light sleep.

The hearse stopped sharp. Emmalee lurched forward, and Mr. Fulton threw his hands against the dashboard. "Lord, Hester." Mr. Fulton stared at his wife, but Mrs. Fulton had already snatched the key from the ignition. She opened the car door. Then she stopped, pulled it closed, and faced her husband.

"After thirty years of marriage, I know you, Basil Fulton," she said. "And I know what you're going to ask of me." Her tone was coarse, and Emmalee curled away from the front seat. "And I won't do it. I have taken care of the dead and dying and their families for you all these years and never once complained. But I will not claim any one of those Bullards as my own."

Mrs. Fulton stepped out of the car, slamming the door shut behind her.

For a moment, Mr. Fulton and Emmalee sat without speaking, and Emmalee found herself wishing she was back in Red Chert. "Well, I guess we both know where my wife stands on this," Mr. Fulton said at last, breaking the mounting quiet. He tried to smile, but his expression fell blank. "Let's go on in and get you settled. I bet you are worn out." Mr. Fulton opened the rear door and stuck his head inside. "Come on. Hester won't bite, I promise."

"You sure about that?" Emmalee asked as she moved across the sidewalk, her back hunched and her walk slow. She followed Mr. Fulton up the concrete path. Ruthie Thornton stood on her front porch acting as though she was tending to a plant already shriveled and browned. She even held a watering can in her hand, but Emmalee caught her staring.

"I'll take her up," Mrs. Fulton snapped as she waited inside the door. "But that's it." Mrs. Fulton gripped the rail and headed to the second-floor hall. Emmalee looked back at Mr. Fulton.

"Go on," he mouthed and waved her along.

The upstairs hall was wide, at least three times the narrow space in Leona's trailer. Emmalee felt out of place here, and she wrapped her arms around her body, trying to comfort herself in the strange and open space. Mrs. Fulton stopped in front of a room painted a soft shade of blue. She opened a closet door and began pulling out blankets and towels. She did not seem to notice Emmalee paused behind her, staring into the room where the bed was spread with a plaid cover.

Curtains out of the same material hung on the large window overlooking the street. A pine dresser was topped with five or six photographs of Billy dressed in a different athletic uniform. An assortment of large and small trophies, and red and blue ribbons, covered a long wood shelf mounted on the far wall. Felt pennants with names like *Braves, Indians,* and *Dodgers* decorated the space above the bed.

Billy appeared near perfect, judging by all the remnants of his past successes, and Emmalee guessed Mrs. Fulton saw her son that way, too.

She also guessed it would be near impossible for a son to disappoint a mama, especially one who thought so well of you. Seeing his room, Emmalee knew she had done right to push Billy away after that day by the Sequatchie River when he spread a blanket along its grassy bank. They had picked blades of grass and tossed rocks into the water before Billy asked her to be his girl. He covered their bodies with another blanket and ran his fingers through Emmalee's long hair. He pulled her blouse back and kissed her bare shoulder and whispered in her ear.

"I love you, Emmalee Bullard."

Billy kissed her neck and loved her in a way that was gentle and tender. Emmalee closed her eyes and snuggled in his arms while the sun dropped below the horizon.

"What's your mama going to think about me being your girl?" Emmalee asked, her head resting in the crook of his arm.

"Mother? She doesn't understand these kind of things."

"What *kind* of things are we?"

"You know my mother's crazy," he said and leaned over and kissed Emmalee's nose.

"You didn't answer my question, Billy." Emmalee pushed her hands against his chest.

" 'Cause this isn't about my mother."

"How do you figure that? Nolan says people don't ever change the way they think about a Red

Chert girl. He says I'll die there like my mama. But if you love me—"

"Emmalee, hang on there a minute. What are you getting at?" Billy rolled onto his side and stared at Emmalee. She grew careful with her words.

"You love me, Billy. You been telling me so. You even talked about putting a ring on my finger one day. Remember that? The other day when we were riding over to Jasper?"

"Emmalee, I'm not planning on marrying any-body right now." Billy sat up next to Emmalee and tossed a rock into the river. "Hell, I'm only eighteen. I'm going to college at the end of the summer. You know that. I'm sorry if you misunderstood what I was saying."

Emmalee scrambled to her feet. "Then why'd you crawl on top of me like that? I ain't some wild cat in heat."

"Hell, I figured I could care about you without marrying you. Can't I do that, Emmalee?"

"Care about me," Emmalee said, the words seeming to float away on the water's surface. "Sure. You can care about me all you want." Emmalee snatched up the blanket and wrapped it around her body. She begged Billy to take her back to Red Chert, and when he did, she told him not to come for her anymore. She ran alone down the gravel road back to her father's house, tears streaming down her face. Billy called after her. He begged her to stay and talk things out, but Emmalee ran on, knowing there was no amount of talk that would ever change where their roots were first planted.

She had worked hard to forget Billy in the months following that afternoon on the river-bank and she never once believed she was pregnant with his child. She was tired most days but working at the factory and taking care of Nolan always left her that way. She had bled some in the months afterward, but she hadn't kept track of its timing. She hadn't gained much weight either, nothing that a loose-fitting shirt couldn't hide. But now looking at Billy's bedroom, she could see he hadn't been any more ready to admit he was a parent than she had been.

"You are not to go in there," Mrs. Fulton said and pulled her son's door shut. "You will be staying over here in Rachel's room." She pointed to the other side of the hall. "Bathroom's down there. Here are clean towels. A terry robe's hanging right inside the bedroom closet. But don't go touching any of her other things." Mrs. Fulton spun around and headed toward the stairs.

"Oh, and Emmalee"—Mrs. Fulton kept her back to Emmalee as she spoke—"don't confuse my husband's kind gesture as anything more than that."

Emmalee stuck her tongue full out of her

mouth. She was growing to hate that woman and was eager to see her go. She was worn out and wanted to sleep. It had been nearly four days since Leona had passed, and she hadn't slept much since hearing the news. Her eyes burned and her body hurt, tired from sewing and grieving and caring for Kelly Faye.

She inched toward the bed draped in a crisp white coverlet with a large *F* stitched in the center and a smaller *R* and *W* on either side of it, all done in a golden yellow thread. Emmalee lifted the pretty cover and folded it back toward the foot of the bed. She overheard Mr. Fulton speak in muffled tones and another set of footsteps sounded up the stairs. These steps were uneven and slow, and Emmalee greeted Mr. Fulton at the door. He held a plate in one hand and a large glass of water in the other.

"Doctor said you need to eat and drink plenty of fluids. Here's your medicine." Mr. Fulton set the plate on the table by the bed and fished in his pocket for a bottle of pills. "Go ahead and take one. You'll take another again after supper." He handed Emmalee the glass.

"Thank you," Emmalee said and swallowed a large drink of water.

"I'm about ready to head out to talk to Runt and Mettie. Figured they'd both be home this time of day." Mr. Fulton motioned for Emmalee to sit down. He sat next to her, careful to dust the seat of his pants before sitting on the mono-grammed coverlet. "Look, Emmalee, I'm not trying to convince you of anything. But I do want you to consider that sometimes letting go is the most loving thing you can do for somebody. I've seen it in the eyes of the sick and dying too many times to count."

"You ain't trying to tell me I'm dying, are you?"

"No. No." Mr. Fulton laughed. He leaned across Emmalee and picked up the china plate. "But you do need to eat some food, or you're going to waste away right here in front of me." He handed it to Emmalee. "All I meant is that if you were to decide to let Runt and Mettie keep the baby, nobody's going to think less of you."

Emmalee pushed away the plate. "I'm not sure anybody could think less of me than they already do."

"Stop that talk. Everybody makes mistakes. Billy's got a part in this, too. No matter what his mother thinks."

Emmalee laughed. "I'm sorry," she said, putting her hand to her mouth. "But I'm sure Mrs. Fulton would like to think I did this on my own."

"Well, it is a little bit funny, hon," Mr. Fulton said. "Good not to lose your sense of humor, even in the darkest days. That's another thing I've learned from burying the dead all these years." Again, he passed the plate to Emmalee.

Emmalee lifted the piece of white bread covering the slices of meat and cheese. "Nolan ain't bought ham in months."

"You enjoy it then," Mr. Fulton said and placed the plate in her hands. He stood and straightened the cover where he had sat. "And by the way, Hester'll be downstairs in case you need anything else."

Mr. Fulton turned toward the door and stopped. "You know, Emmalee, you've got a lot of living to do yet. You need to finish your education, make something of yourself. You're no more than a child yourself."

"I ain't been a child for a long time."

Mr. Fulton's smile faded.

"I want my baby," Emmalee said. "I want her more than anything and not just because I birthed her and got a claim to her. I love her."

Mr. Fulton nodded.

"Take me with you. Please. I want to go with you. I need to talk to Mettie."

Mr. Fulton shook his head. "I really do think it's best if you stay here and rest, like Dr. Greer said." Mr. Fulton took hold of the doorknob. "Let me talk to them first. Everybody's emotions are running pretty high today. And you getting upset and Mettie getting upset won't help the baby at all."

"But I'm her mama. It ain't right what she's done. Mettie said she'd keep Kelly Faye for me while I worked on the dress. I didn't leave her there for good. Mettie promised to give her back. She lied right to my face. She knew she was staking a claim to my child."

"Like I said, you'll have your chance. But not right now." Mr. Fulton's voice sounded firm. "Eat up. I didn't make that sandwich for it to sit there and get stale," he said and pulled the door behind him.

Emmalee set aside the sandwich and rushed to the door.

"Wait. Mr. Fulton."

He turned to look back at her.

"I just wanted you to know Kelly was your blood. With all the dying going on this week, I guess I needed her to know she got some family of her own. More than me and Nolan." Emmalee hesitated. She leaned against the doorframe.

Mr. Fulton nodded and pointed to the sandwich. "Eat."

Emmalee dozed for a bit but never fell into a deep sleep. Every creak inside the two-story house stirred her awake, and she lay there anxious for any sound of her baby's return. There was no clock in the room, but Emmalee had grown good at judging time by looking at the sky. She figured Mr. Fulton had been gone nearly two hours when she heard the creaking sound of the front door open and close.

She ran to the top of the stairs, jumping down two at a time to reach the first floor. Mrs. Fulton was already standing on the porch. She ignored her husband, who struggled to push the car door open.

Emmalee saw no sign of her baby girl. She slumped against a porch post before catching a flash of pink, a piece of blanket across Mr. Fulton's dark suit. Emmalee ran toward the wagon, but Mrs. Fulton quickly ordered her back.

"Don't make another scene out here," Mrs. Fulton hissed, standing on the concrete walk and casting a long shadow across the lawn.

Emmalee ignored Mrs. Fulton and ran to the street, meeting Mr. Fulton as he stepped onto the curb. She reached for her baby, scooping Kelly into her arms and rocking her back and forth, kissing her tiny head. "I missed you, baby. I missed you," she repeated between kisses.

"Emmalee, quit carrying on like that out here in broad daylight." Mrs. Fulton kept one hand on her hip and waved at Emmalee with the other. "Or maybe I should knock on Ruthie's door, and we'll make it a party right here in the front yard." Emmalee clutched the baby tighter and brushed past Mrs. Fulton as she walked back to the house.

"Basil, what have you gone and done?" Mrs. Fulton stood face-to-face with her husband.

Mr. Fulton sidled around his wife and followed Emmalee into the living room.

"Why don't you go on upstairs, Emmalee, and get the baby settled," he said. "I'll be up to check on the both of you in a minute."

"Thank you, Mr. Fulton."

Emmalee carried the baby up the stairs. She heard Mrs. Fulton carrying on behind her, but she did not look back. She kissed the baby's neck and stepped down the hall.

Emmalee eased onto the bed, resting against one of the large monogrammed pillows placed along the headboard. The baby slept in her arms, and even though Emmalee was growing tired, she refused to put Kelly down. She kept her close and watched the baby's back rise and fall with every little breath.

Emmalee dozed a bit and then jerked awake at the sound of Mrs. Fulton's voice growing louder and louder until every angry word seemed to be gurgling up through the bedroom floor.

"I don't care what Dr. Greer thinks. You had no right to bring that baby into this house. What were you thinking, Basil? You know as well as I do that child is best off with Mettie and Runt. That girl can't be trusted with a newborn."

"Hush, Hester." Mr. Fulton's voice rang loud and strong and for once it frightened as much as it impressed Emmalee. "I'm going to tell you what I told Runt and Mettie. Let's get Leona buried first."

Emmalee pulled the pink blanket over her baby's head. "Don't listen to that talk," she said and stared into her baby's eyes and kissed her tiny lips, leaving wet tears on Kelly Faye's cheeks. Kelly Faye scrunched her nose as if she was going to cry but her face fell into a smile. In these rare moments of her daughter's contentment, Emmalee marveled they had made it this far, especially now with just about everyone plotting to take her baby. She rolled on her side and placed Kelly Faye on the mattress beside her. She lifted her shirt and pulled the baby to her breast.

"You'll be nice to your mama, won't you?"

Emmalee flinched as the infant latched on to her nipple. But this time she took a deep breath and shoved a pillow behind Kelly Faye's back, determined to find a more comfortable position. Emmalee did not hurry things along. Instead, when her baby's eyes started to droop, Emmalee tickled Kelly Faye's feet and encouraged her to drink some more as Dr. Greer had instructed her to do. "There you go, pretty thing. There you go. Dr. Greer called you a nip-and-napper. Is that what you are? A nip-and-napper?" She patted her baby's back.

Emmalee hummed a lullaby, making up words to the tune she had heard long ago. She snuggled closer to her baby. And there on the second floor of the Fultons' home, a few feet from Billy's room, Emmalee drifted back to the day when Kelly Faye was born, and Leona was there to help her.

LEONA

Tennewa Shirt Factory

Two Months Ago

Leona had dropped five bundles, each one at least four dozen collars thick, in Emmalee's basket this week alone. Still she suspected Emmalee would fall short. Mr. Clayton had been patient with Emmalee, but even Leona wasn't sure how much longer his good nature would last.

Mrs. Whitlow stood by the time clock and took note of Emmalee's tardy entrance, the third in a row. She studied Emmalee as she settled behind her machine a few minutes after the morning whistle blew. Even Georgia Lewis pointed to the clock and twisted her lip in a smirky manner. Emmalee's thin cotton dress was soaked with sweat. She had walked to work, she told Leona, and the morning broke hot. "That's all it is," she said, her tone turning sharp. Leona offered to fetch her a glass of cold water, but Emmalee shooed her away.

Only when Wilma stood up for her morning coffee break did she get a good look at Emmalee,

311

her tanned skin turned white and her blue eyes glassy. Wilma leaned forward and gently placed her hand on Emmalee's forehead. "You got a fever, hon?" she asked, staring into Emmalee's eyes. "You don't feel too hot but your eyes sure look sick."

Emmalee pushed away Wilma's hand. But Leona could see Emmalee's arms and legs shake, and she had listened all morning to Emmalee's machine stopping and starting in awkward fits as her foot fell and relaxed against the floor pedal.

"You're wringing wet, girl," Wilma said.

"Machine's running hot. That's all." Emmalee pointed beneath the table where the motor coughed hot air. Leona knew the motor could scorch bare legs, but she glanced over at Emmalee as though she did not believe her.

"Leona, you think Emmalee done caught that summer flu going around?" Wilma asked. She leaned farther over her machine to make her voice heard. "You and I both know that machine ain't been running long enough to make a body sweat like that. Besides, she barely finished half a bundle. Easter said the crud's been going around Cloverdale Loop for more than a week. Maybe it's done spread to Red Chert." Wilma stood up and shoved her chair beneath her table. "Maybe she ought to go on home," she said. "No sense getting us all sick." Wilma walked to the other side of the room carrying an empty mug in her hand.

Emmalee's face grew flush and her hair wet with sweat. She dropped her head on the machine and turned her cheek to its metal searching for a cool surface. She held her arms around her stomach and screamed for Leona. She screamed again, long and slow, piercing the noise of the machines' spinning fast. She crawled onto the floor, her body twisted up tight.

Leona rushed to Emmalee, and she spotted Gwen Whitlow running from the front office on the other side of the factory. "Oh Lord, is it her finger?" Gwen hollered as she sprinted across the sewing room floor to the corner where the collar makers worked. It had been only three days since Naomi Johnson placed three perfect stitches in her left index finger. Gwen near fainted at the sight of the long shiny needle piercing the woman's flesh and coming out clean on the other side. She knelt by Emmalee with her hand over her mouth, checking her body for open wounds.

"She ain't bleeding, Gwen." But Gwen paid no attention to Leona and searched Emmalee's hands for an open cut while Leona studied Emmalee's eyes and her full belly. Most of the other women stopped their sewing and turned their attention toward the collar makers.

Easter scurried across the wide aisle separating

the lapel makers from the other seamstresses and hunched behind Leona as if she were ready to take orders. "What's going on here?"

"She's about to have a baby," Leona said firmly, never once taking her eyes off of Emmalee.

"It's just a virus." Emmalee moaned and held her arms across her stomach. "Wilma said so. I need to get home is all. I want to go home." Emmalee fixed her eyes on the ceiling, and her breathing turned fast and shallow. She pulled on Leona's hand. "Make them go away. Please make them go." Emmalee tightened her grip and moaned some more. "Leave me be," she yelled at Gwen, who was still searching Emmalee's fingers for a broken needle.

"Damn it, Gwen, she ain't cut," Leona said. "And Emmalee, this ain't a virus. Surely you know that by now." Leona stroked Emmalee's head and pulled the stray hairs from her face. She pressed the palm of her hand against Emmalee's stomach and promised this pain would pass soon. "Easter, go fetch a wet, cold cloth." Easter scrambled from the crowd of women huddled around Emmalee.

"Leona, what are you doing?" Gwen asked, sounding frantic.

"Lord, Gwen, the girl's pregnant. Hadn't you figured that out?"

"No, no, I'm sick. That's all," Emmalee

screamed as the pain took hold of her. "I got a virus. I need to go home is all."

"Honey, it ain't worth arguing about. You'll see soon enough." Leona balanced on her knees and looked up at Gwen. "Call Mrs. Fulton and then call the rescue squad. Hester and Basil may not run the ambulance service no more but she's only a block from here. I saw her and Billy out watering in the yard on my way to work. Besides, she's done this kind of thing a hundred times, and I don't trust those men from the rescue squad delivering a baby."

Gwen listened to Leona but did not move.

"Go on, Gwen. From the looks of things, I don't think we got much time here." Leona glared at the crowd gathered around Emmalee. "Everybody, get back. You're going to suffocate the poor girl." Gwen took to her feet and ran toward the front office.

Emmalee sobbed and squeezed Leona's hand. "I don't need an ambulance. I don't need Mrs. Fulton. Not her," Emmalee begged. "Please, not her."

Leona stroked the girl's head and held her hand tight. She thought of her own son's birth. He had come into the world too soon and too fast. He tore his way right out of her belly and never had a chance. If she closed her eyes, she could still feel his limp body lying across her chest, his skin turning cold. She looked at Emmalee and reassured her everything would be fine. "It will all be fine."

With the sound of the ambulance ringing close to the factory, the women who had gathered on the picnic tables for morning break rushed inside the sewing room. Several of them forgot to stub out their cigarettes on the way and stole a final puff as they watched Emmalee writhing on the floor. "Give her room to breathe," Leona shouted.

The seamstresses obeyed and widened their circle but quickly swung forward, their curiosity nearly swallowing Emmalee whole. Some stood vigil, their hands clasped together in prayer. Others whispered in each other's ears. Leona knew they were already spreading gossip too juicy to wait until the end of the day to share. A few returned to their machines, not willing to miss an opportunity to stitch another bundle of pockets or lapels. And Laura Cooley held her hands tight to her ears. The color siphoned from her face and beads of sweat collected on her nose, leaving some to think maybe she was the one who had taken ill.

Shortly Mrs. Fulton stormed into the factory wearing a pair of long pants and black rubber shoes speckled with wet grass. She shouted at people to move out of her way and pushed aside those who did not obey. She was taller than most women, and her voice was strong. Billy followed behind his mother, although his pace slowed when he saw Emmalee on the floor. A man from the cutting room, dressed in dirty coveralls and holding a metal wrench in his hand, followed close behind the boy as if there was a piece of machinery needing to be tweaked.

"Let's see what we got here." Mrs. Fulton knelt by Emmalee, wedging between Gwen and Leona. She took Emmalee's wrist in hers and monitored her pulse. "Emmalee, what's going on with you?"

"Flu," she mumbled. Leona caught Emmalee staring at Billy with his eyes wide and his skin white as chalk.

Mrs. Fulton shook her head. "Lord, girl, what have you gone and done?" she asked as she touched Emmalee's hard tummy. Emmalee screamed, and Billy winced at the sound of her cries. Leona patted Emmalee's forehead with the damp rag. She told her to squeeze her hand a little tighter.

Mrs. Fulton yelled for someone to bring her some cotton sheeting as the sound of the ambulance wailed even closer. She folded the fabric in half and placed it over Emmalee's waist and legs. "Leona, I'm not sure we're going to get her to the hospital in time. You lift her right leg, and Billy you come over here and lift her left one so I can slip this other piece of sheeting under her bottom." Billy stood frozen. "Son, what's wrong with you? You've seen a baby born before. Come on."

"Yes, ma'am," he said. He inched closer and touched Emmalee's thigh. She hollered, and Billy yanked his hands back and wiped them dry on his jeans.

"Billy," his mother said, her tone growing angry. Again, he placed his hands under Emmalee's thigh, this time touching her as though he was handling a piece of fine porcelain.

Emmalee screamed louder and pulled her leg from Billy's hand. "Don't touch me!" she cried. "Leave me be. Just leave me be." Her crying grew stronger and stronger like a thunderstorm about to split wide open over the valley till Emmalee was gasping for her next breath. "Leona, please. Make him leave."

Leona looked at Billy and then at Emmalee. She patted Billy on the shoulder. "Son, your mama and I got it under control," she said. "Why don't you go and check on the ambulance. Show them where we're at."

Mrs. Fulton did not notice her son slip out of the room. "Gwen," she said, "call the hospital and tell Dr. Greer we got a baby about to be born. Tell him I don't know how many of us are going to be in the ambulance when we get there." Gwen stood and pushed her way through the circle of women holding firm on the sewing room floor.

Mrs. Fulton kept about her work, not once letting Emmalee's pain distract her. She raised half of the stark white cloth covering Emmalee into the air and directed Leona to pull off the girl's panties. Emmalee wailed like an animal in a trap, begging Leona not to touch her there.

"There's no turning back now, young lady," Mrs. Fulton said, her tone strict and resolute. "You got yourself into this mess, and you're going to have to birth this baby. Good thing is these babies come on strong like this tend to come fast. So get ready." Mrs. Fulton turned and looked for her son. "Where'd Billy go?"

"I sent him out to wait for the ambulance. He's coming. I see him," Leona said. She watched as Billy pushed through the women. Wilma put her hand on the boy's shoulder and asked if he needed to sit down.

"Mama, rescue squad is here," he said. "They want to know if you need them or if they should wait outside."

"Tell them we got it under control for now. We'll holler when we're ready to move her," Mrs. Fulton said.

Billy slipped away from the women and disappeared through the factory door.

Emmalee rocked her head from side to side and screamed as her belly contracted. Leona looked up to see Gwen with a magazine in her hand, her blond hair falling from its place high on top of her head. "Doctor's been called. They're ready when you are," she said and fanned

Emmalee's face with a new copy of *Ladies' Home Journal.*

Emmalee turned toward the cool air splashing over her while Mrs. Fulton tugged on her body, pulling her legs apart, pressing on her belly. With every touch, Emmalee screamed to be left alone, to be carried back to her house, but Mrs. Fulton demanded she open her eyes and follow her commands. The woman knelt on the wood floor between Emmalee's legs and told her when to breathe and when to push. Emmalee panted and screamed louder, squeezing Leona's hand as a small head pushed its way clear into the world.

With one more contraction, a baby girl was born with more than two hundred women there to greet her. The seamstresses clapped and cheered, but Emmalee closed her eyes. Mrs. Fulton placed the baby on her stomach, but Emmalee pushed her away. Leona took the newborn in her arms. She wrapped her secure in some fresh cotton pulled from another bolt on the cutting table nearby. Tears clouded Leona's cheeks as she held the baby in her arms. "You're one pretty girl," she said and pulled the baby close.

Leona heard the other women talk as she passed them by, holding the baby in plain view to be admired. Some said she was beautiful, the prettiest baby they'd ever seen. Others had already named her *Viruslee* and held their hands to their mouths to stifle a laugh. Leona paused in front of Billy. He took a long look at the baby and turned and walked out the factory doors.

The next day, Leona carried a pink crocheted blanket trimmed with pink satin ribbon to the hospital. She had stayed up late finishing it, figuring Emmalee had nothing prepared for this child. She carried bibs and cloth diapers, bottles and a few plastic toys, all gifts from the women at Tennewa. Leona held the baby while she sat in a cushioned rocker in the corner of the stark white room. She cooed and talked silly to the baby, who slept through it all. She soaked in her sweet scent and kissed her forehead with tender lips.

"She's beautiful. And I can see you in this girl plain as day."

"She looks like her daddy."

Leona looked at Emmalee but did not press her for any details. "Have you named her yet?"

"No. Nurses keep asking me the same thing." Emmalee adjusted the hospital covers across her body. "They want me to call her Sarah. Means princess or something like that. I'm thinking Kelly. No reason. Just like it."

"It's pretty too."

"Kind of wanted to name her after my mama but didn't want to be reminded of her every time I call this girl to supper. So maybe Kelly Faye."

"Kelly Faye," Leona repeated as if she was letting it float about the room. "That's a very pretty name."

"It'll do fine."

The nurses' voices could be heard clear from out in the hall. A nurse laughed out loud and then their voices dropped to a mumble. Emmalee looked at Leona. "I heard the bottom hemmers was the ones nicknamed her *Viruslee*."

"Don't go listening to them. Just a bunch of fool talk. They don't know when to shut their mouths most of the time."

"It don't bother me much," Emmalee said, her cheeks flushing pink. "A nurse come by this morning wanting to know if I wanted to give her to some nice couple wanting a baby of their own."

"Adoption?"

"Guess so."

"You thinking about it?" Leona asked.

"Nolan said Ballards don't give nothing away."

"Nolan's been here? At the hospital?" Leona smiled down at the baby.

"He come by last night," Emmalee said and scrunched farther under the covers. "He was making a stop at the Trail Ridge and had to pass by here anyway. Heard I'd had a baby and wanted to see it for himself. He said Runt already come by the house asking about me and the baby."

"Runt and Mettie want to take her?" Leona asked.

"Funny, ain't it? Runt and Mettie can't have one no matter how hard they go at it, and then I have one not even trying."

Leona pulled the baby to her chest. She wanted to shield Kelly Faye from this talk. "Emmalee, let me ask you something. If you could wish for anything in the world right this minute, what would it be?"

Emmalee sat quiet in the bed. She looked out the window and back at Leona. "I'd want to be her," Emmalee said and pointed to Kelly Faye. "I'd want to be somebody else's little girl."

Leona dabbed her eyes with the tip of her calloused finger. She guessed she had wanted the same thing once, a chance to start over. Leona kissed the top of the baby's soft head and felt her tiny heartbeat pulsing beneath her lips. She placed her in the cradle next to Emmalee and covered her with the crocheted blanket.

EMMALEE

Fulton-Pittman Funeral Home
- -

Mrs. Fulton picked at the wreath of white roses she was readying to hang on the front door. It rested across her forearm as she searched Rachel's room for a wide satin ribbon she remembered storing in the bottom dresser drawer. She plucked at another petal with browned edges and placed it in her pocket.

The visitation was set to begin at five thirty, Mrs. Fulton reminded Emmalee as she rushed about her daughter's room. She tapped her watch front, complaining she had less than an hour to finish the final preparations. It was an earlier start than she had wanted, especially for a gathering surely to be so heavily attended.

"Best to get on with it though," she added. "People have been calling nonstop since late Wednesday night."

Mrs. Fulton confessed to Emmalee that her husband was not pleased with Curtis's face. He had resorted to taping a white bandage over the right cheek to hide the raw wound and missing bone he had not managed to fully disguise with wax.

"My husband's a perfectionist, and he feels like he has let the poor man down here at the very end." Mrs. Fulton spoke softer. "Thankfully, the worst of his injuries were below the waist."

Emmalee grimaced and focused her attention on Kelly squirming on the bed in front of her. "I think you grown some. Look at your belly," Emmalee said and blew a bubble on the baby's round tummy. The baby kicked her legs and flailed her arms while Emmalee dusted her bottom with powder. Mettie had packed an assortment of ointments, lotions, and creams in a paper bag along with some new clothes and other supplies. Emmalee was not sure what to do with all of these products, but she was afraid not to use them since Mettie placed them there. Besides, they smelled real good.

She set a dry diaper under Kelly's bottom and struggled to push the point of a safety pin with a yellow duck on its head through the thick cotton cloth. She had never gotten comfortable pinning a diaper, always afraid of sticking her own finger as much as she was the baby's bottom. She wished Mettie had packed some disposable diapers like the ones she had found at Leona's. And she wished she hadn't left those she had back in Red Chert. Only when Kelly started to fuss did Mrs. Fulton set the wreath on the bed and snatch the pin from Emmalee's hand.

"First of all, you keep your pins stuck in a bar

of soap so they'll glide through the diaper. That's why you always have at least two sets of pins, one set in the diaper and one in the soap." She steadied her grip on the pin and held it to the diaper. "You push the point toward the back, not the front. If it comes undone, the pin'll do less harm to the baby if the head is at the back. And like it or not, you keep your hand against the baby's skin so she doesn't get pricked. See any blood, it better be yours."

Emmalee nodded.

Mrs. Fulton hurriedly removed the pin from the other side of the diaper and replaced it properly, facing toward the back. She patted the baby's tummy and combed the baby's hair with her fingers. "There," she said, "I think you can finish dressing her." Then she pointed to her watch again and reminded Emmalee the visitation would be starting soon. "It's not necessary you come down for the whole thing. In fact, it might be best if you stayed up here and gave your daughter your full attention."

"No, ma'am, I'm coming," Emmalee said. "I need to feed and dress the baby first, but I'll be down in a minute." Emmalee rubbed her hands down the front of her blue jeans, the same pair she had worn for the past five days. They were faded and dirty, but everything else she owned was back in the holler. Her long hair was clean but hung loose and tangled about her face.

"Take your time. Take a good long time." She smiled sweetly. "I haven't even gotten this wreath on the door, but I have a feeling Cora Hixson is already sitting there in the living room. She never misses a one of these anymore. For somebody old and lonely like Cora, I guess this is her only entertainment." Mrs. Fulton held the white bow to the wreath. "This'll do fine," she said and she walked out of the room admiring the roses.

"Mrs. Fulton," Emmalee called after her.

"Yes." Mrs. Fulton stood in the hallway staring back at Emmalee.

"I ain't got nothing nice to wear."

Mrs. Fulton examined Emmalee from head to toe. "You look fine to me," she said, the sharp tone returning to her voice. "And by the way, do not say one word to anyone about that baby's daddy. You understand me?" She walked on down the hall, stopping to check that Billy's door was shut and secure.

"Fine," Emmalee repeated. "Ain't nothing fine."

Emmalee stepped back into the bedroom. She slipped the plastic pants over the baby's dry diaper and lifted her onto her shoulder. "There you go," she said and patted the baby's back. "You're such a pretty thing, Kelly Faye Billy Fulton." Emmalee laughed. "Yeah, I think that sounds perfect. Let's tell your grandmama we've got a new name for you, and we're going to have it stitched plain on a blanket like the letters on this bedspread here." Emmalee held the baby in front of her and blew on her belly again. Kelly kicked her legs and cooed.

With a full tummy, the baby grew sleepy, and Emmalee rushed to dress her as Kelly Faye dangled in her arms like a favorite rag doll. She slipped a cotton gown trimmed with rosebuds and lace over her tiny head and placed white cotton socks on her feet. Mettie had wrapped several other new dresses in pieces of tissue and packed them inside the paper bag along with new sleepers and undershirts. Her aunt had wasted no time, Emmalee thought, making this baby her own.

Emmalee swaddled Kelly in the pink crocheted blanket Leona had made for the baby and held her in her arms. Kelly's head flopped to the side, and Emmalee kissed her cheek before lowering her into a cradle that had once held the Fultons' boy and girl. Kelly gurgled and offered a silly grin.

Emmalee had not stopped staring at Kelly Faye since Mr. Fulton had brought her home. It was as if she was looking at her baby for the very first time, studying every detail of her face—her heart-shaped lips, her pink-kissed cheeks, the wisps of blond hair sprouting from the top of her head. A newfound sense of pride and happiness was starting to take hold, but Emmalee worried this feeling would fade when she took Kelly back to the holler and mothered her all alone.

Emmalee sprinkled some of the baby's sweet-smelling powder on her own skin. She tucked her blouse into her jeans and ran the brush across her head, working through tangles and knots until it hung straight and shiny. She took a thin satin ribbon from the bottom of Kelly's bag and tied it around her hair. Emmalee wanted to look special for Leona but figured this was the best she could manage with what she had.

The muted sound of men and women greeting one another in the Fultons' living room filtered through the floor and began to surge louder and louder. People had arrived early as Mrs. Fulton promised they would, and the stench of cigars and cigarettes already tainted the air. Undoubtedly, Cullen's men had begun to gather on the front porch. They were likely blowing bands of smoke into the air between moments of laughter and conversation. Emmalee had seen them sitting on the banister doing just that when walking through town.

"I guess it's time," she said as she took the baby in her arms.

Downstairs in the living room, Curtis and Leona rested side by side in their matching black caskets, both lined with a slick white silk. Curtis wore a navy suit with a crisp white shirt and a red tie around his neck, all things that had come from Mr. Fulton's inventory.

Leona wore her crimson dress with the blue-and-lace trim; the bracelet of spoons on her wrist reflected the room's low light. They both looked handsome, Emmalee thought, as if they were preparing to celebrate a special birthday or anniversary. Even Curtis looked handsome, despite the bandage on his cheek.

A black velvet curtain had been draped across the bay window behind them, something the Fultons did whenever there was a viewing in their home. Flower arrangements of every size and color covered the tables set about the house and much of the floor around the caskets. To Emmalee, it looked like a beautiful spring garden had bloomed in the Fultons' house.

A large cross, made of yellow carnations and fixed on three stiff wire legs, sat between the two caskets. Tacked in the center of the cross was a plastic telephone, and a satin ribbon stretched from the tip of one arm to the other. There on the ribbon, printed in glitter, were two words: *Jesus Called.* It was a gift from the lapel makers and Emmalee's favorite arrangement.

With Kelly balanced on her shoulder, Emmalee scooted a tall stool next to Leona's casket. Mrs. Fulton had told Emmalee the stool was always intended for the grieving spouse. But from her perch there by her friend's side, Emmalee counted the people as they walked into the room to pay their respects. She kept a tally in her head, a full record of attendance. Seventy-eight in the first hour. Thirty-four Tennewa women in all. Emmalee imagined Leona would want to know who had come to tell her and Curtis a proper good-bye.

Emmalee knew many of the women who filed by the caskets and lingered about the living room were gossiping about her. She saw them chatting among themselves and pointing her way. But she did not budge. Instead Emmalee straightened her back and turned her gaze toward Leona. She had sat by Leona for three years at Tennewa, and she was not leaving her now.

Another hour passed. One hundred and thirty-three.

Husbands held their wives' hands. Seamstresses whispered in one another's ears. Most were already busy sharing their versions of the accident and special memories they had shared with Curtis and Leona. Some women cried outright, and some men wiped their eyes. Some stepped close and studied their faces. Others kept their distance, but everyone commented on Mr. Fulton's expert work. And all sang a similar refrain: "My, my, they look real handsome *considering* . . ." Then they stuttered and stammered, not sure how to best finish their poorly started compliment. "Well, *considering* everything."

Emmalee even overheard some talk of the

beautiful dress Leona was wearing while others made fun of its color.

"The Bullard girl made Leona's dress," one woman told her friend.

"Red, can you imagine? For a funeral? I thought Leona took in sewing, not men," the other woman said. They both stifled a laugh. Emmalee ignored them and looked only at Leona's face, peaceful in death. No more wounds. No more dark, sad circles under her eyes.

The preacher clutched his Bible as he passed by and thanked Emmalee for her steady sewing hand. The sheriff mumbled a few quiet words. Mr. Clayton straightened his tie and was quick to leave, his wife pushing him along from behind. Gwen Whitlow hugged Emmalee and began to sob, crying till she struggled to catch her breath. She asked Emmalee something about a cross, but the preacher led her to the sofa on the other side of the room before Emmalee could answer. They bowed their heads in prayer and spoke of Leona's generous spirit. Emmalee had never heard Gwen compliment Leona like this.

Mrs. Fulton walked through the room every half hour, tidying the pillows and offering visitors tissues and hot coffee. She stopped and glared at Emmalee. "Do you really need to sit so close to the body, especially with that baby in your arms? Good Lord, Emmalee, you're not even that woman's family."

"I ain't leaving." Emmalee sat a little taller. "And if you got a problem with your grandbaby being here, then you take her." Emmalee held the baby up.

Mrs. Fulton stepped back, careful to keep a smile on her face while she glanced about the room. She nodded at Cora sitting in the blue velvet chair placed opposite the casket, her body wedged into the narrow seat.

"Hey there," Cora called to Emmalee. "That your baby there?"

"Yes, ma'am."

"How you been doing?" Cora popped a cheese wafer in her mouth.

Emmalee shrugged her shoulders.

"Being a mama ain't easy, is it?" Cora asked and swallowed hard.

"No, ma'am, it ain't."

"People say the first one's the hardest, but my third about put me in the grave." Cora glanced at the casket. "Lord, that child was work, cried all the time, sick most of the winter. Boy turned thirty last week, and he's still causing me to worry."

Emmalee shifted Kelly Faye to her other shoulder. "How'd you take care of them all and work a job, Miss Cora?"

"Not much choice. Had to feed 'em. Mama helped me some, till her stroke. Then I had her to care for too."

"I had no idea," Emmalee said.

"Oh, I'm not so different than any other woman around here." Cora lifted her pocketbook onto her lap. "Besides, the oldest one helped when she could. I never would let her miss a day of school though. Sometimes there was no choice but to leave a couple of them home alone." Cora shook her head. "I never liked doing that. But they survived."

She opened her purse and pulled out a book of pictures. "They all grown up. Got families of their own. Not a one of them lives in Cullen no more. Got two in Jasper. Alma, she's my baby, moved down to Mississippi and wants me to come for a while. She got a real pretty house there near Oxford." She handed the photographs to Emmalee. "But that ain't my home." Cora opened her pocketbook wider and fished for a mint candy. "You going back to the factory, Emmalee?"

"I want to. Don't got it all figured out. Don't got no one to help with the baby and sure can't be leaving her with Nolan."

"Lord, no." Cora laughed, her jowls and neck jiggling as she spoke. She set her pocketbook back on the floor. "Can I hold her?"

"Yes, ma'am." Emmalee stepped off the stool and placed Kelly in Cora's open arms. The old woman hummed as she lifted the child to her chest. Her large breasts hung low, and Kelly squirmed as she nestled in between them.

"Oh sweet baby, sweet baby girl." Cora repeated these words, adding a made-up tune as she went along. Even stuffed into the velvet chair, Cora managed to rock her body from side to side and lull Kelly into a sleepy trance. Emmalee liked seeing her baby in Cora's arms. She stared a moment longer and then opened Cora's picture book.

Mr. Fulton appeared from behind the kitchen door. "Good evening, Mrs. Hixson. It's good to see you here as always. I see you found yourself a baby to love on." He hugged Cora's shoulder as he moved through the living room. "She's a pretty thing, isn't she?"

"She sure is."

"Speaking of pretty things, did you see the dress Leona's wearing?" Mr. Fulton walked to Emmalee and stood beside her. Emmalee grinned, surprised Mr. Fulton had drawn attention to her work.

"Prettiest dress I ever seen, and for sure the prettiest dress I ever seen on Leona. Didn't know she'd spend a penny on anything as nice as that," Cora said, her body swaying back and forth.

"She didn't. Emmalee made it for her," Mr. Fulton said.

Emmalee smiled even bigger. Mr. Fulton was always kind with his words. He reminded her of Billy in that way.

"I think we might have to hire this girl more

often. Custom wear for the heavenly bound perhaps." Mr. Fulton laughed. "There's good money in this type of ready wear, right, Emmalee?" He leaned in to hug Emmalee. "You done good. Real good. And I know it's not been easy."

"Thank you." Emmalee fixed her eyes on Leona. "Funny, you know, Leona's got this sweet smile on her face. But when she was living, she never looked happy like this." Emmalee smoothed Leona's collar as if she was placing a warm iron to it one last time.

"Maybe that's it. Maybe she's finally happy," Mr. Fulton said.

"I sure hope so. Hope she's found Curtis, Jr."

"I'm sure she has, hon," Mr. Fulton said. "And I bet Curtis is admiring her in that red dress right about now. Just wish I had done better by him."

Emmalee had no memory of what her mother was wearing the day she was buried, but she wished she had a nice memory like this one to carry with her. Emmalee understood she'd never shake loose the image of Cynthia Faye struggling for a last breath, her skin yellow and paper thin. That image would be seared on her thoughts forever, like a rancher's brand on a cattle's hindquarters. And she figured it was up to her to fill her baby's head with pretty thoughts, not ones that would haunt her and startle her awake at night for the rest of her life.

"You think everybody ends up happy?" Emmalee asked, her hand still resting on Leona's collar.

"I like to think so," Mr. Fulton said. "But I think for some of us it takes a lifetime to get there. For others, I think it takes dying."

Emmalee's eyes swelled with tears at such a kind reassurance. She pinched her nose tight.

"Hon, I've heard from Runt." Mr. Fulton leaned closer to Emmalee. "He and Mettie are coming to the visitation." He paused. "They want to see the baby."

Emmalee's body stiffened. "You said they were going to leave Kelly Faye be until after the funeral."

"They're not taking her." He patted Emmalee's back as he might the baby's. "They just want to come pay their respects. Curtis was a friend of Runt's."

"That may be, but Kelly Faye ain't part of the visitation."

"I understand that," he said. "Let's not worry about that now. They probably won't get here till tomorrow anyway."

"You seen Nolan?" Emmalee asked, her voice turning anxious.

"No. Not yet. I'm sure he'll come around eventually. He usually stops by to see if I need a hand with anything." Mr. Fulton laughed a little. "You know your father, no matter how mad he gets, it never seems to last long. His mood changes like the wind."

Emmalee nodded and pressed her fingers against her eyes, trying to push the sadness back inside.

"Basil," Mrs. Fulton said, the sound of her voice causing Emmalee to shudder. "We got at least fifty people in here, and I see more walking down the street. You keep a close watch on things. You, too, Emmalee. Curtis's got some good people on his side, but I don't know who all will show from Leona's." Mrs. Fulton picked up a porcelain figurine and held it to her middle. "I'm not staying up past midnight keeping track of my things while these men sip their liquor and swap their filthy stories."

"Hester," Mr. Fulton said.

"You can Hester me all you want, but I don't want to find anybody passed out on the sofa in the morning or empty whiskey bottles under the cushions like happened when Frank Dawson passed on," she said, her voice growing louder.

"Quit worrying, Hester. These are all good people," Mr. Fulton said.

The telephone rang, and Mrs. Fulton motioned for her husband to answer the door as she ran for the receiver on the other side of the living room. "Fulton-Pittman Funeral Home. May I help you?" Mrs. Fulton answered, looking stern at her husband and pointing her finger toward the front door.

"Yes, the wreath went up. Yes, it was the Lane couple. Yes, ma'am, it was both of them, Curtis and Leona. On the way to church supper. Yes, ma'am, they're dead," Mrs. Fulton said and rolled her eyes while she placed the figurine inside a cedar box sitting on the floor. "Yes, it was a tragedy sure enough. Yes, that's right. The service will be on Tuesday with burial to follow right there at the Church of Christ. That's fine. Thanks for calling."

She replaced the receiver and walked back into the kitchen. "Lord, I don't hang that wreath on that door just to be announcing bingo."

Emmalee hid her face behind her hands, camouflaging her laughter. She stepped across the room and knelt next to Cora, sneaking a quick peek at her baby. "Mrs. Hixson, would you mind hanging on to Kelly for a minute? I want to stretch my legs outside, and I don't want her smelling all that smoke."

"Love to. But call me Cora, hon."

"Yes ma'am."

Emmalee steered through the crowd of people gathering in the hall, relieved to be in the cold air and out of the dimly lit room smelling of both death and fresh lilies. Several men from Tennewa who worked on the loading dock and in the cutting room stood on the porch, enjoying their cigars and conversation. She pushed her way to the far edge and leaned over the banister. The moon was nearly full, and she scanned the sky for the stars often hidden from her view back in the cover of the holler.

An engine suddenly sputtered and coughed down the road. Emmalee stretched her neck forward to get a better look. It sounded familiar, like Nolan's old truck. But when it passed in front of the funeral home, Emmalee could see it wasn't their beat-up Ford but a better-looking Chevrolet. She turned back toward the house and spied Ruthie next door, standing in her kitchen window. She was washing the evening's dishes while her husband stood behind her, holding their daughter in his arms. Ruthie chuckled about something, and her husband kissed her neck. She smiled and continued about her chore.

Emmalee walked back inside the funeral home and took her place next to Leona.

The next morning Emmalee woke early with Kelly Faye. The evening's last mourners had not left the funeral home until after midnight just as Mrs. Fulton had feared. Fortunately, the baby had slept soundly in the cradle next to Emmalee even though loud outbursts of laughter peppered the talk downstairs.

Emmalee placed the baby in the bed next to her and rested her finger in the palm of her infant's tiny hand. Kelly Faye squirmed and tightened her grip. Emmalee had missed the feeling of Kelly's soft skin next to hers during the time they had been apart. The baby kicked and cooed as if she understood her mama's sadness and was trying to brighten her mood.

Hours later, Emmalee diapered and nursed her and rocked her in the cradle till she drifted back to sleep. The house was still, but Emmalee was too awake and pulled the robe over her shoulders and headed downstairs to fix an egg and a cup of fresh coffee.

The Fultons' kitchen walls were covered in paper with flowers and vines painted all over it. There were two ovens, one set above the other, and the water poured fast from the sink's shiny faucet. China plates and bowls were stacked neatly and stored in cabinets with glass fronts. Every pot and pan had its place. Every surface was wiped clean.

The Fultons slept late this morning as they had warned Emmalee they were prone to do after a long visitation. So she moved quietly about the kitchen. She started the coffee and opened the refrigerator and searched for the carton of eggs. A jug of fresh orange juice caught her eye, and she placed it on the counter.

The telephone rang, and Emmalee jumped, not accustomed to the harsh, trilling sound. She hesitated but reached for the phone mounted on the kitchen wall, hoping the sound had not disturbed the Fultons sleeping upstairs. She lifted the receiver to one ear and tucked her hair behind the other. Emmalee pulled the robe farther over her shoulder as if she needed to cover herself before speaking to the caller on the opposite end of the line.

"Fulton-Pittman Funeral Home. May I help you?" she asked, reciting the greeting she had heard Mrs. Fulton offer over and over the night before.

"Who's this?" a man's voice asked.

"Fulton's Funeral Home."

"I mean who's this on the phone?"

Emmalee's stomach fluttered. She had heard this voice before, and she reached for the back of the kitchen chair. "This is Emmalee. Emmalee Bullard."

A long pause filled the distance between her and the caller.

"Emmalee? This is Billy. What are you doing there?"

His voice sounded deeper than Emmalee had remembered. "Billy? Is that really you?" Emmalee asked.

"Yeah, it's me. But what are you doing there? Mother didn't mention you staying at the house."

"Not surprised. Your mama ain't too fond of me," Emmalee said.

"Don't pay her no mind. You okay?"

"Yeah, everybody's fine. I been a little sick. Baby has too." Emmalee poured a cup of coffee and put it on the table. She sat down and pushed the coffee away.

"But you're okay? You're both okay?"

"Yeah." Emmalee rested her elbows on the table as she held the receiver tight against her ear, desperate to inch closer to the boy she had convinced herself she didn't care about any more.

"Mother told me you say the baby is mine."

"You know she is, Billy Fulton. Don't act like you don't."

Another long pause drifted between them.

"I know, Emmalee. I know."

"You coming back to Cullen . . . to see her . . . the baby, that is?"

"I don't know. Mother wants me to stay here in Knoxville and finish the semester. Exams'll be starting in a few more days."

Emmalee stood and shoved the chair underneath the kitchen table. "And what about you, Billy? What do you want? You got a thought in your head that don't belong to your mama first?"

"Emmalee, come on. This is a hell of a lot to deal with. I don't know what to think. Hell, a baby. It's kind of a big surprise."

"A surprise? Really? No kidding, Billy." Emmalee's tone was growing shrill. "You didn't have a thought before yesterday that she might be your own? You saw her being born, for crying out loud, Billy. Or you figure I sleep with any boy come my way? Is that what your mama's told you? Is that what you think?"

"I don't think that. I never thought that. Good Lord, Emmalee. You should know me better than that."

Emmalee nodded. She did know that about Billy.

"Look, I'm real sorry about all of this. Real sorry. Hell, I never thought this would happen," Billy said. "But you're the one got up and walked off."

"Walked off." Emmalee was shouting now. "Shit, Billy, you didn't love me enough to tell your own mama about me, even when there was no Kelly Faye." She paced the kitchen floor as far as the telephone cord would allow. Again, she heard Billy say he was sorry. She wished that was all she really needed from him, an acknowledgment he had, if only for an evening, if only for a moment, truly loved her. But Emmalee needed more than that now.

"Well, Mother knows everything about us thanks to your daddy," Billy said. "But that doesn't change the fact that I'm not ready to be stuck with a baby. I'm sorry, Emmalee. I'm just not."

Emmalee held the receiver out in front of her. She wanted to bang it on the table but took it back to her ear. "Take your time, Billy. I wouldn't want to rush you into anything. But so you know, this baby can't take care of herself. They don't come that way. And I got my own blood nipping at my heels trying to steal her from me. But if'd you come back to Cullen, they'd leave me be. I know they would."

Emmalee swore she could feel Billy's fear and frustration blowing through the telephone line, a wisp of warm air sweeping right past her cheek. She could hear his breathing as if he was standing right by her. She swore she could smell him, maybe even reach out and touch him.

"You should have done something, Emmalee, done something so this never happened in the first place."

"Done what?" Emmalee asked.

"Look, I can't talk about this right now." Billy sounded angry. "Either one of my parents awake?"

"No. They're both sleeping. And the baby's starting to fuss." Emmalee got up and placed the receiver back on the telephone, never bothering to mention Billy's call.

Emmalee hadn't expected Billy to come and rescue her, but her cheeks burned from the embarrassment of just asking. She tried to stifle a cry, but the tears rolled down her cheeks. She sat back down and laid her head on the cold kitchen table.

A soft knock sounded at the back door. Emmalee looked up to see Cora standing there, her face visible in the glass set in the middle of the door.

"Cora. What you doing here?" Emmalee asked. She hurried over and fumbled with the lock.

"Hey there, little mama," Cora said as she waddled into the Fultons' kitchen. "I knew the visitation would be picking up early today, and I figured you might need some help with the baby." Cora looked around the kitchen. "Where is the baby?"

"Upstairs. Sleeping."

"Grieving's exhausting work, even for a little one, I guess." Cora juggled her large purse and a black umbrella in one hand and a paper bag in the other. "Here, hon, I had a few baby clothes left of my own," she said and handed Emmalee the bag. "Don't know what I been keeping them for. They ain't nothing special or fancy like I hear your Mettie done bought you, but I made every one of them myself and they'll sure keep Kelly Faye warm on a cold day. I can promise you that."

Emmalee looked at the clothes folded neat and stacked high inside the paper bag. She opened her arms wide and welcomed Cora into the kitchen. "Thank you." Emmalee pulled another mug from the cabinet and poured more coffee. She handed it to Cora. "Can I ask you a question? But you got to promise to be honest with me, even if it means hurting my feelings."

Cora nodded and took a sip from the mug. "Sure."

"It's just that you know so much about babies and mothering, and I was wondering if you think I can take care of a baby on my own?"

"Of course you can, sweetie," Cora said, sitting her mug on the counter and reaching for Emmalee's hand. "But you ain't alone."

Emmalee brushed away another tear.

Many of the day's visitors were the same men and women who had come the night before. They picked up their conversations where they had left them and carried on. Others like Sissie Boyd and her mother visited for the first time and took their turn filing past the Lanes' caskets. They hugged Emmalee and doted on Kelly Faye. Even Mrs. Cain from the welfare office came for a short visit. She studied the baby and complimented Leona's red dress, but she did not mention Mettie or Runt.

Grieving the dead, Emmalee thought, brought Cullen together like the Fourth of July parade through the center of town or reunion Sunday at the Baptist Church, and Emmalee enjoyed being in the midst of all the activity. This was a part of death she had never known before. She enjoyed sharing her sadness with everyone else, even if the thought did sound strange.

Emmalee saw no sign of Nolan. She hadn't

really expected him to come pay his respects after he stormed out of the funeral home, leaving her in the Fultons' care. But she figured he'd be eager to flaunt the news he was the Fultons' kin, that Basil and Hester shared his grandchild, birthed by his own Emmalee. She felt of great value to Nolan for the first time in her life, more valuable than any piece of junk he had ever hauled back to the holler. Surely he was pleased he had found a purpose for his daughter after all these years.

Every so often Emmalee walked to the porch's edge to look for his truck. She hoped he would be there when Runt and Mettie came by. She wasn't sure if Nolan would help or hurt, but she wanted him there all the same. But Emmalee always hurried back to her post, afraid Leona would be missing her if she stayed away too long or Mrs. Fulton would take her stool and shoo her back upstairs.

"Hester, why you keep pestering this girl about where she sits?" Cora finally asked her. "She ain't hurting no one, especially not Leona and Curtis." Cora clutched her pocketbook, something she tended to do unless she was holding the baby. Mrs. Fulton said nothing and stepped into the kitchen, the door swinging closed behind her.

"Good. I'd had enough of that." Cora laughed. "Don't know what's gotten into her. She don't usually act like such a crazy woman, especially around a baby. Speaking of baby, bring that precious thing here to me."

Emmalee watched in awe as Cora situated Kelly on her chest and rocked her into a deep sleep. She wished she could handle her own baby so good. Cora promised, as she had that morning, that it would come with time. Emmalee was beginning to believe this, but she sure wished it would hurry along. She looked at Leona, resting so peaceful, and straightened the collar on her dress. "I know I could do it if you were here."

"What'd you say?" Cora asked.

Emmalee twitched as if she was shaking off her thoughts. "I said I think it's going to be real lonely without her."

"Sure it will. Especially at first."

Emmalee said nothing.

"You know Leona and me could sure go at it, but I loved her, sure did. And I'm going to miss her too. But this little one here will fill your days up. I can promise you that." Cora laughed again and her chest jiggled. Kelly squirmed but settled quickly in Cora's arms.

Emmalee spotted Easter and Wilma walking toward her. Easter was carrying another casserole. Wilma was carrying both their purses. Emmalee rushed toward them. "Where you two been? I was looking for you both last night. I thought for sure you'd be here."

"Oh, sweetie, I think we were the only ones in Cullen didn't know the wreath went up. We drove by about five in the evening and didn't see it. So we went on home. Easter started cooking, and I started a crossword," Wilma said, setting their purses next to Cora's. She checked on Kelly Faye snuggled under the blanket and then looked at Emmalee. "About ten o'clock we got a telephone call from the preacher."

"That's right," Easter said. "He wanted us to know he had talked to Leona's sister Tempa and she won't be coming. She hadn't been well and didn't think she could make the trip." Easter placed the casserole on the dining room table with the other food a few feet from the casket. "Didn't really surprise me or Wilma. Neither one of us expected her to show. Those two never got along too well, even when they were little. Tempa always thought she was a bit too good for Cullen."

"Now, Easter, we don't know all that. Tempa's got a real bad knee. And Virginia's a long ways from here. Could be just bad timing," Wilma said and stroked Emmalee's chin. "You feeling okay, hon?" Emmalee nodded and hugged Wilma a second time.

"Yeah, well, flying off a mountain on the way to church supper is real bad timing," Easter said and rolled her eyes. "Preacher did say she offered to send a dress down if her sister needed one.

But I told him there was no need since Leona was already wearing the prettiest dress I'd ever seen."

Emmalee's eyes brightened. She looked over at Kelly Faye, who was starting to squirm in Cora's arms.

"When you feed her last, honey?" Cora asked.

Kelly fussed some more. She kicked her legs and stiffened her tiny back, but Emmalee did not let go of Wilma's arm. Her eyes narrowed as she looked past Cora and into the next room.

"Emmalee, you hear Cora?" Wilma asked.

Emmalee nodded. "Yes, ma'am. But Mettie. She's here."

Mettie and Runt were speaking with the preacher. They were surrounded by a herd of other women and men who had come to pay their respects. Emmalee watched as Mettie leaned in close to the preacher's ear. He smiled and shook Runt's hand.

Cora turned the baby in her lap, resting her against her own thick tummy. "Sh. Sh. Sh. There you go, baby girl. She knows people are talking about her."

"I'm going to feed her before she starts bawling," Emmalee said and stepped in front of Cora. She reached for the baby. "Miss Fulton don't like to hear her crying down here."

"That's what I been telling you. This girl's hungry," Cora said.

Emmalee scooped Kelly Faye into her arms and hurried toward the kitchen door.

"Emmalee," Runt called out. "I want to talk to you." Runt and Mettie hurried past Wilma, Easter, and Cora and the two black caskets by the growing mound of flowers.

Emmalee turned her back to the swinging door and clutched Kelly Faye tighter against her chest. "You ain't taking my baby from me, Mettie."

"Calm down," Runt said in a low voice. Cora wiggled her body out of the velvet chair and stood behind Runt and Mettie. "We ain't here to take her. We're here to say our good-byes to Leona and Curtis. That's all."

But Mettie raised her hands, her palms facing up. "Can't her aunt hold her? Just for a minute?"

"No," Emmalee said, her tongue sounding sharp. "No, you can't. And you ain't her aunt no more. Never have been."

Mettie dropped her hands, and her arms fell rigid by her side. "Runt, take care of this," she said, her expression turned cross.

"Take care of what, Mettie?" Cora asked. "Lord, I've never seen one bitty baby cause such a fuss in all my life."

"Excuse me," Mrs. Fulton interrupted as she pushed her head into the living room from behind the kitchen door. "Emmalee, can I see you for a minute?" she asked, her tone sounding saccharine.

Emmalee kept her eyes on Mettie and Runt as she slipped backward into the kitchen. "Thank you, Mrs. Fulton."

"For what?"

"For getting me out of there."

Mrs. Fulton turned to the sink and pulled a small glass pitcher from the soapy water. "I told you I don't want a scene in my house. Get upstairs and take that baby with you."

LEONA

Old Lick

- - - - - - - - - -

Two Weeks Ago

"Hush little baby, don't say a word," Leona hummed as she stood in front of the closet in what was meant to be her son's bedroom. In all the years of living in the trailer, Leona never thought of this room any other way. *"Mama's going to buy you a mockingbird."*

She stepped back so she could take a better look at the baby things stored there—clothes, high chair, a couple of Little Golden books—all things intended for Curtis, Jr. Leona had never thrown out any of it, guessing other babies would come along. Then after a while, she couldn't imagine these things not there, including the soft blue gown buttoned onto a plastic hanger resting on a hook on the back of the closet door. She had made another gown much like this but had buried Curtis, Jr., in it long ago.

Leona had driven all the way to Chattanooga to buy the fabric for the baby's gown, determined to find more than the inexpensive cottons and poly blends surely available in Cullen or Jasper.

She had even spent a few dollars more on a pattern from the Butterick book instead of making one out of newspaper as she would have otherwise done. She wanted the baby to have a couple of special things to wear for going to church. Curtis insisted on driving her over the mountain. He didn't want her behind the wheel of the truck then with her belly so full.

Now all these years later, Leona had worked the tiny pearl buttons set on the back of the gown between her fingers and lifted it from its hanger. She was excited to welcome a new baby into her home and pictured Kelly Faye wearing this dress, even if it was blue. Maybe she'd make a frilly new bonnet to go with it.

"Leona, what are you doing in here?" Curtis asked. He tapped lightly on the bedroom door. "You okay?"

"I think I am, Curtis," Leona said. "But I do need to talk to you." She sat down on the bed and patted the mattress next to her.

"You're scaring me, Ona."

"Don't mean to be. Nothing bad has happened. In fact, I think it might be something good." Curtis sat down, and Leona placed her hand on his knee. "You know Emmalee had a baby, a little girl, about six or seven weeks ago."

"Of course, I do," Curtis said. "Pretty dramatic entrance into the world. Think everyone in Cullen heard about it."

"Well, Emmalee needs help, Curtis. She needs a lot of help." Leona picked up a pillow off the bed and pulled it against her stomach. "I think she's really struggling to care for the baby on her own. She lost her mama when she was so young, and, the thing is, I want her to come here. I want Emmalee to come here and stay with us for a while."

Curtis rested his elbows on his knees and clasped his hands together. "How long you talking about, Ona?"

"I don't know. Don't want to put a date on it." She hugged the pillow tighter.

Curtis pulled his clenched hands underneath his chin. Leona stood and dropped the pillow on the bed. She walked to the window and looked out over the bluff. "The valley always seems so pretty from up here, don't it? Almost perfect. Like I could see all the way to Kentucky." She smiled and turned to find Curtis smiling sweetly back at her. "But nothing about living down there is pretty or perfect for Emmalee."

"Have you been down there to the Bullards' place without telling me, Ona?" Curtis asked. "Have you already asked her to come?"

Leona kept her gaze fixed on the valley. "I had to, Curtis. I had to see her for myself." She walked back to the closet, the blue gown in her hand. "But Nolan met me outside and ran me off. And I've been worried sick about that girl ever since. I can't leave her there. I can't. Not sure that baby will make it if I do. Not sure either one of them will make it."

Curtis followed Leona across the room. She leaned into him, and he took her left hand in his, careful to avoid the fresh blister brewing on her index finger. "You're a good woman, Leona Lane, and I know you want to help this girl."

"I do want to help her, Curtis. I really do."

"Well, I'm going to be honest with you." Curtis kissed Leona's hand. "Runt's been real concerned about Emmalee and the baby, but Nolan is so fiery about everything he said the only way he could help was if he made a legal claim to her. He said Mettie wanted to take the baby from the start."

"But that ain't their baby to take, Curtis. Emmalee loves that girl. I know she does. She just can't do it on her own,"

"I hear you. But are you doing this for the right reason?"

Leona looked up at Curtis and pulled her hand away. "What other reason could I be doing it for?"

Curtis stared toward the hanger and then back at Leona.

"I need to know you're doing this for Emmalee, not for you. I need to know you aren't trying to fill that hole in your heart with someone else, even if it is a teenaged girl and her baby. So I'm going to ask you again, who you doing it for?"

Leona's eyes grew teary, but she did not cry. She pulled Curtis's arm across her middle. "It feels good here, Curtis. Right here. I ain't lying to you about that."

Curtis drew Leona deeper into his embrace and kissed her cheek. "If Abraham and Sarah could do it, I guess we can too."

Leona laughed real soft. "We ain't that old, Curtis Lane." She rested her head against his shoulder and closed her eyes, still fingering one of the gown's tiny pearl buttons.

The next morning, Curtis drove the truck to the small house at the far back of Red Chert, careful to navigate the narrow path, deeply rutted and muddy from recent rains. The trees hugged the small piece of land around the house, and it felt wetter and colder back there. "Things ain't changed much," Curtis said as he pulled close to the front door.

"Wait for me here," Leona said.

"Are you sure, Ona?"

"I'm certain of it. That old coot don't scare me. Besides, you'll be right here if I need you."

Leona walked around the front of the truck, staring at the diapers and undershirts hanging on a short line. She climbed onto the runningboard and motioned for Curtis to roll down his window. She leaned in. "Thank you," she said and kissed his cheek. She jumped down and hopped from left to right as she made her way to the door, dodging the mud and dirty pools of water.

"Emmalee, it's Leona. I want to talk to you. Only take a minute of your time." Leona knocked hard on the door, and the sound echoed in the holler. She touched the broken-down refrigerator, remembering it all these years later. "Emmalee, please open the door. It's Leona, and I need to talk to you right quick."

The door swung open, only far enough for Leona to see Emmalee's face.

"Hey there. I come by to check on you. And the baby. Can I come in?"

Emmalee hesitated. She scanned the hills in front of the house before stepping outside. She pulled her sweater across her chest and nodded at Curtis sitting in the pickup. He nodded back. "Look. I appreciate the visit, Miss Leona, but Nolan's real funny about people coming around here."

"I won't stay long. Me and Curtis, we got something we want to ask you is all," Leona said. "I know you're here alone. I mean raising that baby on your own, and we got a room." Leona pointed to Curtis. "It ain't much, but we want you to come and live with us. You can stay as long as you want. Curtis and I done talked about it."

Emmalee looked past Leona, setting her attention on the hillside in front of her.

"I guess it sounds crazy coming out of the blue

like this," Leona said. "But I've been thinking about it since the day Kelly Faye was born. I know it ain't easy mothering on your own." Leona paused and glanced back at Curtis. "Well, I can only imagine it ain't easy."

Emmalee ran her hand up and down her arm as if she were trying to warm herself against the cold. "You want me to come with you? Right now?"

Leona smiled. "As soon as you're ready. But I was thinking soon. Today. Tomorrow maybe. Or the day after. Anytime."

Emmalee glanced back inside the house and pulled the door closed behind her.

"You know I've been here before, Emmalee. Your mama stood right where you're standing, but you was in her tummy. She needed someone. She needed help. I could see it in her eyes. I should have done more all those years ago. Let us help you and Kelly Faye. In a strange way, I'll feel like I'm finally doing right by your mama."

"Nolan'll come looking for me."

"Don't worry about Nolan," Leona said and pointed back at the truck. "Curtis can handle him. If not, I got a .22 of my own that'll keep him in his place."

Emmalee laughed, but it faded fast and a serious expression returned to her young face. "He ain't really got no one but me."

"You're doing what's best for your child. Got to get your priorities straight now that you got a baby. I wasn't always good at that." Leona drew a deep breath and blew it out into the holler. "Curtis, there, wants me to be happy. That's all he's ever wanted. And I know what will make me happy. That's doing right by you, by your mama, and by that sweet baby girl of yours. Please, let me do this."

"You got to go. Go on. Go," Emmalee said, her face turning white.

Leona looked confused and reached out for Emmalee's hand.

"You got to go. Please, go on. Told you, damn it, Nolan don't like people coming around," she said, her body shaking hard.

"Honey, calm down."

"Go!" Emmalee backed into the house and slammed the door shut.

"Emmalee!" Leona said, her mouth pressed to the door. "We'll be waiting on you. You hear me? Thursday morning. Just outside the holler on the main road. Don't worry about bringing nothing. Just bring yourself and the baby. You hear me?"

There was no answer. "Emmalee," Leona repeated as she drew back from the door.

Emmalee pulled the blanket to the side and showed her face and then disappeared. Leona rushed back to the truck and climbed inside. Curtis revved the engine and pulled away while Leona spotted Nolan standing on top of a rocky ledge farther up the mountain.

EMMALEE

Fulton-Pittman Funeral Home

- -

"Emmalee," Mrs. Fulton said as she knocked on the bedroom door. "You're going to be walking to the church alone if you're not ready soon. Your daddy will be here soon, and you need to be downstairs when he pulls in the drive."

Emmalee said nothing.

"You hear me in there?"

"Yes, ma'am," Emmalee answered from behind the closed door.

"Listen here. Your father ran over to Pikeville first thing this morning to borrow a second hearse from Heritage. We're expecting him back any minute," she said. "Any minute. And I want you riding with your daddy. Emmalee Bullard, are you listening to me or not?"

"Yes, ma'am." Emmalee stood in front of a long mirror mounted on back of the bedroom door. She studied the skirt she had taken from Rachel's closet. She had admired all of Rachel's old clothes but she favored this skirt best. It was a pretty shade of gray, so warm it looked almost blue. It fell just above her knee, and Emmalee guessed it was perfect for a funeral.

"What are you doing in there?" Mrs. Fulton asked, knocking louder on the door.

"Nothing."

Earlier in the morning, Emmalee had washed in the Fultons' tub. She had scrubbed her skin and lathered her hair, wanting to look her best for the church service. She had never been inside a church building for preaching. She woke nervous, her fingers trembling, knowing she'd see Runt and Mettie, knowing they'd be looking to take her baby home. Kelly gurgled happily in the cradle, and Emmalee pinched the skirt's waistband between her fingers, adjusting for a better fit. She pulled the waistband tighter, folded it, and fastened it with one of Kelly Faye's diaper pins.

She slipped on a matching gray sweater, one trimmed with gray ribbon and silver buttons. She fastened the sweater so only her shirt's collar poked its way free around her neck, and then pulled the sweater down to hide the skirt's pinned waistband. She admired herself in the mirror again, wondering if Leona would recognize her dressed in these fancy clothes. She wondered if Runt and Mettie, maybe even Mrs. Cain, would think better of her dressed like this.

She pulled on her wool socks and worn-out boots, lacing them tight around her ankle. Rachel's shoes were too big and Emmalee couldn't figure a way to make them fit. Ready to go, she turned her attention to the baby, who was working hard at her first smile and waving her hands in front of her eyes as though they were something she had never seen before. Emmalee slipped her fingers underneath Kelly's diaper to check if it was dry and wrapped her baby girl snug in the pink blanket. She lifted her from the cradle and hurried to meet Mr. Fulton in the hall.

"Emmalee," he said, "my, my, you look nice."

"Thank you. I borrowed something of Rachel's. Hope you don't mind. I know Mrs. Fulton didn't want me going through her things."

"Rachel doesn't wear those clothes anymore," Mr. Fulton said. "That's what she left behind when she moved to Birmingham. I keep telling Hester it's time to give all that to the church or the Goodwill, but that woman would hang on to a paperclip if she thought it might serve a purpose someday." Mr. Fulton laughed. "I was coming up to tell you that it's time. We need to be at the church a good hour before the service begins."

"Yes, sir. I'm ready. So is the baby."

"I see that, and you both look beautiful," he said. "I think your daddy just pulled into the drive. You going to be okay?"

Emmalee nodded as a bell rang downstairs.

"There's Nolan. How's that for timing?" Mr. Fulton scooted toward the stairs, reaching for the wall for added support. "Come on, girls, we got a funeral to go to."

• • •

"Excuse me, Doris," Mrs. Fulton interrupted, "but I'm with Mettie here. We need to get things back to normal as fast as we can."

"That's right," Runt said, "and I want the sheriff involved in this. Everybody here knows you can't trust my brother not to do something crazy." Emmalee heard her uncle's voice clear in the kitchen rising above the others. "And we all know Nolan ain't going to take the news of this very good."

"I understand that," Mrs. Cain said.

Emmalee stepped into the kitchen behind Mr. Fulton. There stood Runt and Mettie. Mrs. Cain sat at the table; a clipboard and ballpoint pen were set in front of her.

"What's going on here?" Mr. Fulton asked.

"Runt and Mettie came by with Doris to check on the baby," Mrs. Fulton said.

Runt reached out to shake Mr. Fulton's hand, and Mettie moved toward Emmalee, trying to sneak a look at Kelly Faye. But Mr. Fulton turned to Hester. "What have you gone and done?"

"Basil," Runt said, "Mettie and I called Mrs. Cain. We think it's time something official is done about the baby. We wanted to wait till after the burial, but when Emmalee wouldn't even let Mettie get a look at her yesterday, well, we got to worrying that something wasn't right."

"That's right, Basil." Doris Cain picked up her pen and made a note on the clipboard. "Runt and Mettie called me over to their house this morning because they wanted my opinion." Mrs. Cain motioned for Emmalee to join her at the table, but Emmalee refused. "Mettie and Runt do have some real concerns about your ability, Emmalee, to care for a child, especially given your current living conditions and Nolan's consistent refusal to accept help of any kind."

Mr. Fulton cleared his throat. "Sounds like you've all decided Emmalee is never going to make a fit mother. I thought we were going to give her a chance, a real chance to do right."

"Basil, I always give the mother a chance," said Mrs. Cain. "But I've seen too much of Nolan and Emmalee Bullard through the years to think this baby's got much of a future back in Red Chert. And it was my understanding from Hester here that Emmalee would be heading back there after the service."

Hester glared at her husband, her body growing stiff. "That baby is not our concern."

"Hester," Mr. Fulton said and shook his head.

"Don't be upset with Hester, Basil," Mrs. Cain said. "I explained to Runt and Mettie that you and Hester do have more claim to this baby as the grandparents than they do as aunt and uncle. So part of my reason for being here this morning is to let you and Hester weigh in on this."

Mr. Fulton stared back at his wife but remained silent.

"So does that silence mean that you, as grandparents, are not interested in supporting Emmalee or taking in the baby?"

"That's right," Mrs. Fulton said.

"What the hell?" Emmalee clutched the baby tighter to her chest. "I ain't lying about your precious Billy. Like it or not, Kelly Faye is as much Fulton as Bullard."

"Don't go cussing like your daddy, Emmalee," Mr. Fulton said softly, keeping his gaze fixed on his wife. "Babies hear everything, you know."

Mettie sat a little straighter and smiled.

Emmalee's voice started to quiver. "But Dr. Greer said the baby needs to be with me. I heard him say it. I'm the one that feeds her. She's mine. She ain't even your blood, Mettie. She ain't got a drop of your blood in her. Not one. You ain't got any claim to her."

"Emmalee," Runt said. "Kelly Faye's got my blood in her and that gives me and my wife every right to take an interest in her."

"No it don't," Emmalee shouted and the baby started to whimper.

Mrs. Cain rocked forward on her seat, her short legs barely touching the floor. "Let's all calm down here." Again, she motioned for Emmalee to sit. "Runt and Mettie called me out of concern. I've known you for a very long time, young lady, and I'm going to be honest with you. At this point I cannot recommend that you keep the baby on your own, especially given Kelly Faye's care up to now and your current living conditions." Mrs. Cain stood and stared at Emmalee. She held the clipboard at her side. "Honey, I've been to your house. Many times. Remember? The big difference between back when you were a child and today is that we've got a nice couple willing to care for this baby."

Emmalee looked away. "Funny how they never wanted to take me."

"It was different then, Emmalee, but I am your family, Em," Runt said.

"Shut up, Runt," Emmalee said. "Nolan's right about you. Everything comes easy for you, and when it don't, you take what you want. You stole my daddy's mill, and now you think you can walk right in here and take from me too."

Runt jumped forward.

"Runt," Mrs. Cain said, holding her hand up in the air. "Don't do that. This is not the time for theatrics."

Runt settled back next to Mettie.

"I think all that Runt is trying to say, Emmalee," Mrs. Cain said, "is that surely you don't want that sweet little baby girl to grow up like you had to—no running water, no fresh food, no heat, no clean clothes. Have you forgotten all that? Kelly Faye can have better."

"But I'm her mama." Emmalee heard Kelly Faye squealing. She tried to rock her body like Cora had, but she felt cemented to the floor.

"Yes," Mrs. Cain said gently, "but you are also a very young girl."

"I'm sick of hearing that. I ain't that young."

Emmalee felt everyone's stare boring down on her. "Nolan said I'm getting better at being a mama."

Mrs. Fulton rolled her eyes. "Nolan."

Emmalee wiped her nose on her shirtsleeve. "You seen her being born, Mrs. Fulton. You know this baby's mine."

"That's right, I was there," Mrs. Fulton shot back, "and you didn't act like you wanted her then. You remember that? Besides, Mrs. Cain is right. There's a lot more to being a mama than giving birth. I don't see how a girl who couldn't even figure out she was pregnant can raise a baby on her own."

"Hester," Mr. Fulton said, "what kind of meanness has come over you?"

"Mean. Really, Basil? You're the one prolonging the inevitable."

Mrs. Cain set the clipboard back on the table and folded her arms. "All right. I'm sorry about all of this, I really am, but this is how it's going to be. Runt and Mettie have agreed to let you keep the baby till after the funeral. They're very sensitive to what you're going through. But after the service, the baby will go home with Runt and Mettie. You understand me? We'll need to decide where to go from there in a couple more days. But I need to know the baby's safe, and I need you to look at me and tell me you understand what I've said, young lady."

"You can all go to hell," Emmalee cried and ran out of the room toward the front of the house where Leona lay in her casket. She leaned over Leona and begged for her attention. "Kelly Faye is my baby. She ain't Mettie's. Leona, she ain't Mettie's."

Emmalee felt Mr. Fulton behind her.

"Leona, tell them. Tell them I can be a good mama. Tell them how you were going to take me in and help me raise my baby." Emmalee reached for Leona's hand. "Tell them," she yelled.

"Emmalee, what are you talking about?" Mr. Fulton turned her around with his good arm, and Emmalee fell against his shoulder.

"Leona and Curtis were coming for me." Emmalee sobbed while the others gathered behind Mr. Fulton. "The very next morning after the accident. They were coming for me, for me and Kelly Faye. She knew I could be a good mama. She trusted me."

But all Emmalee knew for certain was that most everything had been taken from her. Her mama and Mama's cancer stole her childhood. Billy Fulton stole her heart. Runt and Mettie were trying to steal her future. And Nolan, sure and slow, had stolen her soul. Truth be told, she wasn't sure who had done her the most harm.

"Leona, you're the only one who wanted to give me something back," she whispered, still bound in Mr. Fulton's arms. "Leona, tell them." But by then Emmalee was crying so hard, no one understood what she'd said.

Both caskets were closed, ready for their procession to the church.

Mr. Fulton said the preacher had talked to Leona's sister earlier in the morning, and she had made the final decision that the caskets be open during the service. "I'm not real sure of her reasoning, but it's her decision to make." He pulled a white handkerchief from inside his suit jacket and wiped his brow. "I don't really think that's what Curtis or Leona would've wanted, not with Curtis looking the way he does. Sure wish I could've done more."

Emmalee offered no reassurance. Still dazed by Mettie and Runt's demand, she stood silent by Leona's casket while the baby fussed in her arms.

Mr. Fulton talked on. "Preacher said that Mrs. Lane looked real pretty in her red dress, and he wanted you to know that. He said he had no idea you were such a talented seamstress. He's even bringing a Polaroid camera so he can take a few snapshots of the bodies in the church to send back to Tempa."

Emmalee stared ahead, her gaze locked on nothing specific.

The bell rang again at the back door. Emmalee shook and clutched the baby. "No," she said, her eyes wide. "They said after the funeral."

"Calm down," Mr. Fulton said. "It's probably Nolan." He pulled the blanket back from Kelly Faye's head and admired his grandchild. "You know, you got every right to tell your daddy about what's going on here. He deserves to know. After all, he's Kelly's granddaddy too. Of course, out of respect for Leona and Curtis, it might be best to wait and tell him after the burial."

Emmalee said nothing, Leona's casket behind her.

Mr. Fulton went to open the kitchen door. "Come on in here, sir," he said to Nolan.

Emmalee walked into the kitchen to find her father shaking Mr. Fulton's hand. Instead of reeking of corn liquor and snuff, Nolan smelled good, like pine and fresh cedar. He had washed his face and put on a clean shirt. Emmalee had forgotten he was a very handsome man. She was surprised.

"Morning, Mr. Fulton," Nolan said, not taking his eyes off his daughter. "You look real pretty, girl, like your mama."

Nolan tipped his hat. Emmalee adjusted her

wool skirt and fiddled with her sweater's top button. She was undecided how much to tell her father.

Mrs. Fulton shoved the door open, slamming it against the wall. She stared at Nolan and then at Emmalee. Her jaw twitched and tightened, and she picked a piece of lint from the sleeve of her navy-blue dress.

"I guess I'll start gathering the flowers," she said, her voice colored sharp. She spun around on her high heels and left the room.

"Poor Hester didn't get much sleep," Mr. Fulton said, "but it sure couldn't be a prettier day. Cool and clear. Perfect for a funeral. Good thing too. Curtis told me once to make sure he was buried on a sunny day. Said if there was rain or snow on the ground, I was to keep his body in the fridge till the weather turned. This day, Curtis Lane, is for you." He pointed out the kitchen window. "Of course, I'm not real surprised the Lord cleared the skies for Curtis."

"Yes, sir," Nolan said.

"Okay, you ready to give me a hand here?" Mr. Fulton slapped Nolan across the shoulder.

"Yes, sir."

Emmalee jostled the baby in her arms as the men set about their work.

Mrs. Fulton came back in. "It's about time."

Curtis's casket rested on top of the rolling cart draped with a red velvet skirt for the visitation.

Mrs. Fulton nudged her way between the two men and yanked the cloth free. She moved to Leona's casket and did the same.

The men wheeled the long shiny box from the living room. Nolan was extra careful not to scrape a wall or bump into a piece of Mrs. Fulton's antique furniture. Mr. Fulton helped as best he could, guiding the front of the casket along, pressing his weight against it as it moved across the carpet. "There you go. There you go," he encouraged as they pushed the casket into the kitchen and past the table and chairs. Emmalee could tell Nolan had done this many times before.

The concrete stoop sloped toward the drive. Nolan hurriedly positioned himself in front of the casket, then kept slow and steady as he guided Curtis's casket onto the asphalt drive.

Mrs. Fulton scurried about carrying flowers from the living room to the drive. She piled as many arrangements as she could around and on top of the casket locked in place in the back of the first hearse. The scent was so sweet. Emmalee had never smelled so many flowers at one time, not even in the spring when the fields outside the holler were blooming full with wild honey-suckle and jasmine.

Nolan opened the door to the second hearse, the one Mr. Fulton had him bring over from the funeral home in Pikeville. This hearse was new, and the chrome trim shone bright in the morning sunlight. The wagon stood a full foot taller, and the rolling cart carrying Leona's casket could not be adjusted any higher. Nolan shifted the weight of Leona's casket onto his right shoulder. He bent his knees low and drew in a deep breath. He straightened his legs slowly, exhaling as he placed the corner of the casket onto the wagon's floor. He crawled underneath it and did the same on the other side, taking another deep breath as he sucked in the strength needed for the task. He pushed the box forward. It slid off the cart and into the back of the hearse.

Mr. Fulton patted Nolan on the back. "Well, done, sir. We'll get the rest of the flowers loaded up, and then we'll all head over to the church. You and Emmalee take Miss Leona. We'll drive Curtis."

EMMALEE

Cullen Church of Christ

- -

Emmalee scooted into the front seat of the hearse, holding the baby on her lap. Nolan pulled his shoulders back and gripped the wheel. "Here we go," he said and turned right onto the street. He glanced in the mirror every few yards. "I can't get too far ahead of Mrs. Fulton or she'll go to flashing those headlights," Nolan said.

"Not too surprised by that." Emmalee could see Mrs. Fulton liked to keep everything to her way of thinking and doing.

"You look real nice, Emmalee," Nolan said without looking at her.

"Ain't once ever heard you say that."

Nolan's compliment sounded strange to Emmalee, but with Runt and Mettie scheming against her, she liked hearing it. Her father's kindness offered some unexpected comfort. And with Leona nearby, even sealed up tight in the back of the hearse, a calm washed over Emmalee.

"Never seen you looking so cleaned up neither," Emmalee said.

"Never had a reason," he said. Nolan stroked his clean-shaven chin.

Emmalee picked at the skin around her fingernail. She felt the tears coming again. She pinched her nose and stared straight ahead.

"You hear me? How's the baby?"

"Good. Getting fat."

"They grow like weeds once they get going," Nolan said. "You look like you're doing good. Sure got some pretty clothes."

"They ain't mine. Rachel's. Mrs. Fulton's pissed at me for wearing them."

Nolan laughed and kissed Kelly's head. Emmalee cracked the window. A burst of fresh air poured across her face. Nolan glanced in the rearview mirror.

"There ain't too many days that bitch ain't pissed at something. Like now. Shit, old woman, I ain't going but five miles an hour. Quit flashing your damn lights."

As they drove closer to the church, Emmalee picked harder at her finger till the cuticle bled. She held her thumb to her mouth and tasted blood.

"What's wrong with you? They not feed you at Fulton's?"

Emmalee dropped her hand. But she still picked at her finger where Nolan couldn't see.

"Nolan," she said. "I didn't tell you about Billy before 'cause I didn't want to ruin things between you and Mr. Fulton. I figured you'd go off and do something—kind of like you did."

Nolan eased his foot off the accelerator. "Billy going to do right by you?"

"I don't think his mama would let him do *right* by me, even if he wanted to." Emmalee pushed her index finger against her thumb. "Truth is, he don't want a baby."

Nolan glanced again in his mirrors. "Mr. Fulton going to do right by you?"

"You mean take me in, take care of me and Kelly?"

"Hell yeah, that's what I mean."

"Hey, you know how Mr. Fulton feels about cussing around the dead." Emmalee pointed to the back.

Nolan kept his eyes on the road. "With you chewing on your finger I know you ain't telling me something. Now spit it out."

Emmalee hesitated, but for once, she believed her father was the only one left who could help her. She felt Leona behind her, but Leona was cold as stone and not going to be much help to her now.

"Runt and Mettie say they're taking Kelly Faye." Emmalee's words strung together so tight she barely stopped to catch her breath. "They brought Mrs. Cain to the Fultons' this morning. They're thieves, like you said, Nolan. Thieves." Emmalee commenced to rocking Kelly Faye. "Runt's planning on taking her. Right after the funeral. He called the sheriff."

Nolan's anger swept through the air like an electrical current sparking and burning her skin. "That baby is yours." He pounded his fist on the steering wheel. "What the hell is Doris Cain doing in our family business? She's been butting in where she don't belong for too long. I swear that woman thinks she's God Almighty. Shit."

Nolan's talk grew more fierce, and for the first time, Emmalee found her father's anger reassuring. The hearse rolled on past the post office, and a couple of men standing out front stopped and saluted.

"You ain't giving that baby to Runt and Mettie. How many times I have to tell you that. Like your damn head's made of concrete or rock or something."

"I'm scared it ain't all that simple anymore."

Nolan steered too fast into the church parking lot. The tires screeched as they made the turn. People gathered around the front of the sanctuary looked toward the road. Emmalee could see in the side mirror Mrs. Fulton flashing the wagon's headlights off and on. Off and on. Off and on. They strobed faster and faster. Nolan shot down to the end of the drive. Emmalee clutched Kelly Faye to her so she wouldn't bounce out of her arms.

"Shit," Nolan said, steering the hearse to the

church door and throwing it into park. "Hell, Emmalee, I dropped you right there at the Fultons' door thinking you'd be able to make this right. Now I got to deal with Runt and that damn Doris Cain. Shit, girl." Kelly Faye's cries had grown shrill and Nolan held his hands to his ears. "Can't you shut that thing up for a damn minute and let me think?"

Emmalee shoved the door open. "That thing's name is Kelly Faye, you old sonofabitch." She rushed up the brick stairs past a small gathering of men and women singing softly in front of the church. She slowed down as she stepped inside and scanned the room for Runt and Mettie and Mrs. Cain. When she didn't see them, she hurried deeper inside as one hymn rolled into another, the final note of the first blurring into the next. She hoped Nolan didn't follow her.

Some women were already seated. Some whispered in their friends' ears. Others held a handkerchief to their noses. Others smiled as if to offer some unspoken comfort to those around them. The men shook hands with other men and led their wives to an empty pew. Emmalee bent her shoulders forward and lowered her head, trying to melt away among the gathering crowd.

The walls were a creamy white, and the windows were clear, not all different colors like they were at the Baptist and Methodist churches in Cullen. Emmalee darted like a field mouse trying to find cover. She longed to be back in Red Chert, hugged tight there at the mountain's base. At least there she understood the landscape.

Emmalee dropped her head against the baby's soft crown and tried to hide behind the pink crocheted blanket while everyone settled in their seats and waited for the preacher to begin. She pretended to pray and wiggled her toe against the hole in her right boot. Cora and Mrs. Whitlow sat three rows from the front among the other collar makers collected there. Mrs. Whitlow's hair looked even taller today, and a shiny gold pin shaped like a butterfly was clipped near the top. It looked to Emmalee as though it might flutter away from its well-teased perch. Cora waved. Her eyes were red and wet, but Emmalee pretended she did not notice and scooted farther down the hard wooden pew.

Most of the lapel makers sat on the other side of the church, also near the front. Pattern makers, machinists, even the boys working on the loading dock found a place in the Cullen Church of Christ. And every woman and man from Tennewa held a finished collar in her or his hand. Emmalee wept at the sight of it all.

Wilma and Easter left their seats and took a spot on either side of Emmalee. Easter took Kelly Faye and held the baby on her lap. She whispered in Emmalee's ear. "I sit with those women every day. Much rather be back here with you two." Emmalee relaxed a bit with Wilma and Easter there. She even rested her head on Easter's shoulder.

Mr. Clayton and his wife sat on the pew two rows in front of her, next to Dr. Greer and his wife. Mrs. Greer looked to be holding a basket filled with fresh baked muffins, and Emmalee's mouth watered imagining a taste of the sugary treats. A few moments later, Mrs. Cain and her husband walked down the center aisle and took their place behind the collar makers, and Emmalee's stomach grew ill. She wrapped both her hands around Easter's thick forearm and snuggled closer to her body.

"You'll be okay, hon," Easter told her and patted her hand.

Sissie and her mama stepped into the church late and filled the space next to Wilma. Emmalee was glad to see them. Sissie reached across Wilma and handed Emmalee a red carnation. "Been thinking of you," she said and faced the preacher, who had taken his place at the front of the church.

Emmalee did not see Runt and Mettie. Still she hunkered against Easter.

The preacher opened his Bible, and the room fell quiet. A few women could be heard stifling their tears. Even Mr. Clayton coughed and wiped his eyes with the back of his hand. His wife, who held her purse clutched tight in her lap, cut a stare toward her husband. He placed his arm around her shoulder, but she turned her back to him.

"We are gathered here to celebrate the lives of Leona and Curtis Lane, beloved members of the Cullen Church of Christ," Brother Herd said. He looked more like a grown man today in his dark suit and dark tie. "It wasn't but a few days ago Curtis and Leona were headed here for Wednesday-night supper. Curtis had already chopped a pile of wood for us earlier in the morning. Leona had made another one of her famous hash brown casseroles to feed our bodies." He closed his eyes and lifted his face upward a bit. "I can still smell that casserole. Can't you?"

The preacher's words jumbled in Emmalee's head. As his voice carried on about the Lanes' good deeds and their strong Christian faith, she made less and less sense of what he was saying. The preacher's message was meant to offer solace, but Emmalee's thoughts took her from the church back to Red Chert Road and the morning Leona had come to see her.

Nolan had taken to the woods before sunrise, but Emmalee feared he was lurking about. She had begged Leona to go, afraid what Nolan would do if he found her and Curtis there.

"I'll be coming back for you. Thursday morning. On the main road," Leona called to

Emmalee. "Thursday morning. You hear me? We'll be waiting for you."

Emmalee nodded as she peeked at Leona from behind the thick blanket covering the front window. Leona had looked back at her and smiled.

"Shall we bow our heads in a closing prayer," the preacher said, and heads dropped low. People shifted in their seats while the sound of women crying grew stronger. "Dear Lord, we know you understand the loss we are feeling. We know you can heal our hearts. And we take comfort knowing you have welcomed our brother, Curtis, and our sister, Leona, into your heavenly kingdom. In all your gracious goodness, you have prepared a special room for them, and we look forward to reuniting there someday, in your heavenly mansion. In all things, dear sweet Jesus, we give you thanks. In your name, Lord, Amen."

Emmalee did not close her eyes like the others. Instead she watched the preacher grow red-faced as he pleaded with the Lord to care for his friends. A mumbled *Amen* swept through the room, and the men and women who had sung before the service offered a closing hymn. Everyone stood. Some sang along with them. Others wept. The preacher kept his place between the caskets and watched as a dozen men came forward and first carried Leona and then Curtis out of the building. The preacher followed behind Curtis's casket and everyone else poured from the pews and fell in place behind him. Emmalee kept close to Easter and Wilma.

Granite headstones dotted the ground to the side of the church. Bunches of flowers decorated most of the markers while a few others stood bare. Emmalee wondered if their families had moved on and forgotten them. As mourners fanned out among the gravestones, a gathering of gray-feathered chickadees scurried across the cold ground and flew in unison to a branch hanging low just beyond a rickety iron gate. *Tsic-a-de-de-de,* they called back to the crowd, singing a final dirge.

Wilma and Easter escorted Emmalee through the cemetery toward the tent pitched above two graves carved into the dirt as if they were guiding her through an intricate maze of corn. *FULTON-PITTMAN FUNERAL HOME* was printed in bold white lettering across the tent's edge. Cora and Gwen followed Easter and Emmalee. Easter paused to place a red rose on her mother's grave, and the bevy of women all bowed their heads for a silent moment.

Other mill women walked past Emmalee, but she did not recognize them at first dressed in finer clothes than she had seen them wear at Tennewa. A couple of lapel makers stopped and spoke to Easter and Wilma. They hugged Emmalee even though they had never said much to her before.

Together they walked a few feet more and stopped in front of a tiny tombstone with a lamb resting on top. The marker read CURTIS, JR. "You're with your mama now," Easter said and wiped another tear. Easter pulled Emmalee close and the women huddled on the land's gentle slope before turning their attention toward the two mounds of fresh dirt, each covered with a blanket of fake grass. The caskets rested on four thick canvas straps, each stretched across a large rectangular hole.

Two men dressed in identical green jumpsuits stood quietly apart at the back of the cemetery, both leaning on the long wooden handles of shovels kept by their sides. People collected around the caskets and the mound of flowers, following Leona and Curtis everywhere they went.

Emmalee scanned the faces at the graveside. She knew Runt and Mettie were there, hidden among these people, keeping a close eye on her like Nolan did when he lurked about the woods. She held the baby tightly in her arms and kept close to Easter.

The preacher read Scripture from the first book of John, chapter five, verse twenty. He thanked the Lord for the beautiful day, choosing to ignore the clouds rolling in from the west. He thanked the Lord for his faithful servants, Leona and Curtis Lane, and lifted his Bible into the air and said *Amen.* The service concluded, and some of the crowd shuffled back toward the church where tables ladened with food awaited. A few looked to the darkening sky and quickened their pace toward the parking lot. Some lingered behind, chatting to one another or visiting other graves. One old man in a dark coat knelt beside a marker, picked stray weeds, and dusted a tombstone with his handkerchief.

Emmalee remained by Leona's grave, finding it hard to leave her friend behind. The other seamstresses stood faithfully around her, never once urging her along. Some other mourners stopped and complimented Emmalee on her beautiful sewing. One or two reached out to hug her. Others only paused and stared. A few spoke in hushed tones.

Mr. Fulton leaned close to Nolan and pointed to the sky. He motioned for the men at the back of the cemetery to come forward. One walked to Leona's grave and knelt on one knee. He placed the shovel on the ground and bowed his head. He mumbled a few words before turning a large metal crank. The crank squealed as the straps began to lengthen, and Leona's casket dropped slowly into the dark, damp ground.

Emmalee tossed the red carnation Sissie had given her on top of Leona's casket and said her final good-bye. Emmalee couldn't help but wonder if Leona and Curtis were as terrified at this moment, packed close in their silk-lined boxes, as they had been when they drove off Old Lick a few days ago. She liked to imagine they had reached for each other and died in one another's arms. Emmalee wondered if maybe they were happy to have said good-bye to this world now that they walked together on the golden streets of heaven. Leona was a woman of simple means though, and Emmalee worried she would be unhappy living in such a fancy place. She waved her hand as if she was pushing the thought off into the clouds, not convinced those gold streets even existed.

"Hey there," a man's voice called out among the others. "Emmalee, hang on there a minute." Emmalee's heart thumped. She clutched Easter's arm, the baby snug between them.

"You okay, Emmalee?" Easter asked.

Runt called again, his voice thundering amid the gravestones as he pushed his way past mourners drifting away from the cemetery.

"Emmalee," he yelled. Mettie marched behind him.

Easter's body stiffened, and Cora threw her hands on her hips, further widening her thick frame.

"We need to talk to you," Runt said, his tone firm and a little too loud. Emmalee's milk dropped, wetting her blouse and the pretty gray sweater underneath her coat. The baby would be rooting for her next meal any minute.

Nolan lurched forward, but Mr. Fulton yanked on his arm. Nolan quickly fell back in place. Wilma covered the baby's head with the pink crocheted blanket.

"Emmalee," Runt repeated more softly. "It's time."

"Time for what?" Easter asked. "What are you talking about, Runt Bullard?" She held her right hand to her head, trying to hold her hair in place, as the wind gusted stronger.

"I don't mean to sound rude, Mrs. Nichols," Runt said. "But this ain't your business. This is between me and my niece."

Emmalee spotted Doris Cain walking toward them from outside the cemetery's gate. Emmalee tried to bury her face behind Easter's arm.

"Well, I know you got this girl shaking in her boots. And since she's glued to me, I'd say it's some of my business."

Runt ignored Easter and reached for Emmalee's arm. "Why don't we finish this in the parking lot, Em."

"Why don't you leave this girl alone," Easter said, growing excited, the large jellylike lump on her neck starting to shake.

Norma Barker, another lapel maker, came from behind and reached out to hug Wilma. But Wilma kept her eyes locked on Runt and Mettie, and Norma walked on. A few others paused as they walked past them, trying to decipher what was happening there among the dead. Even Mr. Fulton moved closer, but he kept his grip tight on Nolan's coat sleeve.

Runt took Mettie's hand. "Look ladies, Mettie and me are taking the baby home with us. Emmalee knows it. This ain't no surprise to her."

Easter narrowed her eyes and carefully pushed Emmalee behind her. "Why would you go and do that, Runt? Emmalee's a good mama. She had a rough start for sure. There's no denying that. But she can do it." Easter looked toward the fresh graves and shook her head. "Leona knew she could, and I bet Curtis felt the same way."

Mettie squeezed Runt's hand. "Mrs. Nichols," Runt said. "I believe even you would agree a baby don't need to be raised in my brother's house, no matter how good the care."

"She don't have to be raised there," Easter shot back. Wilma tried to say something, too, but Easter cut her off. "Emmalee can live with any of us. She don't have to go to Red Chert."

"She ain't living with strangers," Runt said. "The baby ought to stay with the best of its family."

Easter leaned toward Runt. "Emmalee's proven she can do anything she sets her mind to. You seen that dress she made. She could make a good living doing things like that. I tell you this girl can do whatever she wants, even raising a baby way back there in Red Chert if she has to. But like I said, she don't have to be in Red Chert if she don't want."

Runt exhaled, his breath blowing white against the graying sky. Mettie nudged Runt's ribs, and he drew in a deep breath. He grabbed for Emmalee, but Cora swatted at his hand.

"Oh, Lord, you don't need to get Cora going," Easter said and laughed. "Don't let her age fool you. She can throw a pretty mean punch, and she'd think nothing of doing it right here on the church grounds." Easter clapped her hand over the cross she was wearing around her neck. "See, I can't do that. I'm a real Christian woman. But it wouldn't bother Cora none, would it, Cora?"

"Nope. Wouldn't bother me at all." Cora inched toward Mettie, her arms by her side. "And I don't think you want to get into it with an old woman here, with the preacher standing by. Do you, Runt?"

Mettie dropped Runt's hand and crossed her arms across her middle. "I'm sorry, Emmalee, Mrs. Nichols, Cora," Mettie said, her tone harsh, "but I can't leave without the baby. I got to know Kelly Faye is safe."

Emmalee turned away from her aunt and faced the men in the green jumpsuits. They handled the shovels as if they were children's playthings, pushing the metal tips into the pile of red chert and easily tossing another bit of earth back into the open graves. Their motion was steady, and their brows were moist with sweat even though the temperature outside remained cold. With every shovelful of dirt, Emmalee watched Leona sinking farther away. She was disappearing right there in front of her, like her very own mama had done all those years before.

"Are you even listening to me, Emmalee?" Mettie asked. "We're talking about your baby here."

Emmalee handed the baby to Easter and stepped toward her aunt. "Funny how you never paid me a bit of attention till I got me something you wanted."

"That's not so," Mettie said, her voice frantic. "Me and Runt are doing this for you and the baby."

"For me. Hell, Mettie, you never cared about me." Emmalee pushed even closer till she could feel Mettie's breath on her face and smell the jasmine perfuming her skin. "You know, I can't help you're drying up and ain't got no baby in your house. But Kelly Faye ain't your baby, no matter how bad you want her to be. So go on and get the sheriff," Emmalee said and took her baby back in her arms. "This ain't going to be as easy as you think."

Mettie stood quiet, swaying on her high heels sunk deep in the wet ground.

"Go on," Emmalee said, her voice so soft it was nearly swept away in the wind blowing stronger and colder than it had in the morning. Mettie's coat slapped at her thighs, and she extended her arms like a tightrope walker trying to regain footing.

Mrs. Cain held her hand to Runt's ear and said something in private. Runt nodded. He placed his hand at the small of Mettie's back and slowly led her away. Mettie's shoulders slumped forward and shook. Runt stopped and wrapped his arm around her waist, and Mettie leaned against her husband. Runt didn't bother speaking to Nolan as he passed him by.

"Oh hell, Doris," Cora said, interrupting the quiet, "you know I ain't got much. My place ain't much better than Nolan's, I imagine, but I raised three kids there with nobody ever trying to take them from me." Cora kept her hands on her hips and stepped toward Doris. "Like I said, my place ain't much but it's clean, and I'll take in more if I need to."

"That's right," Easter said. She stepped up next to Cora, and Wilma fell in behind her. "Me and Wilma got room. We'd help. You know that. What's got into you, Doris? I've never known you to go around yanking babies from their mamas. You gave up on Emmalee before she ever got started."

Doris shook her head. "Maybe I've just seen

393

more than you three and don't have that kind of hope anymore."

Brother Herd and Mr. Fulton stood by the women, listening to their offers to take Emmalee and Kelly Faye home. Mr. Fulton looked to his wife, but Hester ignored him and walked back to the church, disappearing through the front door.

None of them noticed Nolan sneaking up until he grabbed Emmalee around the arm and pulled her from them.

"Come on, girl," Nolan said, "we're going home."

Cora shifted her pocketbook to her right hand and cocked her arm as if she might hit somebody. The preacher and Mr. Fulton stared at Nolan, who was tugging harder on Emmalee.

"Let go of me," Emmalee said and jerked her arm free.

"Come on," Nolan repeated. "I said we're leaving. The Lanes are in the ground, and it's time to go home."

Emmalee stood firm in her own space.

"You gone deaf, girl? Come on."

"I ain't going with you."

"The hell you ain't."

"Did you hear anything I said this morning, Nolan?"

"I ain't heard nothing about you not coming home."

"Well, I ain't. I ain't making the same mistakes

Mama did. I ain't leaving my baby girl, and I ain't raising her in Red Chert." Emmalee lifted the loose corner of Kelly Faye's blanket back up to her head, protecting her baby from the wind and cold.

"Hell, girl, your mama didn't leave you. She died. What kind of fool gibberish are you talking?"

"I'm talking the truth. Mama gave up on me long before she died. You'd already sucked everything out of her. It wasn't me." Emmalee was shouting now and the baby had begun to squeal. "You didn't give her no choice but to die. And you ain't doing that to me. Leona planned something better for me and for Kelly Faye, and I ain't letting her down. So like I told Mettie, go on. Leave me be."

Mr. Fulton cleared his throat and Nolan looked up to see him standing there with the preacher by his side. Emmalee jostled the baby in her arms, and her cries hushed. Nolan stuck his hands in his pockets and raised his eyes to the sky. "Hell, you'll die in Red Chert, girl, just like your mama. You ain't no different than her." He shot another wad of spit and walked on to the hearse.

"Nolan," Emmalee called after him, but he did not look back.

The women huddled around Emmalee once again.

"Honey, you done the right thing," Cora said.

"That's right," Wilma said. "You did the right thing by you and your baby girl. You see that, Doris? You see what she did?"

But Emmalee knelt on the grass and bent her body over little Kelly, who was rooting for her mama's breast. The preacher knelt beside Emmalee and placed his hand on her shoulder. "I've been praying for you," he said and pressed his hand firm against her back. "You got to know God helps in unexpected ways sometimes."

The preacher opened his Bible and ruffled through tissue-thin pages. Right then Emmalee would have taken help from anybody, especially God, but she dreaded the sound of the preacher reading Scripture to her, reciting all those words that never seemed meant for her.

The preacher flipped to the back of the Bible and pulled out a crisp white envelope. "It's important to have faith in God, Emmalee, but you've also got to believe in yourself. Now let's have a look at what's in this envelope."

LEONA

Old Lick

- - - - - - - - - -

Three Days Ago

"Sorry I snapped at you, Curtis," Leona said. She looked straight ahead as Curtis steered the truck down Old Lick. "I'm tired is all. I worked too many bundles today. I even barked at Wilma for sewing the wrong thread. It wasn't none of my business. She don't even work collars."

Curtis shifted into a lower gear. "Wilma knows you don't mean nothing by it. But I know you, Ona. You're worried about something else. I can tell by the way your mouth is turned down."

Leona shook her head. "You cannot." She leaned across the seat and shifted the rearview mirror toward her. She smiled, erasing any obvious signs of worry.

"You can't fool me," Curtis said as he readjusted the mirror and glanced behind him. "We've been married too long for that."

"Oh, hush up." Balancing the casserole on her lap, she rested her head against the rear window and stared out at the open sky and the full moon rising in the east.

Curtis reached for Leona's hand. "You sure you not wanting to change your mind about Emmalee and the baby coming tomorrow?"

"Oh no, it's not that." Leona spied Venus shining bright overhead as she thought of the bedroom in the trailer ready for Kelly Faye and Emmalee. She had spent most of the money saved in her shoebox on pretty things for the two of them—clothes, fabric for new curtains, plastic diapers, bottles, a stuffed teddy, even a college savings bond for Kelly Faye. Curtis never once asked how she funded her generosity.

"I always wanted a baby," Leona said. "You know that."

"But that ain't what I asked you, Ona."

"I know," she said and looked at Curtis. Leona placed her hand on his thigh. "You know better than anybody I always figured a baby was the one thing I was missing. The one thing that'd make me happy. Damn near drove me crazy not having one."

Curtis raised his eyebrow at her cussing.

"Sorry," she said and flashed a weak grin.

Curtis turned the steering wheel sharp to the right as he guided the truck farther down Old Lick Mountain. He pushed the accelerator and eased into the turn; then he slowed his speed as the road straightened out. He nodded at Leona but was careful to keep his eyes fixed ahead.

"Maybe I got so used to wanting something,"

Leona said, "that somewhere along the way I didn't realize I didn't need it no more. That make any sense?"

Curtis glanced at Leona. "We can do it, Ona. You ain't alone. You never have been."

"I know that now." She closed her eyes. "I love you, Curtis Lane."

Curtis reached for Leona's hand. "I love you, too."

EMMALEE

Old Lick

- - - - - - - - - - -

Mr. Fulton had told Emmalee the logger headed up Old Lick the night of the accident took Curtis's and Leona's deaths real hard. They had to carry him to the hospital over in Chattanooga, and the doctors pumped him full of drugs to calm his nerves, the whiskey the sheriff had given him earlier in the night not proving enough. He admitted he had drifted into the other lane but thought he righted his rig in plenty of time. Mr. Fulton said the Lanes' pickup had four bad tires, and the poor trucker could not be blamed for that. From studying a long stretch of the road, Mr. Fulton believed the Lanes cut too far to the right and got caught up in a patch of loose gravel. There were no tire marks indicating otherwise.

Now heading up the mountain in the backseat of Easter's Buick, Emmalee remembered that conversation, and she imagined Leona sitting in the truck next to Curtis with the hash brown casserole on her lap. Curtis probably rubbed his stomach and told her how good her cooking smelled. She surely thanked him and took his hand in hers. Emmalee hoped so. She had seen Leona talk harshly to Curtis too many times when he came to the factory, but she liked to imagine things differently there at the end.

Wilma slowed the Buick and tapped on her side window. The two white crosses stuck in the dirt by the mountain road were nearly swallowed whole by fresh and artificial flowers, ribbons and balloons, teddy bears, even a large wreath made of collars.

"Look at all that," Wilma said, stopping the Buick in the middle of the road. "Everybody in Cullen must have come up here to leave something."

"It's a shame Leona ain't going to see this," Easter said. "She'd never believe it. What do you think of that, sweetie?" Easter shifted in the front seat so she could look at Emmalee. "You been mighty quiet back there since we left the church. You doing okay?"

"Yeah, I'm doing good," Emmalee said and scooted to the edge of the seat. Kelly Faye sat next to her, buckled in a brand new car seat, a gift from Mr. Fulton. He even tied a pink ribbon around it and told Emmalee his granddaughter was not riding around town in a cardboard box anymore.

Emmalee tickled Kelly Faye's belly and then leaned against the front seat. She held the white envelope the preacher had given her in her hand.

"Easter, you think the deacons'll approve me staying in the trailer for a while?"

"It does say right there on that piece of paper Curtis wanted the church to use the trailer to help those that need help. I'd say you're one of them."

Wilma steered the car on up the mountain.

Emmalee studied the trees passing by. "It's all so beautiful up here."

Emmalee woke in the back bedroom. The window's metal frames clattered one against the other as the wind pushed its way up Old Lick. She had slept off and on during the night. Her thoughts drifted from the dark folds of Red Chert to the days ahead there on the mountaintop. Emmalee pulled the baby closer.

Leona had prepared the room down the hall especially for Kelly Faye, but the wooden crib, decorated with frilly pink-and-white bedding, stood empty. Emmalee wanted the baby next to her.

Kelly Faye's eyes were closed while her tongue suckled at something that wasn't there, and Emmalee wondered where her baby's dreams had taken her. She kissed Kelly's head and eased out of the bed. She tucked the blanket around Kelly Faye's body and then placed a pillow on either side of her baby. Emmalee tiptoed down the hallway past the photograph of Leona and her family and what was left of Leona's silver spoons.

Easter and Wilma had offered to stay with her the first night or two, at least till she felt comfortable mothering on her own. Emmalee thanked them both but admitted she was looking forward to waking in the trailer just her and Kelly Faye. Still, Easter and Wilma promised to be back soon, admitting there would be plenty of need for their help in the days to come. Emmalee already pictured them standing in the kitchen reminding her not to wander off too far what with the baby sleeping there alone.

Emmalee slipped on her wool coat and stepped out the door, eager to see the sun rise big and full over the valley. The trailer was beautiful to Emmalee, and she swore it sparkled there underneath the clear blue sky. She looked to the bluff and the sun popping over the horizon and wondered if she might see some Kentucky bluegrass after all. She looked toward Leona's garden and pictured her own crop of tomatoes and beans growing there soon. Emmalee imagined herself walking through the cool grass come spring, carrying Kelly Faye in her arms. By then, her baby girl might be crawling.

Dry cornstalks clapped around her. Would she hear Leona there, like she had heard her mama calling to her among the pines down in Red Chert? Emmalee hoped Leona might take her time leaving that place, leaving her and Kelly Faye.

Emmalee searched the ground around the garden plot and collected twigs, snapping some in two as she put them in her coat pockets. She kept an eye on the trailer as she walked closer to the bluff, picking up more sticks. In Red Chert, the sun had not been surrounded by nearly so much sky as on Old Lick.

With her pockets full, Emmalee ran back to the trailer and placed her collection of twigs on the counter. The baby was still quiet. She shaped two crosses from her bounty and bound them with crimson thread.

The binding done, she took a ballpoint pen she found near Curtis's reclining chair and carved a name on the back of each cross. *Curtis* on one. *Leona* on the other. Emmalee reached for her mama's cross, which she had kept safe inside an old sweater since leaving the holler, and arranged the three crosses on the kitchen counter.

Whatever happened in the days to come, Runt and Mettie would always be casting their eyes on this mountain, waiting for Emmalee to fall short.

Emmalee looked at the damask slipcovers needing to be finished. Cora promised to come up in the next few days and show Emmalee how to shape the slipcovers Leona had started. When the hateful woman in the green suit showed up at the trailer next, Emmalee would be ready for her. Cora said if the woman was pleased, she'd spread the word. Cora promised Emmalee could make decent money with that kind of work.

The baby whimpered, and Emmalee walked back to the bedroom. Kelly Faye slurped her mama's milk, making sweet notes, draining away the worry.

Author's Note

During its zenith in the 1950s and 1960s, the shirt factory in Dunlap, Tennessee, employed more than seven hundred seamstresses. It was the largest employer of women in Sequatchie County at the time. Many of the female employees worked for twenty and thirty years as collar makers, hem setters, top stitchers, and lapel makers. Often daughters, mothers, and grandmothers worked side by side. Those living and interviewed for this book never spoke of the boredom of routine. Instead they talked of community and self-reliance. This book is written in honor of their commitment and determination to improving their own lives and those of their families.

Acknowledgments

This book took me on a ride into one of Tennessee's most picturesque valleys, and I'm grateful to those who volunteered their time to come along with me. I want to acknowledge the following:

Anne Edelstein, my agent. From our first meeting over a New York City breakfast, I had a hunch she would not only be an extraordinary agent but an amazing friend. She has been both.

Christine Kopprasch, my editor, whose gentle hand made this a better book. And the entire Crown team, specifically Molly Stern, Sheila O'Shea, Jay Sones, Annsley Rosner, Chris Brand, Danielle Crabtree, and Mary Coyne, whose enthusiasm and dedication have been deeply appreciated.

The many people of Dunlap, Tennessee, who generously shared their memories—specifically Jim Jones, one-time Spartan Industries manager and his wife, Linda, also a Spartan Industries employee; Anna Faye Heard, who has been *doing hair* for fifty years at the Bouffant Salon and still only charges $11.00 for a wash 'n' set; Sarah Jo and Roy Joe Walker, who buried many of Dunlap's residents with love and sincerity; Betty

Worley and her hardworking staff at the Sequatchie County Library; Susan Greer, considered an outsider even though she's lived in Dunlap for 40 years and is one of the town's most dedicated citizens; Carson Camp, former mayor and town historian, and the late Marea Barker, who worked as a lapel maker at Spartan Industries for 27 years.

My Southern friends, Darnell Arnoult, Lynn York, Jim Minick, Virginia Boyd, Rachel Unkefer, and Christy Strick who read, instructed, guided, and advised, always with wisdom and patience.

Kelly O'Connor McNees, a beautiful writer, who was first a Twitter friend and now a trusted confidant.

Ann Watkins whom I've leaned on through the years whether strolling our babies together or relying on her critical eye and sharp red pencil.

Shaye Areheart, who is my friend.

Lee Smith, who will always teach me more.

Annaliese Araw, who took her camera and showed me things I would have otherwise missed. And her husband, Albert, such a kind man.

Lawton Haygood, who has supported me in all things whether I'm serving up ribs and turnip greens or a novel about the Southern home we share.

Rosie Von Canon, who has made hard days so much better.

Kelley Hawk, who gave her name to Kelly Faye Bullard and a generous donation to the Georgetown Lombardi Comprehensive Cancer Center.

Cindy Cofer, whose friendship through these many years has never wavered. Cynthia Faye was honored to share your name.

And, of course, my family. I have a big, wonderful family, and this journey would have ended a long time ago if it were not for their continued support. My husband, Dan, and my girls, Claudia, Josephine, and Alice, you are the reason for it all.

About the Author

SUSAN GREGG GILMORE is the author of the novels *Looking for Salvation at the Dairy Queen* and *The Improper Life of Bezellia Grove*. She has written for the *Chattanooga Times Free Press*, the *Los Angeles Times*, and the *Christian Science Monitor*. She has three grown daughters and lives with her husband in Chattanooga, Tennessee.

The Funeral Dress

A Reader's Guide for
The Funeral Dress

Please note: In order to provide reading groups with the most informed and thought-provoking questions possible, it is necessary to reveal important aspects of the plot of this novel—as well as the ending. If you have not finished reading *The Funeral Dress*, we respectfully suggest that you may want to wait before reviewing this guide.

Questions and Topics for Discussion

1. Eudora Welty wrote, "Every story would be another story, and unrecognizable if it took up its characters and plot and happened somewhere else. . ." With this in mind, do you think the Southern Appalachian setting of *The Funeral Dress* is integral to the telling of its story? And in what ways does Emmalee's life in the holler and Leona's life on the mountain affect their attitudes and their relationships, particularly in the face of hardship and loss?

2.	Why is it so difficult for Emmalee to leave Nolan and Red Chert Holler, even though her day-to-day existence is difficult and her father's abuse emotionally and physically painful? How does Nolan's grim work, assisting the town's funeral director, affect Emmalee's outlook toward the living and the dead?

3.	Emmalee gives birth to her baby girl on the shirt factory's floor. A single, teenaged mother, Emmalee feels burdened by her daughter's care. Only as Cora, Wilma, and Easter embrace Emmalee does she begin to see herself as a mother. How do you imagine attitudes toward teen pregnancy have changed in the past thirty-five years? Do you think TV reality shows highlighting teenaged pregnant moms have affected our attitudes toward teen pregnancy?

4.	When Mr. Fulton learns that Emmalee's baby is his own grandchild, he faces serious moral and ethical decisions. How does Mr. Fulton negotiate his relationship with his wife, son, and Emmalee while also dealing with the scrutiny of a small town?

5.	Southern textile mills and factories pro-vided many women a first opportunity to earn money of their own and gain some financial independence. What types of challenges at work and in the community do you think blue-collar working women like Cora, Wilma, and Easter faced? And how do you think these challenges have changed since the mid-1970s?

6. Religion, church, and God mean very different things to Leona and Emmalee. Leona attends Sunday and Wednesday services regularly, but it seems an obligation, whereas Emmalee doesn't attend church but faithfully makes her crosses for every Cullen resident who dies. What do you imagine the relationship with God and church may mean to someone living in a small town versus a large metropolitan area? And what do you think it would be like to feel alienated from formal, organized religion in such a place?

7. References to birds are made frequently throughout the book. The first mention is "A redbird rapped at the trailer's far window, but it flitted off before Leona could blow a kiss and wish for something better" (page 25). More than good luck, what do these birds represent in the telling of this story?

8. Many of the characters in *The Funeral Dress* have dealt with loss of one kind or another: the loss of a child, the loss of a friend, the loss of the way a relationship used to be, the loss of a spouse, the loss of dreams. Do those who are experiencing loss seem connected in some way, even if on the surface their lives are very different?

9. Mr. Clayton and Leona's adulterous relationship was judged harshly by the other seamstresses at Tennewa. Do you think these women were unfair in their judgments?

10. Leona's death was sudden and tragic, and no one felt her absence more acutely than Emmalee. Do you think Emmalee became a stronger, more independent woman because of her friend's death? And in what ways do you think Emmalee's making of Leona's burial dress affected her and her relationship with her baby girl?

11. What do you see ahead for Emmalee? Do you think she will be up to the challenges she'll face while raising Kelly Faye?

A Conversation with
Susan Gregg Gilmore

Q: What inspired you to write *The Funeral Dress*?

A: I stumbled across a 1960s Kodak photograph of my great-aunt and -uncle sitting in
their single-wide trailer, the very same trailer
they shared for fifty-two years. This one
photograph got me to thinking about family,
familial relationships, and specifically my
ancestors and the land we've all shared. From
that one image, *The Funeral Dress* took root.

Q: Is there a Cullen, Tennessee, and if so, was
there a shirt factory there?

A: Cullen is fictional. But I did spend time
researching in Dunlap, Tennessee, just about
thirty minutes from my Chattanooga home. In
fact, some of my most favorite days while
writing the book were those spent with my
friend and Dunlap native Vallerie Greer.
She'd pick me up and we'd drive over Signal
Mountain down into the Sequatchie Valley. We
spent countless hours walking through ceme-
teries, driving deep into hollers, and talking to
people about their lives there at the southern-
most tip of the Appalachian Mountains. And

we always finished the day with a late lunch at the Cookie Jar, where you can get some of the best chicken 'n' dumplings and lemon meringue pie.

There was an operating shirt factory in Dunlap at one time, and I spent a wonderful afternoon with Marea Barker, a twenty-nine-year veteran lapel maker. I kept asking Marea, had she found the work monotonous, tedious, boring? Thinking surely she must have. But she just looked at me as if she didn't understand the question. For Marea, working at the shirt factory meant community and friendship and some financial independence. Sadly, Marea died not long after our last visit together, but she was sewing quilts for her family up until the very end.

Q: Do you sew?

A: Oh, no. I can place a button if need be or a very simple hem, but I had to take sewing lessons to understand the proper construction of a dress. I was making a linen dress as part of my research. Unfortunately, I cut it too short. But it still hangs in my closet, reminding me of what's possible if you really put your mind to it . . . and have a great teacher.

Q: Do you think, as Leona does, that redbirds bring good luck?

A: Of course! My daddy taught me that when I was a little girl. When you spot a redbird, you make a wish and blow a kiss.

When I first moved back to Tennessee after ten years in California, I would see redbirds everywhere and was convinced that every one of them was a sign from my father. Maybe they were, but I've come to realize that there are a *lot* of redbirds in Tennessee. But it's still a comforting thought.

Q: Do you have any ideas about your own funeral; what you'd like? What kind of dress you want to wear?

A: Sure. I have a growing file where I put songs I'd like sung or verses I'd like read. But I know I want it in a church, and I want someone who really knows me delivering the eulogy. I don't want money spent on an expensive casket. I would just as soon be wrapped in a white sheet and cremated or placed in a pine box and buried in the quiet Tennessee woods. But if I'm going to get all gussied up for the affair, I want a simple dress, tailored, not black, but something that still complements my white hair! Maybe even pants and a nice top. And of course good food and good fellowship afterward. Other than that, it can all be a surprise.

Q: While you were writing, did you identify with Leona or Emmalee or both?

A: I identified with both women but definitely felt more connected to Leona. Truth be told, it was probably more of a bonding. Leona had worked so hard all of her life and was still longing for something more. Even though I try very hard to find peace in the moment, no matter the circumstance, I understand that longing, that desperate need for something not yet attained. Even now, I find myself thinking about Leona and wondering what her life would have been like, with or without Curtis, had her situation been different. I hope she's well wherever she is!

Q: You write eloquently about the difficulties of raising a baby. Do you have children? Do you think having a newborn is overwhelming no matter what the circumstances?

A: Thank you, and I do have children. I have three amazing daughters and several nieces and nephews that I love on, too, as if they are mine. I do think having a newborn can be very overwhelming even with a good support system in place. When my second was born, she was small and struggled to nurse. They called her a nip-and-napper like Kelly Faye. Had it not been for a community of women here in Chattanooga that reached out and supported me, encouraged me, cooked for me, I probably would have quit breastfeeding. That's a very physically demanding experience for a new mother, and I so empathized with Emmalee, who had no one teaching her, coaching her, loving on her.

My oldest niece, Mary, had a baby while I was writing *The Funeral Dress*, and I went to help her for a few days. Boy, that brought back a lot of memories, and I felt Emmalee was there with us, watching our every move, soaking it all in.

Recommended Reading: Books on My Desk While Writing
The Funeral Dress

A few reference books, different-colored Moleskines filled with research notes, and some classics from John Steinbeck to Willa Cather were stacked about my desk while I worked. But the most important books I kept close were those of my friends. It was a comfort during the writing process to be surrounded by their beautifully crafted stories.

The Good News Bible, New International Version, and Revised Standard

The Celebration Hymnal: Songs and Hymns for Worship

The Synonym Finder, J.I. Rodale

Our Southern Birds, Emma Bell Miles

Sufficient Grace, Darnell Arnoult

Midwives and *The Double Bind*, Chris Bohjalian

One Fell Swoop, Virginia Boyd

Memoirs of an Imaginary Friend, Matthew Dicks

Commemoration, Lisa Dordal

Moon Women, Pamela Duncan

The Book of Marie and *To Dance with the White Dog*, Terry Kay

Creatures of Habit and Going Away Shoes, Jill McCorkle

The Lost Summer of Louisa May Alcott, Kelly O'Connor McNees

The Blueberry Years, Jim Minick

Whistlin' Dixie in a Nor'easter, Lisa Patton

Fair and Tender Ladies and *Mrs. Darcy and the Blue-Eyed Stranger*, Lee Smith

The Sweet Life, Lynn York

Center Point Large Print

600 Brooks Road / PO Box 1
Thorndike ME 04986-0001 USA

(207) 568-3717

US & Canada:
1 800 929-9108
www.centerpointlargeprint.com